A Twisted Reality

Is forever real or just in fairy tales…

Deb Laubach
Ray Caragher

Cover Design ©Christopher Hawke - CommunityAuthors.com

ISBN-13:978-0-9985290-2-8

Acknowledgments

We cannot thank The Powers That Be, the Cosmic Tumblers, Open-Mindedness and Awareness enough.

We thank our spouses and our children for *understanding who we really are* and believing in our dream. Thank you for loving and supporting us, while accepting each time we said, "Just one more chapter," knowing that it would turn into countless more hours and one less plate to set at dinnertime. We love you.

Endless thank yous to our visionary team of experts at CommunityAuthors.com: Traci Hall and Christopher Hawke for their tireless assistance.

May we all be filled with Love: Consideration, Compassion, and Compromise. Love is timeless and always reveals Herself and She knows no boundaries - for She is Love.

Chapter 1

Grant Robinson's hair ruffled in the spring breeze as he rested against the railing of the 34th floor balcony, watching the Upper West Side start to wake up. *The world looks good from up here!* Broadway was already filling with the sights and sounds of a typical mid-June morning and his view of Central Park was as beautiful as the first day he'd moved in.

Grant still wore his workout clothes as he drank his coffee, waiting for Ginger to return home from her jog in Central Park. Tomorrow, his daughter Lyla would graduate from high school with honors as the class Valedictorian. *Not only beautiful but smart as a whip!*

He remembered how the previous summer they'd reviewed applications from six colleges she had been accepted to. Finally she'd decided to attend University of Wisconsin, partly because it was his alma mater, with the added bonus of how close she'd be to home in Chicago. *She must have hugged me a million times.*

Grant sipped his coffee, enjoying the morning's blue sky. Thoughts about his kids filled his mind. How lucky he felt that they were still so close after the nasty divorce they had endured six years prior. Their mother was just a nightmare.

Jason, his son, was a typical fifteen-year-old who teased his sister endlessly about everything, even joking that he would take her room after she left for college.

Lyla had confided in Ginger during their visit in April how tough Margo was on her. *I hope she doesn't crack under all the unreasonable pressure.* The main reason Lyla had gotten a part-time job at Victoria's Secret, according to Ginger, was to stop her mother's bitching over "being broke." He would have intervened, but Ginger said Lyla loved the work. Better yet, his daughter and new wife shared a common interest in fashion, to the point that Ginger'd asked Lyla's advice on a couple of designs she was working on last spring.

Grant straightened and looked out toward the park. He'd have to see Margo tomorrow, which brought up memories of her and the reasons for their broken marriage. Always jealous of him and his successes, she now hated that he had made it in her world and had become a Head Designer. He truly believed the only good thing that came out of that marriage were his children.

The sound of an ambulance passing by on the street below snapped him back to his reality. He set his cup down on a small table and raised his arms up into the breeze, taking a deep breath of early morning air. Then he released his breath along with the bad energy that had crept into his head.

He immediately felt better when he pictured how Jason and Lyla would go with him on their yearly autumn adventure to make a wish by tossing coins into the Buckingham Fountain in Chicago. *Perhaps Lyla will let Jason take me for a spin in her car.* He laughed out loud when he recalled how pissed off Margo had been when he'd flown to Chicago for Lyla's sixteenth birthday and taken her car shopping. After she'd picked out a brand new 1987 blue Camaro, he bought it for her on the spot. Other happy memories of his kids filled his heart. *Why am I so deserving of all this happiness?*

Ginger quietly walked out onto the balcony with a mug of dark roast, joining Grant. She had her workout towel draped around her neck and her long auburn hair in a braid.

"I didn't even hear you come in." He placed his cup on the small table, wrapping his arms around her waist, and kissed her flushed cheeks and lips.

"Where were you, my love?" Ginger gently touched his temple.

"I can't believe my little girl is graduating from high school tomorrow. I'm proud of how hard she's worked."

Ginger just smiled at him.

"You know what else I love?"

"Me?" Ginger teased.

He gave her a look that needed no words.

"Go on." Her smile stayed on her lips.

"The happiness it brings to my heart that you and the kids have such a great relationship."

She sipped from her mug. "You know how much I love Lyla and Jason."

He placed her coffee on the table next to his empty cup and pulled her into his body, holding her tightly against him. He brushed a tender kiss back and forth across her lips, while he inhaled her breath. The almost kiss was as soft as the breeze of the summer air around them.

Ginger pulled back. "Join me in the shower, my love?"

"I'll be right in…"

She squeezed his ass before walking inside, depositing her cup on the shiny granite breakfast top as she headed down the hallway.

Grant took a last look at the park and then followed his wife, making a few last-minute work-related phone calls. Their flight to Chicago left in five hours.

⊷⊶ ⊙═⊶

Ginger slipped out of her robe and admired the beautiful master suite. They had just finished remodeling their entire three-bedroom, two-bath, 1,400-square-foot apartment. The master bath was their favorite—everything was custom designed to suit their taste esthetically as well as sensually. She stepped into the oversized slate-tiled shower with an L-shaped teak bench long and wide enough to comfortably stretch out on. There were two showerheads plus a removable wand to pamper each other's body with pulsating water pleasure.

The cleansing warmth of the water engulfed her body and soothed her muscles as she stood directly under the showerhead. *God, in August Grant and I will have been together for six years. Who would have guessed that we would have ever briefly met, only to find each other again after ten years – and then fall deeply in love? He still treats me like a queen.*

She laughed out loud realizing that she could star as the main character in a Hallmark production.

I always wanted to have children, but I enjoyed my career as a model and fashion designer which never gave me the luxury of a family. And now, not only am I in love with the most beautiful soul, but the Masters have brought together both my dreams of a career and two beautiful children that I will always call my own. Lyla and Ginger were very close, just like Ginger and her own mother, Lois. *Lyla is the daughter I always wished I would have had, and Jason is a son who reminds me of my childhood with my younger brother. I adore him.*

Ginger rinsed the shampoo from her hair and added the honey bark and almond-scented conditioner.

Lyla was a very sensitive, sweet, and caring person being raised by an extremely unhappy human being; her mother, Margo. Margo was jealous of Lyla's relationship to both her father and Ginger. Many times over the years Lyla had called Ginger to hash out her feelings about the way she was treated at home by her mother for seemingly nonessential things.

Jason just rode atop the waves of life with ease. He was as cute as could be with many of his father's features and he knew it—with a simple hug and his charming smile he could win anyone over. He had sprouted up during the last few years and the girls at school were beginning to hound him. Yet he didn't let that go to his head at all. Jason was a kind kid, very smart, with a loving heart.

She contemplated telling Grant that Lyla had actually chosen New York University—a last-minute decision that Lyla had trusted only Ginger with. *Lyla, baby girl although I didn't birth you, I love you like you are my own daughter. I wish you wouldn't have made me promise to keep this secret from your father. Grant is going to kill me if he finds—*

Her thoughts were interrupted by Grant joining her in the shower. He wasted no time cleansing his perfectly chiseled body to focus on hers with his skilled fingers, playing with the hot spot between her legs...

"Gin, where's your head?" He whispered in her ear and she shivered.

"Oh, baby, nowhere but with you." She refocused on him and what he was doing to her wet, naked body.

Their bodies tangled into one, with the steamy water rushing over them. He leaned her back to sit in the corner of the bench and spread her legs. Grant knelt down to lick her inner thighs and parted her lips with his fingers. Slowly sucking on her clit, he inserted two fingers, and she slid her hips forward, silently begging for more. Ginger twisted his wet salt-and-pepper hair in her hands and pulled his face deeper into her slick wetness.

"How can—we still be this hot—for each other—after all these years?" Her voice quivered as her climax started to build.

Grant knew her body so well, he didn't stop to answer; he just continued to lead her down the path of passionate pleasure until she exploded on his face.

Once her jolts of ecstasy subsided, he finally said, "Because I'm your sweet Tommy, Rachel." He kissed her inner thighs.

"Right. Oh, wait. What?"

"You just asked me how we can still be so hot for each other after so many years…" He laughed at her perplexed expression. "Well, anyway, it's more than these past six years that we can count. What we have spans at least two lifetimes…maybe more."

Grant and Ginger affectionately referred to each other from time to time as "Rachel" or "Tommy." They had discovered they were together in their last lifetime shortly after they were reunited by chance, or fate. They knew their names were Tommy and Rachel from their past lives when they were lovers, but their bodies and souls were separated by death during WWII.

"And I love and still constantly lust for you, my sweet Tommy." She grabbed his wet ass.

"As I you, Rach. But sorry to disappoint—it was all for you this morning. We really need to be downstairs soon. Evan will drive us to LaGuardia."

Ginger pouted her full lips and batted her lashes, looking up at his gorgeous face and blue eyes. It would take more than a half hour to tame her long auburn hair, so she begrudgingly hopped out of the shower.

⟶⟞◉⟜⟵

Once they walked into the lobby of their building, the doorman, Andreas, helped Evan, Grant and Ginger's personal driver, load their suitcases into the limo. He congratulated Grant on Lyla's high school graduation. "One down, one to go, Mr. Robinson. I only have five left…"

"Yes, Andreas," Grant said. "Time flies."

"What are your daughter's plans for next year? She going to school here?" Andreas looked at Ginger, which caused her to freeze, and then break out in light perspiration.

She peeked at Grant, but thankfully, he didn't notice Ginger's reaction to the simple question and responded before she could, taking her off the hook.

"She's chosen the University of Wisconsin, my alma mater," Grant replied with pride in his voice.

Ginger quickly excused herself into the limo to avoid being involved in any further conversation about Lyla—she wasn't good at lying.

As they rode toward the airport in a comfortable silence, hand-in-hand, Grant inquired, "Why are you so distracted, Gin?"

"Maybe just a gut feeling, preparing for something big, I suppose."

"Like what? Dealing with Margo? Please don't let her—"

"No, no. She doesn't get under my skin anymore. I'm way beyond that stage, love."

"Is it business related then? Things seem to be going fine with Gabriel and Gabe and—"

"Life is not always about work," she said as she grabbed his crotch, desperate to change the subject.

"Aren't you ambitious?"

"Challenging me, cowboy?" Ginger knew just how to keep his attention.

"If only we had time."

They shared a passionate kiss, which gave promise of what was to come when they settled into their hotel in Chicago.

Ginger sat back to catch her breath.

"On a totally different note, did you know that Gabe's son, Aksel, has been attending Northwestern University? Should we reach out to him since we'll be so close by?" Grant inquired.

"I think it's really just a family celebration with Lyla and Jason." Ginger wasn't sure what Lyla might want to do and hated to make plans for her.

"He and Lyla really hit it off a few summers ago, you remember? He seems like a good kid."

"It's been a while since I've seen him, but I'm sure he is. He comes from good stock." Filled with gratitude, she squeezed her palm over Grant's knee. "You know I adore the entire Portier family; they helped shape our lives."

Chapter 2

Friday afternoon Grant, hand in hand with Ginger, exited the concourse at O'Hare International Airport and headed to the luggage claim, where he spotted Charlie, his personal driver when he visited Chicago. Charlie waved at them as they came down the escalator. Charlie stood over six feet four inches and probably weighed in at nearly 250 pounds. He looked like a retired linebacker from the Chicago Bears.

"Mr. Grant and Ms. Ginger! How are you?" Charlie shook Grant's hand and gave Ginger a kiss on the cheek.

"Fine Charlie, fine. How's Betsy?" Betsy was his 1980 black stretch Lincoln Continental that he had named after his late mother.

"She's doing well and waiting just for you. I must admit, your timing is perfect with the weather. It's the best we've had in weeks, clear and sunny!"

An hour later Charlie dropped them off at the Park Hyatt. "What time do you need me back so we can pick the kids up for dinner?"

"Actually, Charlie, Lyla is picking us up in her car. So, you're off for the night, but we'll need you to be here at 11:30 tomorrow morning."

"Oh, Lordy, Mr. Grant, I forgot she drives."

"Tell me about it," Grant laughed. "I'm having trouble remembering she is eighteen already, with a mind of her own."

After checking into one of the Water Tower Suites on the twenty-second floor, Grant collected on Ginger's ambitious promise of sensual pleasure.

Their suite had a full-size living room, dining room, kitchen and two bathrooms, with one inside the bedroom suite. It also boasted four bay window seats that overlooked Lake Michigan and the Magnificent Mile—the place where high-end shoppers spent their money.

They tore each other's clothes off and quickly made use of the oversized couch in the living room area, on one of the widow seats, then moved into the bedroom where they continued to make love until the clock told them they had to stop.

Both bare-assed naked, Grant began to unpack his suitcase as he tried to decide what to wear for dinner.

"You better take a shower and cover up that hot body of yours, or you're going to look too well-fucked," Ginger gently suggested.

Grant quickly showered and upon entering the bedroom he saw Ginger making the bed. "We're just going to mess it up again later." He was getting aroused just looking at her naked body.

"Okay, okay. We need to get dressed. Remember who will be here in less than a half hour—your children! I'd prefer that our bedroom looks tidy…that's all."

"Gin, you really think they're going to notice the bed?"

"Let me do this, just in case they haven't lost their eyesight. My shower will only take a few minutes."

⊹⊱◈⊰⊹

Lyla and Jason knocked on the hotel suite door a few minutes early—it had been over six weeks since Grant and Ginger had seen them and they all teared up while hugging.

Breaking the sweet tension, Grant asked, "Where would you like to eat? I made two reservations; one at the

No MI Kitchen upstairs or the new Gibson Bar and Steakhouse?"

"I really don't have a preference, Daddy," Lyla responded and hugged him again.

"Well, we can walk to Gibson's and window shop along the way, or you can drive us there."

All four decided on Gibson's and to walk the half-mile since the weather was so pleasant. On the way, they passed the high-end shopping boutiques. Grant was amazed at how close Lyla and Ginger were in height. They were so wrapped up in talking to each other that they didn't even seem to be window shopping as they strolled down the clean city streets of Chicago, arm in arm.

"No shopping? That's a first," Grant said to Jason.

"Girls…can't ever figure them out, Dad," Jason observed.

They arrived at Gibson's a half hour earlier than their reservation, as Grant had built in time for shopping that went unused. Shortly thereafter, they were seated at a round table in the large dining area surrounded by windows. Their view overlooked the famous Rush Street. The tantalizing scent of grilled steaks filled the room.

Dessert trollies continuously rolled past them and were so mouthwatering that Grant joked, "Should we have dessert first?"

"I'm in on that, Daddy." Lyla laughed. "And the chocolate triple layer cake is all mine!"

They enjoyed appetizers of large shrimp cocktails and oysters on the half shell while sharing small talk. Jason was discussing the Chicago Cubs pitcher, Greg Maddux, and a right fielder, Andre "The Hawk" Dawson, with his father. Ginger and Lyla had their heads close together while talking softly to each other. Jason continued yammering on with his dad about the rest of his summer plans, which included a month at football camp and perhaps a long weekend in New York in early July.

Grant nodded at Jason's plans but at the same time noticed Ginger and Lyla still in quiet conversation. *What are they talking about?* "Sounds great, Jase! You should clear your visit with your mother and then work out the dates with Ginger."

Grant was getting ready to ask Lyla about her summer plans when the food arrived. He and Jason devoured the ribeye steaks like two hungry lions. He glanced across the table at his daughter's full plate. "Ly, is the Mahi okay? You haven't touched it."

Lyla looked at Ginger and then Grant looked at Ginger, whose face suddenly flushed. Lyla's eyes widened and she trembled as if afraid. Neither of them said anything—even Jason stopped eating and put down his fork and knife.

Lyla shook her head "no" at Ginger before looking up at her father.

Grant sat back in his chair. "What the hell is going on here? Is there something I need to know?"

Ginger said nothing as she gently rubbed Lyla's arm, prompting her to speak. Grant sipped his Jack and Coke. Lyla straightened in her chair, took a deep breath and looked directly at him as Grant stabbed his steak with his fork. "I'm enrolled in NYU."

"NYU?" Grant, shocked, almost choked on the words. "As in New York University?" What had happened to his old alma mater?

"Yes. Is it okay? Meaning, can I move in with you and Ginger?"

Grant, overwhelmed by the announcement, felt uncertain and looked at Ginger for direction; she nodded her head in approval.

Live with him? "Yes, yes, of course!" The cut of steak on the tines of his fork trembled. "Oh, Lord, what did your mother say?"

"I haven't told her yet," Lyla said. "She still thinks I'm going to UW. I'll tell her, but I'm waiting for the right time." His daughter spoke with a determined expression.

"When are you planning on telling her, *before or after* you graduate from NYU?" His tone held layers of sarcasm.

"Grant!" Ginger scolded.

Lyla turned to Jason with a pointed finger. "No spilling the beans, okay lil' bro?"

"Are you kidding? Just make sure I'm around when you tell her, she's gonna lose it!" Jason laughed.

"One more thing," Lyla said, making eye contact with all three of them. "This is between me and Mom. I'll take care of it."

They all agreed while Grant chugged the rest of his Jack and Coke and ordered another one.

⟿━◉━⟾

The next morning, after a sleepless night, Lyla looked at her reflection in the full-length mirror in her bedroom. She had a towel wrapped around her hair and one loosely draped over her five foot nine inch, one hundred and fifteen-pound body. She dropped the towel and let it pool around her feet, studying her image as if a stranger. She didn't see herself as exceptionally good-looking. Her cobalt-blue eyes started to tear up while she mentally made note of what was wrong with her body for the umpteenth time.

Removing the towel from her head released her chestnut brown hair that reached just past her nipples. It didn't help her fragile ego that her mother constantly told her she wasn't pretty enough or have the shoulder line to be a model. Her dream since childhood had been to be a designer like her dad and maybe be a model for a while.

However, after all the years of criticisms she'd heard about her body, she'd eventually dropped the idea.

The regional manager from Victoria's Secret had asked her if she would be interested modeling in their summer catalog and while Lyla had been flattered by the offer, she'd turned it down to avoid dealing with the fallout from her mother over how silly that would be when she didn't have a perfect model's body.

Lyla wiped her eyes and pictured her mother's portfolio. *Mom is so pretty with the perfect shoulder line and the perfect model height. She never compliments me on my looks, except to say something negative, even though I always compliment her. When did she last even tell me she loves me? But Jason, on the other hand, can do no wrong, even when he does! I love my little brother to bits, but I'm sick of hearing how wonderful he is when I get nothing emotionally positive from her. I wish I would have moved in with Dad and Ginger years ago.*

Thank God I turned eighteen a week ago! I can finally do as I please and it feels like the end of my prison term, especially once I land in New York!

Lyla, angry and hurt, threw her hairbrush across the room. "I hate you, you bitch!"

⊷⊶⊷

Margo watched the planners prepare for Lyla's graduation party out the back window with cool detachment. She recalled meeting Grant in Chicago for the first time—she'd been five feet, eight and a half inches tall, with blonde hair, brown eyes, and perfect fit model measurements of 34-26-37. She never modeled before the camera, but behind the scenes to assure the garment manufacturers' sizing and fit were correct.

She'd worked with Howard Golden, owner of H&M Designs, one of the top private label houses in New York, for years. Margo sipped from a crystal glass of water. It was her connection that eventually led Grant to his unexpected success. After he'd returned from his tour of duty in Vietnam emotionally fucked up, Grant needed a change to restart his life. She'd begged him to move to New York, and to appease her, they'd left Chicago just after Lyla was born.

Howard, at her request, had offered him a position as an assistant designer. Grant had previously struggled in the industry before being drafted and was only doing piece work at the time that hardly paid the bills. In an awful twist, Grant became successful as her career as a fit model came to a screeching halt during her second pregnancy.

After their divorce, Grant married Ginger Madison, a five foot, eight inch auburn-haired glamour model who had successfully transitioned into a fashion designer. What upset Margo most depended on the day…it was a toss-up between knowing that both her children loved Ginger, and that Grant and Ginger lived in the same apartment she and Grant had once shared. To add to her loathing of life, she'd just turned forty-two with no eligible suitors on the horizon. Lyla's recent birthday represented a sizable reduction in her monthly child support payment from Grant.

Margo viewed her daughter as a competitor and resented Lyla's beauty. Glamour models were slightly more curvy and voluptuous, like Lyla, and it pierced Margo's ego to think her daughter might succeed where she hadn't, so she'd done her best to dissuade Lyla's interest in modeling.

Jason, at fifteen, was already five feet ten inches and a near doppelgänger of Grant in his younger years. He had the same raven-black hair, which he was growing long in rebellion against her, with the same blue eyes that Lyla and Grant shared. It was hard for Margo to look at Jason at times without thinking about her failed marriage. Although she constantly doted over him, he was distant and moody. *Typical teenager*, she often told herself, never considering it could be her own fault that he avoided showing her affection. There now was less than three years left of a constant cash flow on Jason's behalf, which fueled her jealousy of Grant and Ginger even further. What was she going to do, old and alone?

⤝━◉═━⤞

Seated at her bedroom vanity, Lyla's thoughts wandered as she combed her hair in preparation for the ceremony later. *If he could only know how much I still love him, still want him, what I would do for him—even after he left me the way he did. Guess Mom was right, he was just using me.*

It was love for me, but was it for him? Or just lust? I truly believed he loved me. Either way, he'll always be my first, and one great love. No one can take that away. I wonder where he is now… Wonder when our paths will cross again…? It doesn't matter anymore; I'm following my dreams in New York. I will prove to everyone that I'm more than what they think…especially Mom! Maybe I will become a model after all. Lyla laughed lightly and smoothed a curl.

But thank God for Ginger! She's someone I feel like I've known forever. She handles obstacles and bumps in the road so smoothly. I wanna be like her when I grow up…My news at dinner last night about moving to New York was well received thanks to her. I thought Dad was gonna choke on his drink when I said I was going to NYU! I can't wait to be where I can have the freedom, love and understanding I've been craving for so long.

⊷═◉═⊷

Later that day, Saturday, June 10th, at one p.m., Mr. Anderson, the principal of Glenbrook South High School, greeted the audience and announced the commencement of the senior graduation ceremony. The backdrop of the Watson Center for the Performing Arts Auditorium was draped with a forest green and gold banner across the stage with "1989" in sparkly gold sequins. He made some preliminary remarks and then turned toward Lyla.

"At this time, it is my pleasure to introduce the valedictorian for the class of 1989, Ms. Lyla Robinson."

The crowd applauded. As Lyla stood before nearly five hundred people, her knees began to shake. She took a deep breath and found her inner strength as she locked eyes with Ginger.

"Welcome, parents, grandparents, extended family, and friends. We thank you for joining us on this extraordinary day in our young lives.

"Fellow classmates, today is our day to celebrate the passage from childhood to young adulthood. Today marks the day when we begin walking on the path to realizing our dreams.

"Loved ones, we thank you for all the love and support that you've given us over the years—especially the last four years, our greatest time to make memories as teenagers. While we look to the future with excitement, anticipation, and at times fear, please know we will still need you…"

Nearing the end of her speech, Lyla stared directly at her mother and paused long enough for Margo to read her face— Lyla was smiling, but she knew her mother correctly interpreted her smile as a look of sheer defiance.

"I too have decided to follow my life goals in New York City, where I will proudly be attending New York University. Friends, if you don't believe in yourself, why should anyone else?"

Lyla looked away from her mother's shocked expression. "Don't give up on yourself, your dreams, and your passions. Tragically, just days ago, college students abroad in Tiananmen Square in Beijing were killed as they peacefully and nonviolently protested in their pursuit of dreams for their futures. Let us take a moment of silence in their honor." After a few moments, Lyla wrapped up her speech with: "We need to be as brave as them in the pursuit of our future, and contribute to society the way the students who lost their lives can't any longer. Congratulations to all of us!"

The crowd applauded with a standing ovation— except for Margo—who sat with her arms folded, glaring directly at her daughter, who smiled directly back at her…a small silent "fuck you" victory for Lyla.

As she walked back to her seat onstage, someone caught Lyla's attention. She noticed him standing at the back of the auditorium near an exit, clapping, then wiping tears from his eyes. She blinked to refocus just to be sure—but he was gone…almost as if a figment of her imagination.

Why would he be here? She was lost in thoughts of him for the rest of the ceremony.

When graduation was over, Lyla proceeded from the stage intent on finding her surprise visitor. Outside the auditorium, Grant grabbed her arm with Ginger right beside him, grinning proudly. "Hey, where's the fire?" he asked. "Are you leaving without us?"

"Oh, of course not, Daddy. I was just looking for someone." Lyla smiled sweetly.

"Who?" Grant turned his head as if he even had the foggiest idea of who he was looking for.

"Just someone I thought I recognized. But maybe I should get an eye exam, because I'm sure it wasn't him…"

"*Him?* Him who?"

"No one, Daddy. Did you like my speech?" Lyla abruptly changed the subject.

Lyla had seen Jason sitting with their grandparents on the opposite side of the auditorium chatting with some girls he knew, so she had no ally when Margo arrived.

Her mother joined them just as Ginger wrapped her arms around Lyla and said, "You were great, baby girl! I'm so proud of you." Ginger's bright green eyes were filled with tears.

Margo scowled at Ginger. "As if you have the right to take any credit. You're barely her stepmother!"

Lyla rolled her eyes. Ginger squeezed her extra hard, winked, and took a step back as Margo swooped in to hug her daughter.

Her mother hissed in her ear in a tone completely opposite of her body language: "You should have told me about your plans. Like you're going to New York without my—"

"Lyla Robinson!" Mr. Anderson interrupted. "Congratulations again. What a speech! It was a nice tribute to the college students in Beijing." Turning to Margo, he said, "You must be so proud of your daughter, Mrs. Robinson."

"It's Thompson," Margo retorted.

"Oh, right, right. My apologies, ma'am. NYU, Lyla! Thought maybe you'd follow in your father's footsteps by going to UW."

"Just because I'm not going to UW doesn't mean I'm not following in my father's footsteps, sir."

Grant couldn't hide his smile while Margo tried to fake hers.

Her mom finally cornered Dad. "And exactly when did you know Lyla decided on the Big Apple? You put her up to this, didn't you? You bastard!"

"Mar—"

"Couldn't wait until she turned eighteen, could you, just to rip my little girl from my arms!"

Grant laughed. "Seriously, Margo?"

"Fuck you, Grant!" Margo spat.

"What do you want me to do, Margo? Tell her no? Tell her she can only come to New York if she lives on the streets?"

"Again, a fat fuck you, Gr—"

"Spare me the drama, *Ms. Thompson.* She's going to grow up whether we like it or not. I plan to help her follow her dreams and be successful. Within reason, of course."

"Oh, *now* you want to be there for her? Where have you been the last five years, other than gallivanting around the world with your mistress?"

Lyla looked from her mom to her dad—both parents seemed to be losing their cool. "Ginger is my *wife.*"

"Like that word means anything to you," Margo remarked, rolling her eyes.

"What's your issue, Margo? Your life? My life? Our divorce? Because I thought we were talking about our daughter's future, not rehashing—"

"You think that putting her up and giving her a credit card to shop will make you father of the year?" Margo's face was red, teeth gritted, and hands clenched in fists on her hips, three inches from Grant.

"I'll let you know when the award ceremony is scheduled. Otherwise, we're finished with this subject."

Just then, Jason ran up and hugged Grant. "Dad, where's Mommy Gin? I want you both to meet someone."

"Of course, son. She's right over there. I'll walk with you." Grant smirked at Margo and disappeared with him into the crowd. Unfortunately, this left Lyla alone with her mother. She quickly ducked after her dad.

Chapter 3

Lyla's graduation party started later that afternoon in the backyard of Margo's house. At the far end of the limestone pool deck was a string trio playing jazz and soft rock music. On the other side of the pool, a handsome young bartender with a slight British accent flirted with Margo from behind the make-shift bar. An assortment of appetizers under the roofed pagoda and cabana house had been arranged by caterers.

Having been so busy with finals and working, Lyla finally noticed that all the raised flowerbeds around the pool had been filled with red and white geraniums—the school colors for the University of Wisconsin. Her grandparents had given her a UW football jersey and sweatshirt along with a sizable check. Most of her mother's friends had also given her school-related gifts and checks. The young bartender sneaked Lyla a cucumber martini while her mother wasn't looking and told her if she wanted another, just tell him. Uncle Frank, her mom's brother, took her aside and gifted her three joints before he disappeared for a while.

At some point in the evening, her grandfather Fred looked around to make sure they were out of hearing range. "I really like your dad," he said, pausing to make sure he could continue, "and I'm surprised that he's not here with Ginger. She seems really nice…" He stopped mid-sentence when Margo walked up sipping a drink, with a slight stagger in her gait.

"So, what are you two whispering about?"

"Oh, nothing of importance, sweetheart, just how beautiful the yard is." Her grandfather's face flushed slightly.

Margo stared at her daughter. "Well, Dad, I'm glad you like them because the geraniums were for Lyla. But since she will be going to a different school, the gardener will be called first thing Monday morning to rip them out."

Margo held up her glass as if to toast them but instead turned back to the bar.

"Sorry for that," her grandfather said. "I should have been tougher on her as a dad."

Before Lyla could say anything further her grandmother Patricia showed up. "Tough on what, Fred?"

"I was just commenting on how tough it must have been for Lyla working *and* taking her finals at the same time." He winked at Lyla as he pulled his wife by the arm and steered her away from Lyla before Patricia could add one of her famous unfiltered comments.

Lyla went into the house to use the bathroom on the second floor, locking the door behind her. She pulled out one of the three joints that her uncle had given her from her bra. She stood looking out the small opened window in the bathroom where she could overhear her mother telling the young bartender how she had been a glamour model, rather than a fit model, and maybe later she could get his opinion on some photos from a recent shoot.

She decided to take a few tokes on one of the fatties, feeling the resentment toward her mother grow. "This fucking party is all about her showing her off!" *Fuck this shit, and where are my dad and Ginger?* Lighting the candle on the counter before turning on the fan, she inhaled a long drag deep into lungs, holding it before coughing her head off.

Suddenly there was a knock on the bathroom door. "You okay, sis?"

Lyla took a slug of her drink before answering between coughs. "Yes, are you alone?"

"Yeah, why?"

Popping the door open and quickly pulling him in, she locked the door behind him in one swift movement. She smiled at him as she held up the fatty. "Want a hit?" Jason grinned as he took the joint and sat on the edge of the bathtub while taking a puff. Lyla's eyes teared up. "I'm going to miss you when I go off to college, JJ."

"Stop, sis. We still have most of the summer before you leave. And besides, in a few years, I'll be joining you in the Big Apple, okay? I'll see you every time I come visit Dad and Gin."

After she hugged him and gave him one of the fatties for another time, Lyla instructed Jason, "Hey, go down before Mom begins to hunt for us, I need to get something in my room."

Lyla went into her bedroom, locking the door. She pulled the bottom drawer of her tall dresser all the way out and removed an envelope from the back. Contained within were four pictures she had hidden from her mother. *There he is.* She sat on her bed, looking at the pictures from her most favorite time they'd spent together in Central Park. A tear rolled down her cheek as she held the pictures against her heart.

"Lyla, get down here! We're ready to have your graduation cake!" Margo yelled from the bottom of the stairs.

"Coming, Mother!" she yelled back as she put away the pictures.

Fifteen minutes later Lyla stood in the backyard on the deck by the pool as the graduation party began to wind down after serving the cake. She pretended to enjoy all the family, close friends, and neighbors who had come to celebrate her moment. Yet she noticed that two very important people never made an appearance, so she cornered her mother.

"Mom, why didn't Daddy and Ginger show up?"

She looked away from Lyla. "They were busy, I suppose."

"What could they be *busy* with on my graduation day? Wait! You didn't invite them, did you?" She glared at her mother.

"Well, honey—"

"Don't 'honey' me, Mom!"

Margo was caught off guard and Lyla could tell. "It's always about you, isn't it? God, you're such a bitch! Thanks for such a great party, but I'm outta here!" She walked into the house and grabbed her car keys.

"Young lady, you get back here right now!" Margo shouted as she followed her into the house.

Lyla slammed the front door loud enough for everyone to hear. Let her mom face the remaining guests and explain why her daughter had left!

Lyla revved up the engine and the tires of her Camaro screeched on the street in front of her house in the tranquil Chicago suburban of Northbrook. She had no idea where she was headed, nor did she care—she felt ready to explode and had to get as far away from her mother as possible. Pulling away from the gatehouse, she turned up the radio volume to full blast. The Traveling Wilbury's song "End of The Line" was on and she found comfort in the lyrics: "You can sit around and wait for the phone to ring..."

Flying on Interstate 294 with the windows down, her cares dissipated slowly... Subconsciously she had been driving toward Evanston, Illinois and suddenly she realized it. Lyla hadn't been there in almost two years.

I wonder if he's still in the same condo? She pushed the cassette into her tape deck—the *Green Thought* album by the Smithereens played. The lyrics were perfect, she thought, singing along to words of "Only a Memory."

"But It's / Only a memory / Of what our love was going to be / Broken bits of you and me / Only a memory / Only a memory / Why should it matter if I cry / I sit around and wonder why / Now I feel much too weak to live

/ And I've got nothing left to give / Now it's / Only a memory…"

She slowly drove around the apartment complex parking lot. *Can I even find it? Do I really want to find it? What will I even do if he's here? I still have the key he gave me. Will it still work? Should I dare try?*

Lyla pulled into the empty guest space next to a wild strawberry–colored Ford Mustang LX convertible. It wasn't exactly the same car she remembered; this was a 1989—the newest model. But it was obviously his: it had a small French flag on the lower right corner of the rear glass window and a Northwestern student parking sticker on the opposite side.

"FUCK ME! NOW WHAT?"

The blood rushed to her head and as it throbbed, she nearly vomited as her heart started pounding rapidly. Her emotions were bouncing around like a ping pong ball making its way down a long set of stairs. She wanted to run up to his condo, break down the door, and scream and yell and slap him for what he'd done to her. The next second she wanted to kiss him endlessly.

How could he just leave me so easily? No good-bye words were spoken. He just completely disappeared. And how dare he show up at my graduation today? I know it was him.

Lyla cut the engine of her bright-blue Camaro, and sat in silence. She was so engrossed in her thoughts she didn't realize how stuffy it was getting in the early night.

Jesus! Air! I need air!

She threw open the car door. Lyla jumped out and stared up at his condo. She briefly closed her eyes and found her footing, then raced up the stairs and pounded her fist on his door. Her heart was pounding just as loud.

A few seconds went by. *Maybe he won't answer. That will be my sign to leave and—*

The door opened. Aksel Portier stood there wearing a sweat-soaked Northwestern Wildcats muscle T-shirt and gym shorts with a roll of packing tape in his hand and a box cutter in the other. He tossed both aside as soon as he saw her.

His light brown eyes were exactly the same as she remembered—the only thing different was the almost cartoonish expression of shock on his face. He wiped the sweat from his brow and ran his fingers through his thick, dark brown, wavy hair, taking a deep breath.

In his sultry French accent, he spoke nervously, "Lyla? What are you doing here?"

"Oh, so you *do* remember my name? Thought you forgot all about me," she spat out in a resentment-filled tone, with her hands on her hips.

"*Forget* about you? How *could* I?"

"So why *were* you at my graduation today? Now is not the time to lie to me!"

"You saw me?" His cheeks turned red with embarrassment.

Her tone softened. "How did you even know I was graduating today?"

"My grandfather knows everything."

"How perfect. So, Papa Portier sent you." She shook her head in disbelief. "Then where's my gift? Why did you even bother coming? Was it so you could tell him you did? Guess it is all about business, isn't it?" She turned to leave, but Aksel grabbed her wrist.

"Don't touch me! You broke me!" She tried to wrestle away from him, but he was stronger than her.

"Stop. Listen. Please?" he begged.

Tears silently rolled down her cheeks. He let go of her wrist only to pull her close against his sweaty body. Lyla struggled for a moment and then fell into him, reaching her hands up into his hair and pulling his lips toward hers. She was in a mental battle between *wanting him* and *wanting to kill him*.

He displayed his strength and agility by picking her up as she wrapped her legs around him, and he kicked the door shut behind them. Lyla was instinctually grinding into his thick erection, easily felt through his nylon gym shorts. Their kiss deepened, and their tongues danced in perfect rhythm just as before…like they hadn't been apart for nearly two years. Aksel laid Lyla on the couch and kissed her tears away. He took off his shirt, and she took off her purple panties. Their passion hadn't faded into nothingness—it was more intense than ever, finally in each other's arms after such a long time.

Wildly kissing him, she recalled the lovemaking they'd shared, the tenderness of their relationship. He was the only one she'd ever loved, the only one to whom she'd given her body, heart and soul. With her panties off and her dress up around her neck, she pulled his shorts and boxer briefs off, springing free his huge, hard cock.

Suddenly her brain caught up with her…*He left me stranded that day…never to be heard from again!*

"Like what you see, *bébé?*" she whispered into his ear.

"*Magnifique, ma chérie,*" he responded with a kiss.

"*Fantastique.* Now fuck off!" She pushed him away while landing a solid slap across his face. It stunned him as he jumped back from her, holding his cheek which had already turned red.

"Lyla?" he asked, perplexed.

"That's all I ever was to you, a good fuck. You're the biggest asshole I ever met!"

Lyla shoved him again and pulled her dress down, throwing her panties at him. "Keep them and we'll call it my gift to you, so you can prove to your family you went to my graduation!"

She ran toward the door, grabbing her keys from her purse, but lost her footing and tumbled to the floor. Every negative emotion from the past two years erupted into one hell of an emotional explosion, and she burst into tears. Aksel tried to help her to her feet.

She stood up and pushed him away from her. "You left me to suffer alone," she sobbed. "Stuck with a judgmental mother. And now all you want to do is fuck me? Well, fuck you! Find someplace else to stick your dick!"

"Lyla, stop. Listen to me, please!"

"Not a chance! This time I *will* make you a memory!" she screamed through her tears.

Aksel stood there naked and speechless as she slammed the door in his face.

He wanted to run after her, but he didn't. He didn't move an inch toward the door, as badly as he wanted to. Wanting to tell her everything, especially why he hadn't contacted her since that day.

I was such the bad boy before I met her…if she only knew how much she changed me. God, I love her! I cannot live without her…without at least a real shot at us. This just makes me want to move to New York now more than ever. She's finally eighteen. Maybe she'll grant me one more visit…then I can tell her everything. He slumped on the couch, holding her panties in his hand.

Since their separation, Aksel had tried to move on from her but couldn't. Regardless of the countless offers he had in college, he never connected with anyone. It's not that he lacked opportunity—Lyla owned his heart. He was still in love with her. Waiting out their separation had been the longest two years of his life. The night's confrontation was not what he'd envisioned for their reunion.

How could I lose control with her? You stupid shit!

The scent of her ginger-flavored body lotion was on her crumpled-up panties she had thrown at him. *I didn't want to desert her—it wasn't my choice…*

He recalled in vivid detail what happened that day as if it was yesterday. October 15, 1987. Lyla was inside the women's clinic terminating their unplanned pregnancy. Aksel arrived late after having a flat tire and sat down in the waiting area, worried sick, when a tall, attractive woman wearing a yellow Liz Claiborne dress entered the waiting room. He hadn't met her before but from pictures knew immediately that it was Lyla's mother. He stood up to introduce himself.

He'd reached out his hand. "Mrs. Robinson, I'm Aksel Portier and—"

"Ms. Thompson. So, you're the reason I'm here," Margo said. "I'd like to say it's nice to meet you, but truly it's not." Margo folded her arms across her chest. "Trying to keep it all in the family, Aksel?" Her words sliced his heart.

"I just want to be here for Lyla. I know this cannot be easy for her. Or you, ma'am."

"Easy? Think hiding and terminating your sixteen-year-old daughter's pregnancy is easy? If I told her father— or your father, for that matter— what do you think your status in your precious family business would be then? How dare you? She's just a baby!"

"I cannot apologize for loving Lyla. But I am so sorry this happened. We used pro—"

"Protection? Don't even bother! You've fucked with the wrong mother. You were screwing my daughter, an underage girl!"

"Ma'am, please. I—"

"You're over eighteen, little French boy. How would you like to see some of the darker parts of America, like prison?" Margo got within inches from his face and stabbed his chest with her fingernail. "I can get you locked up for statutory rape with just a phone call. And I will, too, if you so much as send her a fucking card, write her a note, leave a mysterious flower on our doorstep, or even call her from a fucking payphone!"

"I love your daughter," he uttered softly. "I always will. Would you please tell her I am sorry?"

"You think that loving her is some kind of consolation prize? As if you even know what love means. Get lost, you fucking little Frenchman," she shooed him away with a flick of her long red nails and a wrist adorned with a gold tennis bracelet.

"May I just say good-bye to her before I leave?"

"NO! Get lost, you fucking rapist! NOW!" Margo screamed at him, and everyone in the waiting room looked at them. He'd lowered his head in shame and quickly left.

Aksel snapped out of his daze. The heartache he still carried for putting Lyla in that position, not being able to say good-bye or tell her how he felt, tore at his chest. He shook his head. *Not this time.*

He called his father in France. "Dad, I've decided to transfer to NYU."

Chapter 4

Grant's office was located on the twelfth floor of 1350 Broadway in the heart of the garment district. The building was where he had worked for almost a decade at H&M Designs, one of the largest private label companies in the city. His current office, a floor above, represented the growth and happiness that Ginger had helped him achieve.

It was just after three p.m. on July 25th when he looked at his desk calendar where the 28th was circled and highlighted in green. The words read "Lyla moving here!" He couldn't believe how quickly fall was approaching or that his daughter would be starting NYU. He'd just returned from spending the week with his son. He and Jason had gone camping with Grant's cousin, Dan, and his daughter, Amiee. Grant rubbed his sore arm muscles. They'd all had fun fishing, hiking and riding dirt bikes, but he was still paying for it physically.

The last three days he'd been with both Lyla and Jason in Northbrook where they lived. Margo had begrudgingly allowed him to stay at the house since she was on a girls' weekend get-away. She resisted everything that had to do with her daughter moving to New York, so Grant helped Lyla pack up her stuff, and they took it to Terri, one of his closest friends, at TerRae Sportswear, her outside clothing manufacturing company, to be shipped to his apartment.

The time spent being a fulltime parent to both his kids in their own environment was eye-opening. Lyla had come home late a couple of times drunk or high, and when he tried to talk about it, she stonewalled him. Then one early morning, he caught Jason sneaking back home around five a.m. after being out with his girlfriend all night. Grant hadn't even realized his son had left.

"Where the hell were you?" he'd asked.

"Dad, I was out," Jason said. "I gotta get ready for football practice."

Grant didn't reply as Jason walked out of sight and it made him aware of the gravity and challenges of being a fulltime parent of a teenager. He wondered how things were going to unfold when Lyla moved in. At one point, he began to have second thoughts as to whether or not he should have set Lyla up in the dorms or a place of her own, but Ginger reminded him that Lyla wanted the time to be with them and to get acclimated to the city.

Grant swiveled around in his black leather office chair to look out from his twelfth-floor office window. The old double-hung sash was halfway opened to allow the warm summer breeze inside. Looking down onto the view of Broadway, bustling with people, cars and noise, he began to miss where he'd grown up, and had most recently visited, the pristine woods of Door County, Wisconsin.

A stack of mail from the ten days he had been away was sitting on his large mahogany desk. He was trying to get back into the groove of his city life, but it seemed as if the more mail he opened, the larger the pile grew.

The highlight of his day was the uplifting and unexpected phone call from Aksel Portier. He'd called Grant to see if he could do an internship for a business class since he was enrolled for the fall semester at NYU. Grant replied, "Absolutely! Just get me the paperwork." He told Aksel about Lyla attending NYU in the fall as well. After setting the date to start his internship, they ended the call.

Grant picked up the phone and dialed Nick's. "Nicky, I'll need a table for four Friday night."

"Sure! So whas da occasion?" Nick asked in his thick Brooklyn accent.

"Your goddaughter is coming home, *paesan.*"

He heard Nick yell with the phone against his chest, "Hey, Tony! Hey, stupid! I'ma talking to yooz!"

"Wha?" Tony screamed back.

"My goddaughter is coming home!"

⋆⟶◉⟵⋆

The summer flew by more quickly than Ginger had anticipated. She spent countless hours redecorating Lyla's bedroom, turning it into a space fit for a college-aged princess. She was putting the finishing touches on the tiny details before Lyla's arrival Friday night and found herself wondering how their life would change with another person living with them for the first time. Ginger loved the spontaneity of a clothing-optional lifestyle, not to mention the sexual activity they enjoyed whenever and wherever in their apartment.

It was going to be a challenge, she anticipated, for them to suddenly become fulltime parents of a teenager. A teenager who for a long time had fantasized about what life would be like living with them instead of with her mother.

Ginger sat on the edge of the unmade bed folding towels, looking mindlessly out the window past the freshly painted yellow walls. She pondered how she was going to manage Grant and Lyla since they both were so strong-willed. Knowing she was going to be the one caught in the middle, making her the "go to mediator" for both sides, she sighed deeply.

Her gaze was drawn to a framed picture of fifteen-year-old Lyla, and Ginger smiled as she remembered that day perfectly. Grant had taken them all sailing on the Hudson River for the ship parade on Fourth of July 1986, the celebration of the hundredth anniversary of the Statue of Liberty. Ginger set aside the towels to give the photo a kiss. "I love you and I'm so happy to have you here with us." She returned the picture to the dresser.

She heard the apartment door open and shut, then, "Gin, I'm home!"

"I'm in Ly's room making the bed."

His long stride went into the kitchen and she heard the smack of mail landing on the counter. "You want a glass of Pinot Noir?" he called.

"Sure, that would be great." She stuffed a pillow into a fresh pillowcase.

Grant walked down the hallway carrying the two glasses of wine but stopped midstride in the doorway: Ginger's ass was in the air as she bent over Lyla's bed, stretching the freshly washed fitted sheet atop the mattress.

"Let me help you make the bed, Gin." He placed the wineglasses on the dresser and slapped her ass lightly. She did not respond verbally; instead, she just wiggled her butt—she could tell that he wasn't going to help her *make the bed* when he placed his hands on her ass.

"Whoa, let's go to our room," Ginger said. "This is Lyla's bed! And I'm almost finished. I've been at it all summer, and this bedding is the -"

Gently grabbing her waist, he said, "She's not here now. Besides, somebody's gotta break it in… might as well be us, because it sure as hell *won't* be her!" He pulled down her shorts and panties from behind, leaving her bare ass exposed to him. Dropping to his knees, he ran his tongue around her cheeks.

"My sweet Tommy, we really shouldn't…" She feigned protest.

"Then maybe you shouldn't have worn these short shorts and this tank without a bra."

"I'm only doing my chores, Prince Insatiable!"

"Take a break, Cinderella. What do you expect from me when your sweet, beautiful ass is so enticingly up in the air?"

She flopped backward onto the crumpled sheets. Grant tore her thin pink racerback tank top off, literally. "Great. Now I have to go shopping *and* wash the bedding again," she purred as she wrapped her legs around his neck. "My sweet Tommy, you're so naughty." She lost her breath as soon as he buried his mouth between her legs and began sucking gently on her clit.

Her body quickly responded to his expert tongue, but she wanted a pounding orgasm and so she pushed his head back. She flipped over to grab one of the upper corners of the queen-sized bed and began taunting him with her backside. "You were almost there."

He had a surprised look on his face. "Are you complaining?"

She slapped her bare ass with her hand. "So maybe you need to spank me a little harder."

Grant smiled as he slapped her ass cheek, leaving a red handprint on it.

"Mooooore, please! Make it even."

He gave her other cheek a matching handprint, and she yelped with pleasure. She spread the lips of her pussy, "Now fuck me. I need a good fucking! I'm soooo ready!" She felt her feminine excitement roll down her bent legs pooling at her knees, before dripping onto the sheets.

Grant spanked her one more time and held tightly onto her hips, admiring her heart-shaped ass. He dragged her body down to the edge of the bed. "Now! Please?" Ginger begged.

Before she could take her next breath, she was overcome with the physical sensation that only Grant could treat her to. He slid deeply inside her and began thrusting in their perfect sexual rhythm. With her position on the bed, she was able to stimulate her clit on the edge of the mattress. Minutes later, they shared an orgasm that left them both breathless and sliding onto the floor next to the bed.

They leaned against the bed and he reached over to the dresser and grabbed their drinks. "I love you, Gin." Clinking their glasses together, they sat drinking the wine without another word spoken, both quietly realizing that their interlude probably marked the end of their sexual trysts of "whenever or wherever." He kissed her as he began to stand, then reached down to help her up. It was their last few nights of being a married couple without children.

They went out to the balcony, still naked. The early evening thunderstorm had already passed so they cuddled on one of the chaise lounges and sipped more wine while the sun set.

"I made a reservation at Nicky's for all four of us on Friday night," Grant said.

"All four of us?" she asked, watching the orange rays of the sun kiss the billowing clouds.

"Well, I spoke to Aksel today and he just moved into his apartment in SoHo on Tuesday. And I thought it would be nice for them to hookup again." He chuckled. "Remember how the two of them were thicker than thieves a few years ago? You know, the summer they were both here for the month?" He kissed the back of her neck.

"Great idea! I'm sure Lyla will be thrilled to see him."

"Let's make it a surprise."

"For Aksel also?" She kissed his hand.

"No, just Lyla. He has decided to attend NYU as well."

"Really? Wonder what made him decide to switch schools?"

"He's studying international business and they have a highly recognized business department. Also, he's going to intern with us part-time for one of his classes."

"When does he start?" Not letting Grant answer, she said, "He's really a great kid."

"I agree. So I thought, I'll pick her up alone on Friday night and give her some excuse about why you're not with me. I can't wait to see her face when we walk into Nick's and she sees Aksel with you!"

"Fun!" They *clinked* glasses, and Ginger smiled. She felt an uneasy sadness suddenly, knowing they were probably going to have to wear clothing the next time they were outside on the balcony.

Chapter 5

Lyla and Jason were alone in the foyer of their house, and she reached up on her tippy-toes to hug her little brother and whispered in his ear, "I love you so much. If you ever need me, I'm just a beep or a phone call away."

Jason continued to hug her, not wanting to let her go. "You know," he choked back his tears as he spoke, "this is the first time you're not just going to a sleepover or to visit Dad without me–you *won't* be back in a few days." His voice quavered as he held his sister tight.

She took a step away from him, reaching into her purse to pull out her car keys. "I know, baby bro. But here are my car keys. I want you to have them. You have your learner's permit. What better way to practice, right? I expect you to know that car inside and out by February so when you take the driving test, you can pass with flying colors."

"Lyla, it's your—"

She cut him off. "I can't have a car in New York, silly. Just let me use it when I come home on vacations."

"Mom won't let me have it." He attempted to give her back the keys.

"Hey, Mom," Lyla barked out loudly, "Jason's gonna learn to drive on my car—he has the keys now."

Margo entered the foyer with a hard smile. "Well, I guess I can't argue with that or I'll look like the bitch mom, won't I?"

"Yep, you would." Lyla looked back at Jason, held his shoulders, and finally let her tears flow. "You have no idea how much I love you. Be safe, JJ."

"I love you too, sissy."

"Come on, it's time to go. It's not like you won't see each other again," Margo grumbled, her jealously of their relationship evident in her sharp tone.

"Mom!" they both yelled, then they hugged again. Suddenly Lyla felt like a part of her was being left behind.

He had always been there for her and had tried to protect her since he was little.

"I'll keep her in line," Jason whispered to her as he gave her a final hug, "Love you, sis."

"Good luck with that. Love you too."

After the siblings said their farewells, Margo drove Lyla to O'Hare International. "Don't forget, your *fake father* has no idea what you put me through over the last couple of years. I covered your ass."

"Why do you always say that to me about Dad being fake, Mom? He *raised* me and *loves* me! Jesus, I've heard you say that like a million times since I was little. You need to get over your past." Lyla looked out the window of her mother's tan '86 Audi 5000 as they flew down Interstate 294.

"I only wanted you to know the truth, Lyla, so you would have options. Howard is a wonderful man and took care of me during a tough time in my life."

"Stop, Mom! PLEASE! You are really upsetting me." She put her hands over her ears, almost tempted to jump out of the moving car.

They arrived at the terminal. "Well, you're eighteen now and off to New York. All grown up. May I suggest you get on the pill ASAP? You wouldn't want a repeat performance, after all." Margo pulled a piece of paper out of her purse. "Here's Howard's phone number and address. He told me he would like to meet with you. And keep this in mind, he can open more doors for you than Grant can. Trust me."

Lyla shoved the piece of paper into her purse. *Like I'm going to actually call him?*

"Whatever, Mom. Is *this* how you want to say good-bye to your daughter? Why don't you add a 'kiss my ass' to it, and tell me that you hope I fail?"

"Lyla Robinson! You know I love you. How dare you speak to me like that?"

Margo parked in the departure zone but didn't even get out of the car. Lyla went to the popped-open trunk of the Audi, grabbed her suitcase and carry-on like she'd done every time over the years when traveling to New York.

Lyla stood by the open window of the car and leaned over to kiss her mother good-bye. "I *do* love you, Lyla," her mother said.

Lyla took a deep breath. She believed her mother loved her—to the best of her ability.

She said, "Love you too. I'll call you when I get there. Or I'll just send you a "two-one-two" on your pager. God only knows what Daddy has planned for tonight."

"Fine," Margo uttered. Her mother's expression was blank, as if she wasn't even there emotionally, like she was just dropping off a package at the post office.

Lyla almost ran to the curbside counter check-in, feeling like she could finally breathe, despite the hot July weather and the exhaust fumes filling the air from the multitude of cars. She relished her momentary solitude. *Freedom!* Lyla didn't even look back and wave good-bye; it didn't cross her mind. She had already left.

She was only focusing on the future—*her* future.

Lyla spotted her handsome father waving at her as she walked onto the concourse from the American Airlines bridge. *God, I love his distinguishing salt and pepper hair.* He wore a huge, welcoming smile as she made her way through the dozens of people all looking for loved ones. "Daddy! Daddy!" Lyla squealed with outstretched arms. She wrapped her arms around his neck and squeezed tightly.

"You are looking good, Dad. Still working out I see." She hugged him tightly again.

"Thank you, sweetheart. And you look like a model, absolutely beautiful. You always do."

"Yeah, but you're biased." She placed a kiss on his cheek. "Hey, where's Ginger?"

"Just picking up a last-minute surprise for you."

They started walking down the concourse toward the luggage claim area side by side. "Oh, Daddy enough already. You both have spoiled me rotten. *But,* I can't wait to see how you—ahem, *Ginger*—redecorated my room.

She called me with all kinds of questions over the last month about colors and whatnot."

"We are so excited to have you with us… Ginger wanted your room to be perfect."

She noticed that her dad kept looking around them as they retrieved her luggage. "What's the matter, Dad?"

"You, my dear, are attracting a lot of attention, most of it male. I'll have to keep my eye on you." He put a protective arm around her shoulder as they hurried outside. She had no idea what he was talking about.

Lyla saw Evan, the chauffeur, waiting by the gray Lincoln stretch limo. "Evan!" She said loudly as they approached him in his crisp white shirt and black pants. Standing on her tippy-toes she placed a gentle peck on the side of his wiry, white-haired Black face.

"My, my, Miss Lyla, congratulations on your graduation and a job well done. You know your daddy, Ms. Ginger, and I are all so very proud of you."

Lyla hugged him. "Thanks, Evan. You're the best."

Evan sighed, holding her hand and slowly spinning her around in her cotton printed sundress just like he had when she was a little girl. "How have you grown up on me? Wasn't it just last spring when I saw you?" He turned to Grant. "Mr. Grant, are you sure this is our little Lyla? Because if it is, I'm afraid she's become a young lady on us now," he teased.

Grant agreed, jerking his thumb toward the baggage claim. "So I've noticed, Evan."

Evan removed his black driver's cap and took a slight bow. "Princess, welcome home." Smiling, he held the door open for them while they climbed in. He put the luggage in the trunk before sliding in on the black leather seat behind the wheel of the limo.

Evan had always been in her and Jason's life with a kind word here and there. He remembered their birthdays with small surprise gifts. How many conversations had he listened to yet never said anything, or even judged? Evan just drove her and her family safely through New York and had since she could remember.

"How about some of Nick's noodles?" Her dad grabbed her hand with a smile on his face.

"Perfect! I'm starving! Ginger will be there, right?"

"Of course. Wouldn't be a proper welcome-home dinner without her."

A half hour later, Evan dropped them off at Nick's Italian Ristorante, a small storefront restaurant located on West 44th Street near Times Square. The aroma of fine Italian cuisine filled the air as they walked under the red canopy toward the door, and Lyla's mouth instantly began to water.

The restaurant hadn't changed since she was a youngster sitting on her daddy's lap. The autographed picture of Elvis Presley still hung proudly on the wall, along with countless other paintings that looked like they were gathered from random garage sales. The long wall had the mural, although a bit faded, of Napoli, as Nick and Toni called it. Countless knickknacks cluttered every open flat surface. Pictures of Nick's grandchildren covered any open wall space, including the walls in the kitchen area. Since she could remember, there was a statue of a big fat Italian chef holding a pizza, which greeted the patrons upon entry. The vinyl, red-checked tablecloths probably hadn't been updated in at least a decade.

Looking across the T-shaped dining room, she was filled with excitement as soon as she spotted Ginger's auburn hair. Her stepmother sat with another man whose back was to her—*who is that?* When he turned, the sight of him caused Lyla to lose her footing. She grabbed onto her dad's arm, trying to make it look like she'd missed a step down.

"Aksel?" she whispered.

When Ginger saw Lyla, she jumped up and yelled, "Lyla!" from across the room, then waited for them with arms wide open, doing a little happy dance. Aksel stood as well, a half-smile on his face. *What the fuck?* Lyla screamed inside as they walked toward the table. She leaned over to her dad. "I know I'm only eighteen, Daddy, but can I order a martini?"

Grant smirked at her. "Aren't you funny, baby girl."

"I'm dead serious, Daddy!"

"Then don't call me 'Daddy.'"

"Then don't call me 'baby girl.'"

Grant laughed. "I'll see what I can do. After all, it's your first night in New York as an *almost* grown-up. But don't get used to it."

As they reached the table, Ginger said, "Surprise! We thought you would love to see Aksel again."

Lyla kept a tight smile as she hugged Ginger whispering, "What's *he* doing here?" She winced at her irritated hushed tone.

Ginger whispered back, "Oh, I take it we made a mistake?"

Lyla nodded at Ginger, then turned to Aksel, who remained standing. He lightly hugged her and pulled back the chair next to him for her to sit.

"Thank you," she said flatly. "Good to see you, Aksel. What are you doing in New York?"

"I transferred to NYU for international business."

"Really? Wow. How nice," she responded politely. *Great, now he's stalking me.*

Aksel's eager expression confused her, but she refused to be taken in again—did he think they could just talk things out and all would be well?

65

Lyla felt Ginger's gaze as she and Aksel conversed. Her dad told Nick that Lyla wanted a martini. Ginger had to know that there was more going on between them than met the eyes.

Beloved Nick, a hearty bald Italian in his early fifties with a booming voice, arrived at their table. He wiped his hands on a sauce-stained apron he wore over a navy Mets T-shirt with white pants. "Lyla!" He yelled in a thick Brooklyn-Italian accent, "Ah, bambina!" He pulled her up from her seat while holding her hands. "Look at how much my goddaughter has grown!"

She hugged Nick with a huge smile.

"Bambina, with those shoes, yooz almost taller than me." He planted a kiss on her cheek.

⊷⊷═◉═⊶⊶

The restaurant was busy as usual, but Nick always had time to walk by and check on his guests, especially the Robinsons. They were like family to him. He'd watched Lyla grow from a small child—he'd taught her how to spin her spaghetti with her fork and spoon—to a beautiful young woman. Noticing she hadn't eaten much of her meal, he became concerned.

"Hey wats up wit' you? Yooz watchin' your weight or somethin'?" Nick stood next to Lyla and peered at her half-full martini glass. "If I didn't know any better, I'd say you like your liquid appetizer more than my pasta," Nick said, winking at Grant, folding his hands across his apron.

"I'm just not that hungry, Nick."

"So now I'm 'Nick'? What, are ya too grown up to call me Nicky no more? Is it da food? Don't it tastes like it should?" Nick turned toward the kitchen and hollered, "Tony, what didja do wrong with the chicken cacciatore ova' here?"

The cook appeared in the kitchen window and yelled something back, then waved him off dismissively and disappeared.

Turning back to Lyla, he said, "Piece of work, that Tony." He pointed at Aksel's plate. "Look, your Frenchman over there loved it."

"It's *perfecto*, Nicky," Aksel responded.

"Thank you. But I'm talking to my goddaughter here." He added a note of protectiveness in his voice.

Lyla sipped from her second martini as if uncomfortable.

"Hey, what's da matter wit' you?" Nick asked Lyla again. "Why you so quiet? Yooz betta not be pregnant or somethin'." He laughed, thinkin' he was being funny.

Aksel dropped his fork.

Lyla almost spat out her drink. "Things have changed, Nick. *Nicky*. A lot."

"Hey, Tony," Nick teased Grant by yelling across the restaurant again, "Grant's gonna be a nonno!"

Tony yelled back as he tossed pizza dough in the air, "Grandpa Grant! So who's da fatha?"

⟡

Standing outside of Nick's as they were getting into the limo, Grant offered to take Aksel home. "No, no, *Monsieur* Robinson. I cannot impose any more on your hospitality tonight," he said. "Thank you for dinner. The company was great. I can take a cab to my apartment—it's downtown from here."

"Aksel, Evan is waiting. Get in." Aksel hemmed and hawed before Grant teasingly pushed him into the limo.

Lyla climbed in, sitting against the far door. "Daddy, sit next to me, please?"

"Sure." He slid across the leather seat.

"Evan, we're going to Aksel's apartment first, then home," Ginger announced in her sweet yet strong tone.

"Yes, of course, Ms. Ginger."

"Great," Ginger said. "Thanks, Evan. Where do you live, Aksel?"

"In SoHo." Grant's new intern seemed upset as he gave the address—what was going on?

An uncomfortable silence fell upon all of them. Grant couldn't figure out what was wrong but the quiet was deafening.

Grant cleared his throat. "So, do you have the penthouse?"

"Not really, it's the top, the sixth floor. I do have a view of the city. But no doormen though." Aksel laughed nervously and glanced toward Lyla. Did the kid have a crush on his daughter?

Lyla leaned into her father, and closed her eyes—effectively ignoring the conversation—she even pretended to be dozing when they dropped Aksel off at his apartment. Grant exchanged a questioning look with Ginger, who shook her head. Kids.

Chapter 6

Saturday morning Lyla woke from a night of twisting and turning in her newly decorated bedroom. She stretched, her body stiff from traveling and the unexpected tension-filled evening. *And to actually think I was looking forward to a new start in New York. God, what a fucked up night last night was! Aksel, you're such an asshole for following me to New York. I can't figure out if I hate you or love you. Or both!*

She began to cry, holding her hand over her mouth so no one would hear her, finally burying her face in her pillow. *I'm so confused. He left me! Why do I even care about him? What's wrong with me? I always knew we would see each other again—eventually! But my first night in New York?*

Lyla had pretended to sleep in the limo so that she wouldn't know where Aksel lived—in case she was tempted to ream him a new one. Sitting up and slipping out of the covers, she lifted her suitcase onto the bed and started to unpack.

A gentle tap sounded and Ginger peeked from behind the partially open door, "Good morning, sunshine!" She came all the way into the room. "I made some coffee, if you need a caffeine fix."

Lyla hoped Ginger wouldn't comment on her puffy red eyes from tears and flashed a halfhearted smile. "No thanks. Haven't started that habit just yet." Lyla continued to unpack with no enthusiasm.

"Tea?"

"Really, I'm okay. I have water." She gestured to her nightstand.

Ginger shut the door and sat on the edge of the bed, amid an explosion of colors from the different clothes that covered the bed from her suitcase—it resembled a watercolor painting.

"So how did you sleep?"

"Not that great, Gin. I still need to adjust to the fact that this is my room again. Oh, and the noises from the street, I forgot about it – even this high up! What the hell, do they pick up garbage *all* night?" She laughed lightly. "That'll take some getting used to, I guess."

"I remember that from when I moved here from Texas."

"But I love what you did to my room, Mommy Gin. And I love these sheets—they are so soft!" She raised her hand to high-five Ginger.

Ginger blushed when she high-fived her back and Lyla wondered what *that* was all about. "I'm glad you like it." Ginger sorted through the tops and finally pickup one up from the pile. "Ly, this is so cute. I'm calling dibs on borrowing this one!"

"Really?" Lyla smiled as an idea occurred. "Cool with me. I can share my clothes…IF YOU WILL!" she said.

"Deal! Glad we can share things." Ginger hesitated and then said, "Speaking of sharing, you obviously know I kept your secret about NYU. I wouldn't share your secrets with anyone."

Lyla stopped separating her colorful clothing and looked at Ginger. "I know that and thank you." She kissed Ginger on the forehead. "You're the best!"

"Not *all* the time, but let's be honest, *most* of the time!" They both laughed, and Ginger reached for Lyla's hand. "Come, sit for a second."

"Okay…" Lyla sat down next to Ginger.

"Can we have some secret girl-talk?"

"Do I get to keep the secret for you this time?" Lyla liked the idea of that.

"We can trust each other with anything, right?" Ginger looked into her face.

"I'll take it to the grave. Do tell!" Lyla was thrilled that Ginger had a secret to share with her.

"Well, it's not about me, Ly, it's about you."

"Uh-oh. *Me?*" Her bubble of excitement instantly burst.

"What's the deal with you and Aksel? Is there something you'd like to tell me? Or *not* tell me?" Lyla felt the blood drain from her face. "Just remember how much I adore you; we've always been connected. If there's *anything* that I can help you with, you *know* I'm always here for you." Ginger grasped Lyla's hand as it went limp. "But considering what I know of your history, what I saw last night between you and Aksel didn't make much sense."

Lyla's eyes immediately welled with tears. She shook her head and looked in the opposite direction of Ginger's caring face. Lyla started to get up, but Ginger grabbed her arm and pulled her back down.

"I know a broken heart when I see one, sweetheart. And somehow your father didn't even notice... men... women's intuition wins again. If you want to talk—" Lyla collapsed onto Ginger's lap. "Oh, baby girl..."

"Where's Daddy?" she murmured.

"He just left to work out for an hour. We're alone. Just you and me." Ginger softly rubbed Lyla's back. Finally gathering herself, Lyla sat up.

"Gin, I-I-I—"

"It's okay. If you want to wait…"

Tears rolled down Lyla's cheeks. "There's so much to tell you but I don't want you to look at me the same way my mother does. Promise me."

"I promise. You can tell me anything."

The floodgates opened as she began sobbing uncontrollably and covered her face with her hands. Ginger retrieved the tissues and sat back down next to Lyla as she composed herself enough to talk. She wiped her tears away with a tissue.

"Remember the summer two years ago when Aksel was here for a summer vacation, when you and Daddy took JJ to the Baseball Hall of Fame in Cooperstown, and Niagara Falls?"

"Of course. You stayed behind to go sightseeing with Aksel."

"Well, that's when it happened… we fell in love that week."

"Really? How did I miss that?"

"We kept it hidden from everyone because he was eighteen, and I was only sixteen."

"Okay."

"God, Gin, it was so perfect! I remember every detail as if it just happened…" She hesitated while looking into Ginger's tender eyes for reassurance before continuing. "We had three nights and four days together, just the two of us. We went all over the city. The first night there was a big thunder storm and it woke me up around midnight. I walked out to get water and found him standing at the window watching the storm. There was a big bang of lightning and we both jumped. We laughed at each other and decided to sit on the couch to chat. He was hungry, and he wanted to have one of Ray's famous pizzas. I told him we had to have the Hawaiian pizza which he'd never had before. There, the two of us sat around at two in the morning eating pizza and talking until early dawn. I think we only had three hours sleep that first night.

"The next day we went shopping on Fifth Avenue, starting at Bergdorf Goodman's where we ate lunch upstairs in the café. We made our way down Fifth Avenue, finally ending up at Saks, where he treated me to a couple of tops I looked at for more than a minute." She laughed and wiped her tears.

"After that, we had appetizers at the champagne bar on the fifth floor at Saks, and finished off two bottles of *Veuve Clicquot* – we tried both the brut and the rose. I preferred the rose." She lightly laughed as she recalled the euphoria in the moment. "Anyway, we took a cab back to the apartment because we were pretty tipsy. And I know what you're thinking, but no, we didn't have sex. Not yet anyway." She blushed.

Ginger smiled. "This is sounding very romantic."

Lyla felt so at ease that she responded with a huge, "Oh, it was!" She began to relive the excitement from the memory. "The next day we had lunch at a corner hotdog stand after getting lost in sparkly things at Tiffany's. Audrey Hepburn is right, nothing bad can happen when you're at Tiffany's."

"Is that when you got that ring that you're still wearing?"

"Yes, he insisted on buying it for me." She looked down at the simple sterling silver band that had a floating heart charm on it, and spun it around a few times. "Then for dinner we walked through the park to Tavern on the Green. Again, it was romantic, but nothing physical had happened yet, except for holding hands and a few cheek kisses.

"We took pictures. Here, look." Lyla retrieved the envelope she'd stashed at the bottom of her purse and handed it to Ginger. Ginger removed the five pictures and scanned each. Lyla stopped Ginger when she got to the last one. "I love this one of us in front of Tiffany's."

"It's adorable. Go on, love."

"So that night when we got back to the apartment, we sat outside on the chaise lounges and talked. It was the second night and we chilled out. Ha, ha," she laughed, "We actually smoked a joint together and drank some of your vodka and orange juice! We laughed and kissed a little, not really making out. But when it was time for bed he came and lay with me in bed. He was inches away from my face and we continued talking, but he stayed above the covers and eventually he petted me to sleep.

"I woke up in the morning to his beautiful face just within reach from mine and I knew I was falling for him. Hard. And I could tell he was falling for me too, but he never made a move on me. So, we spent the full day just roaming the streets, went to the Met, talked about going to a play but we didn't. We ended up in Times Square for a few hours at dusk and it was fun to watch him marvel at the spectacle of lights and sights.

"For dinner we ate at Harry's New York Bar and Steakhouse downtown in the business district. He was dying to eat there since he had been at the one in Paris. Anyway, without discussion when we got back to the apartment, he climbed into bed with me like the night before and he pet me to sleep once again."

She sighed and smiled with tears in her eyes. "But that morning when we woke up, we made love. Gin, he was my first. I loved him so much. It was so tender and passionate, freeing and loving and ugh, I could go on and on. But that was our secret and why he decided to attend Northwestern University so he could be close to me and we could continue our relationship."

Ginger hugged Lyla. "So, why are you two at such odds? Honestly, even though you clearly have broken up, why was it *so* uncomfortable last night?"

"I'm really sorry about that. You'll understand soon, but remember, no judgments, okay?"

"No judgments." Ginger crossed her heart with her fingers.

Then Lyla spent the next half hour telling her as many details of their clandestine relationship that followed, including her accidental pregnancy with Aksel—something she never thought she would speak of with anyone, since she was so ashamed. She told her how her mother took her to the clinic and she expected to see Aksel there, but he never showed.

They embraced, and both cried.

"Gin, he promised me he would be there with me at the clinic… Mom said he called when I was sleeping after."

"God, that must have been just awful for you!" Ginger squeezed her hand.

"All I wanted to do when I got home was sleep and pretend like it never happened. Anyway, he promised me we'd be together forever and ever. And I never heard from him when I needed him most! He's such an asshole!"

Ginger wrapped her arms around her as she sobbed. "I know, my sweetheart. I know."

"Mom said he only called once to tell me that it would have never worked out between us because…I wasn't good enough for him, because I was in a different class than his." Lyla's tears spilled anew.

Ginger consoled Lyla, but asked, "Are you sure that's really what he said, though? I mean, sometimes your mother can exaggerate things."

"No kidding." Lyla halfheartedly laughed through her tears. "I don't really know, but he never called or anything from that day on until suddenly showing up as a shadow at my graduation. He's who I was looking for after my speech. Later when I found out that Mom didn't invite you and Dad to my graduation party, I was pretty steamed and I left. I found myself at his condo in Evanston. And you know what? All he wanted to do was fuck me, Gin! We barely said hello before his shorts were off and my dress was up around my neck. It angered me. I'm SO angry with him! All I really was to him was just a piece of ass," she said through gritted teeth.

After a few minutes of silence, Lyla said, "That's why I can't go to NYU this year. I'm going to defer until next

August. I can't be where he is, Gin, I just can't. But you can't tell Daddy why, okay? Promise?"

"Oh, God. I promise. But we really should talk about this more. A knee-jerk reaction isn't always the best thing to do. Let's sit on it and decide when we're not so emotional."

Thinking about even broaching the subject with Grant made Ginger's stomach flip. Just then they heard the front door open and close. Grant was back. Ginger winked at Lyla, then quickly left her room and closed the door behind her.

Ginger walked down the hallway. *So begins the tumultuous life of living with a teenager. Fuck…this isn't going to be easy.* She held a finger to her lips as she greeted Grant in the hall and whispered, "She's just waking up, my love."

"Oh, okay." He whispered in kind, "I'll shower and then we'll make breakfast."

"Great, baby."

Grabbing her hand and pulling her against him he asked, "Wanna join me?" He wore a naughty grin.

"I'd love to, my sweet Tommy, but we never got the bagels yesterday, so I'll run and grab them. Rain check?" She pinched his ass and grabbed the sweat-covered towel that hung around his neck and pulled his face into hers for a kiss.

"Mmm…if you insist, Rach."

✦⟶⊙⟵✦

An hour later, the three Robinsons were sitting on the balcony chaise lounges enjoying the beautiful day that yesterday's cold front brought with it. Midway through their late Saturday morning brunch together Grant asked Lyla, "So, how soon do classes start?"

"Grant, she hasn't even had a chance to pick her schedule yet," Ginger said as if to deflect his question.

"Actually," Lyla hesitated, "I've decided I'm not starting in the fall."

Grant nearly stopped breathing; Ginger looked toward the sky while downing her mimosa.

Lyla quickly continued, "I thought maybe I'd start school in January, or possibly just take the year off and start *next* fall. A sabbatical, if you will. I can delay my entry for up to a year, you know." She finished her sentence and smiled.

Grant looked at his daughter as if she had two heads.

"It's not *that* big a deal." She drained her mimosa too. "Lots of people take a year off after high school. I'll go, just not yet."

Ginger never said a peep.

Grant blurted, "Ly, I thought NYU was why you are here!"

"You told me NYU was a going to be a surprise for your father," Ginger said.

Turning to Ginger with surprise, he said, "You knew about this before she told us in Chicago?" Grant's voice rose to a holler.

"Uh, well, I—" Ginger shuffled for words.

Lyla put her plate down on the small table next to her lounge chair and jumped up. "Stop it. Both of you. This is *my* life. *My* decision! I'm an adult now."

"A *young* adult who lives here *rent-free!* I hope you have plans on working during your *sabbatical.* Because if you think I'm going to just hand over an unlimited credit card, you're nuts, young lady." Grant heard the stern shock in his tone and didn't recognize it.

"Ohmigod, Dad! Really? I just got here last night! You're going to make a federal case out of this? Can I have five seconds to breathe, or even think? *Alone?* You're acting like Mom!" She stormed off the balcony, leaving Ginger and Grant looking at each other, speechless.

Still dumbfounded, Grant and Ginger sat silently on the balcony trying to digest the news. While gathering themselves emotionally from Lyla's outburst, they didn't speak, afraid to discuss anything in case Lyla was within earshot. They finished their food before gathering the plates and headed into the kitchen. Ginger placed the plates in the sink and Grant spotted a note on the counter. He picked it up and read it aloud:

"Daddy and Mommy Gin,

> *I'm sorry about the news. I didn't think you would take it so hard. I'm okay, or I will be. Just going to take a stroll through Central Park to clear my head. Please still love me when I get back.*
>
> *Love, Ly"*

"Grant, she's young and trying to—"

"To what, Gin? Fuck with our heads? And I can't believe *you knew* she was moving here! And now she's not even *going* to school! That's why you were so calm and reassuring, isn't it?"

"Yes, I did know. She made me promise to keep her secret as a surprise for you. This is new to me about deferring. Grant, babe, she loves you and wants to—" Grant cut her off and continued his ranting as she finished putting dishes into the dishwasher.

"Force me to tell Margo that she was right?"

"Force you to *what?*" Ginger placed her hands on her hips.

"She warned me that I couldn't just swoop in and become the father of the year! Fuck, Gin!" He threw a sponge into the sink and began to pace back and forth.

"Stop interrupting me, Tommy. Sit down before you have a stroke."

"I can't stop thinking about everything I've done wrong as a father. You know what I'm good at? Working. I'm going to go check on—"

"Wait just a second. I have a thought. And sit down, dammit!" She forced Grant to sit down on a stool by the kitchen counter and poured him a glass of water.

"What's your thought?" He gulped the water and collected himself.

"My brother might need a server at his new restaurant. Maybe he can give Lyla a job. It's demanding work, but at least she'll be doing *something.*"

He sighed, "How do you do it?"

"I can just call—" She looked at him with confusion.

"No, no, Gin. How do you always turn lemons into lemonade? I thank God for you, Rachel." Grant pulled her on his lap and wrapped her up in his arms.

"My sweet Tommy, we found each other after being torn apart in our last lives...*this is nothing!*" He squeezed her with his entire body.

"Gin, thank you. I feel better now, but not truly happy about Lyla deferring college. I'm going to clear my head and review the orders from market before Monday's meeting."

"Go. And ask Evan to drive slowly. You need to clear your head. I love you."

"I love you more than you'll ever know."

"I know." She winked at him.

Chapter 7

Ginger stood outside on the balcony after Grant had left with a fresh mimosa in hopes that she could reopen the subject of college with Lyla after she returned from the park. Warm sunlight filled the space and Ginger sat down on the chaise, taking a deep breath before calling her brother. She was glad to have a few minutes alone to digest the news about Lyla not attending college, knowing it had everything to do with Aksel being there. *Yikes. Lyla is so much like Grant, hard workers who carry their hearts on their sleeves*

with that stubborn attitude that they know what's right. I can't wait to corner Aksel and hear his version of this story.

"Thanks, Andrew. You're a lifesaver," Ginger said to her brother. "Love you, too." He had agreed to interview Lyla but assured her that he would hire her. She sat back feeling much more confident in at least having secured a possible job for Lyla. *Now if I can reason with her to reconsider school maybe we can avoid this whole mess.* Ginger went back inside and filled the tub with warm water and just was about to turn the Jacuzzi bubbles on when the phone rang.

The female voice spoke in a terse manner, which she immediately recognized.

"Hi, Margo. No, she's out taking a walk. Yes, at the park." Ginger held the phone away from her ear. "No, Grant is not with her."

"She's alone?" Margo started to speak loudly. "Where the woman jogger was raped and left for dead just this past spring?"

Ginger didn't reply. *God, I forgot to count her into the equation of our new life.*

"She'll be fine." The word *bitch* came to Ginger's mind as she felt her claws coming out. In hopes of deflecting anger away from Lyla, she said, "I might as well tell you—she's decided to take a short sabbatical before she starts college." Margo erupted and Ginger waited for her to finish running Grant into the ground.

When the woman took a breath, she rushed in. "Margo, stop all this blaming bullshit. You and Grant are great parents, but Lyla has a lot of stuff she wants to work through. Don't worry; we've got her covered."

Margo asked, "What does that mean?"

After another pause, Ginger responded. "It means that Lyla's father and I are keeping her best interests at the forefront. I've arranged for her to work at my brother's restaurant as a waitress."

Margo yelled a slew of uncomplimentary words about Grant until Ginger said, "I'm hanging up, Margo. I'll tell him to call you when he gets a chance."

Click.

"Margo, why are you such a bitch?!" Ginger said out loud.

She turned around, and all the blood drained from her face when she saw Lyla standing in the doorway of the master suite.

"Nice Gin, guess I'm supposed to thank you for getting me a job? Thanks for giving me time to look on my own or even decide what kind of a job I want. You're all the same: planning *my* life for me."

"Ly, listen—"

"I need a shower." She walked out of Ginger's room and slammed the door to her room.

◈◈◈

Although any real work could wait until Monday, Grant still needed a change of scenery.

Oh, Lyla, he thought as he stepped off the elevator into a small, dimly lit reception area. The console table had a large vase of flowers brightening the room. Entering the lobby of his office, he took a moment to breathe in as the tranquility of the space he and Ginger had created engulfed him. A *fēng shui* consultant had been called in to design each area to promote creativity and positive energy, keeping negativity at bay.

He rubbed the belly of the golden Laughing Buddha statue and listened to the sound of the cascading rock waterfall positioned in the prosperity corner of the lobby. A small statue of the Egyptian goddess Isis was perched with her wings spread on top of the waterfall.

Standing in front of the water feature, his energy recharged. He walked over to the front counter and grabbed the stack of messages that Sue had left for him in his box. A message halted him midstride when he read: "Howard Golden. Need to talk ASAP—important."

As if I need to hear his voice today. Hadn't had a real conversation since Howard had called Grant a thief, when

Grant would never resort to stealing accounts. *He made more money than he ever dreamed of from the Neiman Marcus account that I brought into H&M Designs.*

Howard was Grant's old boss and now competitor. They'd parted ways after Grant and Ginger landed the Le Printemps account almost six years earlier. The Portiers, owners of Le Printemps, preferred working with Ginger and Grant instead of Howard. They'd offered to form a partnership and back them financially to start their own private-label design company, which they'd proudly named "G Squared."

Ugh, I don't think I can handle him today. Probably had a falling out with Steve or Rebeka at Neiman Marcus. Not my problem.

Grant considered tossing the message, but curiosity got the best of him. He sat at his desk, swiveling his chair to look out the window, and called Howard.

"Howard. Grant. What's up?" He prepared for some nasty comment but was surprised by Howard's ragged breathing.

"Jesus, Howard. You sound like shit. Are you dying or something?" He chuckled to himself as he listened to Howard speak, then straightened. "You're serious—I'm so sorry to hear that… how long do you have…?"

After the call ended, Grant mulled over his conversation with Howard, slightly in shock, when his beeper went off. It was Ginger's message to call home with a 9-1-1.

"What the fuck? What did Lyla do now?" he growled to himself.

He called immediately and Ginger picked up, frantically speaking but he couldn't quite understand.

"Gin, baby, slow down. Aunt Sadie what?" He jumped up from his chair.

"She's in the ICU at Brooklyn City Hospital."

"I'm on my way!" He hung up the phone and rushed out the door, but he couldn't shake a nagging feeling. *Shit, they say everything bad comes in threes…*

⤙�⟞⤚

Grant ran through the emergency entrance at the hospital and found his way to the ICU. Lyla was hovering near the doorway, and he hugged her tightly. "Ginger's inside," Lyla said through tears. "I think Aunt Sadie had a major stroke."

"Has anyone called Ginger's parents?"

"Yes, but they're still out of town."

"Come with me, baby girl." They held hands and walked inside the private room.

Ginger was seated next to Aunt Sadie, holding the older woman's hand. Though hooked up to every machine imaginable, Aunt Sadie had a peaceful look on her face.

"Honey, she's been saying your name," Ginger said, turning to Grant.

"Me? Really?" A sudden cold blast hit him in his core.

At that moment, Aunt Sadie regained consciousness and said softly, "He's been waiting for me, Tommy. Now that you and Rachel found each other again, it's my turn to let you know something…Allen wanted me to tell you that you were the lucky one to come back, to be reunited…I need to go now. It's my turn to be with him on the other side. My soul mate…"

Grant's eyes filled with tears as she neared her last breaths. He turned to Lyla and said, "Let's give Ginger a moment with her aunt."

As they walked out, Lyla inquired, "Who was she talking about, Daddy?"

"It's kind of confusing, baby girl. I'll explain one day, but not right now." He avoided her question, not wanting to open a discussion about past lives right then.

Only a few minutes passed before a beeping sound went off and nurses rushed into the room with a crash cart.

It wasn't long before Ginger stumbled out and fell into Grant's arms. "She's gone. But I know she's happy now. She smiled as she took her last breath, love." Tears streamed down her face. "Grant, do you believe Allen was really there, waiting for her?"

"Yes, my love. I do."

Lyla joined their hug and wept along with Ginger, while Grant tightened his embrace around his two favorite girls.

Andrew, Ginger's brother, a tall, dirty-blond, green-eyed, muscular man, arrived at the ICU, sweaty and out of breath. He stopped running when he saw the three of them. "Gin, am I too late?"

"She went peacefully." She tearfully hugged her brother before he went in.

When Andrew came out of the room after seeing his aunt, there were tears in his eyes. Ginger caught him up on what happened while waiting for the doctor to fill out his paperwork. She then followed a nurse to contact the funeral home. Grant, Andrew and Lyla moved down the hall to the ICU waiting area where they waited for Ginger.

"So, Lyla, Ginger said you are looking for a job?" Andrew asked while sitting next to her.

"Yeah, she mentioned she had talked to you. But I must warn you, I've never worked in a restaurant before. Not sure if I am good enough to be considered help." Lyla didn't look at Grant, who waited for her to try and make an excuse, or back out. Why had she changed her mind about starting college?

"Well, why don't you come over and check it out and decide if you are interested."

"Okay, sounds good." His daughter kept her shoulder to him.

Ginger walked in after she signed the hospital's necessary paperwork, and Andrew offered dinner at his restaurant since Clara was with the kids at her parents. "Lyla, I can show you around and introduce you to the staff."

"Sure," Lyla said.

Grant was grateful that Lyla wasn't fighting them about having a job and quickly agreed.

◦‣═◉═‣◦

Lyla, knowing it wasn't the time to battle Ginger or Grant about working, was impressed with Andrew's restaurant, A. Madison's on the Nue, located on the second floor of a building on Madison Avenue. The advantage of a second floor restaurant was the view of Madison Avenue without the hustle and bustle of taxis or foot traffic. The crown molding resembled architecture from the eighteenth century, complementing the numerous wall murals. Countless chandeliers made of champagne and wine glasses added to the modern eccentric ambiance of the dining room.

She admired the tuxedo-style uniforms the servers wore, knowing Ginger and Grant had designed them. The women's uniforms were more feminine with pleated A-line miniskirts instead of pants; however, all servers wore cummerbunds and bow ties. Every server was gorgeous—would Andrew even want to hire her? It seemed a prerequisite to be strikingly beautiful—that, or it was just New York.

Her mother's negative comments had her concerned she wouldn't be good enough.

They were seated at a table overlooking Madison Avenue while Andrew went to retrieve a bottle of wine.

Ginger tapped Lyla on the forearm. "Ly, hon, I'm sorry about earlier. This isn't meant to be a forever job. What else interests you? You seem so natural with fashion and the latest trends. Would you like to model or work in the fashion industry like your father and I?"

"Wow, modeling? Me? I don't think so."

"Why not?"

"Mom always said I'm not tall or pretty enough."

Ginger sat back in disbelief. "Your height is perfect for modeling, and you're drop-dead gorgeous."

"I'm not gorgeous, Gin." Lyla scanned the room nervously, comparing herself and not measuring up in her own mind. "Look at these people—they're just the servers! It's cool what you and Daddy do, but I don't have any idea how to start in your industry." It was what she'd wanted but now she wasn't sure. Seeing Aksel again had changed everything.

"Remember how you helped me design some patterns last spring? You can do anything, Lyla, and now is your chance. I have connections—I'll see if I can hook you up with the Fashion Institute of Technology or Barbizon, if you'd like."

"Um, I'm not sure." Lyla glanced at Ginger, who she knew loved her. "What if I'm not good enough?"

"That's why it's called school—you'll learn. But I need to know soon so you can enroll, because classes start in a few weeks."

"Would I still have to work?" Lyla asked.

"Yes, Lyla. It's not NYU, which is what we agreed on," her dad said, including himself in the conversation. "I would love to have you learn the industry, though. Maybe intern with us at G Squared."

"Which of those schools would get me that internship?"

"Fashion Institute," Ginger said.

"Then I'll go with Barbizon." Lyla smiled at her tiny rebellion.

Ginger laughed, and her dad rolled his eyes.

Chapter 8

Lyla and Andrew agreed on a starting date that would coincide with the training of other new staff, which gave her almost two weeks off before her job at The Nue. After updating her wardrobe with Ginger during a few shopping sprees, she reorganized her closet, right down to color-coordinating her shoes. She exercised daily in the gym at their building, sometimes twice a day, and walked in the park each morning.

But as much as she tried to keep her mind busy, it constantly drifted to thoughts of Aksel, to how much she loved and hated him. She recalled their intimate moments and how he endlessly surprised her with his passion—which only made everything that happened so much worse.

After a long walk in the park one day, she lay in her bed, on the verge of tears. He'd been so giving. They'd only been able to secretly steal time together in the early afternoons after their classes a couple times a week. It was early fall and the heat of summer still filled the days. Their interludes were both hot and sweaty as they *needed* each other desperately. Their kisses were so passionate and deep, she could barely breathe. The fact that they didn't have much room didn't help—in their familiar place, the back seat of his Mustang, hidden away in some deserted area of any number of parks around the suburbs of Chicago.

It was near the end of the first month of their clandestine relationship, and they'd gotten braver as they explored their sexuality.

She dozed, recalling one of their hottest times in detail.

"Oh, my," he'd said. "Is this for me?" Aksel had pulled her panties aside, feeling her slick wet lips. "How can you give yourself to me so freely?"

"You own my heart, you always have." She felt the heat growing with each touch. She straddled him. They were both topless, skin to skin. She started to grind on him—a prelude of what was to come. She pulled at his long brown hair like a sex-starved maniac, continuing the longest

kiss to date. It had been a week since they shared naked time together, yet it seemed like forever.

Feeling his physical excitement growing, she couldn't get his pants off fast enough to treat him orally. He was so large, and she loved to see how much of him she could take into her mouth, each time a little more. He pulled her head with both hands into him as he thrusted his hips, gently forcing his size deeper into her mouth. He let her have her way with his cock, and they were both entranced with each other.

With bated breath he said, "You are so ravenous. I want to be inside you. Now…"

"I'm not done with you yet. Give in to me, please, Aksel. I want to taste you this time."

"I can't wait any longer to be inside you. Now, baby!"

What sensual power we had over each other, she thought, bunching her pillow behind her head, her body tingling.

Aksel had pulled her skirt up and slowly owned her. As he entered her, he hissed a sound of pleasure: "Ahhhhh, there we go." Each time he entered her was like the first. When he reached the end of her insides with the tip of his cock, it sent shockwaves throughout her body, and she was sure he could feel it too.

After only a few moments of moving in perfect rhythm, very deep and fast-paced, he had pulled out and lowered her head to catch in her mouth exactly what she asked for. "Mmmmmm!" she moaned while swallowing every ounce of the Aksel-flavored liquid.

He quickly sat her on top of him and reentered her, letting her grind on him for her pleasure, while droplets of her sweat dripped onto his face, neck, and chest. Without warning, he pulled out and lifted her sexual apex onto his face as he whispered, "*Ma chérie* needs hers."

With his expert tongue and fingers, she cried out as he brought her to another level of pulsating pleasure between her legs that seemed to last forever.

Basking in their orgasmic afterglow, covered in sweat, he'd held her tightly. "I just can't get enough of you, Lyla." She could only nod in agreement.

Aksel laughed sweetly. "Look at your hair. So sultry." She glanced in the rearview mirror and saw her tousled and thoroughly glistening reflection.

After reliving such a memory, Lyla was sopping wet. She couldn't help but palm herself toward an orgasm that was a ghost of what she'd shared with Aksel.

I thought I looked glorious with strands of my hair sticking to my sweat-covered face and breasts. I really was sultry looking - and glowing. But that was when I was his and he was mine. We had to be the truest equally matched sexual partners possible. And I was in love with him. Guess I still am…God, I hate him! Bipolar much?

⤛══◉══⤜

After calling in a favor through her contacts at Barbizon, Ginger was able to get Lyla enrolled in classes starting the third week of August.

"Thank God!" She sighed and flopped on the bed in the master suite.

The phone rang almost immediately.

"And now what?" Ginger grumbled as she reached for the phone. "Hello?"

"Hey, Ginny Gin Gin! It's Sarah. How are you?"

"Hey, Sarah. It's been a long time. Longer than usual. What's up with you? How's Dallas? Neiman Marcus?"

"Oh, I'm with Estée Lauder now."

"Estée Lauder? That's awesome! Congr—"

"Don't celebrate just yet. I'm at the sales counter at Neiman's."

"Oh."

Ginger went silent.

"Gin? You there?"

"Sarah, what in the world happened?"

"Steve's antics. He dropped me. I landed on my ass, but at least I'm in the flagship store. I suppose I should be grateful, right?"

"Oh, Sarah." Ginger wasn't sure how to respond to her—they'd been friends, of a sort, once upon a time.

"Gin, I want to be like you if I ever grow up." Sarah laughed sadly. "You were so smart to leave when you did." Her voice cracked.

"What can I do?"

"Oh, nothing. You know me, I'll find my way." She sniffled, though Ginger thought she might be playing it up some. "Tell me what's going on with you. Distract me, please!"

"Well, get comfortable, 'cuz there's a lot to catch you up on…"

After a half hour or so, Ginger hung up. Falling into old patterns of gossiping with a friend, she wondered if she'd given Sarah too much information about her personal life—the next time she called, Ginger would make an excuse to end the phone call quickly. She was not the same person she'd been back then—and she thanked her lucky stars for it.

Chapter 9

Grant knocked on the doorframe of Ginger's private office as she went through a stack of orders on her desk. No matter how much headway she made, there was always more to do. He walked in, leaned forward and gently swung her chair around to face him. "Gin, thank God it's Friday! I feel like we haven't had much time to talk all week."

"Ohmigod, you're right."

She looked into his cobalt-blue eyes that always melted her to her core and found just enough energy to respond after a long, emotional roller coaster of a week, with Aunt Sadie's memorial service, Lyla's drama, and all the order deadlines.

Standing up, she gave him a tender kiss. "Thank you, my sweet Tommy, for being so strong this week. I don't know how I would have managed without you." She rested her head against his shoulder.

"Rach, we can get through anything—even death." He held her hands. "Look at you. It's been rough all around and you're still as breathtaking as ever."

"Trying to get laid, fly-boy?"

"Always." He kissed her hands. "However, I hate to add to our already overflowing plate, but it's time to tell you something I've been avoiding because of all the craziness this week."

"Oh, Lord. Now what?" She feared he would say something about Lyla. "It's not *all* her fault, you know. By the way, I've noticed you've kept your mouth shut a lot lately, opting to roll your eyes." She laughed, "Is it possibly a teenager's influence?"

"Probably." Grant reached his hand into her open blouse.

She grabbed his wrist and pulled it back. "Stop trying to razzle-dazzle me. What now?"

"I have to talk to you about Howard."

At the mere mention of his name, she jumped back and wrapped her arms around herself—he'd been awful, when they'd been fair. "Howard *Golden*? Is he still unhappy with what we gave him? That bastard, son of a —"

"Whoa, whoa, love. Listen."

She didn't understand Grant's tone of voice, which usually held fury when he mentioned Howard's name. "Is he dying or something?" She asked the question laden with sarcasm.

"Actually, yes." He held out his palms.

"What? Are you serious?" In her rush back to her desk and Grant, she knocked her chair over. "What's wrong with him? And why did he call *you*?"

"He asked for help. He can't meet his delivery dates with Neiman Marcus."

"What's that got to do with us?" Ginger rested her hands on her hips.

"You always talk about good karma, Gin, and I think we need to help him."

She couldn't believe what Grant was saying—and he was right—except for when it came to Howard. "Give me a minute please." He stood there while she closed her eyes and searched her inner spirit. She controlled her anger enough to look into Grant's face.

"Okay, but I have a question for you."

"What?"

"What are you going to say to Lyla about him? Does she even know?" Ginger's eyes brimmed with tears.

Margo'd had an affair with Howard, which was part of the acrimony between them.

"Lyla? Oh, shit. I don't know if Margo ever told Lyla anything about Howard. I certainly haven't." Grant rubbed his forehead. "Fuck! And I was more worried about helping that asshole get his deliveries done on time. Where's my head at?"

"Oh, Grant! Stop that shit right now—you are a good man."

"I must have pushed the possibility of him being her biological father so far back in my brain that it disappeared." He sighed. "Lyla is *my* daughter."

Ginger believed that with all of her heart. "I believe we need to follow your instinct to help."

"Will you call him, and follow up?"

Sighing, Ginger agreed. "Okay."

"Don't forget that Aksel will start interning with us next week."

"Oh, good Lord," Ginger cried, knocking over her neat stack on the desk. "Can we not tell Lyla about that yet?"

"Why not?" He looked perplexed.

"Just trust my instinct on this, please." *Lyla will hit the roof.*

The first day of Lyla's training at A. Madison's on the Nue came quickly. All three new hires were rounded up in Andrew's small back office of the restaurant. Andrew assigned each of the newbies to the seasoned servers for their first week. Lyla was teamed up with the only male, Darby. Tish and Erin were to train Audrey, and Sarah.

The day flew by, and the only thing that kept Lyla happy and somewhat focused was Darby. She wanted to impress him. In his mid-thirties, he stood about six foot three and had greenish-blue eyes, dark blond hair, and a muscular body that any woman would want. He was cautious in his flirting but flirted just enough to let her know he was interested.

The newbies and seniors were changing in and out of their uniforms in the women's dressing room, checking their makeup and hair. Lockers slammed and loud chatter filled the air.

"You seemed to like your first day." Lyla turned to the sweet female voice. Sarah, five foot nine, blonde hair with fresh red highlights, had bright blue eyes and a friendly attitude.

"So far, so good." Lyla just wanted to go home and take a shower.

"Because you got the cutest trainer, huh?" Sarah smiled and curled a strand of shoulder-length hair around her fingers.

"That didn't hurt." Lyla blushed.

"First serving job?"

"Yes. How could you tell?" Lyla couldn't hide her insecurity.

"Oh, when you've been around the block a few times, you can tell. But I think you did great. I'm Sarah, by the way."

"Thanks. I'm Lyla." She shook Sarah's hand.

"Is this just a part-time gig till you land your modeling contract?"

"Ha, that's funny. Actually, I'm starting Barbizon at the end of August. I don't know how good I'll be, but gotta keep the folks happy." She rolled her eyes.

"I get it. I used to model in Texas. I could always give you some tips. You seem like such a sweetie, so first tip— you *can't* be a sweetie!" Sarah laughed.

"I'll work on that. Although lately I've had some good practice at home." She chuckled. She'd thought living with her dad and Ginger would be so much better than home in Illinois—but she still wasn't free to make her own choices.

"Ugh. Parents?"

"Yup."

"At any age, they can make you nuts. Never good enough, right?"

Lyla sighed. "Nailed it."

"Well, see you tomorrow, Lyla."

"Bye, Sarah."

Sarah winked and smirked, and as she walked away, Lyla felt uneasy about the whole conversation, but wasn't sure why… it was just a gut feeling. Her instincts about people not always being who they appeared to be, told her to be careful.

⋅→≡◉═→⋅

The mayor's invitation arrived for New York's elite annual Labor Day White Party in the Hamptons. Anyone who was anyone attended—it was *the* place to be seen. Grant and Ginger had gone every year since their marriage. The Monday that followed the party would always be the Madison family picnic, so that long weekend was filled with exciting events.

"Ly, come on. It's more than just a party—it's a great social *event,*" Ginger pleaded, holding up three white dresses in her walk-in closet.

"It's just not my thing. Since when am I a socialite? I'm serving at my uncle's restaurant for the love of God. How well will that go over with the mayor and his crowd?"

"Well, with that attitude, it will go over like a fart in church."

Lyla laughed out loud. "Well, *it is* the hottest restaurant on Madison Avenue."

Ginger saw Lyla's demeanor change a bit, so she decided to press further. "If you'd like, I can help you find a date."

"Can't I just go stag?"

"Of course you can. Anyway, there will be plenty of eligible young men there. And I can arrange for you to get a day off from the restaurant."

"You mean the *weekend* off, right?" Lyla smirked.

"Okay, fine. The weekend." The two laughed but Ginger didn't care if she was being played—she wanted Lyla to come with them and have fun.

"Then which dress do you suggest?" Lyla smiled like the Cheshire cat from *Alice in Wonderland*.

"This one, you little demon child."

"It was your idea!"

"True. Maybe this one, then. And we'll need to pick out hat and shoes."

"You know I love shopping!" Lyla's guard lowered a little more.

"Shopping is my favorite thing to do." Ginger winked at her stepdaughter, willing to do whatever it took to make her happy.

Chapter 10

Grant entered Ginger's office to see what she wanted for lunch. A short woman named Trudy, one of the seamstresses, stood next to Ginger, clutching a clipboard while taking notes. Ginger spoke animatedly on the phone, reviewing orders from her desk. Several seamstresses passed him with bundles of cloth, and the receptionist's phone rang nonstop—it was complete chaos as his team worked overtime to fill both companies' Fall II orders. Ginger put the phone on speaker and read off the orders to Terri at TerRae Designs in Chicago, where Grant began his career by interning with Terri many years before. Feeling almost invisible in the middle of it all, Grant waited until Ginger looked up at him, smiled, and handed him a note. He winked at her and left as she continued her conversation.

Once outside, the late August air already held a hint of fall and he decided to walk over to A. Madison's on the Nue instead of picking up their usual lunch from Leo's deli across the street. Besides, he wanted to surprise Lyla.

Grant was greeted by the head hostess, Krissy, who was barely five feet tall, with bright hazel eyes and long blonde hair. "Hi, Mr. Robinson!" She smiled at him. "Your favorite server, Lyla, has an open table."

"That would be great." Grant was careful not to let on that Lyla was his daughter so she wouldn't get in trouble.

"Of course, right this way." He followed Krissy to a table overlooking Madison Avenue—he never got tired of watching the city in action.

Lyla approached with a friendly expression and played along that they didn't know each other. "Welcome to the Nue, sir. Can I start you off with something to drink while you look over the menu, or would you like to hear the lunch specials first?"

"I will start with an iced tea."

"Sweetened or unsweetened?"

"Unsweetened, please." Grant was impressed with how professional she acted as he watched her taking orders from another table close by before ordering his tea. She'd come so far in such a short amount of time. He was taking in the view of the street below when he was startled by two hands covering his eyes from behind.

"That's not very professional, Lyla."

"When have *we* ever been truly professional, Grant?" a vaguely familiar female voice said as he reached for her hands. She whispered in his ear, "Don't worry…what happened in Dallas, stays in Dallas."

Grant whipped around in shock. "Sarah? What are you doing… *here*?"

"I work here. You know how I love the excitement of big cities, Grant. I just couldn't stay away from New York any longer."

She held tightly onto his fingers and sat across from him, tilting her head down to lean her chin on her free hand. More than six years had passed since his old college roommate, Steve Williams, now the head buyer for Nieman's, had arranged for the two of them to spend a night together. It had happened just before he'd been reunited with Ginger and was a memory he would have rather forgotten.

Grant didn't say a word. He looked up to see Lyla holding his iced tea two tables away as still as a statue, staring at him with her mouth slightly agape. She burst into a quick stride, placed the drink between him and Sarah, and abruptly said, "Here's your iced tea, sir. Enjoy."

"Well, hate to cut this short, gorgeous, but I gotta get back to work. Say hi to Gin for me—tell her I'll give her a call." Sarah walked away but turned her head and winked at Grant before disappearing behind the curtains near the kitchen.

✦⟤⊙⟥✦

An hour after her dad left, Lyla was in the dressing room on break, staring in the mirror. It was obvious to her that her dad and Sarah knew each other.

"Hey, lil sis, break time. Man, I need a smoke."

Lyla didn't respond.

"You okay? What's the cold shoulder for?" Sarah stood behind her and started to rub her back. "Oh yeah, thanks for turning that table over to me at lunch."

Lyla's face was flushed with anger as she whirled toward Sarah. "Do you know who that was you were flirting with at *that* table?"

"Flirting? No, no. He's just an old acquaintance from a few years ago. Why?"

"I have to get back to work, Sarah." She hurried away before she lost her temper.

Sarah called after her, "Maybe I was flirting a *little*."

"I bet." Lyla trembled. What was her dad doing with Sarah, when he had Ginger?

⋆⇒═◉═⇐⋆

Grant walked into Ginger's office, thankfully empty for once, and placed the bag of food on her desk without a word. What the hell had just happened? He turned to leave.

"Hey, where are you going?" Ginger said. "I see you went to The Nue. Lyla piss you off or something?" Her brow arched as she waited for an explanation.

"I, uh, Jesus. I don't know if I can form a complete sentence right now." He rubbed his temples.

"Try. Please. Ramble. I can always make sense of what you have to say somehow. Sit down and spill it, fly-boy."

Grant grabbed a chair and sat down next to his wife, raking his fingers through his hair. "Guess who was at the restaurant?"

"Who?" She studied him closely. "Margo?"

"I almost wish it had been her." He paused. "Sarah Gilman."

"Oh, shit..." Ginger fell back into her seat and looked toward the ceiling.

"It gets better." Grant sighed. "She *works* at The Nue… with Lyla. In fact, she became my server."

"Fuck me! It's all my fault. I knew I gave her too much information when she called a few weeks ago. Fuck!"

At least that explained her appearance, but it didn't make him feel any better.

⊶═◉═⊷

Lyla tried to avoid Sarah for the rest of their shift, but Sarah walked in as Lyla was grabbing her bag in the break room to leave. *The story of my life...always followed by a dark cloud.*

"Lyla, what's up? Did I do something wrong?" Sarah pleaded with doe eyes and pouty lips.

"So that customer you sat down with and served at lunchtime is a friend?" Lyla spoke sharply with her hands on her hips and her feet in a wide stance.

"Yes." Sarah nodded.

"You said you two go way back?" She stared at Sarah intently. What her dad did before marrying Ginger was his business, but she had to know.

"Oh, *way* back. Is that what's bothering you? Why would that upset you?"

Lyla couldn't tell if Sarah was really dumfounded or putting on an act.

"You know his last name, right?"

"Of course. But I'm not following you. Help a big sister out here." Sarah gave an awkward shrug.

"I'll give you a clue. We have the same last name."

"You're related to him then?"

116

"I'm his daughter."

Sarah's expression of confusion twisted into shock. She looked her up and down. "No way! Wait, how old are you?"

"Eighteen." Lyla couldn't figure out if Sarah was being sincere at this point.

"Eighteen? I can't believe this! What a small world." Sarah lunged toward Lyla and hugged her so warmly that Lyla lowered her guard slightly before giving her back a hug.

"Wow. And by the way, you are very mature for your age—in a good way. I would have thought twenty-one or twenty-two." Sarah high-fived her. "Then Ginger is your stepmother?"

"You know Ginger *too*?" Lyla dropped her guard entirely. Sarah seemed so excited at the mention of Ginger's name that Lyla let her suspicions go.

"We used to model together in Dallas!"

"Does everyone have a history with each other around here? Jeez!" Lyla grinned.

"Wait, wait, so that means that Andrew Madison is Ginger's little brother? Oh my God!"

"Yes. He's kinda my uncle, I guess. But please don't tell anyone. I don't want to be treated differently." Lyla felt her insecurity creeping in.

"Lil sis, you and I should go clubbing after work. So just know, your secret is safe with me." Sarah held out her pinky.

"Pinky swears work for me."

"Now that whole 'keeping the folks happy' thing you mentioned makes more sense."

Lyla nodded and then looked down, feeling bad she'd said anything.

"Honestly, I love them both dearly, but I get it," Sarah said comfortingly. "They expect a lot from people. Believe me, I know."

"Tell me about it. Speaking of, I really should get home. The guards watch the clock closely," Lyla said.

"A bit of advice, lil sis? Just be the good girl they want you to be—even if you have to pretend. It will make your life so much easier. See if they're okay with you going out with a co-worker after our shift tomorrow."

"Love it. See you later, big sis." They hugged, and Lyla felt as if she'd made a friend.

Sarah did a silent cheer after Lyla left. *I couldn't have planned this any better if I wrote the script myself. I'm just that much closer now to evening the score with those two assholes!* She strolled out of the break room and sat at the bar. Once Darby served a couple their drinks, she waved him over.

"Let's get a drink after your shift," she said.

"Well, I—"

"My treat. Figured you might be interested in some juicy inside info."

Chapter 11

The sudden reappearance of Sarah in their lives worried Grant and Ginger—especially due to the amount of time Lyla spent with her during and after work. Patience was wearing thin with Lyla coming home not only late, but high, several nights a week. Her caustic attitude was grinding toward a showdown—though Ginger did her best to keep Grant in check.

Luckily, the day of the party was one of the good days where Grant and Lyla were able to get along peacefully and Ginger breathed a sigh of relief.

Lyla had been working extra shifts at the restaurant because a few employees had taken off for some end of summer vacation time. Despite working hard, and partying almost every night, Ginger never heard her complain, even when she started classes at Barbizon. Eight-thirty in the morning came awfully early three times a week after working double shifts. Although, Lyla did miss a few classes due to her partying late nights with Sarah.

Ginger thought that the White Party would be a perfect distraction from the nitty gritty nightlife Sarah had introduced to Lyla. *I can only imagine what Sarah is showing her in the city… I hope she's grown up since we lived together. But Lyla seems happy to go to such an exciting event with us. Maybe she'll even see something today that will help click things into balance in her life.*

The trio shared champagne as Evan drove them to the party, laughing like old times. At last, Evan pulled the limo onto the long driveway that stretched a city block before reaching the carriage portico of the mayor's summer retreat in the Hamptons; the elaborate white-stoned mansion sat on an inlet to the Atlantic Ocean. Lyla gasped as the expansive green lawn with a glimpse of the beach came into view.

"Stunning, isn't it?" Ginger asked.

"And *why* haven't I been invited to one of these parties before? It's just…so…wow!"

"Sorry, baby girl. Your mother always had an excuse why you couldn't visit us this time of year," Grant replied.

"Jealous bitch," Lyla said softly under her breath.

"Ly!" Ginger said, though she completely agreed. Grant hid his smirk.

First, Grant stepped out of the limo and surveyed the scene while buttoning the jacket of his oyster-colored three-piece suit. Next, Ginger's white, patent leather, kitten-pump sandals touched the cobblestone driveway. She wore a white knee-length, deep-scoop-neck halter dress that accentuated her shoulders, and a sun hat with a matching shiny leather strap around the brim. Lyla was the last to exit, wearing an alabaster mid-thigh strapless dress, strappy white heels, and a wide brimmed hat with a black sequined ribbon. Ginger couldn't be more proud.

They walked inside the grand foyer which led to a breathtaking view of the pool and the lush, green lawn. The winding staircase off to the left held a large crystal chandelier that sparkled on the marble flooring. White flowers of countless species were in tall vases and placed everywhere. The fragrance filled the home. From the veranda, the sound of the jazz quartet infiltrated throughout the mansion and outside. The air was filled with tunes from the forties and fifties Big Band era.

Couples were dancing wherever space permitted, indoors or out. Every guest was fashionably dressed in white…

Lyla whispered, "I'm rethinking the life of a socialite," and grinned at Ginger as she was handed a glass of champagne from one of the many servers, all of whom seemed to be beautiful men and women.

"Let's enjoy ourselves then." Ginger clinked flutes with Lyla.

Grant chuckled indulgently. "Let me introduce you to a few people."

After an hour of socializing with the privileged class, Lyla told Ginger, "My head is spinning! Gin, how do you remember all their names?"

"When you're an exclusive clothing designer, you have to. You'll get the hang of it." Ginger wasn't worried after watching Lyla charm everyone they'd met.

"Well, I'd like to get the hang of that one, right there." Lyla pointed with her pinky finger as she held a champagne flute to her lips. She gestured to a tall, attractive, dark-haired young man getting out of the pool. His body was toned and tanned, possibly a model.

"Go. But be elegant. His name is Nathaniel. His grandfather is the mayor."

"I've got this." Lyla walked toward him, grabbed a towel from one of the cabana boys, and started a conversation by handing him a towel along with a glass of champagne.

Grant leaned over to kiss her neck and whispered in Ginger's ear. "I have a surprise for you."

"Mmm, what's that, my love?"

"Turn around."

Ginger did, and knew she had to be whiter than her dress when she saw all the Portiers--including Aksel. She quickly turned back toward the pool to locate Lyla, but she wasn't in sight any longer.

"Grant, you should have told me!" *I need to warn Lyla* was all that raced through her head.

"I know, right? I pulled some strings. I love surprising you, Gin."

"Oh, no, no! You should have told me this one."

The five Portiers, Gabriel and Monette, Gabe and his wife, Nina, as well as their son, Aksel, walked toward Ginger and Grant. Ginger collected her emotions and transformed her expression into a smile as Monette greeted her with open arms.

"Ette, Gabriel! What a wonderful surprise!" She hugged them, then Nina, Gabe, and Aksel. "When did you arrive? Where are you staying?" Her eyes darted around, looking for Lyla—she was stuck between a rock and a hard place.

"We landed late last night, and we're staying at the Four Seasons. Aksel's place is nice, but not large enough to hold all of us," Nina answered.

"You look *fantastique, ma chérie*," Gabriel added.

"*Merci beaucoup, monsieur.* How long is your holiday?"

"We have yet to decide. It's been some time since we last were in New York. And the Hamptons, ah, *magnifique!* We may look for a place here," Gabriel said, adding, "Ette tends to do financial damage anywhere in the world."

"A place here? To live?" Ginger attempted to be gracious and not look as frantic as she felt inside.

"Perhaps we wish a family retreat in America! Close enough to you and Grant for our business venture with you. We could share it, as an investment. Business couldn't be better, my friends." Gabriel raised his glass of champagne.

"I agree," she heard Grant say with a broad smile. She tried to hide her panic by sipping her champagne, but she wasn't good at hiding things from Grant. Aksel hadn't spoken much since his initial warm greeting. He was surveying the scene, clearly looking for Lyla.

Gabe, Aksel's father, asked Grant, "And where is your lovely Lyla?"

"She's here somewhere." Grant turned and scanned the crowd.

"I hear she will be attending NYU, as is Aksel. I can't believe she's old enough for college already," Gabe said, turning partially toward the bay.

"That subject is a bit complicated as she has decided to take a year off while attending modeling school." Grant sighed. "Girls. Especially teenage girls. They are the tricky ones, aren't they?"

"*Oui, oui.* In every country," Nina, Aksel's mother, laughed.

Ginger noticed Aksel's reaction regarding Lyla, and her taking a year off. He peered down at his feet and uncomfortably shifted his weight back and forth, as if he wanted to make a dash for the front door. What had happened between them?

"Why don't I look for her?" Ginger offered and quickly disappeared into the crowd. *I've got to warn her. Jesus Christ, she's going to flip when she sees him here!*

After fruitlessly searching through the crowd outside, Ginger went inside, passing through the hallway. She was caught off guard when her arm was grabbed from behind and she was dragged to the closest room, which happened to be the mayor's study.

"How *could* you, Gin?!" Lyla spat. "*Eligible young men?* Just what exactly do you have planned for me? The one you and Dad *really* want for me is Aksel!" Lyla's words came out sharply and coarsely.

"No, no," Ginger said. "I was—"

"Just what? Trying to run my life from behind the scenes? *Again?* Jesus, Ginger! I'm not your pawn!"

Grant entered the room and Ginger was stunned into silence. She'd been doing her best to keep Lyla's secret.

"Perfect, now both of the players are here," Lyla said. "Just to be clear, you two are playing this game by yourselves!"

"What are you talking about, Lyla?" Grant kept his voice down and looked at her quizzically.

"Daddy Dearest, have you betrothed me to Aksel? Trying to guarantee the future of the family business?" Lyla fumed, her pretty face rosy with anger.

"Hey, hey—" Grant started to say when Lyla cut him off sharply.

"This isn't the 1400s when kings and queens negotiated alliances between countries. I guess I'm the sacrificial lamb to the Portiers? I'm not stupid, Dad. You and Ginger planned this!"

"Planned what?" He puffed out his chest.

Lyla didn't reply, she just glared at them. Ginger wanted to calm her, but was helpless as to how.

"You are way out of line, young lady," Grant said in a stern tone.

"No, Dad, you and Ginger are. You act like you own my life or something! Again! I have zero interest in your explanation or reasoning for inviting Aksel and his family here, because I know what you two are up to. And I'm NOT going to be told what to do! I'm done here."

Ginger reached for Grant's hand as Lyla stormed out of the study and left the house.

Distraught, Lyla hurried down the driveway and jumped in the limo before Evan could get out and open the door for her. "Evan, home, please. Now!"

"Miss Lyla, what about your parents?"

"You can drop me off and come back for them. Drive! Now!" Lyla snapped, treating him like he was just a driver, not someone she cared for. She caught a glimpse of her dad and Ginger exiting the front of the mansion as Evan drove the limo down the driveway.

"Yes, Miss Lyla."

She heard the hurt in his voice and rolled up the privacy window to hide the burning tears trickling down her face. *I came to live with them to escape all this bullshit about people deciding what's best for my future. I just want to stretch out my wings and feel life for a while. But everyone wants to direct my future and stop me from doing anything other than what they want. Pleasing them is all anyone wants from me. I refuse to be used by any of them. I need to escape!* She curled up in a fetal position on the limo seat and softly cried as she began to work on a plan for her freedom.

Chapter 12

Aksel watched Lyla, so feminine and ethereal in her white dress, race down the driveway to their family's limo. Sad didn't convey his emotions as Ginger and Grant returned to the Portiers and apologized for Lyla's hasty departure.

"She's been juggling long work hours at her new job and modeling classes," Ginger said.

"Burning the candle on both ends…" Grant added.

"Ah, my friend, do not worry. Most girls her age struggle," Gabe responded, putting his arm around Grant's shoulder, and handing him another flute of champagne.

"*Oui*, Ginger." Nina hugged Ginger. "Try not to worry, *ma chérie.*"

"Gabe, on a different note, we picked up a huge account last week. Aksel has been a lucky addition to our team. He's a quick learner." Grant looked at Aksel with admiration that Aksel knew he didn't deserve. "I hate to lose all the extra time I've had with him when classes begin."

In all of the excuses being thrown back and forth, Aksel knew right away the real reason Lyla had left was because of him. *Ginger knows,* he thought. Ginger glanced at him often, but never broached the subject of Lyla, or talked about her in front of him. He and Grant had grown very close during his internship at G Squared. They would even spend time out of the office together, jogging on weekends in the early morning and after work. It felt like he'd known Grant forever.

⊹⊱━◯━⊰⊹

Lyla redirected Evan to Andrew's restaurant, knowing it was near the end of Sarah's shift. She needed someone to vent to. *Sarah understands me and can relate better than anyone.*

Evan opened the door to assist Lyla out of the limo. "Miss Lyla, will you be okay? Is there anything I can do for you?"

"No, Evan. But thank you. I'm very sorry for how I spoke to you earlier. You know you're special to me. I hope you can forgive me. Just go back for my folks. I'll be fine. Really." She held his hand. "Oh, and if they ask where you drove me, just tell them you dropped me at The Nue."

"Yes, Miss Lyla. Please be safe."

Lyla walked through the restaurant and headed straight to the dressing area. She waved to Sarah, who followed her through the curtains.

"Hey, what are you doing here? I thought you had the—" She cut herself off when she noticed Lyla's puffy eyes. "Whoa! What's wrong, lil sis?" Lyla started to cry again, and Sarah put her arms around her.

"My shift is over in about a half hour. Sit here, relax. I'll bring you a drink." Sarah kissed Lyla's forehead and wiped her tears.

"One of your special drinks that makes the universe feel better, okay?"

"Of course, be right back."

Lyla sat against the wall with her arms wrapped around her knees, quietly sobbing. Sarah quickly returned with a Tequila Sunrise (made with a bonus of powdered ecstasy) and a cold, damp cloth, then she sat next to Lyla on the floor.

"Is Andrew here?"

"No, no. He left a few hours ago. You're safe. Drink up, buttercup."

"Alcohol is supposed to be a depressant, Sarah, but I never get depressed after one of your drinks. What do you do to them? Is it a magic potion?" She laughed softly through her tears and took her first sip.

"You trust me, right?" She wiped Lyla's eyes with the damp cloth.

"Why do you think I came straight to you?" Lyla took another swallow of her drink.

"I'll be done in a flash. Then you have me for as long as you need me. Tell me anything or nothing at all, but I'm all yours tonight." Sarah got up and left Lyla alone to finish her drink.

She stretched out between two chairs in her white dress with her hat and heels on the floor. The drink made her feel more relaxed yet energized all at the same time. The room pulsated with lights, and her mind became numb and filled with unexpected happy thoughts and a sense of peace. She explored the solace and wandered into thoughts of Aksel.

I didn't know such a relationship was possible until Aksel. He worshiped my body...I worshiped his. It seemed as if we could talk about anything!

Lyla giggled to herself. *I never thought I deserved anyone who could have literally walked out of a magazine* ad and into my life, wanting my embrace. I didn't believe I was ever pretty enough for him, let alone worthy of him. Mmmm, now I feel beautiful, my skin feels so soft…

Lyla sat up, looked in the mirror and reveled in the thrill of her reflection, softly touching her lips and cheeks. Looking past the puffiness around her eyes, she focused on the thin line of her irises. They were the bluest blue she'd ever seen, and her pupils were large—extremely large.

Calm… yet invigorated, she lay on the floor and began to reminiscence…

The way he owned me instantly the first time we made love…he made me a woman. It had to be more than just physical for me to continue to be with him, incredible sex or not. I needed to know if he felt what I did that morning.

She pictured that moment when she rested her head on his naked chest, noticing he was getting excited again just by the position of her leg draped across his hips.

I was unwilling to let him take me again until I knew for sure. I looked straight into his deep-brown, golden-rimmed eyes.

"Do you love me?" Lyla said the words aloud.

His response was a deep sigh. I dipped my head to his chest to cover my eyes from his view, mentally preparing to mend my heart as I had already fallen in love with him, many times, but now it was up close and personal, completely different.

She recalled his response verbatim: *"Love you?" he asked as he released his hold on me and put his arms behind his head. "Love is a very strong word."*

Sarah popped into the dressing area and Lyla lifted her hand in in a reassuring wave. She disappeared so Lyla closed her eyes.

All I could do was breathe and let my heart cry instead of my eyes. I didn't move... "Aksel, I've always loved you, on some level." I felt foolish for even asking him; it was too soon. What was I thinking? Stupid little girl.

His silence was deafening. I knew then I had to shut off all feelings for Aksel. But how? If he couldn't or wouldn't or didn't love me, then it had to be over. I knew I couldn't be with him without being loved.

Lyla tried to sit up but couldn't lift her legs or arms and thought a tornado could have torn through the restaurant and she wouldn't have been affected.

Lord! I thought that would probably be the first and last time I'd ever feel him. He was so quiet, and I was devastated, though I'd never tell him that.

But then he said it... "I love you. Lyla, I more than love you. I do. I do. I do."

Lyla sighed. She stretched her arms over her head, feeling the tips of her fingers reaching as far as they could, and pointing her toes in the opposite direction.

Sarah quietly entered the room and Lyla was more aware of her presence—was her friend laughing at her? She was sprawled out on the floor. It was so hard to concentrate…Sarah pulled a chair next to her and gently wiped her forehead with a fresh cool cloth. Lyla's smile widened.

"Sis, that drink was *exactly* what I needed. Thank you. You'll have to give me the recipe."

"Ancient family secret. Let me run and make us two more."

Sarah returned shortly with two glasses on a tray.

"Here's one for you. And one for me because my shift is finally over. Sorry it took so long." Sarah handed her another glass.

"Cheers." Lyla held her glass up to Sarah.

"Cheers, lil sis." After a few sips, Sarah said, "Ready to get out of here?"

"Hell, yeah! But I'm not sure if my body will agree…"

"Let's start by standing up."

Lyla walked down Sixty-Eighth Street the next day in the same white dress from yesterday, though now it was disheveled and slightly dirty. She had her hat tilted over her eyes to hide from the bright midday sun. Her shoes dangled on her finger as she walked barefoot along the dirty city sidewalks, which felt better than wearing her strappy heels. Her body ached, and her mind was caught in the soothing afterglow of a night dancing and drinking—she felt so empowered by the fun she'd had with Sarah. But as soon as she arrived at the apartment building, her mood shifted and her happiness faded.

Deerpak opened the door. "Miss Lyla, how are you this afternoon?"

"Well, I'm here," she half-smiled and headed for the elevator without looking back.

On the elevator ride to the thirty-fourth floor, she mentally prepared herself for the worst reception. Lyla stepped off the elevator and fumbled with the keys to unlock the door to what she had recently started referring to as "her prison in the ivory tower." As soon as she saw her father's agitated face, she was unable to control herself and began to laugh. *I wonder if I should curtsy?*

"Good morning, Your Majesty," she spouted, with no concern for her antics as she paraded past him and Ginger into the apartment.

Grant followed her into the kitchen, and Ginger was right behind him. "Morning was a few hours ago. It's *afternoon*, Ly. Where the hell have you been?" He was failing miserably at hiding his anger with her. Lyla could see he was pissed.

"Father, I left a message with the court's carriage driver." She opened the refrigerator door. "Oh, orange juice! Perfect!" Lyla grabbed the container and sat down on a counter stool, tossing her hat to the floor. She took a large gulp directly from the container. "Any chance we can make this a mimosa?" Lyla asked in a slightly childish voice.

"Are you fucking kidding…?" Grant muttered through gritted teeth. Ginger grabbed his arm, trying to keep him calm.

"Really, you didn't torture Evan to find out? Put him on the rack or anything?" she said with enjoyment as she calmly watched her dad's face turn a brighter shade of red.

"Grant, please." Ginger grabbed his arm and gently pulled him away like a referee in a boxing match trying to get distance between the fighters. "She's home safe. Can't we discuss this like adults?"

"Adults?" He looked at Lyla. "You'd need to *act* like an adult to have an adult conversation."

"Gonna ground me, Your Highness?" Lyla asked sarcastically.

"Listen here, little girl—" He stepped toward Lyla and Ginger scooted in front of him.

"I am *not* your little girl anymore!" she shouted back. "I am eighteen years old. A little girl was, what—when I was six or nine or even thirteen!" Her anger grew as years of frustration was about to erupt.

Ginger, who had been facing Grant, turned toward Lyla. "Hey, hey! How about we take a breather and restart. Ly, would you like to shower?"

"Sounds good to me, Queen Gin." Lyla meandered off to the use the Jacuzzi tub in the guest bathroom.

Enjoying the quiet and solitude of her own space, surrounded by bubbles and the soft hum of the jets, Lyla slipped back into her earlier relaxed state of mind. Moments of the night spent with Sarah popped into her head: she and Sarah had danced like maniacs at several clubs. At some point, they decided to call it a night—or was it day? The sun was fully out when they left that last club. Lyla couldn't remember how many of Sarah's soothing drinks she'd had at that point, but they stumbled into a taxi and somehow made their way to Sarah's eclectically decorated apartment. They were lying on her bed when Sarah had changed into a revealing red silk robe.

"God, Sarah. You're so beautiful. Your body is perfect."

"Thanks, lil sis. You are too." She loosened the red belt.

"Me? I'm nothing like you. You're stunning. I'm just average, pretty enough face, I guess."

"Stop right there. Try this on, then we'll discuss how stunning you are." Sarah handed her a similar robe, only pink in color.

Before she knew it, Lyla and Sarah were standing side by side staring into the mirror. Sarah slipped her shoulders out of her robe and encouraged Lyla to do the same. With each instruction from Sarah, Lyla's inhibitions melted away. She felt more sensuous and comfortable with her reflection. Finally, they were standing nude and holding hands, looking into the mirror.

"Is this a magic mirror? Like 'Mirror, mirror, on the wall'?"

"You are too funny. Stop and look at your breasts for a second or ten. Your nipples are a perfect pink." Sarah reached over and caressed her left one, which became immediately erect. Then, barely touching her right nipple, Lyla turned to face Sarah.

"But *you* really are so…so…"

Sarah cut her off by leaning into her and softly brushed their lips together, which turned into a tender kiss.

✦⟞⊜⟝✦

The brewing storm between father and daughter had calmed, thanks to Ginger reassuring Grant that Lyla was just being a bit rebellious and still adjusting to her new life. Late into the night, he finally agreed with her. "Thanks, Ginger. What would I do without you?"

Monday morning, Grant, Ginger, and Lyla were perched on their favorite spots on the balcony preparing to eat a light breakfast before the annual Madison Labor Day picnic. The blue sky filled with small white puffy clouds was more than one could ask for. Grant absorbed the beauty.

"Daddy, can I have a mimosa also?"

Grant looked at Ginger for guidance—she nodded and handed him the bottle of champagne from the ice bucket. If it was up to him, he'd say no, but his wise wife had counseled patience.

After pouring a bit into Lyla's orange juice, Grant raised his glass. "A toast to my beautiful loves."

"Cheers!" They all smiled and sipped.

Warm with affection, Grant said, "Lyla, thanks for being honest about Saturday night. Am I happy you spent it with Sarah? Not completely, but at least you made it home safely yesterday. I wanted to clear the air between us."

Ginger glowed her approval.

"Anyway, Lyla, the picnic today is a big occasion for us. I still don't understand what your issue is with the Portiers, but please indulge us—no disappearing acts today, okay?"

"Deal. I'm going to get ready." Lyla kissed them both on their foreheads. She refilled her mimosa with mostly champagne and took her plate to the kitchen. Grant and Ginger simultaneously sighed, hoping for a day without issues.

Sarah nearly kicked Darby out of her apartment Monday morning. "See you at work in a bit." He tried to kiss her, but she pulled back and said, "Save that kiss for me. I'll let you know when you can have it." She winked at him and closed the door before he could respond.

Shouldn't he have learned by now what I want in bed? Great size cock and gorgeous body, but obviously he still has to figure out how to use it. Nearly a waste of time, but thanks to BOB, I'm always satisfied. BOB was her battery-operated-boyfriend. She laughed as she turned on the shower.

She washed away Darby and refocused on her next conquest. *Everything is falling into place nicely to even the score with Ginger who stole my golden ticket with Grant. One mission engaged, a few more to ignite.*

Chapter 13

Andrew packed up last minute food items in the kitchen of his restaurant before leaving for the annual Madison Labor Day picnic. He was scurrying around when Sarah silently walked in—he turned quickly and jumped when he saw her, causing him to drop a box full of plastic utensils, which scattered all over the floor.

"I didn't mean to startle you, Mr. Madison. Let me help you." Sarah bent down and purposefully exposed her cleavage. He couldn't help but look, and she caught him. *Perfect*, she thought.

"Call me Andrew." He didn't look away from her breasts.

"I'm sorry I didn't change into my uniform before coming into the kitchen, *Andrew*, but I heard all of this racket back here. I certainly didn't expect to find you as the culprit." She laughed seductively, and he blushed nervously.

His green eyes morphed into a deeper green, and the dark jade rims around his irises turned almost black, matching his pupils. Sarah kept eye contact and slowly stood up.

"I really should get ready for my shift, but you seem like you might need help getting ready for the picnic."

He also stood up and didn't respond. They were inches apart.

"Uh, actually that sounds…" His voice faded into silence when she looked down at his growing erection. He cleared his throat.

She handed him the box of utensils.

"Thank you, Sarah."

Sarah started to unbutton her blouse before turning to go into the women's dressing area, giving him a full view of her sexy bra.

Andrew stopped her. "How about helping me put all this back together and grab a few things from the walk-in freezer, Sarah? That would help."

"Whatever pleases you, Mr.—Andrew. Of course. I, I could use a little cooling off. It's awfully hot in here."

"It is, isn't it?" Andrew responded.

Neither of them had broken eye contact. They continued to pack up the last few items together as he kept looking at her partially exposed bra and breast.

"Do you have everything? What about champagne?" She bent over to grab two bottles, showcasing her perfect ass, looked at him over her shoulder, then *accidentally* bumped against him while she stood up.

"I, uh, have some already packed. I'd better go, though. I'm late. Thanks, Sarah."

As he left with a box of food, he looked back at her one more time, and she smiled.

He's mine.

⊹⊱◈⊰⊹

Labor Day was the perfect day for a picnic. The light breeze had just a hint of fall. The deep crystal blue sky scattered with small, white puffy clouds was reminiscent of a Georgia O'Keeffe painting. The mid-seventies temperature only added to the revelers' high spirits. People were playing tether ball, badminton, or tossing Frisbees. Others sat and enjoyed their drinks and conversations under any one of three tents. Bill, Ginger's father, along with his buddies from WWII, and Grant, manned the grills as they drank beer and told the same old funny stories about their days in the service.

Grant relaxed as he watched the beauty of Ginger laughing with family and friends. Occasionally she would catch his eye and bring him a cold beer with a kiss attached to it. But he was also glad to see how much fun Lyla was having. *Life couldn't be better.*

"Hi Lyla, my love! It's so good to see you! I can't believe you're going to NYU," Lois, Ginger's mother, said as she'd hugged her. Lois was an older version of Ginger. She dressed in a beautiful salmon-colored ensemble, with a matching wide brimmed hat. Her chic style made it obvious where Ginger had first been exposed to fashion.

"Oh, actually I thought Mommy Gin would have told you, but I started Barbizon instead of NYU; I'm deferring for a year."

"She may have. But how wonderful that you're interested in fashion. If I hadn't met Bill I would have pursued that as well, but sometimes love and life gets in the way." Lois laughed out loud. "For better or worse, and he is the best! Though, my thoughts have been a little scattered lately, so many things are changing. We sold the business, started traveling and… let's face it, everything is different without my sister."

"I can't imagine…" Grant was very proud of Lyla when she hugged Lois warmly.

Just then Paulina and Adam ran up to Lyla, their older "cousin" and asked her to join them in kicking the soccer ball around. Lois and Bill had always treated Lyla and Jason as blood grandchildren, which was why his daughter was so at ease around her extended family and their friends.

Grant knew that the only uncomfortable part of the picnic for her was the Portier family's attendance, since she'd made an ass out of herself in front of them two days before. But she was polite, which was all that he could ask for. Two years ago, Lyla and Aksel had been thick as thieves, and now, she was avoiding him. Girls.

⟶⟞◉◉⟝⟵

A few hours into the picnic festivities at Prospect Park, Ginger, along with Grant and Andrew, gathered the crowd together for a toast. Ginger and Andrew's parents joined them as Andrew lifted his glass. "This is the first year we all gather here without Aunt Sadie. But I'm certain her spirit is with us. Aunt Sadie and the uncle that most of us never met, Allen, are now together. He was the love of her life, and I'm sure he was waiting for her on the other side. Let's share a moment in silence to celebrate Aunt Sadie's life and what she meant to us."

Silence fell across the crowd. Grant ended the moment by saying, "Aunt Sadie, we miss you. Cheers to a classy lady who lived an exciting life with a fabulous sense of humor and a heart full of love!"

Bill put his arm around Andrew and said, "Thanks, son. She will always be remembered. Lois and I have been reflecting a lot after her passing. Life's just too short, too precious, not to make new memories. Therefore, I'd like to announce we have decided to sell the restaurant and start living the life we always dreamed of."

The crowd cheered at his statement. Bill held up his glass as if pointing to the sky and added, "Don't worry, though—we'll still host the Madison Labor Day picnic, and we'll send postcards from our trips! Long live our family tradition! Cheers, everybody!"

Clara, Andrew's wife, turned and pulled him around, planting a kiss on him. "I love you sweetheart—that was a nice toast to your aunt."

⊷═◉═⊷

As the picnic continued, Lyla really enjoyed herself. She had managed to avoid the Portiers most of the day. Talking and laughing with her family and friends made her forget all her worries. After chatting for a while with a distant cousin about respective schools, she went to the cooler to sneak a beer. She thought she was being secretive, but when she turned around, Aksel was there right in front of her. Lyla sighed. *So much for my pleasant day.*

Lyla had dwelled on Bill's toast for a while. *Make new memories.* How would she be able to do that with Aksel around?

"Lyla, can we please talk?" Aksel's voice and his French accent melted her insides, but she started to maneuver around him. He blocked her path. She stopped walking and looked off, wishing to be anywhere but here.

"What?" she asked tersely, her arms crossed.

"You've been avoiding me."

"Do you blame me?" She snapped.

"You won't even look me in the eyes now. Why are you avoiding the inevitable? I want to clear the air between us."

She finally looked at him, but she only held his gaze for a moment for fear of giving herself away... her strength was fading.

"What do you want from me, Aksel?"

"Lyla, when I'm at G Squared, every time the door opens, I hope it's you. I hope that you're visiting your parents or dropping off lunch—just so I can look at you one more time."

"G Squared? What are you talking about?"

"I-I've been interning there—wait, did you really not know?"

"No, I didn't. For how long?"

"Almost a month."

Lyla sighed. Could she blame her dad for not telling her? "Well, I'm happy for you. But I can't do this right now."

"Please," Aksel pleaded. "I need you to stop trying to run from me. Please just listen to me. I have to tell you the truth-"

She cut him off. "About why you deserted me?"

"About everything."

He was so sincere that against her better judgment, she stayed in place. "Well, you've piqued my interest, although I would say this isn't the place to discuss a topic of this magnitude. Understand, I have no intention of seeing you again, so I'll give you five minutes. Spill it."

Aksel began to tell her everything about the day she'd terminated her pregnancy, including how her mother threatened him by saying she would alert the authorities that he'd impregnated a minor. She wanted to believe him, but she could still feel the heaviness in her chest from the hurt she'd carried with her over the last two years. All she could remember was what happened the night of her graduation at his apartment, when he couldn't keep his hands off her. She held back her tears—no way would she allow herself to cry in front of him again.

Aksel waited for a response, but she said nothing.

"What else can I say? I just…I just hope that now that you know the truth, maybe…maybe you can stop hating me. And maybe we can be something more again. One day."

She didn't run as she digested his words. What did it all matter?

"You are eighteen now and I do not have to live in jail for being with you. Will you try to remember what we once had? Lyla, I am still in love with you." His eyes welled and he reached for her, but she stepped just out of touch.

"So basically, you're saying my mother lied to me about *everything* and now we can *legally* fuck?"

"No, Lyla, I…" He scrambled for words. "That's not what I meant at all. Please believe me. I wanted to tell you so many times. I had planned on telling you right after your eighteenth birthday, but when you showed up at my condo, you took me by surprise. I had always imagined our reunion, our first time seeing each other again—it would have been much different than that night."

Lyla shook her head. "But it wasn't, Aksel, was it?" She didn't want to believe that her mother would do such an unforgivable thing to her. *She watched as I cried for weeks and never said anything to help me get over him, or even just hold me for comfort.*

"Well, here's how I feel about you, Aksel. *Sing fuier!*" She took her drink, threw it in his face, and ran off.

"I'm cold-blooded?" he shouted after her. She knew in her heart that he was not.

⤙═◉═⤚

Ginger noticed Aksel pull Lyla aside. Crossing her fingers, she hoped things worked out between them…or at the least, they might be friends. Wishing she was within earshot to hear them, she watched their body language closely. She sent a silent prayer up to Aunt Sadie asking for her help. Lyla doused Aksel with her beer and Ginger gasped.

"What?" Grant asked, then followed her line of sight. "Well, there she goes again! I can't deal with this now, Gin. I don't know what the fuck is going on between them, and I'm not sure I want to know, but I can't fucking deal with her acting out every time we are in public."

Feeling awful, Ginger patted Grant, then gathered paper towels and a bottle of club soda and brought them to Aksel. "I didn't mean to pry, but I saw the whole thing."

Aksel shook his head and disappeared into the party without another word.

⤙═◉═⤚

Sarah stayed after the restaurant closed, keeping herself busy by wrapping silverware into burgundy cloth napkins. When Andrew returned to unload the van that night, she was there, and smiled brightly when he came to investigate why the lights were on.

"Sarah? What are you doing here this late?" Andrew asked. It was well after ten.

"Waiting for you to return, of course." She laughed in a throaty tone. "No, I'm kidding. I'm just getting the dining room ready for opening tomorrow." She stopped what she was doing and faced him.

He blushed to the roots of his dark blond hair. "Right. Well, I'm unloading the van." He walked back to the kitchen.

I must be careful in my attack. She ran to the ladies' room, pulled out a vial of cocaine, and sniffed up a couple of bumps. Then she checked her nose twice and looked herself over in the mirror. The cocaine quickly took effect, and she smiled at herself. "Let's go do this," she said to her reflection.

Sarah sought out Andrew in the back.

"Hey, Mr.—*Andrew*, let me help you." She held the kitchen door open for him.

"I think I got everything already, Sarah, but thanks."

Their eye contact lingered a few moments longer than what would be considered appropriate for a married man. He was into her—but she'd have to be the aggressor.

"Well, how was the picnic?" She probed.

"It was a great time."

"You seem a bit stressed, though. How about a drink before you go home?"

Andrew didn't respond.

"I put one of the rosé champagnes aside, just in case you needed something refreshing when you got back."

She walked behind the bar.

Sarah placed two champagne flutes on the freshly wiped bar and handed Andrew the bottle. "Would you like to do the honors?"

"It would be my pleasure." She searched his face, willing to bet he hadn't cheated before.

When Andrew was battling with the foil, Sarah sneaked a bit of her ecstasy powder into his glass. *Pop* went the cork, and Sarah immediately held his flute to catch the bubbles.

"A toast?" she said.

"To?" Andrew asked.

"What's to come," she said coyly.

"I like the sound of *that*."

"Cheers." They looked into each other's eyes while clinking their glasses.

Andrew and Sarah were just about to kiss when she pulled back and dangled her empty glass in the air.

"A little more?" Sarah purred, and he pulled back from her with desire all over his face.

"Sounds like a great idea." They emptied the bottle. "Should I get another?"

"While you do that, I have to use the ladies' room." Sarah skipped away and dipped into the stall to refill her nose. When she returned to the bar, she deceivingly added more ecstasy powder to his flute.

They toasted again, but this time Andrew said, "Cheers to whatever is next to come…and it couldn't come fast enough."

They each downed their flute of champagne—she leaned across the bar and kissed him. She crawled over the counter with the fluid move of a professional, and straddled him, deepening the kiss. She wrapped her legs around him and slowly grinded her hips into his crotch. Andrew's cock hardened.

"I've never been so attracted to anyone like this…" Then he pulled away. "But I've never cheated on my wife."

Just like she'd thought. "You're such a good man. It's my fault, isn't it? I couldn't help myself because you're just so tempting." She pouted.

"Don't be upset with yourself. Attraction is attraction." He grabbed her in a close embrace, and suddenly they were grinding into each other again. "You just feel *so* good. Your body is beautiful. And your lips…"

"Well, let me at least show you what these lips can do…" She dropped to her knees and pulled out his rock-hard dick.

The drug was taking full effect and he couldn't stop her, even if he wanted to. She wrapped her hand around his girth and licked the tip of his cock, and he moaned in response. Sarah took his entire length and stroked his balls until she swallowed every drop of his ejaculation in her mouth.

"God, you taste so good! Mmmmm."

Right where I want him.

Chapter 14

Lyla had taken the subway home after dousing Aksel with beer. *I need distance from everyone right now!* Her mood lifted as she walked around the empty apartment and the thought of being alone for the next few hours. She took an ecstasy capsule that Sarah had given her a few days before and gulped it down with some vodka she had poured for herself. However, soaking in the Jacuzzi tub at the apartment didn't go as planned. Lying in the tub, her mind began to recount how Aksel had taken advantage of their physicality to force her to listen to him. She waited for the ecstasy to take effect, and finally gave up attempting to get him out of her head.

Why do I feel so drawn to him, even when I know he's not good for me? Why do I even care? I want him out of my life—but then again—I don't. It's taken everything in me not to have Evan drive me to his apartment. She sighed. *I just don't know what to think anymore. Did my mother really lie to me or is he lying?*

Around the time she was finally not thinking about anything, just enjoying the bubbles and the hum of the tub, she heard Grant and Ginger return home. *Oh, great. This ought to be a fun night.* But by the time she got out of the bath, Grant and Ginger had retired to their bedroom suite. She went to her room and gently closed the door to avoid a confrontation.

⊷⊶⊷

The next morning, her dad knocked on Lyla's door. "It's open," she said as he popped his head into her room—she was sitting at her makeup station, putting on her eyeshadow.

"Talk. Now." He had a very serious look on his face.

"Dad, I don't have time. I'm already late for class."

"Then you'll be even later. There are a few things we need to clear up. You need to get a grip on real life and quit living in some sort of a twisted reality." He pulled the door shut.

157

Great. She begrudgingly joined them in the living room, where Ginger was already waiting.

"Sit down." Her dad pointed to a chair.

"Fine." Lyla plopped down in a huff on the loveseat instead.

"Ly, take this seriously, please," Ginger said. She said it in a way that was both sweet and stern; Lyla had always found that a fascinating skill. One she hoped to mimic someday.

"We need to discuss how you acted this weekend. You asked to be treated like an adult, and apparently that didn't work. So now what?" Her dad stood in front of her with his arms crossed and a disapproving frown.

"You can't understand, Dad. Why don't you just lay down my punishment and get it over with already? I have places to be." She defiantly crossed her arms and leaned back on the red leather. She turned her head away from his harsh glare and looked out the window.

"I'm over here. Look at me, please."

Lyla turned toward her father with a red-hot look designed to melt an ice sculpture. He didn't budge.

"Before you moved here, you convinced us that you wanted to attend NYU, which clearly wasn't your true intention. We compromised with you, and Gin helped you get into Barbizon. She also helped you get a job. You've really impressed us with how well you've balanced both."

"Oh, I guess I'm supposed to thank you for the compliment." Who was he trying to kid? What did he want?

"Lose the attitude, because it's only going to make things worse. You embarrassed Ginger and me in front of our business associates and half of our clients at the White Party. The Portiers are very integral to our future, and more to the point, they are like family. The least you could do is be nice, even if you're acting."

"Humph. Family to you." She rolled her eyes.

"See? I feel like I'm losing my mind here. What is going on with you, Lyla?" He threw his arms up in disbelief.

Lyla said nothing.

Grant grimaced. "You need to get a grip on real life."

Lyla still said nothing. Of course he'd pick Aksel over her.

"Gin, can you help me out here? I don't know what I'm supposed to do. I've given her everything she's ever wanted. How did I screw this up?"

"Grant, honey; Ly, sweetheart, maybe you both just need more time to adjust to living together," Ginger suggested in a soft tone.

"I have a solution to the problem." Lyla nodded in a quiet, gentle and submissive manner—making up the plan as she went. "I should move out," she said meekly. Inside, she jumped with joy.

Grant laughed. "And where are you going to go? Camp out under a bridge or live in the subway?"

"Dad, *I* am the problem. Sarah told me I was always welcome to use her extra bedroom whenever I needed to. I'll take her up on that offer." Lyla got up and headed toward her room.

"WHAT? Sarah's? Stop right there! This discussion isn't over!"

"Oh, yes it is, Dad. Look at how aggravated you are just talking to me. I never meant to be such a headache." She paused in the hallway and turned toward them.

"Lyla, don't do this," Ginger begged.

"I'm doing what *I* need to do for myself. I left my mother to find myself and clearly we are not in agreement about our relationship. It seems neither of you recognize who I am either. I'm an adult now and I need to stretch my wings. Please understand."

"You think you're an adult? Fine. Let's see if you can afford to live on a waitress' salary. Just remember, when it all falls apart and you find yourself in need of a home, it's here, where you belong. Fuck this shit. I'm out of here. I have a real job to get to." Grant stormed off to the master suite.

Ginger and Lyla stood there looking at each other in silence for a moment. Lyla finally said in a low voice, "I'll be back after classes to pack my stuff."

"Maybe you'll change your mind by then, Ly. Sarah really isn't who she seems to be. Believe me, I know her very well."

"Funny, she said the same thing about you and Dad." Lyla grabbed her bag for school. "I love you both." She left as if her feet had wings, and found a pay phone on Broadway to call Sarah.

"Were you serious about your offer of me using your extra bedroom? Is it still available?" she asked.

"Of course, lil sis. I don't say things that I don't mean."

"You're a lifesaver! Do you mind if I move in this afternoon? I gotta get out of here."

"Sure thing. We're going to be roomies!" Sarah sang.

"Oh, God! I'm supposed to work tonight. Can you cover my shift? I know you were supposed to be off and you worked all weekend already."

"No problem."

⊰⊱

Aksel rode in the elevator to the twelfth floor after his morning classes at NYU. He was an emotional wreck and not sure what to expect from Grant and Ginger. His fear was solidified when he neared Grant's office and could hear him yelling from behind his closed door. Grant yelling wasn't something he'd ever heard before and it didn't seem to be work related. His heart started to pound.

Aksel looked at Sue for some sort of guidance but was she on the phone and flashed a questioning smile. Just then, Grant swung open his office door and saw him. "Aksel, we need to talk. Now."

"Yes, sir." Aksel nervously followed him into the office thinking he must have been told about his relationship with Lyla.

Grant slammed the door behind him, causing Aksel to jump. "I don't know how to deal with this." Grant turned and looked at him. Aksel prepared to make a run for it. "Hey, what's the matter with you? You look like you're facing the firing squad."

"If you would let me explain…"

"Explain what? No, no, no. Listen, Lyla's a mess and moving out. I need to let off some steam, and I trust you with my personal shit." Aksel took a deep breath as Grant continued babbling on about Lyla. He filled Aksel in on the morning's explosion. "You know I love my daughter, but she's like a whole different person lately. I probably sound like an idiot. I wish you knew how frustrating Lyla can be." Grant leaned against his desk and let out a long breath.

"*Monsieur*, she is very young and confused, trying to find her way. She has a lot of growing up to do."

Grant nodded. "You sound like Ginger, and you don't know the half of it!"

"Try not to blame yourself. How about a jog after work?"

"Sounds good. I can run off some excess stress. Thanks, buddy. Want a cup of coffee?" Grant slapped his shoulder affectionately and walked out before Aksel could answer.

Aksel sunk back into the chair and breathed a sigh of relief. Had Ginger chosen not to reveal what she knew to Grant? Or maybe she didn't really know his and Lyla's history. One thing for sure—he couldn't ask.

Chapter 15

Lyla cut her afternoon class and fled straight home to
pack her belongings. She stuffed as much clothing as she
could fit into two suitcases and hurriedly tossed all her
personal toiletries into a large duffle bag. Then she quickly
had one of the doormen hail a cab and left the building. As
she pulled away, that much closer to true freedom, she gave
thanks that neither Ginger nor Grant had interrupted her
departure.

Sarah's place was on Roebling Street in an area of
Brooklyn called Williamsburg. Just off the East River, it

was an eclectic yet quaint up and coming neighborhood to which a lot of young successful people were moving. Restaurants, bars, and shops lined every street and corner, with apartment buildings all around.

Moving into Sarah's apartment was more exciting than she'd imagined. Although she had been to Sarah's place multiple times over the last month, Lyla suddenly felt like she was walking up the stairs to the first moment of her new reality. The superintendent was a good-looking thirty-four-year-old man named Wally. He introduced himself and then helped her take her belongings up to Sarah's apartment on the second floor, and let her in.

"Thanks, Wally. Sarah said you're the best," Lyla commented. She handed him a ten.

"So I've been told." He looked at the bill in his hand and huffed, "Wells, just like I told Sarah, if yooz ever need anythin' at all, don't hesitate to ask." His thick Brooklyn accent reminded her of Nicky's. He was cute—but not her type. She wasn't even sure what her type was anymore.

As the sun set, Lyla finished unpacking and then walked through each room of her new abode with fresh eyes. *This is now my home.* An eight hundred-square foot apartment with two bedrooms and one bathroom, though smaller than what she was used to, seemed perfect.

The bedrooms were similarly decorated yet set apart by the colors or patterns; clear Lucite and black lacquer furniture were the staples throughout. The living room housed an oversized leopard-print couch, a white furry throw rug, and a shiny black coffee table, with matching end tables. The television and stereo were inside a large black wall unit that stretched nearly the length of the entire living room with two freestanding, four-foot-tall speakers on either side.

Exhausted from her day, Lyla turned on the television and passed out on the couch. A little after nine, Sarah burst through the door. "Roomie, I'm home!"

Lyla sluggishly sat up on the couch and blew a kiss at Sarah.

Catching her kiss in the air, Sarah asked, "How about a drink to celebrate your newfound freedom?" With a big smile, she held up a bottle of expensive champagne that she pulled out of her bag.

"Yes, of course." Lyla yawned, wiping the sleep from her eyes, and fell back onto the couch again thinking they would relax. "Looking forward to my first night at *home sweet home.*"

Sarah had different plans for the evening. She gleefully chatted about her day while pouring the champagne, into which she always sprinkled ecstasy powder. "This will wake you up." She handed the drink to Lyla. "Bottoms up, buttercup!"

Lyla drank the entire glass, and Sarah snatched it up, refilled it, and added more X. Halfway through her second glass, Lyla's demeanor began to morph from exhausted to energized, per usual due to Sarah's aptly named Rah Rah Cocktail of ecstasy and champagne.

"So, you met Wally. Like I said, he's nice enough, huh?"

"He's sweet. And cute…until he opens his mouth." Her eyes widened, embarrassed at what she said, and they both laughed.

"Another tip from your big sis? Remember, it doesn't matter what they *sound like* when they open their mouths—it's all about the *benefits you can get from them…*" She paused and sat next to Lyla, who sighed and leaned against her chest. "You seem troubled."

She filled Sarah in on her day, on the blowout she had with Ginger and her father, and her financial concerns. Lyla had finished her drink but still couldn't stop worrying about how she would be able to afford her new life on her limited salary.

Sarah smiled and cooed while softly tracing up and down her spine with her long acrylic, French-manicured nails. "Honey, don't worry about money right now." She looked at her watch. "In fact, I need to get ready for my night job." She pulled Lyla up from the couch and held her hands. "Come out with me tonight. I've already mentioned you to my boss. He can't *wait* to meet you."

"You work *two* jobs? So that's how you can afford this beautiful apartment." She followed Sarah into her bedroom.

Stepping into her walk-in closet, Sarah said over her shoulder, "I have a lot to teach you."

"I guess I have a lot to learn."

Sarah straightened. "Let's start right now. Here, wear this." She tossed a black, see-through, long-sleeve romper and a pair of black stiletto heels at her.

"This? Where are we going?" Lyla looked at her reflection in the mirror while holding up the minimal amount of fabric against her body.

"You'll see." Sarah winked. "Take your clothes off."

Lyla followed her instructions, stripping down to her bra and panties.

"Oh, those panties won't do, try these. And you won't need the bra."

While Lyla started to put on the naughty ensemble, Sarah scurried around her closet, gathering her own outfit for the night job Lyla never knew she had.

"I was asleep when you got here, but now I feel like I can go all night. How does that concoction do that to me?"

"I didn't name it the "Rah Rah Cocktail" for nothing!" Sarah laughed out loud. "I need to get our ride lined up. And another drink for us, sexy?" She left for the kitchen.

Lyla nodded and started dancing to the music Sarah had put on. Her entire emotional outlook had changed from her first drink. No longer was she worried about classes or schedules or money—she felt free and euphoric.

"You look fantastic!" Sarah said. "Glad to see you're feeling better." She handed her another drink.

Lyla spun around in front of the mirror to the upbeat music. "It's so nice to be freeeeee! And braless! I *love* this outfit!" She giggled, looking at herself. "And you! You look *hot*, Sarah!"

Sarah was wearing clear Lucite heels with red sequined straps that had to be at least five inches tall in Lyla's estimation. Her red sequined boy shorts and black halter top with an ultra-deep scoop neck truly accentuated Sarah's beautiful body. She had what it took to turn heads, and she knew it.

The front door buzzer sounded. "Ride's here. Got everything you need?"

"Yes."

"Ready then for a sneak peek into another world? You'll soon think of it as true freedom, lil sis."

"Hell, yes. Let's go!"

When Lyla stepped outside she was surprised to find a black Lincoln Continental Town Car waiting curbside. "I was expecting a cab," she whispered.

"One of the perks of *my* nightlife. I'm so excited to share it with you! Get in, girl!"

They drove for less than a mile when the Town Car turned into a dark alley and stopped at the back of a barely lit building with no signage. There were two doors only a few feet apart. Each door boasted a large, burly man dressed in a dark suit, and hat.

One man walked over and opened the car door for the girls. "Rah Rah, good to see you," he said as he helped the girls exit the car. "And who's your *lovely friend?*" He eyed Lyla up and down.

"Hi, Paulie. This is my little sis, Belle." Sarah winked at Lyla and held her hand, squeezing it. "Hey, Peetie!" she yelled over her shoulder to the other man as she guided Lyla through the door.

The volume of the music penetrated Lyla's body as she followed Sarah down a long, dark, and narrow hallway. She couldn't refrain from swaying her hips back and forth with the beat of the music. A stuffy smell of cigars and cigarettes filled the air, but it didn't bother her as it usually would. She followed Sarah to a red curtain.

Sarah dropped Lyla's hand and said into her ear, "Are you ready for this, Belle? Pinkies, okay?"

Lyla locked pinkies with Sarah and nodded. They walked into a well-lit, cigarette smoke and perfume-filled dressing room, adorned with countless full-length mirrors on one wall and a row of lockers on the other. Couches were sporadically placed around the dressing area with half-naked girls everywhere. Some were looking into the mirrors checking their skimpy bras and panties, adding hats and other sexual accessories, while others fixed their hair or wigs and makeup. A few women were doing lines of cocaine in the corner.

"Hey, girls," Sarah said. Some turned to greet her, while others continued with their own business as if Sarah hadn't said a word. "This is my little sister, Belle. Be nice!"

Sarah then introduced Lyla to Candy, the den mom of the exclusive gentleman's club. Candy was a short, slightly overweight woman in her mid-fifties, with long blonde hair pulled into a tight pony-tail. Her hazel eyes twinkled when she spoke.

"Belle, I've heard a lot about you." She eyed Lyla and nodded at Sarah with approval. "Slim is waiting to meet you."

Lyla's head spun. She was no longer scared, only enthralled with this lifestyle she'd read about but never dreamed she would actually experience for herself. *I feel like I'm supposed to be here, like I've done this before on some level.*

Walking with Sarah toward Slim's office, she asked, "Who's Slim? And why am I meeting him?"

"He's the owner slash manager of this joint. Any girl who works here needs to meet him."

"Work here? Me?!"

Sarah kissed her on the cheek and smiled. "Only if you want to."

"Me, a dancer? Cool!"

"But if you want to, don't forget that you're twenty-one and you forgot your ID tonight because I rushed you out of the apartment."

Lyla could barely contain her excitement as she briefly thought about Victoria's Secret and modeling—this was different, and the idea of being a stripper seemed forbidden and wonderful. "So this is your second job?" Her foggy brain comprehended the situation and she laughed out loud. "So I'm going to be an exotic dancer with you?"

"Like I said, only if you want to. Who needs your parents' money?" Sarah winked and knocked on Slim's door.

"Come in!" a gruff male voice yelled.

Sarah opened the door and sashayed inside with Lyla in tow. "Hey, Slim, darling. This is my little sister, Belle. The one I told you about."

Slim was a heavyset, bald man with a thick mustache, a crumpled suit, and loosened tie. He had dark circles under his bloodshot eyes and a red splotchy nose. Sitting behind his desk in the cherry wood-paneled room, he inhaled a few lines of cocaine before offering some to Sarah. Sarah kissed his cheek as he handed her a rolled-up hundred-dollar bill. She bent over to snort what he laid out for her, and he patted her ass.

Slim stood up from his black leather chair and shuffled toward Lyla. He grabbed her hand, twirling her around.

"Well, your sista sure didn't lie about you. Gotta take your outfit off, though. Gotta see what you got under there, honey."

Lyla turned to Sarah with a questioning look; Sarah encouraged her to do what he said with just a smile and a nod. Lyla meekly started taking off her romper when Sarah interrupted, "You okay, Belle? I gotta get ready for my set."

Sarah kissed Slim on his cheek again. "Thanks for the pick-me-up." Then she left Lyla alone.

Lyla stood frozen with her romper held against her chest. The reality of the situation started to inch its way into her groggy consciousness.

Slim looked her up and down. "First time, huh?"

"Y-yes, sir." She stared down at her feet.

"Here, have some. It'll take the edge off." He handed her the mirror with a few lines of white powder. She held the romper against her body with one hand and took the rolled bill with the other. She was trembling and she hoped Slim didn't notice her hands shaking. "First time for this, too? Must be from the Midwest." He guffawed.

She heard her mother's condescending voice flash in her head and immediately felt a rush of defiance. She smirked at him and sniffed the lines, followed by a small coughing fit.

When Lyla handed Slim back the rolled bill, he said, "Keep it, sweetheart. A souvenir or your first tip—however you wanna look at it. But drop your clothes, please."

All her inhibitions dissipated, and she did her first striptease.

"Very nice. Great panties. I like that you left your shoes on. Now, stand over there." He pointed to the couch in his office. "The next part of this interview gets physical." He unzipped his pants and had her sit on the black leather couch as he stood in front of her with his cock hanging out.

"Now show me what that mouth can do." Lyla did as she was told. And although she didn't enjoy it, she felt empowered when his knees buckled because of her.

Chapter 16

"What the fuck is she doing? Why do I care?" Aksel lay down on his bed and rolled over the papers and diagrams, not caring if he wrinkled them. Opening the top drawer of his nightstand, he took out a photo of Lyla taken one hot August afternoon a couple of years before when he'd surprised her with a scavenger hunt in Central Park. It was their first summer together in New York at Grant and Ginger's apartment—the summer they fell in love.

Aksel had been attempting to finish putting together a business presentation project for his economics class, but he couldn't get Lyla out of his mind. Holding the tattered photo in his hand he recalled that day in 1986. "Fuck me!" he yelled as loud as he could and tossed some of the pages on the floor in frustration.

I'll never forget the scavenger hunt I made for her. I enjoyed surprising her with gifts, and love notes. But this time was different. I left the first clue on her dresser, which directed her to Central Park. Each clue sent her to the next and I scattered them throughout the park. The final destination was a huge weeping willow tree tucked on the edge of an unkempt part of the park, where the last note read: "Wait here."

I left her a bottle of water and a bowl of yellow, pink, and purple flowers at the foot of the tree. I snuck up behind her while she was gazing up at the enormous tree, admiring the vines growing up the trunk and branches looming toward the blue sky. It was like a dream to see her standing there amid the green foliage filled with butterflies flitting about and birds singing in the distance.

She had turned with a smirk, almost as if she knew I had been behind her all along—how did she do that? "You've thought of everything, huh?" she said, then took a sip of water and tucked a purple flower behind one ear. "How did you do all this?" I never answered; I don't think she expected one, anyway.

"What a…breathtaking view," I whispered into her ear. She looked back at me and realized that I wasn't talking

about the tree. Red filled her cheeks as she blushed, and my heart thumped heavier for her—beautiful. She was slightly damp with perspiration as I picked her up and settled her on my back. She wrapped around me like a little backpack.

"The rest of the way isn't easy. I don't want you to get hurt, so hold on, okay, bébé?"

We went through a maze of trees, looming branches, moss-covered fallen trunks. Moving so effortlessly with her on my back, I was falling more hopelessly in love with her and knew I needed her in my life forever.

Eventually we reached a small clearing, and I put her down. "Close your eyes."

She protested, of course, but I knew she was teasing. She had closed her eyes, and I peeled her off my back and lay her down on the softest plush purple blanket, flower petals all around her.

I lay down next to her. "Okay, open your eyes." She looked all around. We were in a hidden area in the middle of New York City. Above us was a canopy of tree limbs.

"Aksel! This is—you are—how did you find this?" she stuttered, and as if on cue, more butterflies appeared, dancing about as the sun began to set, making shadows like moving artwork.

"So what do you think?" I asked her proudly.

"Bébé, this is amazing! It's as perfect as you are, and almost as beautiful, my sweet lover." She kissed me between

each word. *"Thank you for doing this. I only mentioned once wanting to make love to you under the stars, and here you give me the Garden of Eden. How? How did you come up with all this?"*

"You."

"Me?"

"Yes, you. You inspire me in so many ways. I've never felt like this with anyone, ever. What have you done to me?" I laughed.

"You're in love, just like me."

Suddenly I felt like I was having a déjà vu.

"Aksel, that was meant to be a compliment. It just took the right woman for you to find yourself."

I snapped back into the moment. "Speaking of, you still have one more thing to find."

She started unbuckling my belt, "Where? In here?"

"No. Yes. I mean, you'll know it when you see it."

She ripped off her sundress, pulled my shorts off, and straddled me. "You are so delicious…"

After reaching new heights of pleasure yet again, I wondered if this was real. Why did I deserve her? We were outside in the late summer dusk, acting like wild sexual creatures, when she saw it.

"Oh, Aksel, it's perfect," she whispered.

"Took you long enough."

"If you weren't such a delectable distraction, I might have seen it earlier."

We crawled closer to the tree. On its trunk was a heart with the initials L + A inside the heart.

Lyla traced the carving with her fingers. "I feel like we've been together a lifetime, yet it's been less than a month."

"This is our little love nest. I wanted to mark it permanently."

"Mmmm, I love our love nest. Maybe we could add a mirror to see how we look together, outside, naked, like Adam and Eve." Then we continued to devour each other until the moon was our only light...

Aksel stood up, barely able to contain himself after those memories flooded his thoughts. *I love you, Lyla. I always have, and I always will. And now I may never see you again—what will I do without you?*

Chapter 17

It had only been a few weeks, but Lyla's new lifestyle was already taking its toll. The only thing that kept her going was her intake of drugs and the excitement of how financially independent she'd become, from dancing almost every night.

Lyla had just showered and was putting on her makeup as she got ready for what had become her favorite part of the day—nighttime. In spite of being young with endless enhanced energy, she was starting to feel physically overwhelmed with juggling her daytime activities and her evenings.

"My dearest queen bee, where's our wake-up powder?" She bent over the edge of Sarah's bed, completely naked except for her new red stripper heels.

"It's in the second drawer of the nightstand, baby," Sarah replied from inside the closet.

Opening the drawer, she poured some of the white powder onto a small mirror, cutting two thick rails of cocaine with the razor. Lyla felt an immediate burst of energy after snorting it. "Want any?"

"Sure." Sarah twirled a lock of her blonde-auburn hair, standing in a flirtatious position, her lips sultry. "But what I really want is you."

Looking at her, Lyla lay back on the bed, grabbed the cocaine vial, and spread some on her flat, bare tummy. "Well, come and get it." She offered Sarah the rolled-up hundred-dollar bill—her first tip from the night Slim "interviewed" her to work at the club.

Sarah climbed on top of the bed and snorted the powder, then licked the leftovers off Lyla's belly.

"Oh, baby, you're so wet. But my mouth is too numb." Sarah reached into the top drawer of her nightstand and grabbed her huge vibrator.

"Mmm, BOB is so good to us. I like how he takes orders and doesn't talk back," Lyla responded with a giggle, spreading her legs farther apart.

"You've become so naughty, my lil lover. Bend your knees, please?"

"My pleasure. Then yours?" Lyla squeezed her hard, pink nipples as Sarah rubbed BOB around her clit, climaxing when Sarah thrust BOB inside her. Sarah teased her by removing BOB to lick him clean, while Lyla begged for more.

They switched positions after making two Rah Rah Cocktails, and Lyla brought a surprise for Sarah. "Close your eyes?" Lyla strapped on a harness she had bought that BOB fit securely into, asked Sarah to flip over, and slid a pillow under her. The pillow lifted her ass higher, allowing Sarah to have a place to perfectly grind her clit.

"Oh, my...my..." Sarah moaned as Lyla slowly entered her pussy from behind, gently holding onto her hips. "God! Oh, that feels so fucking good! Fuck me harder, baby!"

Lyla began to thrust deeper and faster while Sarah grinded into the pillow. Both girls came simultaneously as BOB vibrated inside Sarah and stimulated Lyla's clit. They fell onto the bed intertwined, giggling and kissing.

"Thank God for the new BOB! Do we even need a man?" Sarah cackled.

"I guess you like the new vibrator?" Lyla kissed Sarah's neck.

"Oh yeah." They finished their drinks after a few lines of cocaine. "We need to get our asses in gear. I think you should wear this for starters tonight." Sarah handed her a lacy bra and matching thong in red. "They go with your shoes, Lyla."

"But you just got those. You haven't even worn them yet!" Lyla protested.

"I actually got them for you." Sarah blew her a kiss and disappeared into her closet.

Lyla, slightly anxious from the cocaine, "Can I have some X to balance me out?"

"Yeah, but not too much. Please don't OD on me." Sarah hurried to her nightstand, and retrieved some X capsules.

Lyla sat back after emptying the contents of one pill into her remaining drink and slammed it back. "Rah, I think I need to cut my hours at Andrew's. I'm starting to fade here. Or maybe I should just quit school."

"If you do that you will be tipping your hand to your father and all holy hell is going to break loose. Right now, they are wondering how you're able to manage without their assistance. You're in charge, babe. No one's telling you what to do." Sarah handed her the rest of her alcohol concoction.

She sipped the drink. "You're right, you're right. I can do this. But I haven't charged anything on my dad's card lately. I'm sure he's curious as to how I'm surviving."

The door buzzer sounded. "Be right down," Sarah bellowed through the intercom.

"We can take care of filling his card tomorrow—maybe get groceries or something. Don't forget your ID again. Darby jumped through hoops to get it for you. Slim's been up my ass asking about it."

"Ewwww!" Lyla took the fake ID wondering how she would celebrate her real twenty-first birthday.

"I know, right?" Sarah wrinkled her nose, crossed her eyes, and stuck her tongue out. Laughing uncontrollably, Lyla did one more bump of cocaine before walking out to the waiting Town Car.

⊹⟞⊚⟝⊹

Grant was in the master suite after taking a shower, getting dressed for their eight-clock dinner date. Lyla had been on his mind again all day. "Have you heard from Lyla lately?" He tried not to sound worried as he picked out a shirt to wear. His daughter's wellbeing was never far from his thoughts. Grant buttoned his cuffs.

"No, hon." Ginger applied makeup at the vanity, meeting his gaze in the reflection.

Tucking in his shirt he continued, "It's been two weeks since I've heard from her, and I can't stop worrying. She hasn't charged anything on the credit card. Gin, how is she surviving?"

She stood up and hugged him. "I know that she's still working at Andrew's and going to school. We just have to give her time to figure things out."

"Jesus, Margo verbally kicked my ass last week when we talked."

"I would think Lyla has been in touch since she moved out."

"No."

They had moved to the kitchen and Gin poured them two vodkas on the rocks since it was only seven fifteen and they had some time. "Would you like a drink, my love?"

"Thanks, babe." He took a sip.

"Grant, maybe you're overthinking this. Lyla's not stupid. She'll be fine. She wants to make a bold statement about herself."

Grant wasn't sure if what she just said was meant to convince herself or him.

They finished their cocktails with conversation on Jason's driving permit, and then Grant led Ginger to the elevator to the lobby. Once inside, he put his arm around her. "I invited Aksel to join us for dinner tonight, but he declined, he's just too swamped with homework." Looking into the mirrored wall of the elevator behind Ginger, he saw her reflection. He pulled her against his body as the elevator would make no more stops after the twentieth floor.

She wiggled away from him and laughed. "I just put my lipstick on!" she said. "I'm so in love with you."

"I am so love with you and wish time would slow down a little for us." He chuckled, "And I'm sorry you are raising Lyla." He kissed her shoulder.

"I want all of you and that includes children, my naughty prince."

⊷⥱◐⥲⊶

Evan was in the lobby conversing with Deerpak when Grant and Ginger walked out of the elevator hallway.

"Break time's over, boys," Ginger teased. She and Grant had a dinner date, just the two of them, at her brother's restaurant—not only to support him, but because the food was wonderful. And yes, a part of her hoped that Lyla would be working.

On the way to The Nue, Grant caressed her arm to pull her attention from the window. "What are you looking for, love?" Grant asked.

"Oh, I guess I'm just hoping to see her walking down the street." Ginger had opened the bill for their credit card and saw that Lyla had only charged a little over a hundred dollars. "Did you give her an extra tip when she waited on you last?"

"No. I almost wish she had approached me for money. At least I would know what's going on and could sleep easier. The thing that worries me the most is her being wrapped up in Sarah's world. God knows what Sarah's got her doing."

Ginger's mind churned—she knew how much Sarah liked to party.

"Hell!" Grant smacked his hand on his knee. "Maybe Margo's just playing us. Think she's sending her money just to make us look bad?"

"Possibly. She always has been devious. Maybe Andrew can shed some light on how she's been?" Ginger hoped that Grant was right, and she slid next to him to grab his hand. "On a lighter note, I heard back from the realtor in England." She smiled ear to ear. "I'm pretty sure it's ours, my sweet Tommy."

"Really, Rach? How soon can we close?"

"It will probably be toward the end of November. Let's make another honeymoon out of it," she suggested. England meant so much to them both.

"Book it, babe!"

Chapter 18

While showering to get ready for his business economics class, Aksel couldn't think straight; he was obsessed with thoughts about Lyla and what she was doing. He'd had a restless night of bizarre dreams about being a soldier in love with Lyla. *What the fuck is wrong with me!? Why can't I accept the fact that it's over between us?* The fact that he had hurt her so badly had begun to affect his heath—he couldn't eat, and couldn't sleep. *I'm such an asshole...I love her so much.* Standing under the showerhead, he wished the warm water could wash away his guilt and pain. *After deserting her to stand alone against her mother, I deserve to be erased from her life.* He'd avoided the last invitation for dinner with Ginger and Grant a few nights before because he couldn't take another conversation about their worry over Lyla. It was killing him, too.

I need to know she's okay. I can't take this any longer. After his shower, he was dressing for class when an idea came to him. *I will follow her after her shift and satisfy my foolish need to make sure she is safe.* He knew he was lying to himself, for what he wanted was another opportunity to beg for her forgiveness.

That night after class he sat in the back of an off-duty cab that he'd secured by paying the driver a large amount of money to park a few doors down from The Nue. When Lyla's shift ended, he saw her leave the restaurant and hail a taxi. His cabbie followed the other taxi to her apartment. Once she stepped out of the yellow vehicle, he watched from the back window of his cab to see which building she walked into.

Aksel's mind swirled. *If she sees me, what do I say? Should I just go ring the buzzer and try to talk to her again? Which buzzer? I'm losing it!*

He paid the cabbie and took a seat at a bar across the street from where she lived. He chose an outside table since it was a beautiful night, where he could see the entrance to her building. He was mentally fatigued from studies, interning, and obsessing over her. *I am really a stalker now.*

Counseling! ASAP! This feels wrong to me. But I must speak to her, at least one more time...

Numerous beers later, he still debated with himself over what to do since it was almost nine o'clock. But after a double shot of Jack Daniel's, he stood with the courage of inebriation and walked across the street. He went up a short set of stairs and stood on a landing. Before he could even press a button, a Town Car pulled up in front of the building and honked its horn. He suddenly felt a nervous gut-wrenching feeling and quickly left the landing to hide around the corner of the building.

The driver got out of the vehicle, went up the stairs, and pressed one of the buzzers. Moments later he saw Lyla and Sarah from The Nue exit the building and get in the Town Car. Luck was on his side—as the Town Car left, an empty cab was coming down the street. He hailed it and jumped in.

"Please follow that car. Just not too closely." Aksel stared intensely through the windshield of the cab and watched as the Town Car turned down an alley. "Stop. I will get out here." He handed the driver a twenty for less than a mile.

Why a Town Car to this place? They could have walked! He slowly jogged down the dark alley surrounded by brick walls on both sides. He saw the car parked and cautiously made his way to where it had stopped just in time to see the girls go inside a door.

What the fuck? What is this place? A club maybe? Aksel reached back into his pocket to get his wallet and remove some cash. Two men in similar attire stood in front of the doors talking to each other and smoking cigarettes. They hovered protectively near the doors—one of which he knew Lyla and Sarah had gone through.

Walking slowly up to the men with two fifty-dollar bills cupped in his hand he attempted to drop his French accent. "So, gentlemen, which door gets me inside?"

They laughed. "Who sent you, Frenchie?" The shorter of the two men smirked and crossed his arms. They both towered over Aksel by at least six inches.

"Obviously I'm from out of town. I thought Mr. Grant would assist with my entry?" He held up the folded bills.

They smiled at each other and the shorter one took the cash from Aksel. The two men faced each other and whispered something Aksel couldn't make out. The larger one turned back to him. "Head on in *missure*." He laughed at his own accent.

"*Merci.*"

The shorter man held the door open to the building. Slowly walking down a long, dimly lit hallway, he heard and felt the loud music vibrating off the walls. He came upon another beefed-up, well-dressed man with white hair standing behind a speaker's lectern. The man barely looked at him as he stuck out his hand. "ID, please."

He handed him his ID, and the man flipped through a few pages on a clipboard.

"Don't see your name here. Our establishment is by invitation only. Yet somehow you got passed the boys in da back." The gatekeeper stared straight into Aksel's eyes, raising an eyebrow. "I wonder how that happened." He smiled and rubbed his thumb against his pointer and middle fingers—the universal sign for cash.

"Ben gave me your address." Aksel handed him a hundred-dollar bill.

"Everybody *loves* Ben," the man said and pocketed the bill. "But how many times did he mention us? I'm sure it was more than *once.*"

"Twice?" Aksel asked, reaching into his pocket, hoping it wasn't going to cost him his entire bankroll just to get inside the mysterious hellhole.

"Really? Usually Ben mentions us guys about *four* times for unknown guests."

Aksel sighed and peeled out three more hundred-dollar bills.

Pretending to look through his paperwork again, he said, "Oh, there you are. Sorry for my confusion. Enjoy your evening, Mr. Smith. And because you've been so accommodating, the next time you visit, the number of Bens will be three."

"Merci."

He took the cash and opened a door adjacent to his podium.

Aksel returned his wallet to his pocket and walked into a dark room filled with music, smoke and a stage where a young woman was dancing naked. He realized it was an exclusive, high-end "gentlemen's club." He readied himself for the worst—an unexpected version of Lyla.

He took a seat at an empty table in the darkest corner of the club where he could see all areas of a U-shaped dancing stage. All three sides of the stage had poles, one in the center and one on each end of the catwalk. A scantily dressed blonde server asked if he wanted anything. The way she said "anything" obviously hinted to more than a drink.

"A vodka tonic, please," he responded, avoiding eye contact. She left a bit disgruntled but returned quickly with his order. The dancer on stage looked like Sarah, who he'd seen with Lyla. He kept scanning the crowd of people hoping to find out that Lyla was just a server and didn't work on stage.

He sipped his drink as a booming male voice sounded through the speakers: "Hands together and open up your hearts and your wallets for Rah! Don't forget to tip the beautiful ladies serving you. Whatever you do, stick round for our lovely Belle next."

Rah Rah danced while removing her clothes… She was definitely the girl with Lyla. Sarah walked around to the tables in her scanty costume after her performance collecting tips from the room full of men, who were all vying for her attention. The music lowered again followed by the voice announcing, "Get ready, ladies and gentlemen, everyone's latest favorite…our one and only, Belle!"

Aksel watched as Sarah sat on a man's lap, teasing him. He seemed to be enjoying it, but when the lights dimmed further, all eyes turned to the stage, including his, and Sarah wasn't even an afterthought for this man. She made a face and faded into the background.

The sound of beating drums bounced off the walls, and smoke vapors filled the area as a spotlight lit up the center pole of the stage. The dancer's back was to the audience—she crouched behind huge red-sequined wings, revealing only her red stripper heels.

The beat of the drums slowly sped up, harmonic chimes fell in tune, and tiny sparkling confetti fell from the ceiling. Angelic voices hummed rhythmically to the beat, further enthralling and enchanting the audience. The dancer slowly stood and unfurled her wings.

The crowd of mainly men, with a few ladies, chanted, "Belle!" over and over as she swayed her hips to the beat, unveiling the rest of her backside. The tempo suddenly changed, and Lyla turned, spreading her wings with her head held high, looking toward the ceiling. He was awestruck and sickened at the same time.

She sensually danced to the slow rhythm as men and women all around threw cash at the stage. They hooted and hollered for her attention as she slowly took off her wings, then bra, then wiggled her ass and bent over. She played with the sides of her thong as if that too would be removed—not that the thong left much to the imagination.

Aksel turned his head away from the stage when the spotlights sporadically lit the crowd. Unable to take another second of watching his beloved sell her sensuality, he stood, placed a fifty on the table, and rushed toward the exit but turned one last time to look at her. She was grinding her hips against the pole. Distraught, he averted his head only to see Sarah escort a man toward what he assumed was the private dance area.

Stumbling outside, he walked down the alley to the street before he vomited. After collecting himself, he hailed a cab and went straight home, emotionally distressed over what he'd witnessed. *What have I done to her? It's all my fault. I am such a piece of shit. No wonder she wants nothing to do with me. I've destroyed her!*

Once safely inside his apartment, he dropped his keys on the console table in the foyer and headed for the refrigerator. He grabbed the bottle of vodka from the freezer. Slouching on the couch, he drank himself into a stupor.

◦❯═◉◉═❮◦

Lyla gathered her cash from the stage after her set and went over to a few patrons who put tips in her garters. She scanned the crowd for any familiar faces, and when she saw Darby's, she walked over to him. "Hey, thanks for your help with my ID."

"Have a seat, *Belle*." Darby patted his lap.

Feeling slightly uncomfortable without Sarah around, Lyla chose a chair next to him. "I didn't know you'd be here tonight." Attempting to be sociable, she asked, "What did you think of my new act?"

Darby placed his hand on her leg and began to rub her inner thigh. Leaning into her ear he whispered, "Loved it. How about we go to a private room and talk about it?" She pushed his hand away from her leg.

"You know Sarah wouldn't like that. You're her guy." She stood up to leave since she and Sarah were friends slash lovers and Darby worked with her at The Nue. Starting to walk away she saw Darby hold up his hand with cash it, signaling a floor manager that he wanted to take her to the back. She knew she was stuck—she had to follow the house rules, so she escorted him to a private room, her mind racing with how she would explain it later to Sarah.

The hallway to the private dance rooms was behind a thick, black velvet curtain. The carpet was black to match the walls, and it lit just enough to see where you were going. Each space had a padded bench and a small half-curtain for what would be considered privacy. The walls did not reach the ceiling, so one could peek in. That was done so the roaming bouncers could keep an eye on every dancer for their safety—or for their own entertainment.

Everyone affectionately called the private rooms "black holes." Lyla warned Darby, "This isn't a freebie. Management saw us come back here. And just so you know, I'm going to tell Sarah that you made me do this."

"Fine. I get it. But honestly, I was just so overwhelmed by your set that I didn't want to hide this any longer." He unzipped his pants, and his huge cock sprung free. He grabbed her hands and held them against his erection.

"Whoa, whoa!" She released his cock. "What are you doing? You said *talk*! Don't be an asshole now!"

"Oh, I see." He stroked himself slowly. "So only talk. Like to your parents, next time I wait on them at The NUE? Or maybe Uncle Andrew?"

"You wouldn't!" She was shocked by his threats.

"Listen, I just want to fuck the shit out of you right now. It will be our little secret, of course." He grabbed at her hips with both hands and lifted her up to straddle his legs. The tip of his dick was against her belly button, and she struggled to get off him, while mentally battling with how to react since his cock excited her.

Darby was Sarah's boy toy. Lyla felt torn by her friendship with Sarah and feared his threat to expose her to her family. Then she decided why not? He was just another guy with a big ego and a cock to match.

Her brain caught up with her. "You got five hundred bucks in your pocket? If not, this isn't happening." *He's just a waiter and I can't fuck him for two pennies.*

"I've got cash. But not that much."

"Then *enough*." She leaned away from his body and crossed her arms.

"You think your family would approve of how you've been spending most of your nights as an underage slut? Snorting coke? Fucking men for money?"

"So wait. You're *blackmailing* me for sex?"

"Listen, sweetheart, I'm just looking to get inside of you. I've wanted you since the day I trained you at the restaurant. Sarah doesn't need to know…"

Lyla's sexual desire started to take over her better judgment, fueled by anger and drugs. And it didn't help that Darby's cock reminded her of Aksel's. "Just this once, right? And *only* if you promise me you won't say anything to Sarah or my family."

"You have my word." He grinned as he crossed his heart.

She began stroking his cock. *This is a huge mistake. But I miss—*

Before she could finish her thought, he picked her up and slid inside her. "No! You have to wear a condom, you idiot!"

Darby laughed, nearly growling, and thrust deeper inside her.

Lyla couldn't stop herself—she began riding his cock and let herself get lost in the moment. Grabbing his hair she feverishly began to fuck him. It had been the first time she enjoyed having sex with a male since Aksel.

"Feel good, baby?" Darby asked.

With her eyes closed, climbing toward an orgasm, Aksel's face filled her head. "Yes, oh yes! Uh-hum! Aksel!" She came hard and quickly. She jumped off Darby, leaving him sexually unsatisfied.

"You better finish me off, you little prick tease! Or should I tell Sarah—or this *Aksel*—how you seduced me?"

With resentment, she got on her knees and did exactly what she thought she had to do to protect herself from anyone ever finding out who, or what, she'd become.

At the end of the night, Lyla realized that she'd danced at Slim's for about a month, but it had never made her feel dirty before, or riddled with guilt. Walking toward her locker to gather her things, Candy pulled her aside.

"Belle, your following has grown so quickly. You should be proud."

"Yeah, I guess so," Lyla replied with a sigh, trying to forget what had just happened.

"Whatever it is that's bringing you down right now, you need to get over it, because we've got an offer for you. Only you, though. You can't mention this to anyone, especially Rah."

"Fine. What's up?" Lyla mentally tried to pick up the pieces of her heart.

"Meet me in Slim's office in five. Jesus, girl, wake up. Here's a bump." Candy filled her long pinky nail with white powder from a vial she pulled from her pocket and lifted it up to Lyla's nose. "This is a great opportunity for you. Not many girls here get *this* offer. See you in five minutes. Alone."

Lyla sniffed it and nodded. She found Sarah leaning against one of the couches in the dressing area, already changed for home. "Rah, uh, I gotta go show Slim my ID. Wait here for me?"

Sarah barely looked up. "Sure. Take your time. I've got lots to count tonight!" She cackled at the amount of money spread out in front of her.

Lyla entered the office with trepidation. Candy leaned against the corner of the desk with a huge grin while Slim cut lines of cocaine on a mirror.

"Here's the deal, Belle," Slim said as he handed Candy the mirror. "I know you've only been with us for about a month now. I'm curious, how much did you make tonight?"

"I haven't counted, but after tipping out, maybe five hundred. Why? Is that not enough?"

"Oh, that's plenty. If that's all *you* want. How would you like to move yourself up a few notches and make five times that in one night with half the work?"

"You've piqued my interest." Lyla sat on the chair facing Slim's desk. Candy passed her the coke mirror, and she snorted the two lines already cut for her.

"We've got a business associate who has nothing to do with the club. She runs a totally different type of operation. And she's always looking for young talent like you."

"What kind of talent?" Lyla wondered where this was heading—dancing somewhere more exclusive?

Slim's face reddened and he stood. "Your kind of talent! A pretty face, a nice body. You interested or not?"

Candy rubbed his arm to calm him down. "Your name has come up several times. Mainly by the men who visit our establishment here. But they don't want to wait to watch you dance or hope to get your attention. They want *you.*"

"So, I won't be dancing, just—" Lyla desperately needed clarification.

"No dancing, unless they ask you to," Candy replied enthusiastically.

"And *five times* what I make here in a night? Hmmm, how often would I *not* be dancing for your associate?"

"Just a few nights at first. If you like it, as often as you want. You game?"

Taking the mirror, she leaned over and snorted a couple of lines. *Why not? I'm the one in control. I can make as much money as I want before stopping.* "Well, I *would* like to make more money..."

"Great. Done deal," Slim said, slamming his open hand on his desktop, as if everything was agreed upon.

"I'll give you more details as needed." Candy clapped her hands and hugged Lyla. "Don't speak of this with anyone, remember?"

"Yes, ma'am."

"See you tomorrow night?" Candy smiled.

"See you tomorrow." Returning the smile, Lyla left Slim's office, realizing she'd always been stressed about being in the spotlight on the stage. *God forbid if a friend of my family ever wanders in here and sees me. And it seems like I won't be dealing with riffraff customers like Darby. It's just sex for a lot of cash. Life is short...*

Lyla grabbed Sarah's arm and kissed her cheek. "Let's go, Rah Rah. I can't wait to get you home!"

"Shower first."

"Always after we leave *here!*" They rushed to their Town Car, where Lyla wondered if she'd finally figured out a way to have the life she wanted. She would have all the money she needed to pursue life as a model or go to college and be beholden to no one. *I could have a place like Grant and Ginger.* She laughed out loud.

Chapter 19

It was nearing Halloween when Aksel realized he had lost all motivation in his studies, his work, and life in general. He constantly blamed himself for the quagmire Lyla was in. The thought that she may *actually* enjoy stripping for strangers he couldn't entertain. He wanted to believe that wasn't who she really was on the inside. But no matter how he tried to rationalize her behavior, he still felt responsible and the guilt continued to wear him down.

It was the third time that week that he'd arrived late for work at G Squared, unshaven, his clothing visibly rumpled. Sue, the receptionist, watched him as he shuffled through the lobby of the office, stopping to knock on Grant's door.

"Come in."

He went inside. "*Monsieur* Grant, I need some assistance."

Grant got up and came toward him from behind his desk. "Honestly, I was hoping you'd ask me before I had to ask you what's going on. Ginger and I have been concerned about you for the last few weeks; we thought maybe school was overloading you." Grant closed the door. "Have a seat." He pointed to the chair in front of his desk as he returned to his.

Aksel slumped. "*Monsieur* Grant, I do not know how to say this. Maybe New York is not what I expected it to be. I just need a little guidance."

"Well, we can cut back your hours. Would that help?" Grant's concern was clear on his face.

"No, no. *Merci.* I love working with you and Ginger. This has been my happy place. Yet I am not as happy as I once was."

Grant paused. "Aksel, is this about a girl?"

"You could say that." Aksel appreciated his perception. He and Grant had a friendship that seemed to bridge all differences.

"Trust me," Grant said. "I've been there."

"How did you get through it?"

"Luck. But I also needed counseling after I discovered the root of my problem. I've been to a great psychiatrist, but he's not the typical type. He looks beyond your current circumstances, you might say."

"May I have his information, please?" Aksel would do anything to get well.

Grant considered this, then wrote down a phone number.

⤙⟞⊙⟝⤚

Grant left the office to meet Howard at Nick's for lunch and review the completed orders. Howard looked even worse than the last time Grant had seen him. His face was sunken, his skin pasty. He had lost a lot of weight and was breathing heavily. Grant wondered why Howard insisted on meeting at a restaurant instead of the building where their separate offices were housed—just an elevator ride away.

After an hour of reviewing work, Howard pushed all the paperwork aside and sighed. "Grant, there's a reason I asked you to meet me here, and it's not work related. My wife has been helping out and I didn't want her to hear this conversation."

"I figured something was up."

"I don't know how much longer I have to live, and I want to clear my conscience." Howard lowered his head. He seemed to be searching for the right words or rehearsing what he'd already worked out in his mind. "At times, I resented your success. Especially when you left H&M and created G Squared."

"Howard, I don't know that we need to rehash-"

Howard cut him off. "Shut up, farm boy! It involves the truth, something I've never been good at, as you may well know."

"No shit, buddy. But don't stress yourself." Grant could see how intense this was for Howard and didn't want the man to die at the table.

"I can still recall the days when you would just say, 'Yes, sir,' and then shut up and listen. Now's the time to reacquaint yourself with that old habit." His breath was labored.

"Yes, sir." Grant held up his glass of merlot and smiled.

"This is about your daughter."

Grant nearly spit out his wine. "My daughter? What about her?" He put his glass down.

"As you know, I hired you as a favor for Margo. She was my fit model at the time. Sure, you ended up being an unexpected surprise—you were and are really good at what you do. The best I've ever worked with." Unable to look Grant in the face, Howard averted his gaze.

"Thank you. Look, I know what you're going to say, and it doesn't matter. I love my daughter, even if you're her biological father."

"That's exactly my point." He grabbed Grant's forearm. "Did I have an affair with your wife at the time? Yes. But Lyla's not mine. She's yours."

"Oh, this is grand, Howard, even for you." Grant felt relieved on one level and in another way pity—Lyla was always his daughter, no matter what.

Howard shook his head. "Grant," he said softly. "Please believe me. I'm not proud of everything I've done. Margo asked me to lie if Lyla ever inquired of me to tell her I was her father. But here is the truth: Margo didn't know I had a vasectomy. I appreciate all you've done for me—in the past and especially recently. You helped me when you didn't have to. After the way I'd treated you, I was honestly surprised that you did." Howard wiped his eyes with a napkin. "And I can't thank you enough."

Grant was uncomfortable for Howard but the man persisted and gave him an envelope.

"It's all in here. Everything I told you is documented. It also includes a copy of the doctor's report from the date of my vasectomy, my blood results, and my DNA information. Don't let Margo poison your daughter with her manipulative lies. You *are* her father, Grant."

Grant sighed deeply, holding the envelope against his chest and whispered, "Thank God." He felt some hope in restoring his relationship with Lyla as he stuck the envelope in his briefcase and parted ways with Howard.

⁘

The soft music playing in Dr. Leonard Ritzius' office, along with the warm and homey décor, immediately put Aksel at ease. A gray-haired, middle-aged woman handed him forms to fill out and he took a seat on a brown leather couch in the waiting room. The doctor that Grant had recommended the day before had been gracious enough to squeeze him in.

About ten minutes after he had finished filling out the paperwork, a tall, thin man in brown dress pants and a light-blue shirt with a relaxed collar entered the room. He had a receding salt and pepper hairline, and wired lenses. "I'm Dr. Ritzius. And you are Aksel Portier?" He spoke softly while reaching out his hand. His manner was calm and controlled, making Aksel feel like he was seeing an old family friend.

The doctor led him back to his office, which was sparsely decorated with a leather recliner and a couple of overstuffed chairs that had two accent tables with lamps. He chose the recliner next to the chair the doctor had sat down in. Aksel began unraveling his story as the doctor took notes and periodically interrupted him for clarification, or to ask questions.

"In the end, I really feel at fault for who Lyla has become. I can't get her out of my head. I'm not even interested in other women. It doesn't help matters that I work for her father, and we have become very close over the last three months. Actually, now that I think about it, I have always felt close to him, ever since we first met when I was a young adult in France." He couldn't hide his despair. "I'm just crazy right, Doc?"

Dr. Ritzius shook his head as he scribbled something down on his pad. "No, Aksel, we all have confusing emotions brought on by events in life."

"I really need help to figure out how to get her out of my mind, out of my system. My future waits for me. Yet I feel paralyzed by the unhappiness that fills me."

"How about we start with the idea that you need to stop judging yourself?" Dr. Ritzius smiled at him. "Because there is no judgment here. You have come to me for guidance and to provide you with some tools to figure out how to handle an overwhelming situation."

"Yes, I understand."

"You say you feel responsible for who this young lady has become, correct?"

"Yes."

"You took away her virginity, and later on in your relationship, she became pregnant. Part of your struggle is with not having the ability to act responsibly at that time, and since you feel you ruined her life by taking her virginity from her, you're the villain. Does her father know this information?"

Aksel's stomach flipped at the thought. "I don't think so—he's never mentioned it."

"Do you believe you can do something now to rectify what you did to her?"

"I suppose, I mean," he looked at the floor. "I know I can't."

"You understand, we all make our own choices. Did she choose to be intimate with you?"

"Of course. We were in love," he said in an exasperated voice.

"And recently, Lyla told you to forget about her?" The doctor looked him in the eyes.

"Yes. So why am I still so drawn to her? Even understanding that I cannot fix anything, as you said."

"Perhaps you have an emotional tie with her that may go beyond what your conscious mind is aware of. In addition to traditional therapy, I do what is called past life regression therapy. At times it opens a door that only your soul is aware of. I can help you reach a state of relaxed, focused concentration. Would you be interested in pursuing that route?"

Aksel sat quietly and took a deep breath as he thought about what it might do to him. "I am willing to do whatever it takes to feel happy again."

"Then let's begin. I want you to relax your body. You will need to free your mind of everything that presently causes you angst. Including any thoughts of this young woman."

Aksel relaxed into the comfortable leather lounge chair. Dr. Ritzius turned down the lights and turned on soft music in the background. At Dr. Ritzius's direction, he closed his eyes and allowed his breathing to become smooth and calm. The doctor walked him through the relaxation of each part of his body.

"Imagine breathing out all the negative, stress, tension--then, when you breathe in, picture the light and let it fill you. Now allow your mind to expand to wherever it wants. Don't try to analyze it, edit it or understand what you see. Don't try to overthink anything. Just see. We will figure it out together. Follow my instructions. If at any time you feel uncomfortable, all you have to do is open your eyes and you will be here."

Then Dr. Ritzius told Aksel to visualize a staircase that led down.

"Aksel, go down the stairs. They lead to a garden. Please open the door and enter." Dr. Ritzius waited while

Aksel followed his instructions before asking him, "What do you see?"

Aksel hesitated for a few moments. The door opened into a pub where people talked and laughed, and the smell of food filled his nose. He felt nervous as his mind's eye looked at the young woman he was with. "She's beautiful, wild, and full of spark. My best friend just introduced us, hoping we would like each other, and he was right."

"What are you doing?"

"We are playing a game of darts, and she is wearing my flight hat…"

"Are you a soldier?"

Aksel hesitated as he looked at his arm with his eyes closed. "Yes. I am wearing a uniform."

"Do you know where you are?"

"We're in a pub somewhere…in England maybe? She has a British accent. My buddy and the girl of his dreams just left. She wants to leave with me…"

Aksel grinned as she spun with her arms stretched out pretending to be a plane. The woman kept smiling as she circled around him.

Dr. Ritzius asked, "What are you seeing?"

"We are now walking together through a small village back to her flat. We can't keep our hands off each other…We're barely inside and she's already kissing me more passionately than I'd ever been kissed before. That kiss was something else...she owned me the instant that our lips touched. I am hers!"

Aksel fell silent as she began to undress. With more prodding, he continued speaking. "I am sucking her toes. I-I've never done that before. She's watching my tongue and mouth slowly and sensually wrap around each toe. At no point have we lost eye contact. This is the hottest, most explosive physical experience I ever had with a woman...all this before I've taken off my uniform.

"I can barely breathe because of how sexually exciting this is. And my mouth is watering." Aksel's lips were slightly agape as he spoke without a French accent. "I'm licking her top lip and gently biting her bottom lip. I am so full of anticipation of what I could do to the rest of her body. This...this is my first time having sex... *Wait.*'"

"Do you want to take a break, Mr. Portier?" the doctor asked.

"No. I just told her to wait. We are finally both naked on her bed, and she is ready for the rest of me, something I've wanted to experience for years. But I want to look at her, to take her all in. I'm tracing the outline of her face. I want to commit it to memory, to keep it in my mind forever. She closes her eyes and lets me explore her skin as my fingertips lightly touch the rest of her body...her beautifully full breasts, her perfectly smooth stomach. I am mentally and physically devouring every inch of her. In this moment, there is no war, no violence or hatred. It's all about us.

"Her eyes open. I'm spreading her legs with my knees. I wrap my arms around her shoulders yet keep my weight just above her on my elbows. I enter her slowly yet passionately, perfectly balancing the two. How we embody both feelings of strength and tenderness at the same time, I don't know.

"It's like I'm on drugs or something—every second is the most incredible first sexual experience a man could imagine. We are moving in perfect sync in desperate need of the other. With each thrust, I am deeper and deeper until I am buried inside of her. It feels as if we are one body, only focused on pleasing the other. I can feel her body starting to explode within minutes of being inside her.

"It is mind blowing. Each minute inside of her sends me out of my body and keeps me in a state of ecstasy for what seems like forever. But this is my time finally—no, our time, together as one. Our breathing is one, literally and sensually, as if she could suck the air from my lungs.

"So quickly again she comes undone, this time looking into my eyes, as much as she can keep them open, reeling from the ultimate pleasure." *I have so much exploring to do.* "I touch her lips with my fingertips. I slowly kiss her, dip down between her legs, and drink her. With two fingers, she explodes again. How so fast, I am thinking as slurred versions of my name escaped her lips like a prayer."

"Do you know your name?" Dr. Ritzius asked.

"Alex."

"Do you know what her name is?"

"She likes to be called Izzy..." Aksel's eyelids started to flutter.

"What's happening now?"

"She's holding my shoulders, and my arms are wrapped under her backside to keep the connection of my mouth, tongue, lips, and fingers inside her."

Aksel grew silent.

"What's happening now?" the doctor asked.

"I'm back on top of her. And I'm thrusting inside her again." He moaned. "I exploded deeply inside her...I cannot describe it. There simply are no words to describe it."

Aksel's breathing hitched, then slowly returned to normal.

"Do you recognize her from this life?"

Aksel searched his mind.

"You may not. It's okay if you don't," the doctor said.

Aksel's eyes flew open. "Yes!"

Chapter 20

It was a busy night at the strip club; Sarah opened her locker in the dressing room to change into her outfit for the third set. Candy, on her rounds, stopped at Sarah's side. The older woman still had a decent body for someone who drank, did drugs, and smoked like a chimney. "I see your other half isn't here yet. Is she coming in tonight?"

"I don't think so."

"Okay. Just checking." Candy shrugged and continued on her way, pausing to share a word or two with the other girls.

The conversation with Candy unsettled her as she recalled Slim's similar behavior the night before. *I thought I was going to have to defend her last night but Slim didn't care either. What's she really up to? Over the last few weeks, she's missed about three nights a week. And that excuse of needing to reinvent herself, and changing her stage name to ZeZe? What's with wearing wigs and masks…there must be something more to this bullshit. There always is. What's going on with that little bitch?* Suddenly filled with rage, Sarah slammed the locker door closed. "She's lying to me!"

The excuse Lyla had for skipping nights at the club had been "side work" with an agent she'd hooked up with from modeling school. Sarah hadn't given it much thought until Slim and Candy had both asked how she was doing. The weird part was how nonchalant they'd been—it wasn't their usual attitude regarding someone being a no-show at the club.

⊷⊶⊙⊷⊶

Nearly three weeks had gone by since Lyla started working for the Manhattan Madam. At times she enjoyed the opulence of the brothel and its clientele, yet on another level, it disgusted her. She felt dirty, and had no respect for the entitled people who paid for her. *Men only want to fuck me. I might as well get paid for sex since that's all people want anyways.* Her attempts to rationalize her behavior fell flat.

The clientele at the brothel were at least upper class, some she'd remembered meeting briefly at the White Party in the Hamptons; she was glad they didn't recognize her. *Dad was so upset with me for embarrassing him that day at the White Party. If he only knew the truth about some of those people!*

Lyla downed another drug-enhanced cocktail as she sat on a plush turquois couch waiting for a client to request her. She marveled at how much she'd adapted, once again, to the newest version of herself over such a short period of time.

The apartment from the prewar era was located on West 70th and Amsterdam, and took up the entire third floor of the building. It was located around the corner from where her father lived on West 68th. The décor had twisted wrought iron throughout; even the chairs were intricately designed with cushions covered in rich red velvet. The chandeliers glistened like diamonds, which played well for the ambiance. Candles flickered at almost every turn of the eye, expensive artwork hung on each wall, all with detailed, expensive framing. She giggled, recalling her first night...

The madam told me they were all going to be beautiful strangers to me. I was so stressed my first night as I got ready to go to the brothel and be a part of a secret sexual society. Looking into my full-length mirror in my room, I felt pretty with my loose, dark-brown curls framing my face—pale, but with dark ruby lipstick. I was wearing white Edwin Jeans, a blue blouse with cutout shoulders to accentuate my bright-blue eyes, and low-cut black boots. I grabbed my full-length coat and left the apartment feeling both exhilarated and frightened at the same time.

When I arrived at the brothel they escorted me to the back area. All the girls were stunning, like movie stars. They were changing into their lingerie provided by the madam. I saw their expensive handbags, shoes, and clothing being folded for them by the assistants who worked there. And for the first time in a long time, I felt out of place, out of my league being younger than everyone there.

My nerves were shot! I gulped down a second glass of champagne, which I had added ecstasy to. A young woman helped me change into my uniform: a white mesh thong and a matching push-up bra and camisole, all accented with deep red. I stepped into matching red stilettos and told myself I was ready.

At the doorbell's first ring, my insecurities had me checking the mirror again, in spite of the fact I'd heard countless times that I exuded sensuality so naturally that people were drawn to me.

I tried to look relaxed as I sat on the plush couch and studied the frescoed ceiling that reminded me of an 18th *century rococo painting of a country side with nude nymphs sitting along a river bank, something that Boucher might have painted. Everywhere I looked, all I could see was beauty. Even the servers and assistants were stunning. Where the hell was I?*

She recalled watching as the men and women walked around, engaging in conversation with the different girls in the brothel sitting area. The clients represented both old and new wealth which they felt entitled them to whatever they wanted in life.

Logan was my first client. Six foot, strong, gorgeous, and smart, in his mid-thirties. He was actually great in bed and knew exactly how to arouse a woman. That night I made three thousand dollars after splitting sixty/forty with the madam. And she invited me back!

Lyla snapped from her drug-enhanced recall as a tall, handsome younger man approached her and asked if she was available. He looked familiar—she realized she had interacted with him at the White Party. It was Nathaniel, the mayor's grandson. She took his hand and led him to a suite. *I would have fucked you for free a few months ago.*

A few hours later, Nathaniel was leaving. "Hope to see you again soon," she said seductively.

"Of course. Sooner than later. By the way, in December, I have some charity events I must attend. Would you be interested in being my plus one?"

Lyla smiled. "You'll have to clear it with the madam, but I would be thrilled to escort you."

Nathaniel had barely left the room when she flopped back on the bed. *Well, I'm glad he paid, because that was lame. He's got a few things to learn about being a lover… if I wanted to get fucked like a rabbit, I would be a rabbit!*

Lyla finished cleaning up, changed into fresh lingerie, and met her next suitor. She desperately hoped he would be more pleasurable. During her working hours at the brothel, she'd only reached an orgasm a few times—otherwise she faked it since it helped clients climax quicker.

Though, really, I can't blame them. No one has ever really brought me to such unimaginable sexual heights as Aksel did. Every time! Damn you, Aksel Portier, I hate you! It's time I stop thinking about you!

She settled with the madam at the end of the night, mentally and physically exhausted. The only thing that kept her going was the drugs and the four thousand dollars in her Gucci handbag—proof she could make it in New York on her own. *Boy, would I love to rub that fact in my father's face!* She snorted some cocaine in the back of the cab hoping to kill her feelings.

⊷⊷◉⊶⊶

Unlocking the door to the apartment around two in the morning, Lyla was caught off guard when she saw Sarah sitting in a cloud of smoke on the couch in her pajamas waiting for her. A pile of coke was on the coffee table next to an ashtray that was full of cigarette butts. Sarah lit up another cigarette, which Lyla was sure she did just to irritate her.

"You're home early. Slow night?" Lyla attempted her sweetest, caring voice, trying to ignore the smoke. "I'm going to slip into some pajamas."

"We need to talk," Sarah said, then blew smoke in her direction.

"Okaaay? I'll be right back."

Sarah looked away and continued stewing on the couch while Lyla disappeared into her bedroom. *Oh, fuck me. She knows.* Lyla quickly stashed her cash in a shoebox and put it on the top shelf of her closet. Then she changed— she decided on a sexy black negligee and matching thong with fluffy heeled slippers instead of pajamas.

Lyla went to the kitchen to make a drink. She watched as Sarah snorted line after line of cocaine, still blowing cigarette smoke carelessly inside the apartment instead of smoking outside on the balcony.

She called out, "Hey, lover, I'm making my favorite drink, the Rah Rah Cocktail. Want one?"

Sarah didn't reply, only glared at her in silence from the couch.

Lyla entered the living room with her drink. "Oh, baby, what a terrible night you must have had. What happened?" She sat next to her.

"Where would you like me to start?"

Lyla leaned over to kiss her, but Sarah turned her head, so her lips landed on her cheek instead. "Must be really bad. I don't think I've ever seen you so upset."

"Probably haven't. This is what I look like when I feel betrayed." Sarah offered Lyla a cigarette.

"I'll kill them! Him! Her! *Whoever!*" Lyla uncharacteristically accepted the cigarette with shaking fingers.

"Where were you tonight? And *don't* feed me that line of bullshit about working with that agent again. Tell me the truth. You only have one chance."

Lyla's mind raced as she lit the cigarette, quickly trying to figure out what she should say. She snorted two fat lines. "I never meant to hurt you."

"Well you have. Candy, Slim, even my boy toy Darby are all asking about you, like they know something that I don't. Spill it. Now."

Tears filled Lyla's eyes. "I *am* working for that woman I told you about, but she isn't really a talent agent like I made her out to be. She's actually a madam of a high-end brothel."

Sarah sighed and put out her cigarette. "Wait, what? Where? How?"

"It was at a job fair at Barbizon." Lyla peppered the truth with lies. "She approached me there. At first I thought she was a legit agent, so I went for an interview at 70th and Amsterdam. But when I got to her flat, she told me the type of *talent* she was interviewing me for. God, Sarah! The place was so beautiful and clean, and the money was so tempting. I agreed to try it for one night. Shit, it's not like we don't already do it at the club, right?"

"Go on," she said with a skeptical tone.

Lyla continued telling her story to Sarah, most of it only a sliver of truth. "I made a thousand dollars on my first night! That's what I average, give or take. But I love how I don't have to work the crowd or screw someone for nearly nothing back in those tiny black holes where the managers watch us. I just have to fuck a few men. And they are different from the guys at the club."

"So, if this is true, then why didn't you just tell me and hook your big sis up?"

"I was going to tell you, but I wasn't sure if it would last. And I still don't know—but once I'm in, I'm sure she won't deny my request to have you join us. I'm starting to gain her trust. I just wanted to wait to surprise you with good news."

"Well, okay." Sarah relaxed back on the couch and rubbed Lyla's leg.

"I'm so sorry you had to find out this way. I didn't want to tell you before I could include you. But God, Sarah, this place is so much better!"

"Who is Aksel?" Sarah stared directly at her.

Lyla's smile faded instantly. "Wh-who did you hear that name from?"

"Just tell me who he is first."

"Fair enough." Lyla filled Sarah in on her relationship with Aksel, leaving out the part about the pregnancy. She still wasn't even sure if she believed Aksel's version.

"Oh, Lord! He followed you to New York? Where does he live?" Sarah sat up with concern.

"Somewhere in SoHo, I think. I hope I never see him again, though."

Sarah blew out a breath. "Sounds like he broke your heart, baby."

"Fuck him. So how did you hear his name?" Lyla took a sip of her drink. How the hell had Sarah found out this stuff?

"Humph. Really want to know? My boy toy."

"Darby?" What an asshole, she thought.

"Yeah. Which brings up another question—why Darby would know about him if you never even told *me*?"

"I don't know. I hardly talk to him at work. Although, there was that first night I did my red butterfly act. You were in the back, and he and I chatted for a bit. I might've brought Aksel up then, though I can't remember why or how." Lyla hoped she convinced Sarah that that's all they'd "chatted" about. "But why would he bring that asshole's name up?"

"He wondered who Aksel was—he said he was just looking to protect you, like a big brother, I guess." Sarah sounded protective, too.

Maybe I should have acted dumb and not told her a thing about Aksel. That stupid fucking Darby!

"So why do you still dance if this brothel shit is so much better? Is that why you changed your stage name and look?"

"Yes, because I told you, I'm not secure enough there yet. I can't leave the club until I know I'm solid. The madam insisted that I change my image because some of her clients go to the club, and they like to see me looking different than when they meet up with me at the brothel—weird, huh?"

Sarah slid over and wrapped her arms around Lyla. "They're rich, they get what they want."

"Exactly."

"Well, you better show up and dance, *ZeZe,* because Slim and Candy are bugging the shit out of me about you.

And keep mum about your second job—they'd fire you on the spot or dump you in the East River!" Sarah laughed.

"I know," Lyla lied.

"Let's come up with a delightful story to cover your ass with them. And, baby, I want in at the brothel!"

"Deal." They hugged again, and Lyla hoped that Sarah believed her lies.

After their conversation, Lyla finished her drink and went to bed. Sarah snorted another line of coke and lay out on the couch. As she rubbed her nose, she thought over what Lyla had told her. *Why would she mention an old heartbreaker's name to my boy toy? Something sounds fishy. I bet Slim has something to do with this as well; he's a businessman after all.*

The next day at The Nue, as Sarah headed toward the kitchen, she heard Lyla loudly whisper, "Well, fuck you, Darby!" Darby grabbed his order from the line and when he turned around, he was face-to-face with Sarah.

"Need help?" she said. "You've never been any good at balancing things." Betrayal twisted her insides as she skewered him with a look.

"I got this."

"You got this? Really? Guess you don't realize that fucking two girls under the same roof isn't good for your health."

Darby stopped in his tracks and shook his head. "Wait, how did you find out?"

"You're so stupid, you just admitted it, you idiot. You're going to regret fucking me over—*and* fucking the niece of the owner." She stormed off into the dining room, and he trailed her, his hands full with a food order.

She fumed. How could they?

Before the dinner rush started, Sarah took a smoke break outside the restaurant behind the kitchen alongside the Dumpsters. The air had a foul odor of rotting food, which matched her mood. Darby joined her for a smoke.

"What do you want, asshole?" she snapped. "Smell out here just got worse."

"Could you just listen for a minute?" Darby tried to pull her closer, but she backed away. "Sarah, please, give me a chance."

She liked the empowerment she felt from his begging and growled, "Well, this better be good."

"Here's what happened. Lyla had come over to my table and sat down. She told me that she wanted to take a break and asked me to take her into the hole to talk. I said that you would be upset, but she just laughed and asked if I was afraid to be alone with her…which of course not, right? So back we went, just to talk, or so I thought. But as soon as we got settled in a private room she started rubbing my leg and said, 'Let me see what Sarah's boy toy has to play with.'

I told her, 'Come on Lyla, we can't do this,' but she dropped between my legs and unzipped my pants. She fucked with me, and I am only human."

"So, *she* seduced *you?*" Sarah tilted her head. Lyla *had* been lying to her. *I know just how to get her back.* She exhaled a plume of smoke. "I'll forget the whole thing under a few conditions."

"And what would those be?" Darby nervously lit another cigarette.

"One, you must ignore Lyla completely. I don't even know if I'll let you come to my apartment anymore. Then again, I don't want to go to your shithole to fuck you...Don't even talk to her at work other than as a need-to basis. And no more sexual escapades with her."

"Okay. Sure."

She was relieved since she really enjoyed fucking him. "Second, you need to find out whoever that Aksel idiot is and get him into the club. I want to see her hot little ass crash and burn for lying to me about fucking you. When she sees me fucking around with her ex, it will destroy her." Revenge was sweet.

"What are you gonna do? Fuck him?"

"Maybe I'll fuck him, maybe not. That's my business."

Darby looked to the ground and kicked a five gallon can they used to butt their smokes. "Babe, I'm telling you, it wasn't my fault. *She* seduced *me*. I didn't want anything to do with her."

"Shut up. I don't care. You have a new mission to focus on. Think you can handle that?"

"Well, do you know anything about this dude?"

"Her father comes in at least one night every week. I can't wait on him." Grant avoided her table. "Maybe he knows something. Make sure you take his table next time. He may be able to lead us to Aksel."

Chapter 21

Grant and Ginger were in a quiet, reflective mood as they rode home in the limo after the funeral for Howard Golden on November 3rd. Howard had been many things to them in life, most of which was unpleasant, but in his final days he had shown them a different man.

"What do you plan to do with the info that Howard gave you that would clarify whatever Lyla thinks?" Ginger asked Grant.

He looked out the window at the few remaining fall colors on the trees as they rode through Central Park on their way back to the apartment. Lyla. He hoped she was okay. Facing his beautiful wife, Grant said, "I haven't decided."

Ginger offered her hand in a show of support. "Has she ever mentioned anything to you about him?"

"No." Grant clasped her warm fingers, drawing strength. "Never. I think I'll keep the envelope in the safe and forget about it for now."

"I think that's a good idea." Ginger pulled free and settled her hands across her lap. "Speaking of Lyla, and I know it's hard because she's almost entirely cut us out of her life over the last month…"

"Yeah, except her monthly credit card bill. But she hasn't ever charged more than four hundred bucks. How is she managing?" The gloom of the rainy day filled Grant's mind.

Ginger scooted across the leather seat so that they were thigh to thigh. "Living with Sarah? God only knows. I try not to imagine the worst and focus on the fact that eventually Lyla will see Sarah's true colors. Lyla's a smart girl—at least she talks to us every couple of weeks. Plus, she's still working at Andrew's, and attending classes. So how bad could it be?"

"That's my point Gin, I don't know. She and Jason are close, yet Jason complained to me that he's only spoken to her a few times since she's moved here. Since he's coming for Thanksgiving, we should remind her that he wants to spend time with her." He turned from Ginger's sweet face to the window as rain cascaded down. "Am I really that awful of a father that she could just, just—"

"Stop it right there." She cut him off with a pat on his knee. "Lyla is emulating her mother's manipulative skills. It's typical Margo style."

"But, Gin." Grant's heart ached with regret. "I wasn't around enough."

"Like you had a choice? Margo took the kids and left for Chicago. You were available as often as possible."

"Was I really, though?" Howard's death, his atonement for his wrongs, had made Grant even more reflective.

"Yes. She'll come around. You'll see." Ginger lifted his hand and kissed it.

"Well, answer me this, since you seem to know so much, *Mommy Gin.* Should we invite Aksel? He lives here in New York and doesn't have any family except for us." Grant already knew that she would tell him it was a bad idea, but she wouldn't tell him why, which meant it had to do with Lyla.

As predicted she said, "I don't think that's a good idea."

"Why not? What's the problem between them?" Ginger sighed but didn't answer. "Gin, I know you all too well. And I know that you know *something.* What is it?

Why do you go out of your way to keep their paths from crossing?" Frustration filled his voice—at the situation, never Ginger.

Squeezing his hand, she said, "My love, I wish I could tell you this one, but I can't. She confided in me, and I don't plan on breaking her trust."

"Just when I think I understand women, I should know better that you have that girl code thing." He shook his head.

"Can you respect it? Understand that this is the way it has to be for now?" Her gaze pleaded with him for understanding. "Besides, it's an issue from long ago."

"Fine. I'll respect the trust she put in you, if you promise to tell me if it becomes an issue that needs to be dealt with. As much as I love Aksel, she *is* my daughter."

"Fair enough."

"Even if she is an ungrateful brat." His heart skipped. "God, I miss her."

Ginger snuggled close. "Well, to change the subject to a guaranteed happy thought, my sweet Tommy, Sue booked our tickets for England yesterday. We leave on the twenty-seventh, the Monday after Thanksgiving. We close on the cottage on the twenty-ninth, and it will officially be ours! Including the furniture!"

Her excitement touched him. "Oh, God, that's amazing! I wonder what it will feel like to walk inside. Think it's the original furniture?"

"From the pictures I saw, it might be. If not, they've kept it similarly decorated from what I can recall. Either way, we can walk through the doors of our past lives. Together."

"I still can't believe it will be ours. How long will we have to reminisce, relive, reenact? Maybe do some gardening?" Memories of their lives together chased away the blues.

"Gardening in November? That will have to wait until a spring visit. But we must be back in time for the Mayor's Holiday fundraiser on December ninth, so we'll come back on the sixth. We need time to catch up with the time change, and I figured you wouldn't want to travel on the anniversary of Pearl Harbor, fly-boy."

"You're so thoughtful, Rach." He laughed as he put his arm around her. "What would I do without you?" She fit perfectly against him.

"We have each other," she said.

"I can't wait to be in front of the fireplace alone with you." Grant planted a tender kiss on her lips. He loved her so much and wondered what memories would be awakened in England.

⊷══◉══⊶

Aksel couldn't believe how quickly a week had passed since his first visit with Dr. Ritzius. He wasn't free of Lyla, but after being regressed and discovering Izzy, he looked forward to seeing the doctor again. He'd made plans for dinner with Grant at The Nue; he hoped for a chance to see Lyla as well as catch up with his boss and friend.

At the office, once Aksel was in the state of mind needed for regression therapy, Dr. Ritzius guided him to search for a time when his heart was broken. "Can you tell me where you are, Aksel?"

"I'm not Aksel." His French accent disappeared. "I'm Alex. And I'm at Izzy's flat again. It's the end of my leave. Something doesn't feel right between us."

"Is there any discussion?" Dr. Ritzius asked.

Aksel was silent for a few moments. He was in her one-bedroom flat; her perfume filled his head with the aroma of flowers. "We're lying in bed after spending the last few days together. I tell her that I hope spending my leave together means as much to her as it does to me.'"

"What is her response?"

"'Of course, it does.' She touches my face gently." Aksel mimicked the movement. "I sigh deeply and say, 'But I'm just not sure why you won't be my wife. You told me you love me already.' She starts to say something, but I interrupt her—needing her to understand. I tell her that it's not random sex for me, just because I'm a soldier—I'm not like that. I want to spend the rest of my life with you, I say again."

"What does she do?"

"I let my words sink in, and she seems to go through a multitude of emotions in a few seconds—including pain. *Pain?* How did I cause my Izzy pain by what I said?" Aksel covered his heart with his palm.

"You know Izzy well. Why do you think you are causing her pain?" Dr. Ritzius asked.

Aksel grimaced. "She just looks so sad. She says, 'I do care deeply for you, Alex. But I'm afraid to marry you because of this bloody war. You're a soldier! What if you never come back to me? I want to be a wife and then grow old with my husband. Maybe I am a hopeless romantic at heart. But I do know this for sure—I am in love with you. Still, I don't know what to do.'" The distress on her expressive face hurts him across time.

The doctor made an encouraging noise for Aksel to go on.

"I wrap my arms around her and she says, 'Maybe we should just see how things go? And...I just don't want to hurt you, Alex.'" He inhaled. "I stroke her hair and say, 'I love you, Izzy.' She says, 'Then make love to me.' We own each other's body in a whole new way. She takes my face gently in her hands and kisses me so tenderly, sweetly, and delicately. We make love to each other in that passionate, all-consuming way. Which confuses me even more. If she's capable of showing me such love physically, why can't she commit to me forever, regardless of how long forever will be?"

Dr. Ritzius must have heard the frustration in his voice because he said, "Let's move forward, Alex."

"I start to dress to leave. She looks sad again. 'Izzy, I feel so close to you right now, and I know I ask so much of you. But I think we could make each other very happy.'"

"'I could never leave my home, Alex.'"

"'I would never ask you to. But I would make England my new home, if you'd be mine. Anywhere you are is my home.'"

"'You really are more than a pretty face, aren't you, fly-boy? You're beautiful inside and, mmm, definitely out. How about we discuss it when you get back?'"

"'That's what you always say…' I reach over to kiss her good-bye. Kissing her hurts. Just the thought of knowing any good-bye could be the last fills me with sadness.

"After a tender and passionate kiss, we stare into each other's eyes, and I ask her, 'What am I going to do with you, Izzy?'"

"'Just love me, Alex. Just love me. I've never been in love like this. Just be patient with me.' She kisses me and gives me a look that leaves me sweetly heartbroken."

Tears rolled down Aksel's cheeks. Dr. Ritzius tapped his arm. "Alex? Is there anything more?"

"No, it's gone. I can't see anything else. But it still hurts. Deeply. More than ever."

"You won't heal overnight, Aksel. It will take a few more sessions to get to the root of your sadness. We haven't found it yet."

The session had ended, but he wanted more. He sat in the chair rooted by the emptiness in the pit of his stomach.

Chapter 22

During the dinner rush a few days later Darby recognized Lyla's dad as he entered the dining room from the elevator, accompanied by a much younger dark-haired gentleman. Business associates, maybe? Krissy started to seat them with another server, but Darby quickly changed tables so that he would be their waiter. He hoped this might provide him an opportunity to get some information about Aksel.

"Welcome to A. Madison's on the Nue, gentlemen. My name is Darby, and I will be serving you tonight.

Would you prefer your water sparkling or still?" He held a bottle of Perrier and one of Evian to choose from.

Grant looked at his companion and responded for them both. "Sparkling please."

Darby poured two glasses of Perrier into their water glasses. "Will anyone else be joining you this evening?"

"No, it's just us guys tonight," Grant replied.

"Very good, gentlemen." Darby removed the extra settings. "Can I start you with something from the bar while you look over the menu?"

Grant asked, "What do you think, Aksel?" Darby tried not to react.

"A red sounds good tonight," the younger man replied.

"Yes. How about a bottle of Bordeaux, Chateau Rothchild?"

"Coming right up, gentlemen."

When Darby walked away to get the wine, he did a silent cheer. *Aksel! Holy shit! This was way easier than I expected!*

Two hours sped by and Darby cleared off their table while they finished the wine. He'd been slammed so he hadn't had time to hover but he wasn't worried—he planned on slipping a note in Aksel's pocket.

"Compliments to the chef, as always," Grant said.

"I'm happy you enjoyed it. May I offer you coffee or dessert?"

"None for me," Aksel said.

"I'll take a double espresso," Grant replied, then excused himself and went to the restroom.

Darby re-wiped non-existent crumbs from the table. He wouldn't even need the note! "Pardon me, sir. I don't mean to be rude, but did I overhear that your name is Aksel?"

"*Oui.* I mean, yes. Do I know you?"

"Not really, no. But I believe we share a mutual friend—Lyla Robinson." He stuck out his hand. "I'm Darby."

Aksel shook, his expression wary.

"I have to ask, are you the Aksel that she keeps confiding to me about?"

"I suppose that would be me. How many Aksels do you know?" His short reply came with a questioning look.

"Frankly, none. Lyla would kill me if she knew I was even talking to you about her. Call me a hopeless romantic, but man, she's still so in love with you."

"Really?" He pushed his chair back to create a little distance between them and exhaled. "I have a hard time believing that."

"She says you two have a long history. But I gather she doesn't want her father to know how she feels about you. It seems complicated."

"You have no idea." Sorrow flashed in his eyes.

The dude had it bad but Darby moved in for the kill. "So, hey, would you wanna get a drink and talk some more? Lyla is falling to pieces." He tilted his head, exuding concern.

"She is?" Aksel glanced toward the men's restroom. "When can we meet?"

Darby scribbled the name of a bar on a napkin. "The rest of my week is slammed. Can we meet next Wednesday night?"

"This is in Williamsburg?"

"Yeah, are you familiar with the area?"

"Not really."

"Well, there're tons of bars around, but I think this is the best bang for your buck—"

"That's fine."

Darby noticed Grant returning. "I can be there by ten."

"See you then." Aksel put the note in his pocket.

God, Darby thought, *this poor mother fucker is desperate and caught in some real bullshit over Lyla.*

When Grant returned to the apartment after dinner with Aksel, he heard Ginger on the phone.

"Oh, Ly, it's been so good to catch up…You sound so happy…"

Grant walked into the living room and sat down across from her. Ginger winked at him and started laughing at whatever Lyla had just said with a blissful smile.

"And I know Jason will be thrilled to spend some time with you also…Sure, you can bring the pumpkin pie…Really, that's it. As long as you're here, it will be a perfect Thanksgiving…Okay, Ly, see you about noonish?" She chuckled again.

Grant held his hand up to his ear and mouthed, *Can I talk to her?* Ginger shook her head. The smile left his face and he was filled with rejection.

"No, no, you never could, Ly. I love you too…Okay, bye-bye." She hung up the phone.

Grant asked, "She didn't want to talk to me?"

"I told her you were out having dinner with a client. It's best that we take things slowly. She also asked who would be here for Thanksgiving and seemed relieved that it would be just the four of us."

"So, okay." Grant took a minute to regain his composure before being too cynical to Ginger, who was only trying to help. "I can't wait to see my daughter in two weeks. In the grand scheme of things, that's nothing, right?"

"Right. Why don't you get us a drink, and we can celebrate?"

Grant headed for the wine cabinet in the kitchen to open a bottle of red. He returned with two filled glasses. "What are we celebrating?"

"To us, *and* that Lyla will be attending our Thanksgiving feast."

They clinked their glasses and took a sip. "Just one question—did I hear you say she sounds happy?"

"Not only does she sound happy, she was getting ready to go out."

"This late?" He downed the rest of his wine. *Jesus Christ, I didn't need to know that!*

"Late? I guess you forgot what *you* were doing at eighteen! Let me remind you in the shower how great it is to be home." She grabbed his crotch and kissed him between words.

⊷⊷⊙⊜⊷⊷

"Dammit. Ginger invited me to Thanksgiving Dinner!" Lyla pressed the end button and ran her fingers through her hair.

"And you're going?" Sarah asked with an obviously fake smile.

"I can't miss an opportunity to spend time with my brother. Besides, he's a great buffer." She leaned over and snorted two more lines. "Let's get our heads into our night. But I'll need two things first."

"What's that?"

"A kiss and some X. I've gotta be solid when I tell Slim and Candy about my 'sick aunt.'"

Sarah kissed her and made two Rah Rah Cocktails. Although she didn't say anything, Lyla noticed a difference in her kiss—it was less intimate and more like acting.

They sat in silence on the drive to the club and finally Lyla said, "Well, I should go talk to them as soon as I get there." She leaned over to kiss Sarah again. This time their kiss was more intense. *Wonder if it's just my imagination or if the X is making her feel closer to me?*

"Want me to be there for a little moral support?" Sarah asked.

"What?" Lyla asked, confused.

"When you talk to Slim and Candy. I could help confirm your story." Sarah rubbed Lyla's inner thigh through her full-length coat.

"I think I can fly solo. I'm feeling much more put together after our second drink. But thanks, big sis."

Sarah immediately pulled away from Lyla. "Fine. Do it your way."

Lyla didn't want Sarah to be upset, but she planned on telling Slim and Candy the truth, that Sarah knew a little bit about the brothel, and it made her anxious. "I'll let you know right away if I need backup."

Sarah didn't reply.

"Hey, what's the matter?" Lyla smoothed Sarah's hair over her shoulder.

"It's nothing. I'm just done with this place, too," Sarah said with a sour tone. "I want into the brothel."

Lyla whispered into her ear, "Shhh, don't let Louie hear you. And *you know* that's on the top of my to-do list. I wish I could make it happen faster. I have an idea on how to make the waiting worth it. Let's go shopping tomorrow and I'll treat you to whatever you want."

"*Whatever* I want?" Sarah whispered with excitement.

"Yes, *whatever*. After all," Lyla said with a sweet smile, "I owe you *everything*."

Sarah kissed Lyla passionately this time. *That's better*, Lyla thought. They were fondling each other's breasts under their bras when Louie interrupted them. "We're here, ladies."

"Thanks, Louie. See you later." Sarah blew him a kiss, and Lyla winked at him. Louie was in on the brothel secret also, and now she had to cover that part in the meeting as well.

After changing into their costumes, Lyla said in a hushed voice to Sarah, "Well, wish me luck. I hope they buy it."

"Oh, I'm sure they will, ZeZe. After all, you're a *fantastic* actress."

Lyla ignored her sarcasm. She knocked and then opened the door to Slim's office—a mist of cigar smoke glazed the whole room. Candy and Slim were doing lines and talking. They both looked up when she entered.

Candy rose from the desk, her nose red and her eyes puffy. She hugged Lyla hello.

"We have a problem," Lyla said. "Rah Rah found out about the brothel. She even mentioned it in front of Louie. She probably even told the guy she's sleeping with."

"What's his name?" Slim asked, a puff of smoke engulfing his whole head.

"Darby."

"He's here a lot, right?" Slim turned to Candy.

"Yeah. He's an asshole." Candy's fist clenched as took a wide stance like a boxer. "I don't trust him."

Slim said to Lyla, "I'll take care of that one. How did Rah Rah find out?"

"She cornered me about where I've spending all my time—I didn't give her exact details, but I had to tell her something."

"You disappoint me, babe," Slim said, shaking his finger at her. "But you told us the truth, and I respect that. So you ain't in any trouble. We gotcha covered."

"Thanks, Slim. One more thing—Rah Rah wants in on the brothel."

Slim put his cigar in the ashtray and laughed. "That ain't gonna happen. Da madam likes young and exciting, not old and used." She heard the contempt in his voice, and it made her wonder what he'd be saying about her in ten years—Sarah was twelve years older than her, but Lyla's closest friend. She'd hoped to get her in.

After she told them everything that she and Sarah spoke about, they reassured Lyla not to worry and she relaxed after their conversation.

As soon as Lyla left, Slim pushed the play button on his CD player. "You Don't Mess around with Jim" by Jim Croce blasted through the speakers. Slim sang along to his favorite part of the chorus, only replacing "Jim" with "Slim": "You don't pull the mask off the old lone ranger / And you don't mess around with *Slim*."

He danced with Candy to the rhythm. "I know *exactly* how ta kill two birds with one stone."

Outside the office in the hallway, Lyla found Sarah leaning against the wall with her arms crossed.

"Why aren't you on the floor?" Lyla asked innocently.

"I wanted to see how it went. That seemed to take a long time..."

"They grilled me. But don't worry—they bought it hook, line, and sinker."

"Awesome. Phase one is complete. Onto phase two—getting me out of this hole! I used to think it was upper class, but your description about the Manhattan Madam's place makes this seem like a shithole."

"Shhh, I will. Just like I promised..." Lyla winked at Sarah. Until that point, she hadn't realized just how good she was getting at lying

Sarah had taken a reprieve from work and was at the apartment alone since Lyla was working at the brothel that night. She decided to organize her closet—she needed the room for all the gifts Lyla bought her that day on their shopping spree. The apartment was littered with tissues, bags and shoe boxes.

A few hours into her project of reorganizing her closet, the phone rang. "Well, I have an update on the whereabouts of Aksel. I suppose I can tell you tonight at the club…" Darby used his most nonchalant voice but Sarah wasn't fooled.

"It's your lucky night. I'm not working—come over and give me every gory detail." She hung up without waiting for an answer.

Within a half hour, the buzzer sounded, and she pushed the button to unlock the front door of the building. She left the door open at the top of the stairs and prepared two Rah Rah Cocktails.

She'd dressed in an Oscar de la Renta black linen evening gown and shoes by Giorgio Armani. Deep plum-colored jewels dripped from her ears with matching bracelets. Darby had just closed the apartment door behind him and his mouth dropped in disbelief when he saw her entering the room with the two drinks. "Wow, you look like a model from one of those fucking fashion magazines or some shit."

"You really are stupid, aren't you? Have you forgotten that I *am* a model?" She put a flippant smile on her face as she handed him his drink, feeling like a model for the first time in years.

"Right, right. Sorry, babe. Just looking at you melted my brain." Darby, underdressed in an old pair of unwashed jeans with a wrinkled tee, made her wonder why she'd settled for him.

"Good answer." She clinked her new Tiffany & Co. cocktail glass with his.

"What's all this?" Darby marveled at all the bags and boxes. "I don't even think I can pronounce some of these names…"

"Well, dahling, over there is Givenchy. There's DKNY. That's all Calvin Klein. Laura Ashley. Coach. Burberry. Dooney & Bourke." He lit a cigarette wearing a deadpan expression on his face. "Oh, clearly I'm boring you."

"I regret asking." He laid out some lines of coke and did them.

"So, please tell me the news, my little detective."

She stepped gently out of her dress, revealing her new sexy black lace undergarments from Victoria's Secret as he started to fill her in on his encounter with Lyla's dad at the restaurant. She held another dress up and got lost for a moment. She was enthralled by the detail of the dress, which she never would have been able to afford if it weren't for Lyla's guilt-driven generosity.

"Earth to Sarah. Did you hear anything I just said?" Darby questioned.

"Sorry, love," she said. She spoke in an airy manner and pouted her lips. "I was having a religious moment." She sat down and crossed her legs, in fashion heaven.

"What's with you?"

"Do you have something to tell me that could lift my spirits higher than everything that surrounds me, or not?"

He stared at her like she had grown two heads. "Whatever shit you're on is whacking you out."

She lifted her chin. "Don't be jealous of the *real me*. Just wait until my lil sis comes through with what she promised. I may not need the likes of you after I move to the Upper West Side."

Darby tilted his head and looked at her as if to see if she was serious. "You're off your rocker, woman. Really think you won't need *the likes of me* anymore?"

"Such a childish response. Now please, pardon me for a moment while I powder my nose." She lifted a shiny flat stone dish and snorted a few lines of cocaine with a new brass straw, holding out her pinky like she was a person of means from a bad B movie.

He grabbed the dish out of her hand and inhaled a huge amount of cocaine, not bothering to cut a line from the pile.

Why was he here again? Oh, yeah. Lyla's mysterious ex. "So? What did you find out?"

"Jesus, Sarah, wake up. I already told you." His jaw was clenched with obvious annoyance. "I found Aksel!"

"What?" Sarah jumped up. She hadn't actually expected Darby to do something right, and the news excited her enough to clear her head. "Who is he? Where did you find him? What's his story?" Sarah was back to the truest version of herself—scheming and manipulative. "Tell me!"

He relaxed into the couch and lit another cigarette. "What's in it for me?"

"Anything you want, hon. Just tell me what you know first, and your wish will be granted."

"Suck me first. Just to prove to me that you know I'm not stupid."

"Darby!"

"Right now, you little slut." She heard the degrading tone in his voice and her cheeks burned.

"Very well." She dropped to her knees before him, sticking his cock in her mouth. She tongued the tip of his cock and swallowed as much of it as she could, bobbing up and down with her fingers tightly jerking the rest of his huge penis. But just before he was about to explode, she stopped.

"Gahhh! Fuck, I'm almost there!" He choked out his words.

"Your punishment. Now tell me what you found out."

"You're a real bitch, you know that?"

"And you love it. So what's the deal?"

"I'm grabbing drinks with him here in Williamsburg next Wednesday night."

"Oh, baby! You're amazing."

"You're fucking right I am. Now I think I deserve something…"

"You've earned this. Now give me that cock of yours!"

He grabbed her head and fucked her mouth so hard, she gagged, nearly vomiting. He pulled out and ejaculated all over her face.

She coughed and spat. "You know I hate that!" She wiped her face with the bottom of his tee shirt, trying to keep it from dripping onto her new bra.

"Ooops, forgot." He laughed, still pumping his cock with his hand.

"You're a fucking asshole!"

"And you love it. Now I think I saw some handcuffs in one of those bags…"

"Forget about those for a minute. We need to come up with a way for you to convince Aksel to get inside the club."

"On one condition."

"What?"

"You don't fuck him. Just fuck *with* him. Because I don't want to share you with him."

"Are you telling me what to do? Because you don't own me, nobody will ever own me again." She glared at him as her hostility toward Darby grew.

"Okay, okay. Relax. Jesus, it just popped into my head – I'm not trying to control you. I get it, okay?"

"Good, because I've had enough bullshit fed to me."

I'm gonna fuck Aksel the first chance I get. How perfect we are for each other, just two fucked up assholes on the same page. Then she flipped over on the floor and let him fuck her from behind, her favorite position.

Chapter 24

Late in the afternoon on the day before Thanksgiving, Aksel had his next appointment with Dr. Ritzius. He discussed his plan to have drinks with Darby, and possibly arrange a meeting with Lyla. If she'd told Darby that she still loved him, then maybe there was a chance for them.

Dr. Ritzius listened for a while and finally conveyed his concern, "I would advise against this—it isn't a well thought out plan. You are allowing yourself to slide down a slippery slope and not weighing the cost. There are many pitfalls that may hinder your journey to the more stable mental health that you desire for yourself. Aksel, you are putting all your hopes for happiness in one basket created by Darby."

Aksel had hoped for a better response from the doctor and rubbed the nape of his neck. "But I love her, Dr. Ritzius! I just can't give up yet." He slumped against the leather chair.

"I understand, Aksel. Let's continue your regression and maybe you will find some answers."

Dr. Ritzius had Aksel sit back comfortably on the recliner. The doctor again led him to a twilight state of mind and directed him to search for heartbreak from his past life.

"What do you see, Aksel?"

Aksel's breathing became rapid and sweat formed on his forehead as he pressed his lips together tightly. He shook his head back and forth. "No! I don't want to go here."

"Who are you?"

"I'm Alex again." His body trembled.

"Alex, what's happening?" Dr. Ritzius leaned forward. "Remember."

"Can't…breathe…" Aksel gasped for air.

Dr. Ritzius spoke in a calm tone. "Alex, you are not in danger. Have you been hurt?"

"No, no. *FiFi* has been hit and she is in trouble."

"Alex, let's go back a little before this event." Aksel's breathing slowed. "Tell me what's happening."

"Cap just told Del to put on some music. Harry James is now playing through our earphones. The music makes me think about Izzy. I'm wondering if she'll marry me when I'm done—I only have five missions left."

"You're flying, and your plane's name is *FiFi*?"

"Yes. The sky is so blue, and the clouds are big and white."

"What's your duty?"

"I'm the navigator." Aksel's breathing again hitched, and he grabbed the arms of the recliner.

"Alex, you are safe. Remember that you are still in the office. Now describe what's happening around you."

"*FiFi* just got hit by antiaircraft fire from the ground. Smoke is filling the plane, I hear all the alarms blaring and there's no oxygen in my mask. I hear on my headset that one of the engines is on fire. We are banking on a hard left out of formation. I hear Ray yelling at Chuck. I think he's using a fire extinguisher or something. Cap sounds like he's hurt. His breathing is…is very ragged. We're diving down now, leveling out I think at ten thousand feet because I can breathe now.

"Luis is screaming something…we've lost engine two. I hear the bell. It rings three times."

"What does that mean, Alex?"

"It's the signal to prepare to bail. Cap has leveled *FiFi*. There's not much time left. Then I hear the final long ring of the bell. Cap yells that he's holding *FiFi* level, so we can all bailout.

"Everyone else has jumped but me, and another explosion shakes the whole plane. I went to help Cap in the cockpit. The captain's body is horribly burnt and he's bleeding badly. I tell him we must go. *FiFi* trembles, and I can hear pieces of her outer skin tearing away. Tommy, the Cap, says he can't leave yet. There's a village beneath us. If he abandons the plane, it'll crash into the village below and kill lots of innocent people.

"I'm going to stay, to help crash-land the plane. But the smoke…it's choking us.

He's so badly burnt, I know that he might not survive, even if we do land. He begs me to go. I want to get back to Izzy, but I want to stay and help. He's my best friend." Aksel begins to sob as tears roll down his cheeks. "I … have to leave him now… or die with him. He makes me promise to tell his Rachel that he loves her and that he'll be back for her the next time around."

Tears stream down Aksel's face. "I jump out. My heart is breaking as I float to the ground, watching *FiFi* spiral into a field just past the little village. But I… I … see no other parachute." Aksel covered his mouth with his hand. "He didn't get out."

Aksel stopped crying and his breathing returned to normal. He was quiet for a long time as reliving that traumatic event explained so much.

"Aksel, do you recognize Tommy as anyone in your life now?"

"I do. Holy shit! I do. No wonder I feel so close to him."

"Who is he now? Aksel?"

"Dammit, Doc, the cap is back! He's Lyla's father, Grant."

⁘

Darby took a cab instead of the subway to meet Aksel, wondering if he'd show up. He hadn't seen him since the night in the restaurant. He walked into the bar and grill to see Aksel already sitting at a table.

"Aksel, glad you made it."

Aksel stood and shook Darby's hand, then they sat across from each other while ordering a round of drinks.

"So, tell me, Darby, exactly when did you start having these conversations with Lyla?" "Let's get right to it, huh?" Darby could tell that Aksel wasn't completely sold on the story he'd told him and knew this could still blowup in his face if he wasn't careful. "Not long after she moved in with Sarah. Sarah and I started dating, and she's been like a big sister to Lyla. Sarah said that Lyla moved in with her to get away from family pressure." Aksel nodded so Darby continued, "She wanted to find herself without the interference of her folks, and finally prove to her ex-boyfriend that she was worthy of another chance."

"She *truly* said that to you, or Sarah?" Aksel tapped the table.

"Well, I'm summarizing, but—"

The server momentarily interrupted Darby with their drinks.

"Thanks."

"*Merci,*" Aksel said.

"Anyway, about a month ago at The Nue, I found her crying in the alley out back where we all take breaks. We're close at the restaurant, like extended family, you know?"

Aksel's expression was guarded. "What did she say?"

"That she probably screwed up and lost any chance of getting back together with her true love. I can't remember word for word, but she said your name. Aksel is not a common name in New York. I first thought of Guns N' Roses, to be honest." He chuckled.

"Like I haven't heard that before." Aksel laughed too but it wasn't friendly.

Darby sensed Aksel's doubts. "Man, if Sarah loved me the way Lyla loves you, we'd already be hitched."

"Honestly, I always hoped that one day Lyla and I could find a way to work things out." Aksel centered his glass on the cocktail napkin.

That meant the man still cared, and Sarah's plan for revenge would cut deep. Darby leaned forward and searched the Frenchman's face. "So, what's keeping you and Lyla apart then?"

"It's complicated. Even more so after today."

"What happened today?"

Just like that, a wall went up. "Nothing I want to relive at this moment."

"Well, then, fuck it." Darby sat back in his chair as if there was nothing he could do. "If you're not sure…"

"It isn't that easy."

Darby drummed his thumb on the arm of his chair, casting his line to see if the man would bite. "Look, I know where she is," he maintained eye contact, "and how she's making extra money. I can take you there, and you two can talk, or we can call it a night. I'm doing this for Lyla."

<hr />

Aksel looked at Darby in disbelief. Sarah's boyfriend sounded like a salesman trying to sell him a rotten bill of goods. Dr. Ritzius's words echoed in his head that this was a bad idea.

Still, he put his beer down and pushed aside all the warning lights. This was about Lyla. "Okay, okay." Aksel slid his chair back and waved at the waitress for the bill. "But tell me where we're going." He handed the woman a twenty and told her to keep the change.

"It's less than a mile away. I gotta warn you, it may not be the kind of place you would expect to find her."

Aksel saw through Darby's concern, and his jaw tensed, knowing exactly what the man was referring to. "What type of place is it?"

"Now, don't judge her—New York is a tough place to survive."

What did Darby want to show him so badly? Was this a test of some kind? "Darby, are you going to tell me or not?"

Darby lowered his voice, his gaze sharp. "It's an invitation-only gentlemen's club. She's an exotic dancer."

Aksel lowered his head. He knew all of this, but it still hurt to hear it. "Darby, I do not believe that is the right place to attempt to rebuild our relationship."

"It's perfect! Think about it—you surprise her, prove to her you still love her regardless of what she's doing, then you can whisk her away from that lifestyle."

Aksel sat quietly—he hated to admit that Darby's idea appealed to him. He wanted to save Lyla.

"Dude, you'll be her knight in shining armor."

His heart beat faster. "I suppose it is worth a shot."

"It really is. And you'd better include me as a groomsman at the wedding—I'd look amazing in a baby-blue tux."

They took the short cab ride to the gentleman's club in silence. Aksel's intuition was telling him to leave but he ignored the bad vibes. He felt a knot in his stomach and his chest became tight to the point where he almost couldn't breathe. If Lyla was still in love with him, there was a slim hope for them to be together—he'd take it. Still, he steeled himself for what lay ahead.

Darby and Aksel walked to the building, heading toward Paulie and Peetie, the two bouncers Aksel had encountered the first time he'd visited the club. Aksel held back a moment, hoping they wouldn't recognize him. Darby took the lead and shook hands with them both.

"This is my buddy, Aksel. He's with me," Darby said.

Peetie looked Aksel up and down. Before he could say anything, Aksel pulled out two fifty-dollar bills and slipped them each one as he shook their hands. "Hello, gentlemen. Here's a little something for you."

"Why thank you, sir. Enjoy your evening," Peetie held the door open for them, which let loose the boom of music from within.

They walked down the hallway filled with music, when Darby stopped midway to scold him for tipping the doormen. "I told them you were with me. You didn't have to do that."

"I really did." Aksel relaxed a little since his cover hadn't been blown. He didn't want Darby to know that he had been to the club before.

"Must be nice to have that kind of cash to throw around."

They rounded the corner and approached the same white-haired man dressed in a black suit standing behind a speaker's lectern in front of a curtain. *Here we go again.* Aksel stressed over his cover being blown. Darby reached out his hand, "Georgie, my man. This is my buddy Aksel, he's my guest tonight, so don't bother checking for his name."

Aksel shook his hand and slipped him four hundred dollars while Darby passed through the black velvet curtain ahead of him.

Georgie tipped his hat and pocketed the cash. "Welcome, sir."

When the curtain opened, the waft of cigarette smoke, cigars, and cheap perfume hit Aksel. He took a deep breath and wiped his sweaty palms on his pants. *Okay, Aksel, here goes nothing…*

Chapter 25

The walls vibrated with loud music, there were men holding up cash to get the attention of dancers, and servers ran around delivering drinks. It was a packed house at the gentlemen's club. Sarah was seated with a drunken client at the bar when she saw Darby and Aksel arrive—their timing perfect since Lyla was in the back getting ready to perform her set. Sarah quickly blew off her client with a lie. "Sorry, my manager's signaling for me, I gotta go, or we need to move to the back area." He released her since he wasn't interested in paying for extra time.

The audience was going crazy for the blonde dancer when she removed her panties and strutted around the stage, allowing patrons to put money in her garter belt as she squatted in front of them with her legs spread. The music was at an eardrum-shattering level when Sarah approached Darby and Aksel, seated at a table near the back of the room. The men had just ordered their drinks. Sarah sat on Darby's lap. "Hey, baby. Who's your cute friend?"

"Sarah," Darby practically had to scream. "This is Aksel. Aksel, this is Sarah."

Sarah smiled as they shook hands, pretending to be caught up with the dancer on stage. She suddenly whipped her attention back to the handsome Frenchman. "Aksel?!" She gasped and covered her mouth with her hand. As if on cue the music dropped. The blonde's act had finished, and she was picking up the cash on the stage floor along with her clothing. "Are you the same *Aksel* who stole my Lyla's heart?"

"I guess I am." He lifted a single shoulder and let it fall.

"Why did you bring him *here?*" She looked at Darby with a shocked expression, but winked when Aksel glanced down at the table.

Darby continued the charade. "You know she wants him back, Rah, even if she won't admit it. I thought maybe this would be a good place to start."

"*Jesus Christ, Darby.* Do you want to cause a scene?" She turned to Aksel. "Quick, honey, order me a drink or else I have to move on. House rules."

Aksel flagged a server and ordered three drinks.

"Fabian, make it quick, baby," Sarah slipped her a twenty and blew the waitress an air kiss.

When their drinks arrived, Sarah tugged at Aksel's arm. "We need to talk. Grab your drink. I'll be right back, Darby."

She led Aksel slowly between tables toward the black holes as the announcer introduced ZeZe's performance. The lights dimmed and the music got loud. Sarah smiled to herself while purposely slowing as they neared the dancer's entrance, her hand on Aksel's arm. Lyla took the stage just as Sarah and Aksel started walking again, to the back. The girls made eye contact and Sarah double-winked at Lyla, their signal telling each other they'd just scored a high roller. Lyla winked back but then noticed who she had with her.

Sweet!

Sarah sat Aksel down on the bench in one of the black holes "The managers can see us in here. I have to be dancing whenever they walk by." She found him attractive and wanted him to want her; plus she had a score to settle with Lyla. Sarah stood in front of him and began to dance, moving her crotch close to his face, swaying to the music. She removed her top but he stopped her.

"What did you want to tell me?"

"What's wrong, Aksel? I'm just doing my job. You can talk and watch me dance at the same time, right?"

"Yes, yes, but keep your bra and panties on, please."

"Darcy shouldn't have brought you to the club, Aksel. Lyla would be crushed if she were to find you here, seeing her this way."

"I have to do this, Sarah. I love her." She sat on his lap, hoping to feel him becoming aroused, but there was nothing happening beneath her ass. "I want to tell her that."

Frustrated, Sarah exhaled. "Fine. But take her back here. It'll avoid a scene. And make sure one of the floor managers see you paying her. House rules."

"Speaking of house rules, take this." Aksel handed her two hundred dollars.

"I don't want to take it, but…thank you. You know, you're more beautiful than she described."

Aksel's smile had a shy quality. "Wish me luck."

Sarah continued to straddle his lap, wishing she'd found someone like him. "She's not the sweet little girl from the Midwest anymore." She switched tactics, grinding down on his lap. Maybe she could hurt Lyla in a different way. "Aksel, she's no longer simple, shall we say. But then, you seem very worldly; someone who can appreciate all the finer things that are on the menu of life besides love." Was he becoming slightly aroused?

He realized what she was doing and looked into her face—not interested. "Sarah, what is going on here?"

"I care enough to tell you that she and I are lovers, along with other people." He didn't respond to that either. Frustrated by his self-control, she stood in front of him. "You need to grow up and stop trying to destroy her with your silly romantic memories that no longer mean anything to her. She's moved on." Sarah lifted the bills. "Thanks for the cash. If you hurry, you might be able to catch the rest of her act." She left him in the dark.

⚜

Stunned, Lyla found it nearly impossible to get her mind into her performance. *Sarah was taking him to the black hole. What's he doing here?* She didn't think she could continue—it was like being punched in the chest. But then she heard the crowd chanting her name, "ZeZe, ZeZe!" and in typical Lyla fashion, she shook off her thoughts about him and channeled her anger into her act.

When Lyla finished her set the crowd made a ruckus at the conclusion. But she was seeing red and didn't pay any attention to the many requests for a lap dance—she ignored all the men calling for her attention, waving bills at her. She looked around for Aksel and Sarah. No sign of them. *I never wanted him to see him again.* Lyla turned on her heels to head toward the black holes and to her dismay, she collided right into him.

"Pardon me, Miss."

Doesn't he recognize me? Maybe with the wig and all the makeup and colored contacts? "May I spend some time with you?" he asked.

She spoke lightly, masking her voice somewhat. "You want a turn?"

"*Oui*, I would like some time with you," he replied in his sultry French accent. "Private?" He motioned to the floor manager toward the black holes.

Seeing the floor manager watching, she replied, "Of course. Follow me." Lyla grabbed his hand and led him to the back.

Even though she was furious with him for so many things, curiosity got the best of her, and she couldn't stop her feelings of excitement just being in his space. *My sweetest, deepest carnal desire is right here. With no one knowing the better, not even him, I could touch him the way I've wanted to since the day I last saw him.*

Going into an empty black hole, she motioned for him to sit on the soft bench and she straddled him. "What type of dance would you like, sugar?" she asked in a childish voice and gently placed her arms on his shoulders.

"Cut the charades, Lyla. What is going on here?"

She chuckled nervously. "Lyla? Was that the name of the girl you were just in back with, big boy?"

"What's happened to you? Why are you doing this?"

She ignored his question and only focused on his beautiful face, eyes blazing with—what? Anger? Frustration? Lust? She didn't know how to react exactly. For the first time, she couldn't move. *FUCK, FUCK, FUCK! He knows it's me!*

She whispered into his ear, "Sorry to disappoint, sir, but you must have me mistaken for someone else, possibly someone you knew a long time ago. If you want a dance, pay up. Otherwise, I have to go back to work."

He held her tighter.

She couldn't help but slowly grind on his growing erection. *As pissed as I am, I still want him. And obviously he still wants me, if I'm feeling this right.*

"Lyla, I have memorized your face, your lips, your walk, your body. I would recognize you if you were dressed in a clown's costume." She twirled her finger through a lock of hair from her wig. "Which isn't too dissimilar to this outfit…" he said.

He stood up and pulled her into his hard, perfect body and softly traced her face with his fingers.

Volts of passion eradicated any traces of anger she had. Her heart pounded so hard, she could feel it in her ears. She leaned into him for a kiss, but he released her.

"Here." He handed her five hundred dollars. "For your time. Figure yourself out, Lyla. I will be waiting for you for... well, forever."

Aksel walked away, leaving Lyla in an emotional shambles. She ran to the dressing room wanting to leave the club—intent on escape.

Sarah saw her coming and prepared to defend herself, but Lyla walked by her without saying a word or even acknowledging her presence.

"You okay, sis?" Sarah called after her.

Lyla kept walking and didn't look back or respond to her. *Oh, yeah, I got her good.*

Chapter 26

Thanksgiving Day, Lyla woke with a pounding head as she lay in bed. *I have so much to do. I need to stop by Andrew's and pick up the pie…face my father and Ginger for the first time in months. At least Jason will be there. And with a little help from my friend in a vial, I won't eat too much so I can make it to the brothel tonight without passing out.*

Suddenly her mind filtered through the unsettling thoughts from the evening before. Lyla hadn't talked to Sarah about Aksel being with her in the hole since she didn't want to appear weak. *But what the fuck was Aksel doing there last night? How did he find out about the club?*

Lyla couldn't sit still any longer and decided to trade the comfort of her bed for Sarah's bedroom. Lyla quietly opened Sarah's door and tiptoed to her bedroom night stand. She grabbed the blue box of drugs and Sarah rolled onto her back.

"Mmm, good morning, sunshine. Feeling any better?" Sarah cooed.

Lyla sat on the edge of the bed and removed Sarah's eye mask, brushed her messy bed-head hair gently away from her face, and kissed her cheek. "Not really. Maybe I'll feel better after a bump or ten." Sarah was no longer a friend and perhaps had never been one—but they could be cautious allies in this crazy world.

"You know where the goodie box is."

Lyla was already holding the large blue box. It held all manner of drugs inside: cocaine, ecstasy, weed. She quickly laid out two lines and inhaled them. Not feeling anything, she opened one of the capsules containing ecstasy powder and instead of mixing it with a drink, she emptied the contents into her mouth, grimacing at the taste.

"What the hell are you thinking? That's a lot all at once," Sarah admonished.

As if she cares.

"I'm gonna need as much help as possible to get through the day. Especially after last night."

Sarah just sighed.

"Speaking of... do you know that one of your clients last night was Aksel?"

"What are you talking about? Which one was he? How *could* I have known?"

She's so full of crap. "The hottest guy in the entire club—with the French accent."

"Lyla, you know I've never seen him before."

"I know, I know. But…it's gonna be hard for me to erase the thought of you two having sex." She flopped back on Sarah's bed. "It really hurts me. But I guess he's just a typical guy, like you said in the past." She opened the conversation to try and get some version of the truth.

Sarah traced her arm. "And Ly, if you ask him what happened, he would lie to you."

Lyla wasn't sure who or what to believe anymore—everything was clouded. "Maybe I should just quit the club."

"Think that one through carefully. I'm not sure how kindly Slim would take to you leaving." Sarah pulled Lyla's naked body closer. "How about a little morning play?"

Sarah's touch was repulsive to her and Lyla jumped out of bed. "Rain check?" She grabbed a vial of coke. "I have to pretend to be happy," then she returned to the box and palmed an additional two capsules. "Just in case."

⤖⟞⟝⤚

Lyla was holding the pumpkin pie in her hands when Andreas opened the door for her at Grant and Ginger's apartment building. "Happy Thanksgiving, Miss Lyla. Nice to see you."

"You too, Andreas." She almost sprinted through the lobby to the elevators. It was one p.m.——she was an hour late already because of the Macy's Day Parade.

Before knocking on the door, she took out her makeup mirror to check her nose and then breathed deeply. She realized she was wearing a shirt that said too much: "I'm not a naughty fairy, the others are just too good," was on the front. "I do what pleases me at the time, while they only do as they should," was on the backside.

She knocked. Thank God, she thought, when Jason opened the door.

"JJ! God, I've missed your face!" She hugged him with one arm until Ginger entered the foyer from the kitchen and took the pie box out of her hands.

"I've missed you too, sissy!" They hugged tightly.

"Look at you!" She stood back from him and slapped her thighs. "You look like you've grown a foot since summer." She wrapped her arms around him and peered over his shoulder at her dad and Ginger. She was relieved that they were smiling at them. "Did you?"

"Something like that," Jason replied with a bashful grin.

She turned to Ginger and her dad. Their expressions welcomed her without recrimination and she hugged them warmly. "Sorry I'm late, the parade had everything backed up."

After pleasantries were exchanged, they sat down to eat. Conversation was easy, surprising her at how much she'd actually missed being with them.

"So, we have some exciting news to share with both of you," Ginger said.

"You're pregnant?" Lyla said excitedly and laughed with Jason.

"Not gonna happen. I already have too many children I love—you and you, monkeys. And you're both a handful," her dad snickered.

Lyla elbowed Ginger, who looked like she could be doing a photo shoot for the holidays. Elegant, confident, and yet warm. Lyla hoped to be like her one day.

"We're buying a cottage in England for family vacations. We leave on Monday to sign the papers," Ginger said.

"A family vacation home in England? That's awesome news!" Lyla said excitedly.

"I always wanted to visit England," Jason added.

"Maybe we can celebrate New Year's there together," Ginger said. "We can watch Big Ben strike midnight!"

"Although we'll have to ask your mother first, Jason," Grant quickly noted.

The family tradition was to stuff themselves and watch football on Thanksgiving, so it was easy for Lyla to sneak off to use her stash of drugs as often as she wanted. The Lions beat the Browns by three. Ginger was glued to the action on the screen with the next game, and all were thrilled to witness the Cowboys getting slaughtered by the Eagles. Lyla enjoyed her family—she'd forgotten how attached they'd been, the love genuine. Between games, Lyla and Jason went to Central Park to toss the football around, like they used to when they were younger. It was a clear day around the mid-thirties mark but warm enough so long as they stayed in the sun.

"Since Dad and Gin have you tomorrow," Lyla said throwing the ball, "Saturday is *my* day for us to spend together, okay?"

"Hell, yeah." Jason caught it, arm poised to toss it back. "Maybe I can stay at your place Saturday."

She felt disappointed that he couldn't. "I wish. But I have a photo shoot. Tonight is the practice run." Lyla looked at her watch. "Actually, I should get going soon."

"Sure, no problem." Jason's easy smile disappeared.

"Hey, don't be upset. We'll have the whole day Saturday." She tucked her hand through the crook of his arm and they walked back to the apartment building.

"But I'm leaving on Sunday, so let's spend as much time together as possible."

She pulled his hoodie over his face and ruffled his head. "You're silly—here's an early Christmas gift." She handed him five one hundred-dollar bills, the money from Aksel the night before, and a joint.

"Wow. Thanks, sis."

"Anything for my little bro, but be careful with the joint. And, don't tell Dad and Gin I gave you the cash, okay?"

Jason shook his head. "Why are you hiding your modeling success from Mom, Dad, and Ginger?"

"It's complicated. Just trust me. I'm better off not telling them yet."

Lyla left around eight p.m. to start the second half of her day. Her vial was empty, but she refilled it as soon as she got back to her apartment. She'd just put on a blue sequined cocktail dress when Sarah walked into her room. She was still in her waitress uniform from her double shift at The Nue.

"I need a pair of shoes for tonight, Ly. Can I borrow a pair?"

Lyla motioned toward her closet. "Help yourself."

As Lyla continued to do her makeup, she watched Sarah tear through her collection of shoes. She silently gave thanks that she'd made it to the bank so her real amount of cash wouldn't be visible. She already had one safe deposit box almost completely full. There was close to fifty grand in that one, and after a few more good nights at the brothel, she wouldn't be able to fit another bill inside. Lyla never thought about what to do with the money but felt she would figure it out down the road.

"How soon can I interview with the madam?" Sarah asked, breaking Lyla's train of thought.

Lyla sighed. *So this is really why she came in here...*"Hopefully within the next week or two. Just trust me."

"Oh, I do baby. I do." Sarah winked at her and left her room without a pair of shoes.

"Fucking snooping!" She cursed under her breath.

⋆→═◉◉═←⋆

On Saturday, Lyla met Jason for lunch at Andrew's. After filling their stomachs, they started wandering from shop to shop. Hours later, they were each holding arms' full of shopping bags of designer clothes and shoes, and whatever else Jason looked at for more than a second.

"Hey, let's drop these at The Nue and keep going. I only have a few hours left with you."

"Sissy, how can you afford to spoil me like this?"

"I told you, I'm doing just fine here in New York. Plus, I got a bonus last night for being early to the practice run for tonight's shoot. Are you complaining about me spoiling you? *Really?*" she teased.

"If you want to spoil me, then let's get a drink—a *real* drink."

Lyla smirked. "I'll see what I can do. Hey, by the way, how about I just send you all your new things and put Uncle Andrew's restaurant as the sender? That way you won't have to explain to Mom or Dad where all this cool shit came from."

"Deal. IF you get me a drink while we're at The Nue."

"You know how to work it, don't you?"

"I learned from the best!" Jason snickered.

"So from me, or Mom?"

"My perfect big sister, who's secretly making it in New York. You've surpassed Mom's expectations." Suddenly she felt dirty about her secret life, and her actual job compared to what he thought she did for a living. It reminded her of her mom, who claimed to be a glamour model all the time when she wasn't.

She pasted on a bright smile. "Good enough. Now let's get you that drink!"

They entered through the back of The Nue and put all the bags in Andrew's office. Lyla scribbled a note and left it on his desk and then they headed to the bar. She was glad that Sarah and Darby had already left for the day.

She maneuvered behind the bar. Jason sat on one of the barstools. Lyla made two Rah Rah Cocktails. *If I'm going to pollute my brother, why not treat him to the best?* She pushed one of the drinks in front of Jason and then sat next to him.

She held her glass to his. "To the greatest guy I know."

They clinked glasses. She took a long gulp of her drink.

"To my bad ass, sis," Jason said, then sipped his drink. "Wow, this is good." He coughed, and his eyes got watery.

"Only the best for my bro."

Emptying the bottle between both glasses, she instructed, "Now finish up—we have so much more to do!"

Later in the evening, as they walked up Fifth Avenue, laden with a few more shopping bags, Jason said, "Is it me, or is the whole world moving way too slowly right now?"

She chuckled. "I think it's you."

"I was just thinking," he said. He smiled and looked up, lost in thought. Lyla waited for several seconds.

"You were thinking what?" she prompted, which brought him back.

"What?"

"You said that you were thinking."

He pointed at her. "I think therefore I am." Then he started laughing.

"Okay, okay. Settle down."

"I just feel so amazing! Let's hang out longer. I could watch you work."

Lyla lost her breath at the reality of her world compared to his and what he thought she was. "I would, but it's a closed set." Her heart broke—she realized what she had become. "What if I ride with you to the airport tomorrow? We can do breakfast and a curbside farewell."

"Good enough, I guess." He stopped walking and yelled, "I love New York!" Jason put his hands on her shoulders and rested his forehead against hers.

Tears burned her eyes.

"I feel so alive! It must be because we are together— you're my first best friend. I love you so much," he continued. "I miss you. Just being with you makes me happy. I should move here and live with you." He wrapped his arms around her.

"I love you more than you know, but let's talk about it *after* you graduate high school. I'll be more established by then."

But his attention was already onto something else, and she realized he wasn't listening anymore because he was rolling on ecstasy. *You've got some fucked up sister.*

"Oh, lil brother," she said lowly and mostly to herself, "I may have overdone it with your drink…"

Chapter 27

Grant and Ginger prepared Sunday brunch for everyone at the apartment before Jason's late afternoon flight to Chicago. After the pleasant meal, Jason, Lyla, and Grant left for the airport while Ginger stayed behind to pack for their trip to England.

Grant listened to his kids banter about Thanksgiving holidays in the past, and before he realized it, they'd arrived at La Guardia. He got out behind the kids while Evan unloaded Jason's bags.

"Let me walk you to the gate, Jason," he said.

"Dad," Jason protested, "I would prefer if we said our goodbyes here. I'm not a child anymore. Do you mind if I walk to the gate alone?"

Grant looked at him for a moment, and then grinned in defeat. "You guys are growing up on me, aren't you?" Grant hugged Jason, handing him some cash. "A little something for you to have fun with. Call me when you get home, so I know you're safe. I love you, son."

"Thanks for everything, Dad. I love you too." They hugged again.

"Work on your mother about New Year's in England."

"Will do," Jason promised.

Grant climbed back into the limo, giving his kids their own space to say their good-byes, though he couldn't help but sneak a few glances.

Lyla stood looking at Jason with a huge grin and tears in her eyes.

"Don't cry, sissy." Jason hugged her.

"I can't help it. You are one of the brightest parts of my life, and now you're leaving."

"Yesterday," he whispered, "was the best part of my visit, not just because you spoiled me rotten either. It was because I spent the day with you alone. I love you so much, sis."

"I love you so much too. But do me a favor? Try not to grow another foot by the time I see you next, will ya?"

Lyla jumped back in the limo, her eyes slightly puffy and red.

"Honey, we'll see him soon." Grant wished he could take her sadness away. "Hopefully for New Year's in England."

Lyla didn't respond. She opened her compact mirror and dabbed cover-up around her eyes as Manhattan came into view.

"You would come with us to England for New Year's, right?"

"I suppose, if JJ will be there. It wouldn't feel like family without him." Grant heard the wobble in her voice.

"I know, sweetheart." Grant tried to comfort her by stretching out his hand in an attempt to bridge the distance between them, knowing it was emotional for her to say good-bye to Jason. She turned her attention out the window and didn't see his offer.

He didn't want to botch his first time alone with her since she'd moved out as they rode back to the apartment. "It was a nice weekend as a family." His words were meant to break the silence. "Ginger and I are very proud of you. You're obviously doing well on your own."

"That sounds like you doubted that I could do it." The animosity in her voice matched the hostile glare on her face.

Grant tried to ignore the tightness forming in his shoulders. "Uncle Andrew told me how great you're doing at The Nue."

"Really. I suppose that means you are keeping tabs on me at Barbizon also?"

"No. I have not checked on you at Barbizon, Lyla. For Christ's sake." The hair on his nape rose to attention.

"For the sake of privacy, maybe I should stop working at *Uncle* Andrew's."

"Why would you do that?" The irritation level in his voice climbed rapidly.

"Really? Maybe to stop the weekly status reports to you and Ginger."

"That's ridiculous!" His body tensed. "I'm your father, Lyla. And I would like to know how my eighteen-year-old daughter is surviving in New York City. I'm only concerned about you."

"*Father*, that's a funny word for you to use."

He put his hand over his heart, as if to stop a mortal blow. Had she meant to hurt him? He sighed. "Yeah. I guess it's time to discuss that. Why don't you come up to the apartment with me?"

They neared the building but their conversation was far from over. Would she come up, or avoid him?

"You really want to discuss this?" Her reply was a snarl filled with scorn.

"Lyla—"

"Stop!" She interrupted him, lips back from her teeth. Her clenched fists were shaking with her anger. What had he done to deserve this?

"I know the truth. You talk about family. You never thought it was important to tell me that Jason is only my *half-brother?* Funny, how he is the only one I really trust. My mother is horrible, and my real father is dead. And he didn't even want anything to do with me." She looked at Grant, her eyes filled with indignation. "And then there's *you.*"

He couldn't form a word.

"That's right. I've known the truth for the last six years of my life. Mom called me that first Christmas we spent in France to wish me and Jason a merry one—with some fucking twisted tale over the fucking phone about my father and it isn't you, *Grant.* Since then she has never ceased to remind me. When I left for New York, her parting gift was the phone number of the asshole whose sperm load she took to make me."

"Lyla," he finally sputtered. "I can't imagine how it must have felt to live with that all this time." Damn Margo.

Evan stopped in front of the building. He got out and took his time walking to the car door.

"Listen, Lyla, you need to know the truth. Your mother—"

"We're here," she said. "Bye, *Grant.*"

She stepped out of the limo on the opposite side and slammed the door, leaving before he had a chance to say anything, or stop her.

Evan opened the door for Grant, but Grant remained inside, shaking his head.

"I cannot begin to apologize for her behavior, Evan." His chest ached.

"Teenagers are complicated, Mr. Grant."

"That's an understatement." He pinched the bridge of his nose. "You know what? I don't feel like going home right now."

"Wherever you want to go, Mr. Grant."

Evan closed the door and got back in, leaving Grant alone in the back as he waited for his instructions. "Evan, let's go to my office for a little while, and understand I need to put up the privacy window."

"Yes, Mr. Grant."

After the window was up, he used the car phone and dialed the apartment. He was relieved when Ginger didn't answer. "Hey babe, just had one of those fucking fabulous moments with Lyla. I'll be home in a bit. Need some time to clear my head. I love you."

My God, how did this happen to her? I remember holding her in my arms for the first time and swearing to myself I would always protect her. And where did I go? Her knight in shining armor, the loving and caring dad, went off on his own journey to find his own happiness. She blindly attacked me and I deserved every word she said.

He hopped out of the limo in front of the office before Evan could assist him. "Evan, go home and enjoy the rest of the night with your family. I'll see you tomorrow."

"Yes sir, Mr. Grant."

He entered his office and sat in his desk chair, looking around the room that held different awards and picture of events in his life. He picked up the framed picture of Lyla and Jason from that first Christmas they'd had in France. He stared into Lyla's twelve-year-old face as tears flooded his eyes. "Sweetheart, Daddy has woken up and I won't let go of you without a fight."

⋅→═◎═←⋅

As soon as Lyla exited the limo, she hailed a cab and quietly fumed during the ride to her apartment. She tore through every inch of her purse looking for any pick-me-uppers that she previously had overlooked. She found a nearly empty capsule of X and sucked the remains of the powder into her mouth. She paid the cabbie, then stood still in the cool night air. Lyla looked up toward the second floor apartment window before going in, and it felt like her blood was starting to boil. *Everybody has used me, lied to me, fucked with my head, or taken advantage of me. I hate them all!*

Lyla burst through the door of her apartment, throwing her bag in one direction and her keys in another. She ignored Sarah, who was sitting on the couch watching television.

She went straight to Sarah's bedroom and riffled through the drawers looking for the blue box. Not finding it, she stormed back into the living room and screamed, "Where's the fucking blue box, Sarah? I paid for most of the shit you keep in it! WHERE THE FUCK IS IT, SARAH?" she shrilled.

Sarah picked it up off the coffee table and held it toward her without a word, her eyes wide and wary.

"Thanks!" Lyla grabbed it and sat on the floor, pouring out all of its contents.

Sarah watched her furious movements from the couch. "Uh, I already have some coke ready to go on the dish, if you want, baby."

Lyla lifted the dish off the table. "Don't BABY me! And yes, give me that!" She kneeled in front of the coffee table and snorted whatever was on the shiny dish. When she finished, she stomped into the kitchen where she popped open a bottle of champagne from the refrigerator, laughing hysterically at the overspill of bubbles. She took the Tiffany & Co. champagne flute along with the bottle and plopped back on the floor. Sarah's gaze never left Lyla as Lyla grabbed two capsules of X and, with trembling hands, opened the first one and emptied it into her mouth. Then she dumped half of the second one into her champagne and drank the entire glass.

Lyla stretched out on the area rug on the hardwood floors and barked, "Turn that fucking TV show off and put on some music for fuck's sake!"

Sarah turned off the television and started flipping through the CDs in the disc player. "What do you want to listen to?"

"Anything that will calm me down! OBVIOUSLY!"

Sarah put on a Yanni CD, called *Chameleon Days*. Lyla stripped down to her bra and panties and inhaled deeply. Exhaled. Lyla felt Sarah next to her on the floor, playing with her hair--Lyla moved away and slapped Sarah's hand.

"Leave. Me. Alone!" Lyla snapped.

"What can I do for you?" Sarah asked sweetly.

Lyla's eyes immediately shot open. "Don't you mean what can *I* do for *you*?" She threw the champagne flute against the wall, shattering it into a million pieces. "Need a new set of Tiffany flutes now? How many? A dozen? I know how much you love your blue boxes!"

Sarah jumped away from her. "What the fuck is wrong with you, Lyla?"

"Everybody wants something from me! It's always take, take, take. Is love even real?" Lyla was screaming and started throwing everything she could grab within her reach. "And all of you are liars! Everyone is a liar! I hate liars!"

Lyla lunged at Sarah with her hands out, ready to choke her, but Sarah crouched in the corner of the living room. "Please, please, stop! You're scaring me! What happened? What did I do?"

Her laugh sounded mean and wicked to her own ears. "Well, *clearly* you *have* done something to hurt me also! But just you wait! You'll get yours! All things, good or bad, come back around! It's called Karma!"

Every ounce of pain that Lyla had ignored for so long, each feeling that she had dulled with alcohol and drugs for months, crashed down on her. Lyla finally crumpled to the floor hysterically crying.

"Just breathe." Sarah went to get her a glass of water and returned. Lyla sipped the water, then crawled onto the couch and wrapped up in a blanket.

After a few minutes, she glanced at Sarah, who looked at her with pity. "I'm sorry for how I acted. I-I just want to be loved for who I really am. But I don't even know who that is." Hot tears spilled down her cheeks. *Who am I?*

Chapter 28

Monday morning before leaving for England, Ginger and Grant spent time at the office with their staff arranging some last-minute details. They had already packed their luggage into the limo, allotting them extra time at the office before leaving on their holiday.

The plane reached its cruising altitude while they were holding each other's hands. The stewardess brought them two flutes of champagne. Ginger noticed how distant and flat Grant seemed to be but contributed it to the end of their family weekend with the kids. Hoping to lift his spirits she raised his hand to her lips and kissed it. "Love," she said, making eye contact. "The kids really enjoyed the weekend. I hope New Year's works out with them in England. What a treat that would be for us all."

He attempted to form a smile and lifted her hand to his lips. They made a toast to the future before he climbed back into his shell—she knew he was thinking of Lyla while he stared out the window. Finally, after five minutes, Ginger broke the silence. "What's up with you, my love? I feel only your body is with me. What flight is your mind on?"

"What do you mean?"

"You should be beyond excited—I thought you were upset about the kids and concerned that everything at work is in order." She paused, taking a sip of bubbly. "But that's not it. So, what's going on? Mind including me, since we will be together for the next seven hours?"

Grant turned his full attention to her. "Sorry. I've been thinking about what Lyla said to me last night on our way back from the airport."

"Like what? You didn't mention anything to me other than you had a moment." She felt her frustration start to simmer. "Are we in this together or not?" She slid to the far side of her seat, attempting to create a space between them.

"I didn't want to ruin our trip…" He reached for her hand, but she pulled it away.

"You can see how well that's working. What the hell happened between you two?"

The stewardess showed up and this time Ginger ordered a dirty martini and he ordered a double Jack. He held out his hand and she finally took it. "Rachel, my love, I'm sorry. I tried to bury it. On some level, I actually understand her anger. I just wanted to find a better time to tell you about what happened since you were so excited when I got back last night. In short, Lyla told me that her mother has told her for years that Howard is her biological father."

Ginger bit back a scream. "That *fucking bitch*!" she hissed. "I'm so sorry, Grant. Any idea when she started telling her?"

"Oh yeah, glad you're sitting with your seatbelt on. You ready for this? The first Christmas we spent with the Portier family and your parents in France... over the phone."

"No! How could she? Lyla was barely a teenager then. That poor baby! You told her that Howard wasn't her father, right? Please tell me you did." She grabbed his hand, spilling some of the martini over the edge of the glass. "Grant, please tell me you told her, sweetheart!" She stared into his face. "Oh, my God you didn't. She must be so confused and angry!"

His eyes welled. "I tried, Gin, but she hopped out of the limo before I could explain." His voiced wobbled. The stewardess arrived with a towel to wipe up the spill. Tears spilled down his cheeks.

"We'll fix it, my sweet soul." She gently dabbed around his eyes with a tissue. "When we get back, you can show her the envelope, tell her the truth."

"The worst part is that she called me 'Grant.' She hates me now—I am no longer her father."

She pulled his face to hers and stared into his blue eyes. "Listen to me..." She waited until he focused on her gaze, adding fire to her voice. "I will make her listen, even if I have to strap her down to a chair!"

Grant sighed. "I wish it were that easy. Don't forget who she's living with. She's under Sarah's influence and probably hearing all kinds of lies about us."

She hadn't wanted to say anything but since they were coming clean Ginger said, "She's under the influence of something else as well. Did you notice how little she ate at dinner on Thanksgiving?"

He gave her a blank look. "Not really."

"I know what it's like to be a model. How do you think a lot of models keep their bodies looking so perfect? No such thing as too thin, right?"

"I never thought much about it."

"I began to notice how often she went to the bathroom." Ginger lifted a brow.

"Actually…now that you mention it, you're right." He sank back with realization. "Fuck."

"I guess we're going to war when we return," Ginger said, ready to fight for Lyla. "She's smart. I hope she figures out how much of a dead-end she's headed for. And if not, we'll make sure she does."

"You are my secret weapon." Grant leaned over and kissed her.

"Damn straight I am." She deliberately exhaled. "Now, please push those thoughts out of your head for a while. We've *earned* this trip to our special place. Just know that we'll tackle this when we return."

"You're right. Nothing should stand in the way of our reunion with the past." He pulled her over and kissed her. "I love you, Rach."

⤖⟞

Nine hours later they'd checked into the Double Tree Hilton in the West End of London at five a.m. They had selected this hotel because it was close to the train terminal at Kings Crossing and the fastest train to Royston, near the cottage. They planned to shop for necessities that they would need for the place—bed spreads, sheets, towels, tableware, the whole nine yards.

It was around six a.m. by the time they were settled in and decided to stretch out for a few hours before shopping.

Grant woke up to an empty bed and heard the shower running. He ordered some breakfast for them and opened the bathroom door. "Rachel, can I join you?"

"Of course, my sweet Tommy! But there's not room in here like at home for play, so I'll just have to take care of you later."

"I'll cash in after the shower and breakfast I ordered for us." He washed her back and ass, making his cock rock-hard.

She squirmed with a sultry laugh. "God, you fly-boys are all the same, aren't you?"

"Yes." He continued massaging her perfect ass, and finally his hands made their way up to her shoulders. "I feel like I need to walk after our long flight yesterday and the weather is perfect. Let's eat and hit it. There's some great stores I'd like to check out."

"Sounds good to me, my sweet Tommy."

⋆⇒◉⇐⋆

Ginger and Grant had found all the items on their list and made arrangements for all to be delivered to the cottage in Royston. They ended up on a street called Rathborne, where they each experienced an odd sense of familiarity in the eclectic neighborhood of row houses and small storefronts. It was late afternoon when they walked into a local pub called Newman Arms. Suddenly Ginger said, "I'm having a déjà vu! We've been here before, Tommy!"

"Really?" He looked around the narrow, dark-chestnut-paneled space, with the old wooden bar to his left. Mirrors everywhere and a stone fireplace surrounded by tables. "I don't recall it…"

"I do! We came here for drinks and dinner."

He squeezed her hand. "Well, what did we order, because I'm starving!"

She laughed at him while they were seated at a table along a wall of white colonial-style windows and ordered two pints of dark ale. They shared fish and chips and a cheese-tomato salad plate with a Manchester Tart for dessert.

Walking back to the Hilton, Grant stopped on a corner and turned to Ginger, pulled her into his arms, and lifted her off the ground. "Now it's my turn for the déjà vu, because I recall kissing a beautiful barmaid right here." He kissed her passionately with no regard for the passersby. They basked in the feeling of reconnection to their past life together.

Their bodies were still adjusting to the time change, and they were exhausted. They took a cab ride back to the hotel and had a snack in their room.

The next morning, Ginger and Grant hopped the train to Royston and the cottage. They had plenty of time to do the final walk-through before the closing. They decided to visit the pub where they'd first met in their past lives for a celebratory ale. The bar was dark and empty, but much of it was the same, which brought back memories from the past; they felt like they were starring in some sort of time travel movie.

Ginger pointed at the bar. "Tommy, you sat right there that first night!" she whispered excitedly.

"And I remember you standing behind the bar when I walked in. Here's where you first kissed me, Rachel, you sassy Brit," he smiled and kissed her, "claiming to be a 'proper English girl.'" Grant reached over and pinched her ass.

The bar top with the mirror behind it appeared to be the same, just a bit more worn—buffed from years of other people creating memories together. The tables, chairs, and booths were updated but still had a vintage look about them, and the same pictures hung on the dark paneled walls—in a way, time had almost stood still.

They sat at the bar and ordered two ales, one dark, one light.

The bartender delivered two mugs. Grant raised his. "Let's make a toast to—"

"To an eternity of love," Ginger said, staring into his eyes.

"Cheers!" They tapped their mugs together.

They reminisced about the experiences they'd shared, each corner of the bar reigniting another lost memory. Before long, it was time to go to the cottage for the inspection.

"Let's walk, Rach, just like we used to?"

"Sure we have enough time, Tommy?"

They strolled in the cool early December air as Ginger continued to reflect about when Grant had been the young soldier she'd loved named Tommy, when her name had been Rachel. It *was* surreal to realize they were together again in England where they met and fell in love in a past life.

They walked hand in hand down the cobblestone street toward the cottage. The narrow street hadn't changed much in the last forty-plus years. Grant laughed and recalled the night he'd returned to the pub to ask her for a date.

"I was pretty sure you were going to say no." Grant snickered.

"And you were so nervous. Yet we ended up making love that first night," Ginger said, almost blushing. "What a slut I was!"

"I don't think that at all—we were just two souls reuniting."

"Oh, Grant Robinson." She sweetly kissed his cold nose.

"You were mine from the moment we met then, and now. We are two souls finally together after being apart from each other in the past."

"So, our bodies celebrated along with our souls."

"Exactly."

"Fabulously, you could say."

Grant and Ginger stopped to kiss again as waves of emotions continued to wash over both of them from the present and the past.

As they ended their passionate kiss, they heard a woman's voice. "Um, excuse me, Mr. and Mrs. Robinson?"

They hadn't even realized they were standing in front of the cottage. A woman watched them from the gate.

"Mrs. Wahlbrink?" Grant said. "I'm sorry. We were—"

"Enjoying the moment. No need to apologize. Please, call me Lindsey. When you're ready, I'll be inside. Take your time." She smiled and disappeared into the cottage.

Grant opened the gate and silently stood in awe at the view. It was as if the curtain of time had been gently drawn back for them to return to the past. They slowly walked up the stone walkway to the front door of the white-washed thatch-roof bungalow. Flowerbeds still lined the path.

"I remember the flowers you planted were of every color and species, Rach," Grant whispered as they approached the green door.

"And you'll help me plant them again, Tommy," Ginger whispered back with a naughty grin.

"Shall we?" Grant gestured toward the opened door.

"Let's take another step into the past."

They walked inside, both trying to hide their overwhelming emotions as they entered.

"Is it what you hoped for?" the realtor asked nervously.

Ginger could hardly contain herself and let out a squeal of delight. Grant rolled his eyes and smiled at Mrs. Wahlbrink.

"I think she likes it," Grant said.

"Well, you seem to be already familiar with the property. Can't say I ever made a sale without showing the property first," Lindsey said in a questioning manner.

"Not to worry. You were highly recommended by our business associates in France," Ginger said.

"Splendid. Let me show you around." Mrs. Wahlbrink went toward the bedroom from the living room.

Their clasped hands tightened as the realtor walked them throughout the two-bedroom cottage. Neither of them paid much attention to what she was saying; they were both reliving the past in their mind's eye.

Grant even chuckled when the wood floor creaked under his step in the master bedroom.

Lindsey said, "It's all original. If you feel the need to update or do repairs, I can put you in contact with some contractors."

"No, no. It's perfect," they responded in unison.

Soaking in their surroundings, they found themselves back in the living room by the fireplace, which Grant had lit when his name was Tommy and her name was Rachel.

Standing in the bay window they lost their breath at the sight of a huge Rowan tree with all the garden beds surrounding the yard. "During spring and summertime, the beds are magnificent," Lindsey pointed out.

"I know. I mean, I can only imagine," Ginger said.

"And all the trees are beautiful. Some old and some new. I am particularly fond of the old Rowan, which I'm told was planted right around World War II."

Ginger smiled at Grant and stopped at the bay window, where she ran her fingers across the wooden bench. *I'm home.*

Chapter 29

Lyla decided to go to The Nue after the blowout she had with Grant to take control of her life. She knocked on the frame of Andrew's opened office door and he motioned her in as he finished up his phone call. He stuck his pen into the pen pocket on the sleeve of his white chef's jacket and stood. His white French chef's hat perched precariously next to the work schedules across his desk.

"Hey Ly! I thought you were off today." He smiled at her while looking down at his desk as if checking to see if he was right, and pushed back his dirty-blonde hair. She always felt short next to his six foot three inch frame.

"I am. But I wanted to talk to you for a few minutes. Is this a good time?" They both sat down.

"Of course, anytime to talk with you is a good time. I got your note and already had the stuff shipped to Jason in Chicago."

"Thank you so much for taking care of that. How much do I owe you for the shipping?" Lyla reached into her purse.

"Don't worry about it." He waved his hand at her, smiling. "He's my nephew."

"No, really. I want to pay for it. Especially because, well," she paused. "I'm here to give you my notice."

Andrew sighed, locking his hands behind his head as he leaned into his high-back leather chair. "Really? I thought you liked it here."

"I do, Uncle Andrew," she replied, realizing how much she liked calling him "uncle" rather than boss.

"I mean, I knew it wouldn't be forever, but has something better come along already? Did you sign a modeling contract?" His green eyes warmed, just like Ginger's.

"Something like that. Actually, I'm just getting overwhelmed with classes and all my side jobs. Most of the shoots I do end up being scheduled right after my shifts and I really need to be on my A game if I want to be successful."

"Lyla, that's great news! And understandable—I remember how long my days were when I attended culinary school and worked at the same time. I'm sure your father and Ginger must be thrilled with your success." Still leaning back, he placed his feet up on a corner of his desk. The aroma of herbs and spices from the kitchen began to fill her head as the restaurant's kitchen prepped food for the day's menu.

She wished she had some ecstasy to give herself a boost. "I haven't told them much about the jobs I've been getting. I wanted to wait and surprise them. Could you keep it a secret for now?"

Andrew returned to a sitting position. "I suppose when you hit it big, they'll forgive me for covering for you. Sure, not a problem. What's an uncle for?" He smiled.

"Anyways, I know the new-hires are ready to be on their own and they could use more hours." She hesitated and took a fortifying breath. "Is it okay with you if I quit without notice?"

He shrugged. "No problem. We'll make it somehow."

"Really? Are you sure?"

"Anything I can do to help my niece be successful in her career."

"Then one more favor?"

"What's that?" He leaned forward and folded his hands across the papers.

"I'd like to keep the reason I'm leaving from the staff."

"You mean Sarah?"

She nodded, quickly realizing that he probably didn't know about Darby and Sarah. "Yeah, and Darby, since he's her boyfriend of sorts."

"Oh, is he?" He looked surprised. "Well, your secret is safe with me. I'll miss seeing you, but I fully understand. And anytime you need a delicious meal, it's always on the house."

"Uncle Andrew, I can't thank you enough for the last few months. I really insist on paying for shipping my brother's things."

"Consider it a bonus." He stood up and hugged her.

She hugged him back. "Love you, Uncle Andrew."

"Love you too, Ly. See you around? Don't be a stranger." She started out the door of his office when he called, "Lyla! Wait."

Lyla turned at the doorway.

"Don't forget Christmas at my house. The kids can't wait to see you, okay?"

"Count on it." Exiting the restaurant, she felt free as the cool afternoon air hit her face. All her senses were filled with the sounds and sights of the holidays. *Merry Christmas to me.* She stretched out her arms, pretending she had wings to soar.

•➤═◉═◄•

Aksel was seated in Grant's office, paging through several papers and scribbling notes on them. He had been left in charge of G Squared during Ginger and Grant's absence. It was almost four, and he still wanted to review two work orders, get updates on a pending design project, and check on some reorders that had come in—they'd only been gone for two days! *How do they manage all this craziness? And it's off season!*

He was about to grab another stack of papers when the intercom interrupted him.

"Don't forget you have an appointment in a half hour, Mr. Portier." Sue's voice through the intercom interrupted his train of thought.

"Thank you, Sue."

He stood and looked over Grant's desk, covered with papers and sticky notes. The chaos would be there when he returned, no doubt. He sighed and walked out to the lobby. "Sue, thank you for all your help these past few days."

Sue smiled at him. "A pleasure as always, sir."

Aksel put his jacket on while waiting for an elevator, wondering what would be revealed to him in today's regression.

In less than an hour he was already drifting into the twilight state as Dr. Ritzius guided him down the staircase to open the door in his quest to unlock whatever his soul knew about his past life.

"Where are you, Aksel?"

"Walking down the cobblestone street to do what I promised Tommy I would. It took me a while to get back from France. Izzy wasn't at her flat, so now I'm almost to Rachel's cottage. I was hoping Izzy was with her, but out in the yard all I see is Rachel, surrounded by all the brilliant flowers in the garden. I hesitate at the gate before opening it. She's turned and sees me, and begins to run toward me. But she stops halfway to me, dropping her basket of freshly picked flowers. It's such a beautiful late summer day with puffy white clouds against the bluest sky. The soft warm breeze is blowing, and the smell of the flowers in her yard permeates the air, but none of this matters because of the news I'm delivering."

Aksel's eyelids fluttered. Dr. Ritzius waited in the silence, allowing Aksel to relive this moment from the past. "I push the gate open and start down the path. But she already knows that I'm alone, and her face turns red and now she has collapsed on the ground. I haven't even said anything yet."

Aksel paused again, reliving the pain.

"I'm kneeling with her and she's crying. 'Tell me he's just hurt, Alex. PLEASE! He'll be okay, right?' I wrap my arms around her—she is trembling. It's so hard to do what I promised, but I have to. 'I'm so sorry, Rach. He's gone.' She screamed, 'Noooooo! My sweet Tommy, no!'"

Aksel sobbed at the memory, which felt as real as if it was just happening all over again.

"It's like he's watching me. I can feel his spirit nearby. Then I told her, 'He saved the entire crew. I would have gone down with him, but he wouldn't let me. He was trying to keep *FiFi* up long enough to save the village below that would have been destroyed if the plane crashed into it. I tell her he gave me a message for her—that 'she's the love of my life and my brightest star in the darkest night.' He said to call you his sweet Rachel. And he's so sorry. He wanted you to know he loved you like he's never loved anyone in his life. He said to tell you that he'll be looking for you next time around. That he'll be back, just not now.'"

Aksel's voice quivered.

"I told her I went looking for Izzy at her flat to come help me tell you, and then I went to the pub, they told me to find you first. Where is she, Rach?'"

Aksel's voice broke, and he started to cry with a heartache that came from the depths of his soul. He was unable to speak. Dr. Ritzius waited and then asked, "Alex, where is Izzy?"

"Izzy is dead. She killed herself by not taking cover in a bombing raid. Rachel began crying again as she told me. 'Izzy lost all hope. The bloody war took its toll on her heart and soul. She thought you were gone. I tried to keep her hopeful that you would return, but I guess I failed miserably. I'm so sorry, Alex. She loved you so much. She didn't want to live without you.'"

Aksel sobbed deeply; streams of tears poured down his cheeks. "I've lost everything—my best friend and the woman I wanted to marry."

After a few minutes, when his breathing returned to normal and his crying had subsided, Dr. Ritzius asked, "Alex?"

Aksel opened his eyes. "No. I can't see anymore." He wiped his tears with a tissue, but the heartache remained. "Why does it still hurt so badly? We found the source of the pain, right?"

"I believe you have identified that Lyla is Izzy in a past life. But there's something you need to understand. Now that you've found the reason that keeps you bonded to her, *you* cannot make up for what happened in your past life. You feel you let her down then, and you let her down now by not being there when she needed you in this life."

"It wasn't by choice! *Either time!*" Aksel protested.

"I understand—but your souls remember each other. Therefore, it's out of your hands. It's up to *her* to forgive you for both times. Unfortunately for you, her soul hasn't recognized that it knows everything which is behind her distrust of you. You must forgive yourself in this life to set *yourself* free from the pain." Pausing, the doctor leaned forward. "Do you understand, Aksel?"

"Very clearly. But what if she forgives me in *this* life?"

"That might help, but it may not bring about the resolution you want. Now that you know, you only have two choices. One, you live with this information, knowing that you hurt her, and you leave her to live her life, no matter her choices. Or two, you try to help her realize that you are worthy of her trust. I can't tell you which path to take. Both are difficult. But I do believe that you two have been brought back together again for a reason. What reason that is, is for you to discover…"

⊶━━◉◖━━⊰

Aksel walked the thirty blocks back to his SoHo apartment from Midtown Manhattan in a daze after his session with Dr. Ritzius, trying to decide what to do about Lyla. The situation seemed hopeless. *I love her and it's hard for me to just stand by. Grant and Ginger are part of my life forever and if I don't act, I will share in their pain over the outcome of their daughter. He saved me in my past life and now I am just going to do nothing?* His brain was spinning with Dr. Ritzius's words echoing in his head. *You will have to accept that it is over.* Acceptance stung—and even so, he had to save his true love from the destructive course she was on.

Exhausted when he got back to his apartment, Aksel had no desire to eat so he went to bed hoping to sleep, but instead he tossed and turned, unable to drift off. He got up to have a drink, making himself a vodka on the rocks, then another, and yet another. With the clarity of thought that only alcohol can provide, he came to a decision: he was going to do whatever he could to save Lyla from herself. She would not, if he could help it, end her life like Izzy had.

Tomorrow night, I will corner her at the club, and attempt to make her understand! Then he passed out on the couch.

Chapter 30

Aksel, headed to the high-end gentleman's club, dressed in a pair of torn jeans, a gray long-sleeved fitted T-shirt, and black loafers—Lyla always preferred a more casual style, and tonight was about her. He added a navy sport coat to dress up his slightly disheveled appearance and to keep warm without a topcoat.

He took a taxi to the building and walked down the dark, chilly alley to the hidden entrance. The bouncers, Paulie and Peetie, sat on stools next to an outdoor heater.

"Hey, Frenchie!" Paulie walked toward him. "Good to see you again." He rubbed his hands together for warmth.

Peetie followed with, "Whacha got for us tonight?"

"A bonus for not blowing my cover last time, guys." He handed them each a hundred-dollar bill.

"Mercy bokoo." Peetie slipped it into his pocket.

"So, who's you comin' to see? She must be worth it, huh?" Paulie asked.

"A gentleman never tells," Aksel replied with a secretive smile.

"Well, enjoy your night, Mr. Frenchie." Paulie held open the door for him.

The percussion of the music hit him as Aksel entered the building and the thump grew louder as he walked down the hallway toward the lectern in front of the black curtain.

"Welcome back," Georgie said from behind his podium.

"I believe you have me on your list…" He palmed Georgie three hundred-dollar bills.

Georgie pocketed the cash and then looked over the clipboard. "Ah, yes. There you are, Mr. Smith. Enjoy your night."

"Enjoy?" Aksel winced. "It might be better to wish me luck."

"Luck'll cost ya extra." Georgie guffawed and slapped Aksel on the back, pushing him through the opened door behind the curtain.

Aksel entered the other world that Lyla lived in at night. After his eyes had adjusted to the dim lighting, he searched for her. He spotted Sarah almost immediately, but she hadn't seen him yet. Sarah was slowly making her rounds after her performance, he assumed, to connect with someone to bring to a private room. He didn't want her to warn Lyla that he was there. The club was not crowded like the last time, making it easy for him to find an empty table in a dark corner.

He ordered a vodka on the rocks. Darby was seated at the same table they'd shared the last time, midway back from the dance stage, almost in the middle of the room. Aksel kept an eye on him, but Darby never looked over; he was too busy watching the scantily clad girls dance while bullshitting with the cocktail waitresses and a few dancers.

Finally, Aksel thought to himself, as Lyla returned from the back area. She flirted with some patrons several tables away from him—but she hadn't seen him. He knew he had to act before she became cozy with one of the other men so he decided to approach the floor manager, requesting her for a private dance.

The floor manager took his money, then went over and whispered in her ear. Aksel watched as she excused herself, then followed the man to Aksel's table. When she saw who had asked for her, she rolled her eyes, then smiled as she reached out her hand and led him to the back to a private room. He could feel her animosity toward him by the way she gestured him to sit on the cushioned bench in the tiny room and braced himself.

⟶⟾◉⟿⟵

"What's your pleasure, Mr. Portier?" Lyla sat down on Aksel's lap only to find her anger cascading away. *Shit!* A flood of emotion hit her. *I still really want him. He's so fucking hot he could have been a model. He's mine!* She quickly refocused herself. "I'm surprised you're back after your last visit. After all, I thought you hated it here." There was no mistaking his body's natural reaction to her being on his lap as his cock began to harden.

"And who told you that?" His voice had a slightly defensive tone. "Darby, or Sarah?" His arousal turned her on.

She laughed cruelly. "And when did you talk to Sarah? While you were fucking her?"

"I did *not* fuck Sarah."

"Sarah said you would deny it." Lyla squirmed against him, and felt his cock stiffen through the thin fabric of her costume.

"Because it's not true!"

She wanted to believe him, but liked being in control. "And I suppose I should just believe you?"

"I wish you would, Lyla."

He wrapped his arms around her waist and looked into her eyes—he cared, she saw that, but it wasn't enough. She settled her hands at the nape of his neck, tortuously pressing her breasts against his chest.

"I can't do this, Ly." He looked over her shoulder rather than at her.

Lyla couldn't believe he was turning away from her. "Wait." Taking his beautiful face in both hands, she forcibly moved his head and made him see *her*. She twisted his hair around one of her fingers. *So bold! But I don't care! I've been secretly dying to do exactly this.* She felt his body responding to her every touch. *It seems like he wants me to touch him tenderly as we used to.* It reminded her of their sweet love from long ago.

Aksel's arms tightened around her waist. "You shouldn't be here."

"Right. You want to save me. And if I don't do what you want me to, you'll disappear like the last time you showed up."

Lyla watched his serious expression as he struggled with what to say. "So, are you a typical stripper, doing the managers, doing God knows what drugs and—"

"How dare you accuse me of things like that?" Lyla tried to pretend that he was wrong by acting infuriated, hating the fact that he was right. "Who the hell do you think you are?" She started to stand up, but he kept his arms locked around her waist.

"Honestly, Lyla! What else am I supposed to think?"

She crossed her arms and looked away. "Why do you even care?"

"Because I love you," he said emphatically.

She pressed her hand against the thump, thump, thump of her heart... *Is that my heart or just the music?*

He might care, but if she agreed to give them a chance, would he let her dance here, or work at the brothel? No. He'd tell her what to do. "There will always be something between us," she finally said. "I will always remember the passion of our kisses, how you taste, and how it felt to be one with you. But I will never allow myself to be hurt again." She heard both defiance and sadness in her words.

A look of defeat crossed his face. His hold dropped from her waist to her hips as they sat silently, looking into each other's eyes.

Lyla's mind reeled. *If what he told me about that day at the clinic is true, knowing me, I'd fall deeper in love with him than before. But it would probably end in disaster and pain. I'm in control of my life and that's the way I like it.*

"I should never have left you that day at the clinic," his voice was a desperate whisper in the near dark. "There's so much I need to tell you."

She retreated behind her shield, guarding herself against his pain. "Don't beat yourself up, Aksel—like I already told you, we will always share the memories of our connection. But you're clearly not pleased with who I am. And I will not change that. For *anyone*. So, I don't know what else to say." Her arms rested on his shoulders.

"I owe you an apology for all the pain you've endured by yourself. I am so sorry. We never should have happened, I guess." His head lowered.

"I'm glad we happened, Aksel." She caught her breath. "Despite some of the bad times…"

He released his grip on her, and suddenly she felt lost, like she was spiraling into empty darkness. He gently pushed her off his lap. He held her gaze for what seemed like an eternity. She couldn't breathe. He took her trembling hands, softly brushed her fingertips against his lips.

"I…" He paused and looked at her. It seemed as if he wanted to tell her something but he stopped as he gazed over her shoulder, staring at nothing in particular. "Again, I am truly sorry, Lyla. I am now wasting your time." He held her chin. "But maybe one day, we can at least be friends."

"I-I'd like that," she stuttered. Had he finally given up on her?

"I wish you would stop working here. You are way better than all this." He counted out five hundred dollars and handed it to her. Tears welled in her eyes. "I will never give up on you, Lyla."

As she watched him begin to leave, she grabbed his arm. "Stay, please." For at that moment, she suddenly felt alone. She whispered, "Stay with me. Please. Let's talk."

Aksel, thank God, turned around. "Just talking, Lyla. I would like that."

Chapter 31

Slim stood by his open door and saw Candy giggling with one of the dancers by the dressing room door. "Candy, get your ass in here!" he growled as he went back into his office and sat at his desk.

"Yes, sir," she answered in her high-pitched voice.

He was lighting up a cigar as he watched her enter, then close the door and sit down in a chair in front of his desk. Slim looked her over, recalling how long she had been with him—to him, she'd always be the pretty blonde, hazel-eyed girl that he'd met on the playground in fourth grade.

He sucked in a long drag on his cigar and leaned forward as he released the smoke. "We needs to talk!" She nodded, body alert as she waited to do his bidding. "It's time we see to da resolution here with the Rah Rah shit and her prick of a boyfriend that keeps showing up wit' his fucking hand out." He slammed his palm down on his desk. "I want it done tonight! Got it?" The vein in his temple throbbed with the force of his anger.

Candy braced her shoulders. "You want me to have the boys kick his ass?"

Slim snarled. "And den wha? He knows too much about tings around here due to his worn-out hag's snooping. The two of dem is messing with my big plan for da future here." He took a few snorts of cocaine. "Tonight's what we been waitin' for, a small crowd with a perfect opportunity looking us in the face." He handed her the coke, waiting as she snorted a couple of lines before he continued. "Sit down and let's review the plan, Candy Cane. Like I says before, we're gonna kill two birds with one stone. You tells Peetie, that moron, to get his ass in here right away, so that we's can all be on da same page. After dat, yous den tells Rah Rah, that flabby old ass bitch, to get in my office ASAP. Yous understand the girls are gonna be scared, so I'm relying on yooz to take care of dems like the mothafuckin den hen that you are and gather 'em up."

"Okay. I'll make sure the girls are safe." Candy reached over and touched his cheek—he kissed her hand.

"I'll go get Peetie," she said.

———◦———

Sarah sat with Darby in the main floor area, when Candy caught her. "Rah Rah! Slim needs to see you ASAP!" Candy spoke sternly and headed toward Slim's office, but stopped, turned back and gestured for Sarah to follow her. Now.

"I knew this was gonna happen! What the fuck, Darby?" Sarah stood up.

"What have I done? I am just sitting here watching the show, buying some drinks."

"You're an idiot— I'll be right back."

What could she do? Sarah hurried down the hall and knocked on the open door. "Come in!" Slim hollered. She found Candy and Slim sitting on the couch.

"Hi, sorry to interrupt. You wanted to see me?" she said, out of breath. Dang it, she knew better than to show Slim her anxiety.

"What's with dat loser boyfriend of yours?" Slim glared at her.

"What are you talking about?"

Slim's cackle turned into a wet cough. "You really tink I ain't known about him? Come on, Rah, you're smarter than that, I hope. He's been here two nights this week and three times last week. That son of a bitch takes up your time from paying customers, and just for the record has stiffed me for drinks!"

Damn Darby, she thought.

The sly smile left Slim's face, and he stared at her, his eyes wide and ferocious. Sarah immediately felt threatened—her boss wasn't just blowing smoke, but furious.

"Look, Slim, I know we're not supposed to let our guys in here when we're working. I just…"

He cut her off. "How about I have da boys take him on a fucking one-way trip?"

"No please, Slim. I'll handle it without a scene and cover anything he's had to drink. Can I have one of the drivers take him home? He's bombed."

"Oh, you'll cover his drinks. How kind of you." He looked at Candy and laughed. "It must be true love, Candy Cane. Too bad all da drivers are busy right now."

Sarah looked from Slim to Candy and back to Slim, afraid of what he would say next—he never backed away from using violence, from the stories she'd heard. "Uh, okay. I'll have him get a cab."

When she turned to leave, Slim said, "Tell ya what I'll do fer ya, girlie, since it's just around the corner from heres. Because I like ya—take my car. After all, 'baby it's cold outside,'" he sang. Slim stood and tossed his car keys to Sarah with a grin.

She caught the keys mid-air but before she could say anything, Slim added, "Tell that cheap son of a bitch he ain't allowed in the club ever again, understand? If he does, you lose your fucking job. And I will personally see to it that he gets da shit kicked outta 'im or worse."

Grateful for the reprieve, Sarah nodded.

"Rah," Slim pointed his chubby finger at her, "dis is his only chance to disappear quietly."

Her voice shook. "Understood. Thank you, Slim." She paused at the doorway. "Where's your car tonight?"

"Where it always is—in da alley, where Peetie and Paulie can keep an eye on it."

"Thanks." She ran out of the office.

As soon as Sarah closed the door, Slim turned to Candy with a smile and rubbed his hands together. "Well, we should start some plannin' for improvements soon." He laughed so hard, his whole body jiggled.

"It's just as easy as that, huh?" Candy said. She shook her head as she got up to take care of her part of the plan—the girls.

"It's all about da timing, Candy Cane. Just be sure da hallway in the black hole is clear for a while." He started bobbing his head and sang, "'And you don't mess around with *Slim*.'"

⊷╌◉╺═╍⊶

Peetie and Paulie guarded the doors when Sarah and Darby walked outside. Sarah spoke to them both, "Hey, boys, I'll be back in a few. Taking Slim's car." She jingled the keys for them to see.

"Enjoy," Peetie said.

"Or should we say that to you, big guy?" Paulie nodded toward Darby.

"I always do. See ya around." Darby flipped them the finger.

Peetie chuckled and whispered, "Sure you will, asshole."

Sarah unlocked Slim's car and got in, only to find that Darby had climbed into the backseat. She yelled, "This is fucking serious, Darby. Get up here!"

"I thought we came out here for some real privacy."

"Slim knows about us," Sarah said as soon as Darby shut the door. "You're being kicked out of the club permanently." She'd waited to get them to the car before telling him the truth in order to avoid a scene.

"Wait, what? He kicked me out of here *permanently?* What the fuck does that mean?"

"What the fuck do you think it means? Slim just confronted me about you. He doesn't want you back in the club. Ever!"

"Bullshit! Why?"

"Because bringing your boyfriend to the club is against the house rules, for starters. And also because he said you're a cheap son of a bitch!" She screamed at him. "If you ever come back, I'll lose my job!"

"Oh, fuck that shit, Sarah! How do you think you're gonna get the extra drugs without me around?"

"I'm not kicking you out of my *life*, just my *workplace*."

"Who cares?"

"I do! And now I've gotta do major damage control. Fuck!"

"Fuck this," he said as he unzipped his pants. "Get back here and blow me in your fucking boss's car. If I'm kicked out of the club, then I'm going out with a bang—right here in that fucker's car. Now blow me."

"Fuck you, Darby."

He sat there with a nasty sneer on his face, stroking his hard dick.

She knew they weren't going anywhere until she did what he wanted—maybe it was time to dump him for good. "Fine." Sarah climbed into the backseat, and swallowed his erect cock. She twisted one hand up and down his length and palmed his balls with the other.

Darby moaned. "Yeah, just like that baby." He leaned his head back and pulled her hair tighter in his hands. "Faster." He wrapped one hand around hers and pumped her hand faster, pushing the length of his shaft down her throat. He growled as he started to cum in her mouth.

Swallowing his semen, Sarah lifted her head and wiped her lips. The car windows were already fogged from the cold air outside and the body heat inside. Sarah climbed over the seat. "I'll take you to my place," she said and turned the key to start the engine.

⊷══◦◦══⊷

Aksel's heart warmed with hope as he and Lyla, side by side on a padded bench, agreed to have a conversation. They'd barely gotten started when a loud boom from outside shook the whole building. It sounded like an explosion, and it was so powerful that pieces of the ceiling tile dropped to the floor, leaving dust in its wake. They looked at each other, unsure of what had just happened. People in the club started screaming so Aksel grabbed Lyla's hand and pulled her up to exit the building.

Within seconds, the percussion from another explosion threw both of them to the floor, with Lyla landing on top of Aksel. His ears rang from the second, louder blast, but he could see and hear all the chaos going on. Aksel quickly pushed Lyla off of him and rolled on top of her, shielding her from yet another explosion.

Flying debris crashed to the ground around them as smoke began to fill the black hole. The lights went out, and for a few moments, it was completely dark. After a few ticks, the emergency lights illuminated the inside of the club, with fire sprinklers spraying water from above them as the fire alarm blared intensely. Aksel and Lyla were covered with dirt and dust, which was caked onto their bodies from the foul-smelling sprinkler water.

Aksel tried to help Lyla up and realized she was unconscious—he scooped her in his arms and carried her. He dodged a few ceiling panels that had begun to topple from above and jumped over anything that was in his way. Aksel reached the main area of the club and hurried with Lyla in his arms through an illuminated exit. He crossed the street, out of harm's way, and rested on the curb with her cradled in his lap. He sucked in a breath of air, checking for Lyla's pulse at her wrist. There.

The sound of the emergency sirens grew louder. He removed his coat and put it over her to keep her warm and began to wipe off the dirt from her cheek just as she opened her eyes.

She reached up and touched his face. "A-Alex? You're here? Oh, Alex, I…" Her voice faded as her eyes rolled back in her head.

She'd called him Alex. "Izzy? Izzy! Baby, I love you!"

But it was too late; she had again passed out in his embrace.

Chapter 32

Grant slipped the key into the lock of the wooden door, now a faded Wedgewood Blue, and unlocked it. Ginger and Grant walked into the cottage that held the stored memories of their past lives from 1944 and for a moment it was as if time ran in reverse. They stood in silence as they gazed at the surroundings, where a young American pilot and a beautiful British girl had fallen in love.

Ginger reached out and grasped his hand as he finally found his voice. "Is this real, my love, or a dream?"

"Real," she answered. The furniture that came with the house had been covered by sheets the day of the inspection and they'd only seen pictures.

The realtor, Lindsey, had made arrangements for the cottage to be cleaned and everything was spotless. The dishes, glasses, and silverware they'd picked out during their first few days in England had been delivered, washed and neatly stacked on the kitchen counter. A bundle of firewood had been placed on the hearth by the fireplace along with a small box of kindling. The new mattress and box springs had also been delivered and were already on the antique poster style Queen Anne bed. A beautiful bouquet of red roses along with a bottle of Macallan fifteen-year-old whiskey had been placed on the dining room table along with a thank you card from Lindsey.

Grant pulled her into his arms. "Home at last," he said softly.

"Tommy, we're back." Ginger's eyes filled with tears. "Please don't leave me this time." Her arms wrapped tightly around him. "I love you, my sweetheart." They shared a long, passionate kiss.

The next few hours she spent, with his assistance, organizing the kitchen. Her mind constantly drifted back to the past as they washed the new bedding and towels. After unpacking their suitcases, Grant opened a bottle of merlot and poured them each a glass before sitting down on the overstuffed velvet armchair with floral jacquard cushions next to the bed.

Ginger finished putting her clothing and toiletries away and joined him.

"You look cozy, my love." She picked up the glass of wine from the small table by the chair and sat down in his lap.

"Much cozier now." Grant planted a kiss on her neck.

Ginger shifted on his lap and felt his cock getting hard. "I'm going to start making the bed since the sheets are finally dry—and then I need what I'm feeling in your pants. So, fly-boy, think you can build a fire to warm this place up a little in case my clothes just happen to fall off? After all, I wouldn't want to catch a cold." She added with a tease in her voice, "Try not burning the place down?"

"Sure—going to remind me to open the damper?" He smiled at their shared memory.

Ginger got up, drained her glass of wine, and pushed him out of the master bedroom.

Twenty minutes later, he had a great fire started, and had poured himself some of the Macallan whiskey before sitting on the loveseat in front of the fire. The wood sizzled and popped as he sipped his beverage, watching the dancing flames in the fireplace.

Ginger walked out in a sheer red robe and jumped into his arms. They kissed and melded together on the couch. Rain pattered against the window as gray clouds opened up, at first in slow, rhythmic drops and then increasing into a heavy downpour.

"I have a surprise for you," Grant whispered into her ear. "I'll be right back." He left her on the couch and walked into the kitchen.

As soon as he left her embrace, she longed for him. "My sweet Tommy, I am so *over* surprises. I can't wait another second for you."

"I'm coming. But close your eyes."

She closed her eyes tightly and waited impatiently for his return. Her lips were still wet from their kisses, and her nipples were fully erect—she wanted him so badly.

She heard rustling, and then Grant sat next to her on the loveseat and said, "Okay, ready."

She opened her eyes and squealed with excitement—Grant's cock was covered with whipped cream, surrounded by decorated lined paper, and topped with a small lit candle, creating a sexy cup-body-cake.

"Happy house warming, Rachel!" His voice was mixed with excitement and an edge of anxiety. "Blow out your candle. And, uh, please hurry. Hot! Hot!"

Ginger laughed so hard, her sides ached. She jumped up to his lips for a quick thank-you kiss and sat back down, gently blowing out the candle. She kissed him again, sharing the whipped cream she managed to lick off. Finally, she slowly removed the candle and paper and devoured her surprise. She slid Grant's cock into her watering mouth and stroked his thick, velvety smoothness, purring the entire time. She gently ate and licked every drop of the whipped cream before focusing on the tip of his fully erect cock.

Grant pulled her up from the couch, carried her into the bedroom, and gently laid her on the bed. He climbed between her legs, bent on his knees, and licked her inner thighs. Then he slowly ran his tongue from Ginger's navel up to her nipples and sucked on each one.

"Oh, my sweet, sweet Tommy."

He moved up to her mouth and softly nibbled on her bottom lip while the tip of his cock pressed against her warm, wet pussy lips.

"Rachel, Ginger, I love you beyond words."

"Grant, Tommy, I more than love you."

He slid his mouth back to the apex of her sexuality. With her feet resting on his shoulders, his mouth on her femininity, he gently pulled on her pulsing, erect clit with his teeth. His tongue danced with the rhythm of her slightly thrusting hips.

"That feels so gooood," she purred.

He slid three fingers inside of her and knew she was climbing toward an orgasm when her pussy tightened around his fingers. She guided his wrist and fingers in and out of her each time as deeply as possible. While he expertly sucked her clit with his tongue dancing on the tip of it, her whole body shook as she exploded onto his face.

"Oh, God! Ba-by! Ba-beeee…" she moaned, her legs locked around his head, grinding her throbbing clit into his mouth.

She soaked in the afterglow of her orgasm when Grant scooped her up from the edge of the bed and hovered over her…just like the first time he entered her…in their past life.

"Please?" she begged.

He kissed her and slid inside her while she wrapped her legs around him. As he thrust inside her, she pulled at his muscular tight ass encouraging him to go deeper.

"There! Yes! Oh, my sweet Tommy…yessss…uh-huh…"

Another orgasm encompassed her body and mind. It felt like she was out of her body watching from above as he pushed deeper and deeper inside her. Finally, he joined her in a simultaneous orgasm, sharing physical ecstasy.

Early the next morning Ginger woke before Grant and gently slipped out of bed. Walking into the living room, she went to the bay window bench and pulled back the cushion. *I need to find what's under here. I dreamt about it all night.* She ran her hand over the wood, finding no loose boards.

She went to the kitchen and started the coffee maker, grabbed a knife and was walking back to the living room when she almost stabbed Grant.

"Whoa!" He jumped back. "Good morning, I hope?"

"Sorry, sweetheart." She leaned into him and kissed him with the knife still in her hand. "Glad you're awake. I dreamt last night about something hidden under the seat of the bay window. It's so weird! I don't remember anything from my regressions about it, but I knew exactly which board to look under. However, it's nailed down and I thought I could pry it up with this." She held up the knife.

"Okay, let's take a look at it." He walked over to the built-in bench and she pointed to the board, then handed him the knife.

Grant attempted to wedge the knife between the pieces of wood to no avail. "Let me throw some clothes on and I'll check the shed for a flat-tip screwdriver and a hammer."

Twenty minutes later he returned with a smile. She saw in his hands a wrench and a stiff-bladed putty knife. "Best I could do, love." Seeing her drinking coffee, he stopped. "You mind if the plumber slash painter has coffee before we start the remodeling project?"

"Fine, fly-boy. Just get a fire going to warm us up, please." She kissed his cheek as she went to get his coffee.

"Yes," he said sarcastically, "Your highness."

"Careful, I still have the knife!" she replied, laughing.

The fire was beginning to take on a full glow of flames, filling the small cottage with warmth. Ginger returned with a tray that held two coffees and a plate of warm Chelsea buns. "My husband isn't here, sir, and he has all the money. I was hoping this would be enough pay for your help. If not, I have another rather naughty idea for payment..." She sat down on the loveseat and placed the tray on an end table.

"I see. Well, let's see how big of a project it is and then we'll decide on the payment. But I'm sure that you'll still need to be naughty." She grinned from ear to ear before kissing him. For the next twenty minutes she sat with him in front of the fire waiting as patiently as she could while he finished his coffee.

"Okay, love, let's see what is hidden below the bench." Before he could put the coffee mug down she was standing by the bay window. He joined her and cracked his knuckles theatrically. "Please stand back." He took the putty knife and gently put it between the seams in the wood. Taking the pipe wrench, he hit it five or six times before the board made a cracking noise and popped loose. He leaned forward and peered down into the dark five-inch opening. "I don't see anything, Ginger."

She pushed him aside. "Out of my way, please! I know where it is." She lay flat on the surface of the bench, and with her slender arm, reached inside.

After a few moments, she declared, "Got it!"

Grant smiled as she lifted a journal from the hidden space. Then she instinctively put her hand back in the hole and felt around. She retrieved journal after journal and placed them on the bench.

"Wow! You've hit the mother lode!" Grant said.

Had she hidden them here a long time ago?

"Hang on, there's something else, I felt it." She stretched her arm all the way in with her chin against the bench. "Yes, got it!" She gleefully pulled out an old cigar box that barely fit through the space.

She stuck out her hand for him to help her stand up and looked at the stack of journals with excitement and trepidation. "I know it's early." She paused, still holding the box. "But I need to have a glass of wine before I look in here."

She stood at the edge of the window bench, clutching the box against her chest.

"Merlot, my love?"

"That would be great." She nodded yes at him as he went to get her wine, her anxious curiosity growing by the second. When he returned, he handed her the glass and placed the board back down on the bench. He put the cushion in place as he stacked the journals on the window bench for her.

She sat down on the window seat, settling the box on her lap.

Ginger, nervous, drained her glass like the merlot was water. Her fingers shook.

"I'll go get the bottle," Grant said.

She couldn't contain herself any longer and she opened the box, discovering an old, yellowed, neatly folded piece of paper that sat on top of all the stuff in the cigar box.

"What's the note about?" Grant refilled her glass and she blinked back tears. "You okay, Ginger?"

"Yes. Well, no." She accepted the wine and patted a spot on the seat next to her. "She knew I would get all this." Ginger handed him the note and cried while he read it. "I died," she said. "I loved you, so much."

Grant finished reading, also in tears. "Should we forget about the journals?"

"No." Ginger touched the stack. "It's important to reconnect, I think. But let's take the next couple of days to go through them." Seven journals, and what she'd hidden within the cigar box.

Chapter 33

Aksel called G Squared from the hospital waiting room Friday morning. Sue picked up the phone with a cheery greeting.

"Hello, Sue." Aksel's voice was hoarse from all the smoke and dust from the explosion.

"Are you okay, Mr. Portier?" Sue asked with concern.

"*Oui, oui.* I won't be coming to the office today. I am at the hospital…" Aksel paused, cautiously adding, "With a friend." Lyla still hadn't woken up and he was torn on what to tell Grant and Ginger, if anything.

"Of course, Mr. Portier. Is your friend okay?"

"*Oui.* I will keep you informed. Did Mr. or Mrs. Robinson leave a number to call them?"

"I have the information for their realtor—would you like that?" Sue quickly gave him the phone number.

"*Merci*, Sue. Is there anything that needs attention?"

"No, not at the moment."

"Excellent. I will check in with you later. *Merci beaucoup.*"

Aksel hung up and headed straight back to Lyla's room. He looked at his watch and saw that it was ten o'clock in the morning, making it four in the afternoon in London. He decided to check on Lyla before he reached out to Grant. A nurse was checking Lyla's vitals when he walked in. "How is she doing?"

"Mr. Portier, she's stable. It might be a while before she regains consciousness." Last night the doctor had given Lyla a heavy sedative to keep her calm. Aksel had been so scared. "If you want, you can go home, shower, get some rest," the nurse said. "We will call you as soon as she rouses."

"No, I'm fine, thank you. I should be here when she wakes." He couldn't let her down again.

"Well, how about a dampened cloth for your face at least?"

He touched his forehead, feeling a bruise. "*Oui, merci.*"

The nurse left and Aksel stood by the side of the bed, his gaze intent on Lyla. Her eyelids fluttered, and her face twitched; she was dreaming. He brushed her cheek. *Now what are you dreaming of, my dear Izzy?*

⊷══◉══⊶

Lyla attempted to wake up, but her ears were ringing and her body ached. In her dream the sky overhead was gray—she seemed to be walking down a street thick with foot traffic. A poster plastered on a building read: "In a raid–open your door to passers-by–they need shelter too." She instinctively knew it was during WWII and she was with a friend who kept telling her to keep her spirits up. She had been convinced by her friend to spend the afternoon shopping, so they meandered from shop window to shop window. It didn't help—her mind was focused on Alex.

I can't shake this feeling that I will never see him again. The same thing happened with my brother—I knew he was dead before he was even declared missing in action! I have that same feeling now. But once I hear the words, it will be the end of me—I will have nothing left to give.

She and her nameless friend were in a shop when a siren cut through her thoughts— an air-raid alarm wailed so loudly, it drowned out the cries of the people scrambling outside the store.

Her friend grabbed her hand and shouted, "Izzy! Come on!" The friend pulled her outside and they made their way through the crowds of people toward a bomb shelter. In the midst of the chaos, she, Izzy, slipped her hand from her friend's grip to avoid running into a family clustered in the middle of the street. That fraction of a second to dodge them was all that she needed—her friend disappeared into the sea of panic. Izzy scanned the faces around her and spotted her friend's auburn hair as she entered the shelter.

A wave of relief washed over her—her best friend was safe. Now she could go where she belonged. There was a bridge in the opposite direction of the mob. "I need to be *right there!*"

She arrived at the bridge and stood with her arms reaching up to the sky; the bomb would be the end to all the pain she had suffered. A plane zoomed overhead and released a heavy object that plummeted right toward her. At the last second, she turned toward the bomb shelter and saw her friend looking back at her.

A blast sounded, followed by a flash, and then crimson darkness overtook her—and she finally saw Alex's beautiful face.

Lyla's eyes flew open, and she sat straight up, gasping for air. "Alex!" she screamed as tears ran down her cheeks.

Aksel grabbed her hand. "You're okay, Lyla. Everything is okay."

"Aksel? Oh, Aksel." She sucked in air and cried as he held her. "Th-the bombs," she said.

Aksel gently wiped her tears. "Shhh, you're okay now. You were hit with some debris and lost consciousness."

"Debris? No, I couldn't have survived…" She looked around, finally taking in her surroundings. Her dream faded from her consciousness.

"The club was bombed last night. They still don't know exactly what happened," Aksel said.

"Right…the club."

"They gave you a sedative. You have been unconscious for a while."

"Are…are *you* okay?" she asked him.

"*Oui, ma chérie.* You are okay. I am okay. We are both okay."

"Then get me out of here!" She pulled at the IV stuck in her arm.

"I was going to call Grant and Ginger to tell them what happened. They'd be very worried about you."

"Aksel, please don't. I'm okay."

⊹⊱◉⊰⊹

The cab stopped in front of Lyla's apartment building, and she climbed out with Aksel right behind her.

She wore his jacket as he assisted her up the steps, holding her arm. It was in the mid-forties, but the sun beating down made it feel warmer as they stood on the landing. "Remember, you have a mild concussion, so you need to rest. Are you sure you will be fine, Lyla?"

"Yes, I'll be okay. I just need a shower and then some sleep in my own bed." She pulled the handle on the door, which was locked shut. "Damn. I was hoping someone had left it open. My keys are back at…well, at whatever's left of the club." She pushed the buzzer for Sarah.

"Is Sarah home?" Aksel asked.

"Probably. If not, our super will let me in. No biggie."

Lyla pressed the buzzer again, but there was no response. She turned back to Aksel. Something seemed different about him. There was a spark of familiarity, a closeness she hadn't noticed before. Face to face at the top landing of the steps, neither spoke. Lyla basked in the rekindled comfort of being in his space. Did he feel it too? Lyla couldn't put her finger on the difference.

"You seem…different." She tilted her head and tucked loose strands of hair behind his ear.

"How so?"

She studied his eyes and nose and finally touched his lips with her fingertips. It was almost there, like trying to remember a dream, but she couldn't quite make it out. She shook her head. "Nope. You're still you." She ruffled his hair and then inched back. "Sorry, I probably sound crazy. Nothing like a blow to the head to scramble my brain a little, huh?"

"Lyla, after the past twenty-four hours, I think we have all changed a little."

"So true." Their conversation in the black hole just before the explosion—he'd mentioned something about being regressed. She'd wanted to hear him, to see if she could get past what had happened between them.

Lyla quickly swiveled away from his searching gaze—it felt like something was trying to reach into her soul. She impatiently rang the buzzer for her apartment again. When there was no answer after the fourth time, she sighed. "Maybe you should just go," she said.

"I will not leave you on these steps until I know you are safely inside your flat. Maybe she is not home, or in the shower, or perhaps busy? I just need to be sure that—"

"I know," she cut him off. "Let me try the super." She buzzed Wally, who answered through the speaker and said he would be right down.

"See? I told you."

Aksel leaned close to her like he was going to kiss her and it seemed right but Wally opened the building door and she immediately stepped back.

"Hey, Wally," she said, glad the mounting desire to kiss Aksel had been interrupted. "Thanks for letting me in."

Wally eyed Aksel. "Who's the stiff?"

"This is Aksel. He's my…my friend." She took off his jacket and shivered in the chilly air while holding down the back of the hospital gown she had on.

The two men shook hands, each exuding mistrust as they maintained eye contact. She wanted to invite Aksel inside but desperately needed her quiet time, feeling exhaustion coming on.

She wrapped her arms around Aksel. "I'll reach out to you soon. Thanks for seeing me home safely."

"*Ma chérie.*" He kissed her hand, then walked down the steps as Wally glared at him.

Aksel stood on the sidewalk with one hand in his pocket and the other holding his sport coat over his shoulder. He couldn't decide whether he should catch a cab or catch a buzz at the bar across the street after the last twenty-fours. She'd been so close to remembering the past.

He decided to hail a cab. *A long shower and a stiff drink at home is what I need.*

⋆⟜◉⊸⋆

Wally, her beefy, somewhat handsome super, unlocked the door to her apartment.

"I heard some shit about an explosion at the club. You okay?"

"I'm all right. I have a mild concussion, so I need to rest."

"Tell me what happened." He followed her inside, and they both looked around. Every light was on and the apartment as messy as it had been when she and Sarah had left yesterday.

"Wally, I don't remember much, though." She swayed, light-headed. "I just need my bed."

"I'm dying to hear—"

"I'd love to talk, Wally, but Sarah's probably sleeping, and I'm beat. I'll catch up with you later." She gently pushed on his chest, forcing him back through the apartment's front door.

"You know I'm always here."

Lyla winced when she nodded. "I can't thank you enough. Good-bye, Wally."

As she shut the door, he said, "Just holla if you need anythin'."

Lyla turned her attention to the jumbled disarray in the apartment. Sarah's bedroom door was shut, but the blue box of goodies had been left out on the coffee table.

"Jesus, Sarah," she mumbled under her breath. She grabbed the box and rummaged around for sleeping pills, finally dumping the contents of it on the floor before finding the bottle.

She gulped down two of the blue-and-black capsules, and then dragged herself into the shower. The warm water washed off all the remaining smoke and debris from the night before, and afterward, she crawled into bed. Silence.

What a nightmare. I hope everyone at the club is okay... She barely finished her thought before she was out cold.

Chapter 34

Lyla woke up in an almost catatonic state from a deep, drug-induced sleep, not even sure what day it was. Lying in her bed, random thoughts about the last couple of days turned into a deluge of memories about people and places that made no sense. The previous day's dream at the hospital suddenly filled her mind. *Whoa, what the fuck was that about?*

She attempted to recall the details about the faded dream made up of a bunch of loose puzzle pieces that didn't fit together. *God, was that caused by the sedatives at the hospital? World War II? Who was that guy? Maybe Aksel, since he stayed with me in the room. But he had a uniform on.* "Get up!" Lyla slowly and carefully sat up in bed. "I can't lay here thinking about all of this nonsense, it's giving me a throbbing headache."

Shuffling down the short hallway, she saw Sarah's bedroom door was still closed. As she entered the living room, a burst of sunlight hit her eyes causing her to squint even though the window blinds were almost shut. Walking into the kitchen, she opened the fridge and poured herself a tall glass of orange juice. Closing the shades, she sat down on the couch in the living room and decided to take something for her headache. The blue box was on the white throw rug where she'd left it the evening before, the contents spilled out next to it.

She finished her orange juice and placed the glass on the coffee table before summoning the energy to get down on the floor and put away the drugs. Seeing a vial of cocaine, she opened it and dumped some onto the glass-top coffee table. She cut four lines with the razor from the box, taking her souvenir rolled up hundred-dollar bill, and snorted the coke. The drug hit her brain immediately. "*Breakfast.* Why the fuck is Sarah still sleeping?" Lyla asked aloud. "It's one in the afternoon. Time for a Rah Rah Cocktail for sure."

Lyla, halfway finished with the second cocktail, was still attempting to piece together the events of the last forty-eight hours. *God, I hurt everywhere.* She pulled a comforter from the back of the couch onto herself and fell back asleep.

It was midnight when she woke up again and went to find Sarah in her bedroom. Rapping softly on the door but hearing no response, she cracked the door open—no one was inside. *I bet she's with that scumbag boy-toy of hers.*

Lyla swung the door open and walked in. It finally dawned on her that Sarah hadn't been home after the explosion— her restaurant uniform was still in a heap on the floor, her bed was disheveled, and the nightstand light on.

This is nuts. Suddenly it occurred to her that maybe Sarah had been injured. *I'm going to beep her.* First, Lyla turned the ringer for their phone back on and then checked for any messages on their answering machine. *Why wouldn't she be home at least to check on me after what happened? For fuck's sake I hope she is okay! And if she is okay, then she should at least pretend to care if I'm alive or dead!*

Sitting on the couch, she turned the volume up on the answering machine that had three messages. She was surprised by the first one, from Uncle Andrew. "Sarah, you didn't show for your shift yesterday afternoon. Hoping you're okay. Please call me as soon as you can. I'm worried about you." The tone of his message seemed a bit too personal, she thought.

The next message was from Candy, and it had been left the day before, after she'd been released from the hospital. "Hey, Lyla. It's Candy. Call me when you get this message. We need to talk." Her voice held an urgent tone. The third message was Candy, just an hour before. "Lyla, Slim and I are concerned about you. Please get back to us ASAP. Thanks, dolly."

Lyla immediately dialed Candy's number, her heart racing.

"Hey, Candy. I'm sorry, I just checked my messages. Yesterday is a blur for me. Is everyone okay? What happened? Have you seen Sarah? I came home…"

Candy cut her off, "Oh, sweetie, slow down. Are you sure you're all right? I rushed to the hospital, but someone was with you—the nurse said you were in shock, with a mild concussion."

Her head still ached. "Yeah, I'm fine, just really tired. But everyone's okay from the club—what about the building?"

"We're all okay, for the most part. We'll need ta shut down for a few days while we rebuild the back area, where most of the damage was, but we got it under control."

"Oh good." She sighed with relief. "Have you heard from Sarah? I don't think—"

"Just come to the club," Candy interrupted Lyla. "I've got your stuff here. Slim and I are going through the mess. We'll talk."

Lyla gripped the phone tighter. "What about Sarah?"

"Like I said, we'll discuss everything when you get here. Gotta go, love." Candy hung up. Lyla knew the den mother was being evasive. *Why won't she answer me about Sarah? They're hiding something from me.* Lyla had a bad premonition about Sarah and tears stung her eyes.

⊷═◉═⊷

Saturday morning Aksel woke up groggy after a sleepless night of churning over Lyla. She had said his name, Alex—his name from her previous life time. *Did she remember it, or did I just fantasize that I heard her say it? Should I talk to her about it?* His thoughts made him dizzy and he needed a caffeine fix before digging deeper.

He sat on his couch, sipping coffee as he recalled her gentle touch when she'd tucked an out of place strand of hair behind his ear. The look she'd had in her eyes as she ran her fingertips across his lips. *I want to run to her apartment just to see her again.* He sighed. *No. Not just yet. I cannot drop in unannounced. But maybe I can get her number and I can at least talk to her some more... That'll have to wait, though. I need to concentrate; I've got finals next week. Plus, I still need to watch over everything at G Squared.*

He got dressed and headed for the office—he'd take advantage of it being closed on a Saturday to study for his mid-terms in peace, and catch up on any paperwork from Friday.

Once there, he called Sue. "*Madame* Sue, I apologize for calling you on the weekend. I am in the office today, doing some studying. Is there anything that you need me to address? Shipping, papers that need to be signed?"

Sue chuckled. "You remind me of Mr. Robinson, you know that? You have the same work ethic."

"I thank you for the compliment."

"The answer to your question is no, there's nothing you need to do by Monday."

He leaned back in Grant's office chair feeling relieved that he had nothing to do but study. "*Magnifique! Madame* Sue, would it be improper of me to ask a favor of you?"

"Of course not, what do you need?"

Why are you doing this?

"May I have Lyla Robinson's phone number? I would like to invite her to a charity event. Business, really."

"It's in my rolodex. Anything else?"

"No, *merci*, *Madame* Sue."

⊶≡◉═⊷

"Sarah's *dead*." Slim felt like an actor as he forced a note of sadness into his voice, dropping his head down like he had during rehearsal with Candy. The practice paid off.

Lyla's hand rose to her mouth, and her whole body trembled, slumping over on the couch next to Candy. Candy wrapped her arms around Lyla and looked at Slim for approval. When he gave it, Candy embraced Lyla like a mother would her daughter when hearing of a dear friend's death. Slim grabbed a box of tissues from his desk and gave them to her.

Slim waited in silence. Normally he wouldn't give a shit about covering his tracks with a dancer, but Lyla was smarter than the average stripper and he had more at stake.

"How did it happen?" Lyla finally asked, obviously in shock. Her nose was runny, and her eyes were watery and red; she wiped both with a tissue.

Candy stroked Lyla's hair and looked at Slim. "Slim, honey, why don't ya get her something for her nerves."

"This shit always helps." Slim motioned to the mirror on his desk with multiple lines of cocaine ready.

"I, I, I," Lyla stammered, "need some ecstasy powder."

"I got that too, angel face."

"Anything to numb the pain." She had a perplexed look on her face as she blew her nose. "How? How did this happen? Tell me!"

"Do dat, and dis, den we'll talk details." Slim added ecstasy powder to the mirror.

Lyla snorted more than she should have but Slim wanted her to calm the hell down.

He sat on the couch with her and handed her a bottle of water while waiting for the drugs to take effect.

"Better, sweetheart?" Candy asked as she continued to rub Lyla's neck and shoulders.

"Okay, I'm ready." Lyla wiped her tears with a tissue and leaned against Candy.

"This is not a pretty story." Slim paused, taking a deep breath as he continued his performance. "People aren't always who they appear to be. You know that, right? And your 'big sister' as she called herself, was one of them people."

"Yeah, that's for sure," Lyla said.

Slim patted her knee. "Well, neither was her boyfriend."

"He's such an asshole." Lyla crumpled her tissue. "Do you have more of the X powder, Slim?"

"For you? Of course. You know I consider you family. Candy and I love you as much as we *can* love someone, without being blood and all."

"And sweetie, that says a lot!" Candy pulled Lyla under her arm.

"You've always been good to me." Lyla's upper body began to sway back and forth on the couch. "So, what happened?"

She had a glazed look in her eyes and a relaxed body. Slim winked at Candy. "Well, Sarah's boyfriend wuz at the club causin' a commotion. We had to throw him out, you see, you know da house rules, boyfriends ain't allowed here for good reason—they see their girls dancin' for other men, then they get all jealous. Anyways, yooz know that."

Lyla's eyes were closed and she nodded.

"So's, I tell Sarah to get rid of him. And I let her borrow my car since she's extended family like yourself, yooz might say. And seein' as how all the drivers were tied up at that time, the two o' them climbed into the car to leave, and then…well…boom."

Lyla's eyes popped open wide and she looked up him. "Boom?"

Slim shrugged. "I'm sorry, sweet cakes, but this ain't the first time someone's tried to take me out. My Caddy was rigged by some bastard to fucking blow me up."

Candy chimed in to help sell the story they'd concocted. "The bomb was meant for Slim. It was a hit on Slim. We still don't know who did it."

"Could be any number of people with scores to settle. It's part of da game."

"Sarah and Darby died in the blast," Candy explained in her den mother voice.

"Oh, God…Sarah." Lyla burst into sobs.

"Candy Cane, fix her a vodka and tonic," Slim ordered.

Candy poured a vodka and tonic on the rocks, lacing it with more X powder, and gave it to Lyla. "Peetie and Paulie saw the whole thing. We're just glad no one else got too badly injured."

Slim eyed Lyla—she didn't question a thing. "Did some damage to the club, though, enough that we have to shut down for a few weeks to do some remodeling of the private dance areas."

Lyla eyes were closed again, and she took big sip of the drink.

"Lissen, honey bun, I don't want you back at the club when we reopen. Stick with the brothel." Slim could see that Lyla was *very* high and gave Candy a wink. "I get my cut and they're happy with you there."

"You're one of their best," Candy seconded as she kissed Lyla's pale cheek.

"Take a few days off and get your head straight. As soon as you're ready, they want you back." Slim patted her shoulder—mission accomplished.

"Okay, I will." Lyla slurred her words.

⊹⊷◉⊶⊹

"Now, on another small business matter, we need to talk about something because of what just happened."

Slim's tone alarmed Lyla enough that she forced her eyes open. "What's that?" Lyla blinked a few times to focus. *Sarah and Darby, both dead.*

"The night of the explosion, you was in the back with a guy, a French fella, I hear. Well, it so happens that when Candy came to the hospital she saw him sitting with yooz." He peered at her as if trying to see into her head. Aksel had taken her to the hospital and stayed with her, making sure she was okay.

Lyla turned toward Candy. "Were you spying on me or something?"

Candy shook her head. "I was just visiting to make sure you were all right. But I recognized him from the club that night."

"And you know that all my girls live in buildings that I own." Slim cleared his throat. "Wally, your super, works for me." Lyla handed her vodka to Candy and picked up the water bottle. She had to wake the hell up, fast, so she took a slug of water.

"He does?" Lyla's drug-induced confusion made it hard to follow the conversation with Slim.

"Well, he says that same French guy brought you back to your apartment." Lyla put the water bottle down as she looked into Slim's face. Despite his words, there was very little sympathy or kindness in it. "Who is this guy and how does he know you?"

"Oh." Aksel's image filled her mind as she scrambled for words that made sense, knowing on a gut-level she had to protect him. "His name is Aksel. He's just a family friend."

Slim stood from his seat next to her to perch on the arm of the couch. "How much does he know about what you do?"

"Only that I work here."

"So, he don't knows nothing about yooz at the brothel?"

"God, no!" Lyla sobered and realized what was at stake. "I wouldn't tell him anything, Slim. I promise." Scared, Lyla held Slim's gaze until he nodded in agreement.

"You gotta understand, sweetheart, you work for a secret society. We can't have any do-gooder sniffin' around, alertin' the cops." He gripped her chin too hard. "So get rid of him. Or else I'll have to. Understood?"

Slim's heartless expression chilled her to her soul and Lyla feared for Aksel's safety. Her heart raced. "O-of course. No problem."

"Good, doll face, 'cause I got big plans for you."

Chapter 35

Lyla sat in the back of the Town Car feeling sober despite all the ecstasy, cocaine and alcohol that she'd consumed throughout the time spent at the club with Slim and Candy. She shivered and not from thirty-degree weather outside. It was what she'd seen in Slim's eyes and had heard in his voice that made her realize how dangerous he was. Her brain busily tried to compartmentalize everything into neat little mental boxes, but it wasn't working well.

The Town Car pulled up in front of her apartment that she now realized was owned by Slim. The driver opened the trunk and handed her two large garment bags—one filled with her personal items she'd kept at the club and the other filled with Sarah's.

She started up the steps to the apartment and reality hit her hard when she saw Wally holding the door open for her. "Putting some salt on those stairs, it might snow tonight. Won't want you to slip and fall now." He smiled at her like he knew she was returning from the club. She looked at him through new eyes: He wasn't a random apartment super but the warden of the jail where she was an inmate.

"Hi, Wally." She greeted him with clarity as she blew past him.

"Hiya, Lyla," she heard as the door shut behind her.

This guy is a fucking creep! I never really liked him. She suddenly felt trapped and wanted to run away—go back home, or anywhere, but she was afraid to even entertain the thought as she recalled Sarah's warning about getting out. Lyla was pretty sure that Sarah and Darby's death had been planned by Slim. He and Candy had said the right words, but the emotion had been fake.

Suddenly Wally was right behind her and snatched one of the bags from her hand. "Let me help yooz wit' those." He followed her up the stairs to the second floor and unlocked the door to her apartment. "I'm sorry about Sarah. I know yooz twos were close and all."

He rambled on and she didn't pay attention. "You can just put the bag on the couch," she said.

"So, you gonna be okay living here alone now?" His tone and expression made her feel insecure about his question.

"I don't know yet." She needed to process everything.

"Slim had me change your lock on the door… for safety reasons, of course." He handed her the new key, and she felt funny about the way he was looking at her—he desired her.

Lyla burned with anger. "Am I ever really alone here, Wally? After all, you have a key and I'm sure Slim does."

"Only to let you in if you get locked out. Yooz should think of me as a guardian angel." He winked at her which made her even more uncomfortable.

"Whatever, Wally. Good to know. Right now, I need some alone time. Please go."

Heading toward the door, Wally grabbed the handle and looked straight at her. "Yooz are one of the special ones, Lyla. Don't be mad at me. We all need to do what we're told to do—yooz should keep that in mind. Reality's a bitch, huh?" He laughed at his statement and sauntered out, leaving the door open for her to close.

She went over and slammed it shut, then sighed with relief that he'd left.

Finally, alone…? Lyla looked around the apartment. She would never feel alone here again and knew now, she'd never been. She was Slim's property until he decided he was done using her.

Sarah made it seem like this was her apartment…Christ almighty, I gave her money for the rent. Wonder what that went to? When I moved in with her and started working with her at the club, I sold my soul without even knowing it! I'm really fucked! Oh, shit, that story about the bomb in the car being for Slim…I got her killed by telling Slim and Candy that she knew about the brothel! Oh, I have royally fucked up my life!

"I need to get high," she said aloud. "First things first, a few lines, a drink, and then I'm changing the outgoing message on my answering machine. And I'm going to get an attack cat to help protect me." She attempted to get high and forget but she just couldn't stop thinking about the conversation with Slim. Lyla was afraid for Aksel. She didn't want more blood on her hands.

Lyla decided to use her pent-up energy to clean out Sarah's room, filling three large construction bags of things to toss out. Lyla kept what she wanted for herself, especially the jewelry, clothing, and shoes that she'd treated Sarah to on their two-day shopping spree.

When she sat down and thought about how Sarah misled her, hatred toward her simmered from below the surface of her psyche, and she quickly did another few lines of coke to dull her emotions.

Lyla rearranged the furniture in Sarah's room, putting the bed against the farthest wall and the two nightstands on either side. All her nightlife accessories were in the walk-in closet, and Sarah's dresser fit perfectly inside it for storage.

She stood back and assessed her new dressing room. Lyla pictured a makeup table like the one she saw at Tiffany's placed perfectly under the window. *This'll have to do for now. I hope—*

Her thoughts were interrupted by the phone ringing. She decided to let the answering machine pick up. "Hi, Lyla. I wanted to check on you. I—" she recognized Aksel's sexy French accent and her stomach flipped from fear. She jumped up and grabbed the phone. "Aksel! I'm here."

"*Bonjour.* So, is this your personal home phone line? Does Sarah have her own number?"

"Sarah doesn't live here anymore," she replied flatly, attempting to mask her fear with indifference.

"Is this a bad time, *ma chérie?*"

"I said *I* would reach out to *you.* How did you get this number?"

"*Madame* Sue gave me access. I thought maybe we could see each other. I have an event next weekend, and I wanted to ask you to—"

"Aksel, let me stop you. I'm not sure that's a good idea. You shouldn't read too much into what happened over the last few days. Catastrophes can bring people closer together, even if only momentarily. And I think ours falls into that category." Lyla made sure her voice was stern and unwavering.

Aksel sighed. "I see. I did not mean to offend you by calling. I truly wanted to just check on you."

"It's not that I'm ungrateful, but it's probably best that we just let go of the past and move forward. You will always be special to me."

There was silence. Finally, Aksel said, "If that is how you feel, I will respect it. Please take care of yourself, Lyla."

"I will. And you do the same."

"Well, I better get back to studying for my finals. Farewell, *ma chérie.*" He hung up before she could say good-bye.

"Oh, fuck you, Aksel!" she screamed. "How can you not see that that I'm in love with you? But in my twisted reality, I'm just trying to protect you!" Lyla threw the phone across the room, and it shattered into dozens of pieces when it hit the wall.

"How did I end up here? Fucking Sarah!" Anger boiled over as she admitted bitterly to herself that it was her own fault, and she knew it. She let out another shout as she pounded the pillows on the couch before throwing them across the room. Lyla sank down with her arms curled around her legs, rocking back and forth, trying to figure out how to escape from this mess. "Even if I took all my cash and ran away how do I know my family would be safe? Slim will never let me go. When, or if, he decides to let me go, will I end up like Sarah?" She began to sob.

⤙⤜◉⤛⤚

Aksel slammed the phone down and dropped into Grant's chair. "What the fuck was that all about?"

He walked to the front lobby of G Squared, called Dr. Ritzius's message line and asked for an emergency appointment, leaving the office number for him to call. He then made a cup of chamomile tea and attempted to relax on the couch. The sound of the waterfall over the cascading rocks was soothing, but his mind wouldn't rest.

I can't figure that woman out! I mean, at the hospital and in front of her building, I could tell she started to remember something. Dammit! Maybe I shouldn't have called...

The shrill ring of the phone startled Aksel, and he jumped up to answer it. He was relieved to hear Dr. Ritzius's voice on the other end.

"Aksel, I received your message."

"Thank you for calling me this late on a Saturday, Doctor." It was after three and Aksel feared he wouldn't hear from the doctor until Monday.

"You sound quite distraught."

"I am, sir. Is it possible to see you today?"

"I don't normally see patients on the weekend." There was silence. "But I suppose I can make an exception, if you can come now. I happen to be at the office for the next few hours."

"I can be there in twenty minutes."

"See you then."

Aksel grabbed his coat and ran down the stairs to exit the building—he didn't want to waste time waiting for the elevator.

⊷═◉═⊶

Lyla knew she'd hurt Aksel with what she'd said—it had hurt *her* to say it—but she knew it was for his own good. *At least he'll be alive. I'd rather wonder about what we could have been for the rest of my life than visit his grave for the rest of my life.*

She picked up the phone and dialed the club, knowing she should tell Slim that Aksel had called her, for both their protection just in case he somehow knew.

"Hi, Candy, can I talk to Slim please?"

"Sure, he's right here, dolly."

Slim's gruff tones came on the line. "What's up, sweetheart?"

"Slim, I took care of the Aksel situation. He's nobody you need to worry about. I told him good-bye and he won't be coming around the club anymore."

"Good news. Hey, Candy Cane, our sweet little girl took care of dat French Fry already."

"But Slim, the only thing I can't control, is if I happen to run into him at family events," she clarified.

"Eh, no worries! But if he ever becomes a problem, you're gonna tell me, right?"

"You know who I'm loyal to." She crossed her fingers like a kid but hoped she sounded sincere, adding the bird as well.

"Don't forget that, cupcake. Case closed."

"Oh, one other thing, Slim?"

"What's dat?"

"I guess this apartment is mine now, or kind of mine?"

"Yes, yes?"

"Will I be getting a roommate?"

"Do you want one?"

"Not particularly."

"Okay, not a problem. No roommates."

"So." Lyla paused, wondering how far she could push. "Can I do a little redecorating?"

"Sure yooz been through a lot, go for it. I'll even give you a big budget. How's bouts five grand sound?"

What? Laughing in disbelief she said, "I just wanted to hear you're okay with it, I didn't expect for you to pay for all of it! I almost forgot, when is the rent due and how much is it?"

Slim started laughing so hard that it turned into coughing. He finally caught his breath. "You sures are having fun with me today. Yooz make me laugh when yooz say tings like dat. It's free, buttercup, yooz works for me and I pay the rent." He chuckled low. Sarah had fucked her for extra cash as well, Lyla fumed. "Ah, go enjoy! You're family, remember? We're all in this together, love."

"Thanks. Love you, Slim." Lyla felt foolish as she realized just how gullible she had been.

Chapter 36

Despite the clear and chilly afternoon, Aksel was lightly covered in sweat from dodging all the holiday shoppers out with their families. It had taken him extra time to get to Dr. Ritzius's office and he was relieved to be settling into the office chair at last.

"Aksel, tell me what's going on."

"I reached out to Lyla…"

Aksel filled Dr. Ritzius in on every detail, starting with their talk at the club the previous Thursday night and what had happened after the explosion. She'd called him Alex and said he'd looked different to her. Followed by her telling him to back off in their most recent conversation and to leave her alone.

"Am I going crazy or what?"

"She called you Alex both times when she was unconscious or semiconscious?" Dr. Ritzius asked.

"Correct. What does that mean? What else can I do?"

"Aksel, when a person is in a semi-conscious or unconscious state, the soul is free of its limitations. Unfortunately, that does not automatically mean that the person's conscious mind knows what their soul knows. It's only a confirmation of what you have discovered through your regression therapy."

Disappointment filled him. "So now what do I do?"

The doctor gave him a serious look. "Nothing. You already know it's up to her to discover the truth buried within her conscience. At this point, I suggest you move forward with your life. Attempt to free your soul from the bond you once shared in both the present and your past life. Maybe you can try going on a date or talking to other women. *It's out of your control.*" Aksel felt like he'd just received a mortal wound as the doctor continued, "Whatever governs our existence has not opened the door for you and Lyla to be together currently, and may never again in this lifetime. You need to accept this."

"I do not believe I can." His heart ached, but he knew intellectually the doctor was right. He had hoped for a different answer.

"What other option do you have?" The doctor leaned back in his chair.

"Regress me again. What if you guide me to a happy time in our relationship in the past? Maybe in learning more about her then, I can find a way to open her up in the present."

Dr. Ritzius sighed. "You must understand this is not magical; you might discover things you do not wish to recall. It can be a slippery slope."

"I am willing to take that risk. Please, doctor."

"I hope we can find peace." Dr. Ritzius proceeded to relax him into the REM state. "Where are you?" Dr. Ritzius asked.

"I'm with Rachel at her cottage."

"Have you told her about Tommy already?"

"Yes. That was days ago. She asked me to stay with her for a while since I had been given a week-long leave—I wanted to stay. We need each other right now. She's cooking dinner and told me to go bathe after helping her out in the garden all day. This feels odd, but we're getting closer. She's been throwing up almost every morning, and off and on with heartburn. She thinks it was something she ate but when I was twelve my mother was pregnant with my baby brother and she was doing the same thing. I think they called it morning sickness."

"In what way does it feel odd?"

"She's so beautiful. We are both so sad. She asked me to come lay with her and we fell asleep spooning in bed last night."

"What are you doing now?"

"I'm drying off. The towel is wrapped around my waist, and I have a hard-on. I feel guilty, but I *want* her. I think she wants me too…"

Aksel was silent for a few minutes, and then his breathing changed.

"What is happening, Alex?"

"We're kissing. Her mouth is so sweet. I pick her up and gently lay her down on the bed where we continue to kiss passionately. She pulls off her dress and I climb on top of her. She spreads her legs and reaches for my ass. I slide her panties down and ask her if she's sure we should do this. She puts her finger on my mouth, 'Just make love to me, Alex.' I'm on top of her, kissing her. We look deeply into each other's eyes. She sucks my bottom lip, pulls at my ass cheeks, and guides my cock inside her. God! She feels so good! She's so wet. Her eyes are closed and she's bucking her hips into each thrust, wildly digging her nails into my ass cheeks. I am about to climax…"

Dead silence until Aksel started crying. "It isn't right. I must stop…she just called me her sweet Tommy. What have I done? I hate myself! How could I do this to him? He was my best friend! I'm a monster. I'm so ashamed."

Aksel opened his eyes, wiped the tears from his face, and couldn't even look Dr. Ritzius in the eyes.

"Aksel, it was a natural human reaction. It's not uncommon for two people who share an emotional tragedy to become physically involved, however briefly."

"But I feel awful." He could hardly breathe thinking about what had happened.

"We can work through that. Do you want to continue?"

Aksel shook his head. "No, no, I'm done for now."

⤟═◑ ◐═⤞

Monday morning Lyla was riding in a cab headed toward Raymour & Flanigan on the Upper Westside in search of the perfect makeup station to add to her new dressing room—anything to clear her head and get her mind off her precarious life. Out the window, she saw holiday decorations everywhere she looked. The Salvation Army Santas rang their bells next to their pots, collecting money on every corner. How many Santas were there?

Traffic wasn't heavy, and the cabbie made good time, but as he exited off the Brooklyn Bridge, Lyla heard a loud *bang* –the vehicle careened out of control, tossing Lyla from side to side in the back seat before coming to a crashing halt against the guard rail.

The popping noise of the tire ignited her fear of dying, and pushed her over the edge after the events of the past few days. She closed her eyes while placing her hands over her ears and started screaming hysterically. "Alex! Alex!" The cabbie tried to get her to calm down by telling her that everything was under control, but Lyla hyperventilated and blacked out.

When she came to, she was stretched out on the back seat of the cab with the driver leaning over her, attempting to revive her by fanning her with a magazine. "We're off the highway, Miss!" he said reassuringly. "We are safe. I had the dispatcher request an ambulance. Please relax!"

She struggled into a sitting position and regained her composure.

"It was just a flat tire, Miss," the cabbie said, speaking rapidly. "Another cab is on its way as well."

"Th-thank you. I'm going to be fine. Please cancel the ambulance—I don't need it." Lyla calmed down though she was still alarmed by the incident. Thoughts of Slim and what had happened to Sarah filled her mind with fear that wouldn't go away.

"If it will help you, I can have the dispatcher contact the Alex you were calling for."

"Alex?" She stared at the cabbie in confusion. "Who's Alex?"

Chapter 37

Over the next few days, Lyla used her time off to do errands, eagerly awaiting the delivery of her new dressing table. She promised herself not to trust anyone as she'd trusted Sarah again and decided to visit Animal Haven, the local animal shelter. A friendly blonde employee named Mariluz escorted Lyla to the back of the shelter. Mariluz led her past a row of cages, explaining how the cats came to be at the shelter, and that each animal was examined by a veterinarian to make sure they were healthy and had all their shots updated. Lyla was standing in front of one of the cages containing a small eight-month-old tabby with green eyes.

The cat looked at Lyla and meowed. It was love at first sight for them both, and an hour later, Misty was on her way home via a stop at the pet shop.

Lyla watched Misty exploring the apartment as she set up her litter box and water. The two of them played with some toys she had bought for the next couple hours until Misty yawned. "Is it nap time, kitty?" Caring for the kitten relaxed Lyla for the first time since the explosion. She carried Misty into her bed while scratching behind her ears and under her chin. Misty's purring soothed Lyla into a deep sleep.

She dreamed that she was a barmaid working in a small English pub and each time a soldier entered, she looked to see if it was him. In the dream, she was sitting with a friend, looking at a picture of a young airman in uniform; but none of it made any sense. She was suddenly standing on a bridge looking toward her best friend when there was an explosion and she couldn't breathe. Lyla woke up gasping for air as she recoiled into her comforter in fear.

Her heart raced so hard that she gave up on trying to figure out the dream's meaning and climbed out of bed.

Her new roommate must have one off to explore while Lyla slept. "Misty? Misty? Mommy loves you…where are you, baby girl?" Lyla pinched a small pile of catnip—a feline's treat— in a dish and placed it on the floor. Seated in front of her new dressing table, she looked at herself in the mirror. Her face was still pale, her eyes sad. She needed a pick-me-up from the blue box, so she swallowed a whole ecstasy pill, hoping it would act quickly.

She climbed into the shower and the warm water soothed as she switched her thoughts to the night ahead of her. It was the next step in her life of only working at the brothel. Each step forward represented one step away from her past with Aksel Portier. *I once thought we'd have a future together but now I need to protect him.* Finished with her long shower, Lyla put on her new thick white bathrobe and wrapped herself in it.

Meow.

"Thank goodness!" Misty emerged with a stretch and a yawn from a pile of Lyla's clothes on the floor. "I was wondering where you went!" Misty rubbed against her leg and began to purr. "You're just so perfect, my baby girl! Come to your mommy." She held her new infatuation against her chest as she danced to Madonna's song, "Like a Prayer," and placed Misty on her dressing table while she sang along with the rest of the album, applying her makeup.

Slim had left a message while she was in the shower— she turned off the music and rifled through the blue box for something to lift her spirits before calling him back. After sniffing few lines of white powder, she picked out her clothing for her evening at the brothel. She then called Slim, letting him know she was returning to work that evening—

but he wanted her to come by the club as soon as possible. She hung up. "Now what?" Her pulse skipped with anxiety.

During Business Economics, Aksel couldn't focus on the video presentation because thoughts about Lyla kept intruding. When the video concluded, and the lights were turned on in the large auditorium, Aksel slipped his notebook into his backpack as he prepared to leave.

A soft, shy female voice asked, "Are you going to the study group today?"

He turned to the girl sitting in the seat across from him—her eyes were almost identical to Lyla's. The bright blue of her irises and matching pouty lips stopped him cold. *Even her hair is almost the same color as Lyla's!* The intense stare she gave him caught him off guard as he tried to remember her name from the group. "Thank you for reminding me. My mind has been somewhere else."

Picking up her backpack and loading it with her things, she glanced at him. "Great, you want to walk together?"

He hesitated for moment and then smiled. "Yeah, sure. It would be nice to have the company. But please forgive me. What was your name again?"

Her faced blushed. "Leah."

"Leia? As in Princess Leia from Star Wars?"

She tried not to laugh. "Not exactly. *Leah* is a Hebrew name. I'm named after Leah from the Bible—she was the eldest sister of Rachel."

"Rachel?" He repeated the name in shock, remembering his past life.

"Have you ever read the Torah?"

"Not really." He tilted his head back, feeling slightly uneasy about her question since he couldn't even remember the last time he'd looked at a Bible.

"My parents are very devout Jews," she said with a pensive smile.

He looked at her with a fresh perspective as she stood in front of him, and stretched out his arm, nodding toward the door. "After you, *mademoiselle*."

⊷═◯═┅⊷

It was mid-afternoon when Lyla met with Slim and Candy at the club. It would be her first day back to work at the brothel after the explosion from the week prior. The club was still under construction, with plastic sheets covering the walls, and hammers and drills echoing throughout the hall. She reached Slim's office, uneasy. Lyla had a sense of dread as she sat in a chair before Slim, seated at his desk.

He took a drag on his cigar and leaned back in his black leather office chair. "How are you doing, my cupcake?

Need a drink? A boost of some kind?" His voice was kind, but she didn't trust it.

"Yes! A drink of whatever you're having and something for my nerves would be nice. Thank you." Just then an anchor gun fired a nail into the concrete causing her to jump. "How do you put up with all this noise?"

Slim laughed as he poured her a whiskey and handed her some ecstasy. Her hands shook slightly as she took the glass.

"I thought you said you were ready to get back to work?" Candy got up from where she'd been sitting on the couch and gently rubbed Lyla's shoulders.

"I *am* ready, just a little jumpy with sharp noises. Just need a little bit of whatever you have the most of to calm my nerves. I don't want to deplete your supply."

"Ain't she da best, Candy Cane?"

"Of course, she is," Candy said. "She's very thoughtful."

Lyla drained the tea-colored liquid in one gulp and followed it with an ecstasy capsule as a chaser. Handing Slim her empty glass, he refilled it while she explained her apprehension. "I think it's just the construction. Loud sounds have been bothering me since the explosion."

"It's called ESPT or STDS or some shit."

"PTSD. Post-traumatic stress disorder," Lyla said, trying not to sound like she was correcting him.

"So, let's talk about a new biz prop." Slim leaned forward, resting on his elbows as he looked at her.

"Business?" *Thank God he's not talking about Aksel.* Her tension eased.

Slim smiled. "Yeah, business."

What could he want? Slim waddled to the front of his desk and sat on the edge with his arms crossed. When he smiled, it always reminded Lyla of the Cheshire cat, a wide, brimming grin—only with a gold tooth among a row of stained ones.

"Okay," she said. "New business. I'm listening, but honestly what else could you possibly do to make me happier than what you've already done for me? I live alone in a beautifully furnished apartment with a driver who will take me anywhere I want to go; someone living in the building who keeps a protective watch over me; plenty of money and drugs. Does life get better than that?"

"How does this sound? Lyla Robinson, movie star?" Slim waved his hands through the air making an invisible marquee. Her mind went blank as he continued, "Lylakins. We said before we're family. And in dis family, there's rules or guidelines yooz might say… but mainly respect."

"Of course. Did I do something wrong?" She forced a smile. She'd done everything he'd asked of her.

"No. Jesus, no." He waved his cigar.

"So, you said something about a movie star?" Lyla was so high she wanted to make sure she'd heard him right.

"Yeah, which leads me to the rules, guidelines and respect of the *family business*. First off, The Manhattan Madam is a distant, but lucrative family member, like a second cousin, where you, you're more like um, a niece."

"Okay?" Confusion muddled her drugged-up brain. "So, you don't want me working at the brothel? I'm sorry, I'm not following you."

Candy sighed. "Slim, just tell her what you're offering her. Stop all this other horseshit about family and fucking rules. Shit, she already knows. Right, Ly?"

"Yes." Lyla tried to hide the new anxiety infiltrating her being, almost tipping her toward a panic attack. She reached for her drink with a trembling hand. She saw Slim notice. "Sorry, I guess the noise is still affecting me." Lyla brought the drink to her lips.

"It's all good, no worries. Let's cut to da chase. Yooz will want to stop working for The Madam at some point. You know all dat nice stuff dat yooz mentioned before comes with a price—ain't nothing for free, ya know?"

Lyla remained silent, nodding her head in agreement while trying to hide the fear that was slowly encompassing her entire being.

"But now is where you need to hit it big for us. The brothel is only a stepping stone. We're talking movies next!"

"Me in a movie? I mean, I always wanted to be a model, but…movies! What kind of role do you have in mind? I didn't know you were in the movie industry too! God, Slim, your world is awesome!"

He nodded. "Yes, yes. My world is awesome. We all can agree on dat. You already auditioned for the lead role." He gestured with his hand as if to refer to her body. "You have lots of talents."

Lyla turned to Candy for answers but heard none. "What do you mean?" Candy wouldn't make eye contact with her so she looked at Slim with a raised eyebrow. "Oh, you mean my dancing? I can dance. But what lead role needs a dancer like me?"

"I *mean*, honey, these roles would focus on your other skills—fucking, and I know you're good at dat. I *mean* for yooz to become the greatest porn star to ever grace the silver screen." The words just rolled off his tongue, his dialect thick with his Bronx accent suddenly grinded on her nerves as she listened to him. Porn star?

"You are da fantasy slash reality for every man. Dats why they're desperate for you to return to the brothel. You won't be nominated for an Academy Award any time soon. Alls yooz need to know is dat the best of the best porn stars write their own tickets. And a lot of us think yooz got what it takes to sweep the industry and knock em dead on their asses!"

Lyla was stunned into silence as she tried to process his statement. She finally managed to say, "Porn? I don't know, Slim…"

"How's it any different than what you already do? You fuck, you get paid. Am I right?"

"But it's not recorded, Slim! What if someone were to recognize me?" Fear filled her voice at just the thought of all the people who might see her or discover what she was doing.

"You wear a wig, use a fake name—ain't no one gonna be the wiser. You think that gorgeous brown hair of yours isn't gonna be covered up with a blonde or red mop? Whacha think, it's gonna say 'Starring Lyla fucking Robinson'? Come on, you're killing me here. And you know I don't like no death threats, eh?" He laughed with irritation. "Jesus fucking Christ!"

Lyla didn't answer. She sat quietly for a moment, recalling Sarah words. *Once you're in, it's not easy to get out.* Slim looked at Candy with a furrowed brow then nodded in Lyla's direction.

"We really think you should consider this opportunity, Ly," Candy said on cue.

"Dis *wonderful* opportunity, I think is what Candy here meant to say."

Lyla rubbed her arms to warm up—she suddenly felt very cold, and dirty, and really trapped. "Can I, uh, get back to you on this? I just need some time to think about it."

"What's there to tink about?" Slim growled. His face turned bright red. "Do you not understand all the money we can make from this?" He turned to Candy. "Help me out here!"

"Ease up, Slim," Candy finally said. "Just give her some space. Can't you see that she has PTSD? It's a real thing," Candy said while Lyla finished her drink and snorted three lines of the white powder in front of her.

Slim exhaled and unclenched his fists. "Fine. Take all the time you need." His meaty paw grabbed her chin. "But I strongly recommend you take it."

She nodded, driven by fear.

"Fair enough then," Slim said. "So how long you need, Lyla-Pop?"

"A few weeks, a month?" Never?

"How's 'bout dis, I give you three weeks—oh hell, wait, the fucking holidays screw everything up." Slim looked at the calendar. "Okay, a month. Then we can start off the new year, new decade, with a bang! So, January 5th, one month from now, we meet with the producers, okay?"

"O-okay. Thank you," Lyla said meekly as her brain spun wildly out of control.

"Sweetheart, you're one of the family, and family takes care of family. I hooked yooz up with da brothel, I pay for your place, your hair," he rubbed her blouse between his fingers "your nice clothes, your everything is because of me. Maybe it's time you take care of me some. Speaking of movies and family, you ever see da movie The Godfather? One of my favorites. Consider me your official Godfather."

The look in his eyes and his sinister laugh sent chills down Lyla's spine.

He snapped his fingers at Candy. "Where's that bag of goodies you put together for our future star here?"

"Here you go, baby. We even picked up some catnip for your kitten." Candy smiled and handed her a medium-sized Chanel bag filled with lingerie and drugs.

"Thank you. And thank you for understanding I need a little time, Candy, Slim." She got up to leave, her head down, when Slim blocked her path.

"Hey," he pointed a fat sausage finger at her. "Yooz do what's right here. Don't go backing out on me." His face was deadpan and a shade of red that she recognized: he was serious and trying to control his temper.

She couldn't look him in the eye for fear that he would know she was lying. "Never, Slim."

"Good girl." He kissed her cheek and let her go on her way.

She almost ran out of the club, just to get as far away as she could, and found herself desperately wishing for Aksel, but for his own good, she had to forget about him.

Chapter 38

Outside the classroom, standing in the hallway, Leah bashfully admitted, "I've been dying to talk to you away from our study group for the past few months. It's almost like you never noticed me before today."

"I apologize for giving you that impression." His gaze locked on her blue eyes. *She's even smart and to the point like Lyla.*

"Aksel, you're always so serious, darting out of class and groups so quickly. Where do you disappear?"

"I have an internship slash job that is very important to me." He maintained eye contact with her. Was he dreaming?

Leah smiled. "It's obviously very important to you."

They walked in silence toward the exit when he stopped her.

"I must apologize once again." Aksel held her hands and brought them to his lips, gently kissing the top of her knuckles.

She blushed and averted her gaze. Was he being too forward?

"What causes you to look away from me, *mademoiselle?*"

"You," she stammered.

He decided to take advantage of her response and spun her around. Aksel analyzed her body from head to toe; everything about her reminded him of Lyla—her figure, her smile, even her height.

With the pink hue from blushing still on her cheeks, she finally lifted her head, no longer looking away.

"Do you believe in fate?"

"*Oui.*"

"*Oui? Parlez-vous français?*"

"*Oui, monsieur.*" Leah gave him an enigmatic smile.

"*Magnifique! Café?*" He looked at his watch. "*Vino?*"

"When?" Her sable brows rose with pleasure.

"What better time than the present? We can blow off study group." He had to get over Lyla, and who better to help him, than Leah?

He helped her into her coat. Walking slowly together he caught himself laughing out loud, as if a heavy weight had finally been lifted from his chest.

A few hours later, they were still talking at a hole-in-the-wall Italian restaurant. An empty bottle of wine and two dishes with nothing but crumbs and some remnants of sauce sat on the table. They went on and on about their lives, their goals and dreams. For the first time in years, Aksel felt a connection with a woman other than Lyla and decided to take it a step further.

"Is it too early to ask you for a second date?" he asked.

"You think *this* was a date?" Leah teased, resting her chin on her hands.

"Then is it too late to ask you for a *first* date?" He grinned, wanting to see her again.

"What were you thinking about doing for our *second* date? So that I can decide which occasion it is."

Aksel laughed. "I have a charity event this Saturday that would be infinitely more pleasurable if you would join me."

"A charity event. As in, evening gowns and tuxedos?"

"*Oui.*"

She hesitated, looking at him across the table. Her smile warmed him. "*Oui*, Aksel. I would be happy to make your event more *pleasurable.*"

"*Fantastique, ma chérie.* We will spend the evening together, starting with a ride to the event in style, and champagne."

He enjoyed the sparkle in her eyes. "I suppose the ride will not be via public transportation if it includes champagne." She giggled.

"Only if you consider a limousine public…" They laughed together and something in him began to hope that he could move on.

"Will I see you before then?" Leah curled a lock of hair around her finger. "Other than in class?"

"Unfortunately, no. As I mentioned, my job is very demanding. The owners return from holiday tomorrow. There is much to do."

"Best get to it then, *Monsieur* Portier."

They exchanged numbers, addresses and finally he placed a tender farewell kiss on her cheek.

"Rosé. I like a rosé champagne," she said as they looked into each other's eyes.

"Duly noted. *Au revoir.*" He kissed her hand once more and turned to open the door of the cab he had hailed.

As they parted ways, Aksel felt a newfound lightheartedness. *Letting go of Lyla is the key.* He jumped into the taxi. *Maybe everything we shared was meant to happen: it all led me to Leah.*

⚜

Lyla unlocked the door to her apartment and threw her keys on the kitchen table. *My God—Slim wants me to make porn!* Her body trembled at the idea. She made herself a drink laced with X and flopped onto the couch. She checked the clock—three hours until time to leave for the brothel.

Her mind reeled from her conversation at the club. *If I agree to do those hideous films, Mom would kill me—and I would want her to! What about my father! Father? Howard's dead. Daddy? Grant? Gah! Who's got serious daddy issues?* "MEEEEE!"

Lyla discarded her black-and-white-striped sweater, jeans, and knee-high boots for her favorite robe and fluffy socks, all the while calling for her kitten. Her new love was nowhere to be found. Curling up on the couch, she opened the gift bag from Slim and Candy.

She tossed the lingerie across the living room and dumped the remaining contents of the bag: cash and drugs. The crinkling from the plastic bag of catnip brought Misty out of hiding.

"There you are," she laughed. "You want to get high? Just like your mommy!" Sprinkling the catnip on the throw rug next to the couch, she watched Misty lap at it and then roll onto the leftovers. Lyla picked the kitten up and scratched behind her ear.

"What happened to being in control of my life, Misty? How did things get so out of *my* control—and how the hell do I fix it?" The kitten purred. "How about we skip town, just you and me? You game?"

Deciding she needed an emotional pick-me-up, Lyla grabbed an unfamiliar capsule from the pile of drugs on the floor, opened it and snorted the entire thing. The results were amazing: she felt both high and extremely relaxed. Misty curled up into a tight little ball on her chest, and Lyla, mesmerized, watched as gold slowly dominated the feline's green eyes.

"Whoa," Lyla said. "Whatever that was, it's good shit."

⸭⸺◐◑⸺⸭

"You're fucking late, you dumb bitch!" Wally's screaming voice woke Lyla from the most peaceful sleep she'd had in a week. She opened her eyes, unable to focus as the room lightly spun around. Misty jumped down from the couch and darted off.

He loomed over her. "Lyla, wake up! It's ten o'clock! Everyone's been trying to reach you. Lyla, get up!"

She tried to focus on what he was saying. "W-Wally? What time is it?"

He crouched down and raked his fingers through the pile of pharmaceuticals and street drugs on the floor.

"Wally?"

"Huh?" he responded.

"I'm calling Slim!" She sat up.

"Fine, call him. He's already kicked my ass—it's your turn." He grabbed a handful of drugs. "Guess you couldn't handle what Slim gave you, huh?"

Lyla finally regained her senses and got to her feet. "What the fuck are you doing in my apartment, Wally?"

"A car will be here in twenty. Get your pretty, dumb ass ready right now, bitch!"

"Fuck off, you asshole!" Lyla screamed.

Lyla was in a full sweat as she ran to her room, slammed the door shut, and quickly got dressed for the brothel. *Fuck me. Slim is going to be really upset with me!*

Chapter 39

After a long evening at the brothel, Lyla put the shower on hot which created steam in the entire bathroom. Once the water cooled she reluctantly pulled back the curtain—then jumped in alarm. Janice, the Manhattan Madam, waited by the vanity, her signature bleached-blonde bob unaffected by the humidity. Lyla covered her breast with her arm, uncomfortable at her boss's unexpected visit.

"Ready for your warm towel?" Janice didn't smile as she selected a towel from a stack on the counter.

"Yes, thank you." Lyla quickly wrapped herself up in the fluffy cotton, her heart pounding from the scare.

Lyla guessed Janice to be in her early fifties. The madam had a cold, hard air about her that most people found intimidating, and Lyla was no exception.

"Lyla, I wanted to personally check on your well-being. How are you holding up?" Janice's tone was matter-of-fact while her deep hazel eyes bore holes into Lyla.

"I'm fine. Thank you for asking." It was highly unusual for the madam to interact with her in such a way after a shift. Would she be reprimanded for being tardy?

"You were late. On your first night back." Cold delivery of facts as the madam assessed her with a critical gaze. "And honestly, you don't appear to be fine—which matches the feedback I got."

Lyla walked over to the sink and picked up her hairbrush, keeping her back to Janice so they only had eye contact in the mirror—it seemed less intimate. She'd done her best to perform. "May I ask from whom?"

Janice's mouth tightened. "The other escorts, assistants…even the two gentlemen you entertained tonight."

"What did they say?" Lyla hated the pensive tone of her voice and nervously twirled a lock of hair around the brush. Would she lose her job?

"The staff said you seemed out of it. Both gentlemen mentioned that you were distant. If you're not ready to be here, I want you to be honest with me and yourself. These men pay a premium price for our services."

Lyla readjusted her towel. Had she been distant? Maybe. She would try harder. "I'm really okay."

The madam turned to walk out and stopped before opening the door. "Your performance today was…inadequate. Are you sure you're up for Saturday night with Nathaniel?"

Lyla opened her mouth to object, but the madam lifted two fingers to halt her response. "Lyla, just a week ago you experienced more emotional and physical turmoil than the average person in a lifetime. I would understand if—"

She held tightly onto her towel with her fists just above her breastbone. "Please don't fire me. I will step up and show you—"

"Oh Jesus, Lyla. Stop acting like a child! I'm not firing you. I have a business to run and my reputation is important. However, since I'm not sure that you understand what is at stake for me, you are on probation for a week."

"That's not fair." Lyla had always gotten top reviews in any job she'd held.

"I have exacting standards because our patrons have high expectations. One week probation—and the date with Nathaniel better reap great compliments." The madam left the bathroom.

Lyla, still wrapped in her towel, realized that *she* wasn't important to anyone unless she did what they expected of her. She swiped some steam from the mirror and studied her image. Were those shadows under her eyes? Her face was too thin. Not good enough. *I've lost all control of my life. And I don't know how to get it back. Aksel is the only one who truly loves me for me—whoever that might be…*

⊷═◉═⊷

Aksel kissed Leah good-bye after class on Thursday and rushed off to G Squared. He was excited to see Grant and Ginger after their absence.

Sue greeted Aksel in a jovial mood, and then gestured over her shoulder. "They are in Mrs. Robinson's office."

He grinned and rushed by Sue's desk, entering with a knock. "Welcome home. How was your holiday?"

Ginger looked up from something she'd been reviewing. "*Fantastique*, Aksel!" She stood and hugged him warmly.

Grant shook Aksel's hand and gave him a slap on the back.

"Please, tell me what you think of my performance in your absence. Was everything up to your expectation?"

"Well, we're still playing catch up with a few things but nothing serious. And yes, you did an outstanding job.

Thank you, Aksel," Ginger replied with a radiant smile as she sat back down and tapped a pile of papers. "I need to make a few phone calls, gentlemen."

"And that, son, is our cue to leave," Grant said. "Let's go to my office and look at the latest shipping reports together. I would like your input on a few things." Grant slipped his arm around Aksel's shoulders in a fatherly manner. They reviewed some paperwork for an hour and found themselves finally just shooting the shit.

Grant suddenly stopped talking about fashion trends to study Aksel's face, then smiled coyly. "Hmmm. Are you the same young man who I saw last week? There's something different about you," he observed.

Aksel looked down and blushed.

"Ah, I see," Grant continued. "Okay, who is she?"

"You are quite astute." Aksel sat so he was on the edge of his seat. "Her name is Leah. She is beautiful and smart. And so funny!"

"When do we get to meet her?"

Was it too soon to introduce Leah around? He wanted to be happy, and she could be the one. "Saturday evening at the charity event."

Grant clapped his hands. "Well, that's fantastic. I can't wait."

Just then Ginger walked into his office with a grim expression. "Sorry for interrupting, boys. Grant, could I see you for a moment?"

"We'll catch up some more later," Grant assured him before joining Ginger.

"*Monsieur, Madame*, I just wanted to remind you that tomorrow I will not be here due to finals next week." He noticed the somber look on Ginger's face and hoped it wasn't something major, like an issue with Lyla. His senses were on high alert.

"Right, Aksel. No problem." Grant barely acknowledged him. Aksel watched them head back to Ginger's office. "What's wrong, Gin?"

"I called Andrew," he overheard Ginger say.

"Okay. Not good?" Grant's voice sounded tense. They went into Ginger's office, but they didn't close the door completely. Unable to help himself, Aksel quietly moved closer to listen to their conversation.

"You don't know the half of it, my love. Is it too early for a drink?" Ginger must have started to cry as he heard her blow her nose. Aksel hated to eavesdrop, but if this was about Lyla, he had to know.

The minibar door opened and closed as two beers were opened. "Here you are, love. What's going on?" Ginger started ranting but Grant cut her off and half-heartedly laughed, "Jesus Christ, slowdown. Should I hide the scissors?" One of the things he loved about Grant and Ginger's relationship was how Grant could lighten Ginger's rare bad mood, and Ginger did the same for Grant. They were true partners. Aksel stepped back to leave them alone.

"Lyla isn't working at Andrew's any longer," she said.

He froze.

"Okay. Well, we knew that it was only temporary. Why did she leave?"

"The reason she gave Andrew was that she's too busy with school and her modeling side jobs."

Modeling? That would be a stretch for what Lyla was doing, Aksel thought. He inched closer to Ginger's door.

"Well, that's good, right?"

"Well," there was a pause as Ginger took a long swig from the beer bottle, the glass bottom smacking down against the wood top of her desk. "I called Debbie at Barbizon. She said that whatever Lyla's doing as a model isn't through the school like she told Andrew."

"Why am I not surprised? But why are you so—"

"There's more, Grant. She hasn't even been going to school. Debbie checked her attendance records. It's been almost a month since Lyla attended classes. I called Lyla's apartment but got the machine. The outgoing message has been changed since Thanksgiving."

Aksel heard Grant sigh, and felt his pain. "She's staying with Sarah, right? Maybe Andrew has her address. We can go check up on her, make sure she's okay."

"No, no I already asked. He doesn't have Sarah's current address on file. She didn't quit; she just didn't show up again. Ever. He's going to check with the other employees and let me know if he hears anything about her."

Grant sounded incredulous. "So, we have no way to find Lyla?"

Aksel had to be a part of this conversation, and maybe offer his assistance. He'd promised Lyla not to mention her hospital stay, but she must not understand how much she was hurting the people who cared about her. He knocked on the door. It creaked open a few inches and Aksel peeked in.

"Sorry to interrupt, but I have a question about a shipping order."

"Sure, Aksel." Grant turned to Ginger. "Gin, I need to take a mental break from—well, I'll be back to help you with the next calls in a few minutes."

"Okay, babe." She swiped her cheeks with a tissue from the box on her desk.

"*Monsieur, Madame*, is everything okay?" Aksel fully stepped into the office, hoping for more information even as he wished to ease their worry.

"We don't know yet, Aksel," Grant said.

"Is it anything I can help with?"

"Thank you, but there's nothing you can do," Grant said sadly.

"It's—it's about Lyla," Ginger explained, holding Aksel's gaze as if to acknowledge that he and Lyla had once cared for each other. "She's sort of disappeared. She quit her job at The Nue and hasn't been attending classes. We don't know where she lives, we don't know where she works, if anywhere."

"I am trying to ignore the pit in my gut," Grant said, "but I feel like something is wrong. Really wrong."

Aksel remained quiet. He knew where Lyla's apartment was, but he couldn't betray her trust.

"I am sorry. I am sure she is alive and well, though." He patted Grant's shoulder. "Do not worry about the order. I will take care of it."

Aksel walked out of Ginger's office, then headed straight for the elevator—he would check on Lyla immediately. He hailed a cab on Broadway to Lyla's apartment building. He ran up the steps, but before he could ring her apartment, Wally opened the door. The doorman stepped out close to Aksel, forcing him off the landing onto the top step.

"Hey, French Fry, you ain't supposed to be here. Lyla don't wanna see your dumb ass."

Blood rushed to Aksel's face at the threat—but this wasn't about him so he kept his temper in check. "Fine. But please give her a message."

Wally crossed his arms. "Nope."

Aksel lifted his fist. "If you give the tiniest shit about her, then you should tell her to reach out to her father. He's worried about her."

"Go fuck yourself. And don't come back, 'cause next time, I ain't gonna be so nice."

Wally slammed the door.

⊷⊶

Lyla was in her bedroom when she heard her apartment door open and shut. Then she heard rustling in the kitchen—glasses clinking, cabinet doors shutting, low grunts. Her eyes widened. *Holy shit, am I being robbed?* She grabbed the bat she kept by her bed and crept down the hallway. When she peeked around the corner, she saw Wally sitting on the couch.

He stuffed his hand into a bag of chips, pulled out a handful, and crammed the whole thing into his mouth with crumbs falling around him on the couch. She was pretty sure he didn't chew, either. She silently watched as he licked his greasy paws and then wiped them on one of her couch pillows.

She dropped the bat and jumped out from around the corner. "What the fuck, Wally!"

He turned to her and lifted the bag. "Chip?"

"What are you doing in here? You can't just show up and walk in whenever you want! I'm gonna call Slim! This isn't what I agreed to. I deserve some privacy, for fuck's sake!"

"Siddown and shuddup," he said. He had a strange look on his face.

"No. This is *my* space, and you're intruding."

"Oh, now I'm a fucking intruder?" He chuckled. "I think your Frenchie is the intruder, bitch."

"What are you talking about? He knows to stay away." Anger filled her voice.

"That's what I told him. A few minutes ago. At the front door of the building."

"Oh, fuck. Why was he here?" Her anger swiftly switched gears to anxiety. Had Wally hurt Aksel, or threatened him?

Wally shrugged, then crinkled the empty bag into a ball and tossed it to the floor. "I suppose to see yooz. Wonder what Slim will think though, eh?"

"Don't tell him. Please." Lyla feared for Aksel's safety.

He leaned back, stretched his legs, and put his hands behind his head. "Why wouldn't I?"

"What do you want?" She would do anything to protect Aksel and just hoped it wouldn't be a physical expectation.

"I'll make a deal with you, doll face. I won't say nothing to the big boss if you fork over a couple hundred in cash and some of the good stuff from your bag over there."

"What? You're going to blackmail me?" Lyla glared at him with her hands on her hips but caught herself.

"Yeah, I guess so. Deal? If not, I make the call."

"Whatever. Take what you want." She threw the bag at him and tossed a wad of cash on the floor. "Now get the fuck out!"

⊷═◎═⊶

An hour later, Lyla's phone rang, and the machine picked up. She was not surprised to hear Aksel's voice. "Lyla, I do not wish to bother you, but you should contact your father. He is—"

She grabbed the phone.

"Aksel, I told you not to come by here or call me."

"I would not have, but your father is worried."

"Just my father?" Her tone softened.

"Look, Lyla, you no longer wish to be friends, and I respect that. But your father is running around like a crazy man looking for you. He needs to know you're alive and well."

"I'll call him. Thanks."

She hung up and then listened to the recorded conversation over and over. His voice sounded different…callous almost.

"Great, just fucking great. Now even he doesn't give a shit about me. It's all for my father—Grant." She held Misty close and kissed her furry face. "At least *you* still love me."

Tears rolled down her cheeks and she reached for her magic box to get as high as she could; it was all she wanted to do when it came to dealing with her life.

Chapter 40

Lyla woke up to Misty's purr, the kitten cuddled against her chest, sound asleep. She rubbed Misty's chin. "Good morning, sleepy girl." Misty yawned and stretched. "Spare me the stare. I suppose you want some breakfast?"

She fed Misty and made herself the newly named ZeZe Zippee, formerly known as the Rah Rah Cocktail, before curling up on the couch in the sun-filled living room. She sipped her drink while gathering herself for the dreaded call she had to make to Grant whom she hadn't talked to since the night in the limo.

Misty was on the floor batting a toy ball without a care in the world. *I just want to be a little girl again when life was simpler, playing in Central Park on the swings…playing hide and seek with my dad the dragon slayer who would search for me in my make-believe dark forest. I always knew he would find me and bring me home. Reading a bedtime story filled with fairies and magical spells where happily ever after was the only ending. And here I sit afraid for Aksel and my family with no magical fairy dust left, only drugs to give me relief from the pain.* She got up and made herself another ZeZe Zippee before returning to the couch. Feeling sufficiently high enough she dialed his office number.

"G Squared. How may I direct your call?" Sue said in a crisp, cheery voice.

"Grant Robinson, please."

"One minute, please. Who should I say is calling?"

"Lyla."

"Oh, hi Lyla. Hang on." She was put on hold, and a melody version of "Here Comes the Sun" by the Beatles played over the line. High, she hummed along to the tune.

The music stopped and then Grant said, "Lyla?"

"Hi, Grant. How was your trip?"

He immediately placed the call on speaker. "I'm putting you on speaker, so Ginger and I can both hear you."

"Okay." She bit her lower lip, feeling anxious.

"Lyla?"

"Yes, I'm here. Hi, Gin." Lyla somehow kept her emotions in check.

"Hi honey, thank you for calling," Ginger said. Her lovely smile was reflected in her caring voice. "We've been concerned about you."

"I'm fine," Lyla said, hoping to mask any of her sadness from them.

"Lyla, what's going on with you?" Grant jumped in with both feet. "Andrew said you left the restaurant, and we know you haven't been going to school…"

His slight rant caused her to go into a defensive mode which was better than feeling bad. "Per usual you've been checking on me. What is it with everyone?"

Grant said, "Lyla, allow me to explain—"

"Explain why everyone needs to check on me? Listen, I am *alive and well.* That's really all you need to know. You have my number and can call anytime you want but I'm not always here so leave a message."

"Oh!" Ginger gasped.

"Where *are* you working? And what *happened to Sarah?* I thought you two were roommates? Why haven't you used my card?" Grant's questions continued to feel like bullets.

"You know what, Grant? Stop!" Lyla screamed as her anger totally took over and she slammed the phone down, causing Misty to run for cover.

--→≡◯≡←--

"Alive and well?" Grant growled. "Those were the exact words that Aksel said yesterday. She's alive...but *well?*"

Ginger rubbed his back. "Grant, honey, she's well enough to *still be her sassy self.* That's something, isn't it?" Ginger's voice sounded raspy. "She's still mad that—"

"She's mad?" He moved away from her coldly. "I'm furious! *"*

"Calm down, Grant."

Grant's face was hot. "Don't tell *me* to calm down. She's my daughter and acting like an ass!"

"Oh, I see. You don't think I consider her my daughter as well?" Ginger countered. "You need to control that temper of yours before you respond and attack her. Or me."

Ginger stormed out of the office, slamming the door behind her.

--→≡◯≡←--

"Fuck you, Grant!" Lyla threw the phone, then shot it the middle finger. "You're not even my father! I just happen to have your last name because my mother was nothing more than a fucking whore…just like me…at least I get paid. And the worst part is, I miss you Dad—Grant." She began to cry while curling up on the couch in a fetal position.

"I'm trapped! I'm sure the car bomb was really Slim's way of getting rid of Sarah…I can't go back to Grant and Ginger, and who I really want to be with is Aksel! I'm so fucked!" When she got out the blue box of drugs she realized how low her supply was getting. She grabbed the gift bag Candy had given her realizing that Wally had taken a large amount of the bag. Lyla emptied her last ecstasy capsule into her mouth.

She spoke aloud to an empty room.

"I'm not getting as high as I used to… I need more." She swept through the apartment for any remaining drugs and laughed with relief when she found Sarah's secret stash under the sink in the bathroom in a plastic container. "Fuck you, Wally!"

She picked up the phone and called the club. Candy answered.

"Candy, can you tell Slim I need new shoes?" That was the secret phrase she was supposed to use over the phone when she needed more drugs.

"What size, honey?"

"Eight. A couple pairs of eights."

"You wore out your shoes already? That's a bit fast, baby."

"My brother's back in town. Been doing a lot of…walking. Do I really have to say more than that?"

"No, of course not. But be careful, you gotta big date tomorrow night. I'll have one of the boys drop your shoes off with Wally."

"*No!* I mean, I really don't want him to know *that* much of my business. Can I meet you at the Rainbow Coffee Shop?"

"About half hour okay? I'm not going to tell Slim, so be careful."

"That works—see you then. You're the best."

⇥═◦═⇤

Ginger understood Grant's emotional state but needed space of her own to figure out the best way to deal with him and Lyla.

I feel like a tennis net that keeps getting hit with balls served from both sides. She layered her body for the freezing temperature outside that night. Grant was sitting on the couch in the living room having a drink.

"Grant, I need a little fresh air. I'm going to go for a walk."

"Okay, give me a second to grab my jacket and boots." He jumped up from the couch and walked toward the foyer.

She waited by the open door. "Babe, I need some alone time."

"Gin, I am sorry about all this shit with—"

She cut him off. "I know. But everyone needs to have some space from time to time. I need my own right now."

"You're really upset with me, huh?" He looked down, his guilt for how he'd treated her evident in his slumped shoulders. "You've never asked me for alone time."

"Haven't I? Please don't worry. Just let me be, okay?" Her smile faltered. She desperately needed her own space before she lost her mind. She shot him a quick half-hearted smile and left.

Outside, Ginger inhaled the cool night air, letting it fill her brain. She walked along Amsterdam Avenue as the holiday traffic flew by. When she got to West 66th Street she found a small wall to sit on as she attempted to release the negative energy that consumed her. In her pocket was the Egyptian amulet that had been in the cigar box in England—it had once been given to Tommy. She closed her eyes, focusing on the amulet in her hand, and whispered, "Do you really care and protect?"

Eyes shut, she held it up in the air. A voice said, "Stop it, Ginger." Her eyes sprung open as she looked to see who had spoken, but no one was near her.

"God, I'm losing it." She placed the amulet in her pocket and checked her watch; it was 9:45. Somehow, she felt more lighthearted, and definitely cold…it was time to get back to the love of her life. A quicker route home was to take 70th Street to their apartment on West 68th Street. The walk relaxed her, and her mental fog began to clear…

If there is something that could help me understand what's going on and how to fix it, please give me a sign. She ran her finger over the curved loop of the ankh in her pocket. *Can you hear me?* Ginger appealed to the Powers That Be—the same powers of the cosmos that had brought Grant into her world.

Passing the playground next to an elementary school, a black Town Car shot up the road and came to an abrupt stop on the far side of the street. Why was it going so fast? Kids played around here. Ginger was walking toward the car when a woman stepped out of the vehicle and began to cross the street. Ginger stopped midstride—it was Lyla, wearing a blonde wig.

Lyla, oblivious to anyone around her, strutted across the street, stepping onto the sidewalk like she owned the city, clad in a rhinestone-fringed full-length wool coat— Ginger knew for sure it was Lyla, because that one-of-a-kind wool coat had once belonged to Ginger. Lyla paused before an exclusive building entrance right in front of her.

The way the doorman greeted her sent chills through Ginger's body—chills that instantly reminded her of the past. Having been a model in her younger years, she'd pushed away the unwanted memories of the many offers to be a gentleman's escort. And all of a sudden in a flash, everything became clear to her—Lyla's disappearance, her attitude, her loss of appetite.

Before she could think twice she blurted, "Lyla!"

Lyla turned, saw Ginger approaching, and said to the doorman, "This will just take a moment, Fritz."

"Oh, my gosh." It was such a relief to see her. "Look at you, Lyla," Ginger said, trying to catch her breath from almost running.

Lyla stood within inches of Ginger's frosty breath. "Please close your mouth. You're embarrassing me."

"Excuse me?" Ginger said, stunned at Lyla's words.

"Look, now is not a good time for a conversation. You need to leave me alone."

Ginger couldn't walk away, no matter how angry Lyla got. "Now is absolutely the best time for a conversation. What are you doing?"

"Give me a break, Gin." Lyla's chin lifted defiantly. "You were just like me once upon a time, so don't judge me."

"I-I'm not judging you." Blood rushed to her face as her fists clenched.

"The look in your eyes says otherwise."

"Lyla!" She didn't want this to get ugly, but Lyla wasn't backing down.

"Well, now that you know, we can drop the pretenses. We're more alike than you think. I mean, let's be honest with each other… Isn't that why you married Grant? So, you could live the life you live? You just don't want to admit it."

"What the fuck are you talking about?"

"How about the truth for once, *Mommy Gin.*" Lyla rolled her eyes.

"I love your dad." Ginger lowered her hands, feeling as fierce as a tiger ready to pounce.

"God! No one can admit the truth… Just like my mother, that fucking lying whore. Would you really have married Grant if he was still some unknown farm boy from the Midwest and not a wealthy Midtown Manhattan asshole?"

"Of course I would have married him!" Ginger leaned forward as her anger reached a boiling point. Lyla had no idea what she was talking about, and it hurt Ginger to hear her talk like this.

"Oh, bullshit!"

"Lyla, his money never meant anything to me. And our success is a team effort."

Lyla scoffed. "Again, bullshit! So, I suppose you'll report to him as soon as you get home, won't you?" Lyla gave her a disgusted look.

"As a matter of fact, NO! THIS, my dear, is between you and me."

"Are you saying you passed on good opportunities when you were modeling?"

"Jesus, Lyla!" Ginger's body tensed. "Quit being a little bitch and listen! Have you really forgotten that I've kept all your secrets? And yes, I've been down this path, but surprise, I passed it up, so I could look in the mirror and like my reflection."

Before Lyla could respond, Ginger wrapped her arms around the girl she considered a daughter and whispered into her ear, "Be safe and smart. Your father has something important to tell you, if you'll listen to him. But remember, you can always trust me. And no matter what happens, I love you."

Ginger left before she said something she might regret.

Zinged by Ginger's words, Lyla watched her walk away; but held her own head high, and wiped a tear from her eye. She took a deep breath, refocused, and turned back to the doorman.

"Sorry about that. She's...somebody I used to know." She handed the doorman a fifty-dollar tip hoping she bought his silence.

Chapter 41

The study group always met at Caffe Reggio a few blocks from NYU. The aroma of coffee and food flooded the air of the quaint 1920s Italian restaurant. Aksel and Leah kept exchanging glances throughout the session. Their attraction to each other was unmistakable—even to the members of their study group. Once the group had covered everything for the finals, they all quickly dispersed, leaving only the two of them at the table.

Leah sighed with relief as she gathered her books. "Finally." She hooked her arm around his, pulling him in for an unexpected kiss. "I'm so excited about tomorrow night," she said. "I can hardly wait to spend an evening with you."

"Would you like to go to my place for a bite to eat?" he asked, his voice deep with anticipation.

Her eyes brightened as a smile filled her face. "Let me call my parents and tell them I'll be later than usual."

⁘

Aksel felt close to Leah throughout the whole meal—watching how her lips moved, the way she said words. They were on their second bottle of red wine when they moved to the couch. Empty cartons, half-eaten fortune cookies, and chopsticks lay on the table. When he started to clear the table, she assisted him, and he couldn't stop from watching the way her ass swayed.

"I have a nice buzz from the wine," Leah murmured when she returned to the comfort of the couch, where she stretched out as he added another log to the waning embers in the fire place.

"Would you like a blanket and some music? Unless you need to go?" He fixed his gaze on her attempting to read her thoughts by her facial expression.

"I think you can keep me warm enough." Then she sang softly, "Baby, it's cold outside."

"I might not let you go then." He slid her close and kissed her. Their physical attraction blazed with each caress.

"You are so handsome, Aksel." She flicked her tongue across his lower lip, a naughty grin on her face.

"And you are so beautiful, *ma cherie.*"

She blushed, then reached over him, pressing her breasts against him as she lifted her wine for another a sip.

Aksel gave her a tender kiss that morphed into heated passion. Before they knew it, they were on the floor with clothes flying in every direction. Leah, naked, straddled him with her body pressing against his groin.

"Are you sure you want me?" He attempted to gain control of their carnal desire that was as hot as the fire crackling in the fire place.

"You have no idea how long I've wanted you!"

He gently rolled her onto her back, slid between her spread legs, and began to eat her wet lips. She moaned with pleasure, having an instantaneous climax, as she pulled his head to the apex of her thighs. After a while, Aksel removed his boxer briefs, revealing his thick erection and gently slid his cock all the way into her.

Aksel's cock had reached the deepest part of Leah's pussy as she had yet another orgasm. Each time he thought he felt the beginning sensation of his own orgasm starting to build, it would quickly disappear. Over the next few hours that were filled with sensuous pleasure she had climbed on top of him, and rode him feverishly, till she cried out, "Yes, Aksel! Yes!"

It didn't matter how much he pleased her physically, his own pleasure was interrupted by thoughts of Lyla. He finally reached his ultimate sensual peak when he closed his eyes and pictured Lyla's naked body from behind.

"Yes, Aksel, fill me! Oh, God, baby!" Leah continued her sexual rhythm as he finally exploded inside of her.

Lying side by side and out of breath, Leah panted, "*Monsieur,* you are *magnifique.* We are *magnifique* together."

Aksel hesitated before responding, "*Fantastique, ma chérie.*"

It was almost eleven when he walked Leah to the cab he had called for her.

"Tomorrow, you will ride in style," he told her. "I'll pick you up around eight?"

"Sounds good, Aksel. Tonight was… magical." She tilted her head back and he kissed her.

"*Oui.* I look forward to tomorrow."

She slid into the cab and he gave her another kiss through the open window, then knocked on the roof of the car. He waved as her cab drove out of sight into the cold night and he slowly climbed the stairs to the sixth floor.

Once inside his apartment, he spoke aloud, "Dammit, Lyla. Will I ever be free of you?"

He opened the freezer and filled a tumbler full of ice and topped it off with vodka. With each sip, the reality became unbearable. He finally admitted to himself what he hoped he'd kept hidden from Leah. "Lyla, you really are the love of my life!" He dozed on the couch.

⭒

Lyla arrived home from the brothel still high from the drugs she had consumed. She scooped up Misty and crawled into bed. Ginger's words rattled around in her head—but Lyla couldn't accept that Ginger really cared. After swallowing a couple of sleeping pills, she closed her eyes and fell asleep.

Lyla and Aksel drifted off into their respective sleep and began to dream, a dream that intertwined into one:

Aksel said he found something new for us to play with. His voice was so sultry and thick when he explained what he is going to do to me tonight. I'm nervous about his size fitting inside me! He promised that with plenty of prepping from his tongue and fingers, I will be fine...

-

The sex we have had has been more than I ever expected, although I knew it would be amazing with Lyla. I just did not know how amazing! Each time we are together, I come undone in earth-shattering, mind-blowing orgasms. She is so sensual that she has unleashed a sexual desire I only hoped one day I would get to feel.

-

He treats my body to the most erotic sexual positions—he brings me to tears with pleasure.

-

I need her like water…

-

I need him like air…

-

We are so perfectly matched that when we are apart, I feel lost. I am completely addicted to her.

-

I want no one else, only him. I just wish he wanted me as much as I want him—however, whenever, wherever. Forever.

⋆═◉═⋆

Late Saturday morning Lyla opened her eyes. Her heart felt heavier than ever before. Misty was curled up into a ball right next to her head. Lyla scratched Misty's ears, which woke the kitten from her slumber. "If I'm awake, you should be too," she said.

Her mind shifted to Ginger... *She really does love me. And what is it that Grant has to say that's so important? Probably some bullshit to try to convince me that he's my father. Short of something signed in blood proving it, it's easier to accept that Howard Golden is my dead biological father.*

She left her warm bed, fed her kitten, and prepared a ZeZe Zippee with her updated stash. Once Lyla curled up on the couch in her bathrobe, Misty jumped onto her lap. In her sweetest voice she said, "I love you! Yes, I do!" Suddenly the rest of her night filled her head—a myriad of dreams starring Aksel.

"Misty, he's a mongrel! I wish I could let him go. Never get mixed up with one of his kind! They consume you—even your subconscious—even when you push them away to protect them. Just remember: Boys are trouble, okay?" She gently kissed Misty's nose.

⤙⟶⊚⟵⤚

Aksel awoke on the couch and quickly hopped in the shower to start his preparation for the holiday party. He had to coordinate the car and driver, go buy the bubbly, and do some clothes shopping. But he couldn't keep Lyla out of his mind. *It was only a dream.* Warm water washed away Lyla, a memory from their past. *She no longer wants me in her life, and I must respect that. But I need to focus on my own happiness, and that now involves Leah…*

Finally clearing his head, he dialed Grant's home number. "Good afternoon, *Monsieur* Grant. I appreciate the extra time to study for my finals."

"Of course, Aksel," he replied. "Studies are important. We will see you tonight, *oui?*"

"*Oui.*"

"And we look forward to meeting this woman who has brought happiness back into your life."

"*Oui*, if I have not scared her off already." He gave an uncertain laugh.

Chapter 42

It was late Saturday afternoon and Lyla had arrived early at the brothel to get ready to be Nathaniel's escort to the ball. She'd secluded herself in one of the brothel's private dressing rooms as she attempted to quiet her nerves about being on probation before the event. She gave her image a critical eye—was her face too puffy? Lyla was startled when the madam entered.

Janice walked past her to inspect the light blue gown Lyla had selected from the brothel house garments. "This is the one you picked?" Lyla immediately felt like a stupid child.

"Yes, it's beautiful. I can't…" She'd thought to wear something understated.

The madam cut her off with a slash of her hand through the air. "This is your first appearance beyond these walls, Lyla. Are you prepared? Remember, no one can know that you are his paid escort—or in my employ."

"Yes, of course, Madam."

Janice strode purposely to the rack of clothing in the room. "I would prefer if you wore this one." She pulled out a garment from a row of designer evening gowns. It sparkled from shoulder to toe. "And these shoes."

Lyla looked up through her lashes and excitedly replied, "I love it. Thank you."

"Remember, tonight is not about you, it's about *who you are with*. You will be on the arm of the mayor's grandson. Photos will be taken." Janice lifted her finger in the air. "I repeat! No one can know that you are an escort! You must blend in. Give him your attention but be charismatic and kind to other guests," she instructed in a severe tone.

"I won't let you down." Lyla's lips quivered—she was not use to failing.

"See that you don't. I have prepared a list of names with some photos of the guests, and information about them. Memorize the details, remember their faces, because some are important clientele. Do not get high even if you are given the opportunity. You need to be able to think your way out of any situation. Fall on your face and that will be the end of you with me." Janice stood with her hands on her hips, her eyes cold.

Lyla's fear stopped her from responding.

"You received raving reviews last night," Janice said. "However, I expect nothing but *perfection* tonight." The madam turned to leave but stopped and looked back over her shoulder. "I know you came from a wealthy family, and you can do this, my little dove. Remember that you were handpicked..." She waited in the open door. "Which reminds me, before you leave, stop by my office so that I can approve your appearance. I might have something special for you."

⊷═◉═⊷

Aksel promptly arrived at eight p.m. at Leah's parents' Upper East Side brownstone home on East 86th Street, near Park Avenue. She answered the door and invited him in. He was relieved that her parents were not home—he wasn't ready for that just yet.

She was dressed in a Christian Dior deep-blue gown and matching shoes. Aksel was used to seeing her in casual wear at school, but now he could not take his eyes off her.

"You are stunning, *ma chérie*." He assisted her with her wrap and overcoat, then walked her down the steps to the Town Car. Settling next to her in limo, he pulled out a chilled bottle of rosé champagne and popped the cork.

"If I didn't know better," she said with a giggle as he poured her a flute, "I might think you are trying to get lucky tonight. A Town Car and rose champagne? You are a very naughty fellow, Aksel. Making a woman's head spin is unfair. Please pinch me so I can wake up from my little girl's dream of being Cinderella!"

"*Mademoiselle,* all I have done is listened to you and remembered what you said. Can I be blamed for anything else?" It pleasured him to see how happy he'd made her.

"You are too much, *monsieur!* I feel like a real princess."

She kissed him intimately. Halfway through their kiss, thoughts of Lyla swirled into his head. He pushed them away, admonishing himself mentally to stay focused on Leah.

They pulled up to the brand new Marriott Marquis, a thirty-eight-story building in Times Square. Their driver opened the car door for them, and they walked into the hotel's massive lobby. Its ceiling was eight stories high, and the whole area decked with red, green, and gold Christmas decorations. A huge Christmas tree sparkled in the center of the lobby and the sounds of music, laughter and conversation permeated the air.

The main event was in the Broadway Ballroom. They entered the room while multiple camera lights flashed as photographers took pictures of couples entering the gala. The Manhattan Orchestra music filled the air with a saxophone, clarinet and piano version of "Santa's Coming to Town." Countless servers in red blazers, black pants, white bow-ties and matching white gloves walked around serving hors d'oeuvres and champagne. The room and everyone in it sparkled under the glow of the crystal chandeliers above.

Aksel could tell the gala was more glamorous than Leah had expected. Her fingers trembled slightly as she handed her full-length wool coat to Aksel to check, keeping her shoulder wrap and small silver clutch with her. Aksel checked his own overcoat and adjusted his Ralph Lauren tuxedo jacket, then put his arm out for her to hold as they entered the festivities.

He was almost immediately greeted by a multitude of acquaintances, a few times speaking in French. Leah, he noticed, was trying to act as if she wasn't overwhelmed with all the glitz and glamour as he introduced her to different prestigious people. Aksel eventually spotted Grant and Ginger amid the crowd and whispered to her, "There's Ginger and Grant. They are like family to me."

He clasped her slender hand and realized it was clammy. He grabbed two champagnes from a server and turned to her as he handed her the flute. "Leah, relax." He toasted her. "And enjoy, because under all this glitter they are all people just like us, having fun." He kissed her cheek and was rewarded with a soft smile.

When Aksel introduced Grant and Ginger to Leah he saw that she was still overwhelmed as she half-curtsied before shaking hands. Both Grant and Ginger exuded class and style individually; looking at them together you saw how awesome of a couple they were—*the* power couple of the night.

"Leah, so nice to meet you. Your dress is astounding," Ginger said with warmth in her voice.

Aksel was proud to call them friends. Grant was extremely handsome in his Christian Dior tuxedo, and Ginger was stunning in her Yves St. Laurent deep-emerald-green velvet gown. The slit on her left leg reached her upper thigh, showcasing her physique. Random crystals sparkled across her flawless figure. The satin bow on the back of her gown matched the mini bows on her stilettos. A Judith Leiber full-beaded green-and-silver crystal bag and black opera gloves completed her look. Her auburn hair in a half-sweep up-do had floating crystals.

After the introductions, the two couples fell into comfortable conversation. Then Grant's attention turned to something—or someone—beyond them. He lost focus on the conversation with Aksel and Leah, leaned into Ginger and whispered, "Look who's here." He nodded toward the winding staircase.

Aksel turned to where Grant was looking as Lyla walked hand-in-arm down the staircase. She was wearing a deep V-neck, skin-toned gown with matching stilettos and a sparkling sapphire-blue clutch. The sporadically placed embroidered stones cast flashes of light with her every movement. Diamonds and sapphires draped from her lobes with a matching inverted heart-shaped necklace.

"Just look at her," Grant said. "She's gorgeous. And isn't that the mayor's grandson?"

"It is," Ginger whispered softly. "Nathaniel."

"They met at the White Party last summer, right?" Grant's voice shook and Aksel guessed he must be in shock at seeing his daughter here. Aksel sure was.

"Pardon me for a moment," Grant said to Aksel and Leah, kissing Ginger on the cheek.

Before he took his first step, Ginger grabbed his arm and he spun around.

"I'm sorry," Grant said. "Did you want to come with me?"

She spoke in a low tone, "No, I'll stay with Aksel and Leah. Please be sweet, Mr. Robinson."

Lyla. Aksel's breathing hitched as his heart raced faster and faster. He observed paparazzi crowding around the couple who were engaged in laughter and kisses. *My gorgeous Lyla…on the arm of another.* Jealousy simmered in his heart.

"Aksel, are you okay? You look like you've seen a ghost." Leah studied him with concern.

"No, yes." He stammered, "I-I need a drink. Let's go to the bar."

Leah put her hand on his arm and looked at Ginger. "Would you like to join us for a drink, Ginger?"

"Thank you, Leah, but no. I'll wait here for Grant."

Aksel and Leah made their way to the bar in silence. He stopped and turned to Leah, but positioned himself at the bar so that he could be in full view of Lyla. He waited for Lyla to look in his direction long enough to notice him, and when she did, he kissed Leah passionately.

He didn't know if she had watched, but the kiss was hot, and he *almost* forgot all about Lyla…

⊷⊷⊷

Lyla gritted her teeth, seeing the kiss. She was sure Aksel had glared at her before planting that not-so-subtle-kiss on his date—and it looked hot! Lyla hoped that Aksel saw her retaliate by kissing Nathaniel. "After so many photos, I believe we deserve something stronger than champagne." She wanted to taunt Aksel by going to the bar with Nathaniel at her side.

"You betcha. I haven't had my picture taken this much since the White Party."

"We met at the White Party, Nathaniel. Remember that's when we started secretly dating?"

"Yes, dear." His tone held a teasing note in it.

Lyla noticed Grant heading in their direction and was grateful when he got sidetracked by a couple who wanted to socialize with him; she quickly slipped passed him with Nathaniel in tow.

⊷⟝⊜⟞⊶

With drinks in hand, Aksel purposely guided Leah within earshot of where Lyla stood with Nathaniel at the bar. He noticed Lyla eyeing him briefly as she ordered two martinis. She lifted hers up in a toast and glanced at him to acknowledge his presence but then looked through him as if he was invisible to her. Nathaniel whispered something in her ear to which she giggled, kissed him, and started to walk away, Nathaniel's hand resting just above her ass on her lower back.

Watching her display of affection, his jealousy finally reached its boiling point and Aksel couldn't pass up the opportunity to make Lyla feel uncomfortable.

"Lyla?" He spoke loud enough to turn some heads.

Both Lyla and Nathaniel stopped and turned around.

"Lyla, it *is* you! Ah, you look *magnifique!* It feels like forever since we saw each other last. Good to see you are alive and well." He sauntered over and kissed her on the cheek.

Lyla played off the ruse. "Nathaniel, darling, this is Mr. Aksel Portier. He's an *old family acquaintance.*"

The men shook hands, but Aksel didn't look away from Lyla, heightening the tension.

⋆═◉═⋆

Leah sensed that something was wrong, and it was hard for her to dismiss how similar she and Lyla looked. She glided toward them to introduce herself. "Lyla, Nathaniel, hello. My name is Leah." She paused for a brief second. "Leah Skyberger. It is such a pleasure to meet you both."

"It's a pleasure to meet you." Lyla eyed her up and down and turned to Aksel with a smirk. Nathaniel, who was drunk already, chuckled. "Leah Skyberger? That's awful close to Leia Skywalker." He kissed her knuckles.

Leah shrugged.

"Sounds like a wannabe starlet's name to me," Lyla said. "Shall we, darling?" Lyla took Nathaniel's hand and smiled at Aksel. "Have a lovely evening," she said sweetly to Leah but rolled her eyes at Aksel.

Nathaniel didn't move until Lyla whispered something in his ear. Then his eyes widened, and he flashed

451

a wicked grin. "Good evening." He nodded to Aksel and Leah.

"An old family friend, huh?" Leah watched the gorgeous, yet arrogant, couple walk off. "With friends like that, who needs—"

Aksel lashed out in uncharacteristic anger. "Do not finish that sentence." Aksel's voice was hoarse and heavy. "*Skyberger*? Why couldn't you have waited at the bar?"

Leah had been having such a wonderful time until that moment. She suddenly felt used and her naïveté fell away as she couldn't believe what was unfolding in front of her. She bit her bottom lip—no way was she going to be treated like she wasn't there.

"Don't you dare, Aksel," she said. "How foolish of me to think I was your *date* tonight and not just a pawn to make another woman jealous!"

Aksel seemed instantly contrite. "No, Leah, let me explain."

"I'm leaving now. Give me my ticket for my coat."

Confusion mixed with guilt across his features and he handed her the ticket. "Please…"

She cut him off and tossed her flute of champagne in his face.

"And don't worry, I can find my way home."

Chapter 43

Aksel stood alone at the bar using a few napkins to wipe off the champagne, feeling like a total idiot for his behavior. He couldn't believe how deeply he had hurt Leah and ordered himself another drink when Ginger sat next to him. "I'll have what he's having," she told the bartender.

"A double Jack on the rocks," he reminded the bartender, then took another sip of his.

"I see you are having the time of your life tonight, just like I am. Those Robinsons can be rough on your heart, can't they?" Ginger commiserated with Aksel as he straightened his bow-tie.

He was about to respond when he was startled by a male voice from behind. *"Those Robinsons?* What do you mean by that?" They were both caught off guard with Grant's stealthy arrival. Ginger and Aksel turned around to face him but neither of them answered his question. Aksel never wanted Grant to know his true feelings for Lyla.

"Bartender, I'll have whatever they're drinking." Grant butted in between them.

"Coming right up, sir." The bartender quickly whisked off like he wanted to avoid the ominous impending conversation.

"Do the two of you know something about the Robinsons that I don't? Let's start with the phrase 'alive and well' regarding my daughter. Then we can go onto the discussion about 'those Robinsons.'" Grant stepped back from the bar, so that he could see both their faces at the same time.

The bartender interrupted them as he placed Grant's whiskey down on the bar. "Sir." He nodded at Grant and left. They all looked at each other and took sips of their drinks. Aksel swallowed and remained quiet along with Ginger, since he didn't know how to reply to Grant.

"What the fuck is going on?" Grant asked under his breath through gritted teeth.

Ginger reached for Grant's arm, finally breaking the silence. "Now is not the time to make a scene, my sweet Grant."

"I don't *feel* like your sweet Grant right now." He pulled his arm away from her hand.

"Nor are you acting like him," Ginger retorted through a tight-lipped smile, her tone defensive.

"Lyla." Grant took another large swig of the deep golden liquid almost draining his glass. "Wait…whose heart is being broken?" He looked back and forth between them.

Aksel cleared his throat. Ginger grabbed Aksel's wrist and pulled him next to her. "Grant, just listen to what I'm saying, now is not the time to sort this out in front of the whole world."

"Well, thank you for reminding me where we are. You both obviously know some things that you don't want to share! What game are you all playing here? What do you know about LYLA?" His voice rose with each word.

"No games, *monsieur.*" Aksel stood up from the bar stool.

"Finally!" Grant clapped his hands together.

"I don't know how to say this, but I am in love with Lyla." It was the last thing he'd wanted to share with Grant, his mentor, his friend—but the last time he'd kept quiet about his feelings, he'd lost Lyla.

"What are you talking about? Since when?" Grant slammed his remaining drink back and held his empty glass up to get the bartender's attention. "Another please!" He looked at Aksel like he had two heads.

Aksel stepped back before answering. How much could he share? "It's complicated. I fell in love with her a few years ago, the summer we spent together here in the city. We dated-"

Grant cut him off. "And you kept that a secret from me? Why?"

Aksel looked down and shook his head. He couldn't tell him about the abortion, not without Lyla's consent.

"I've always treated you like a son, Aksel. Why wouldn't you—wait." He turned to Ginger. "And I suppose you knew all about this?"

"I, well, I—" Ginger's face flushed as the blood raced to her face.

"Unbelievable. I thought there were no secrets between us!" He gulped down his entire drink. "And since you don't want me to make a scene, *my sweet wife*, and *my dear friend* whom I treat *like a son*, why don't you quietly fill me in on how it is that you were both so certain that my daughter is 'alive and well?' As in well-off? How can she afford the dress and jewels she was wearing tonight? Which one of you is supporting her? It has to be one of you since a waitress or a brand new model can't make that kind of income."

"I'm not supporting her, Grant." Ginger finally got a full sentence out.

"Then it's you!" Grant turned to Aksel.

"No, *monsieur.*"

"Well, isn't this just grand? Neither of you will explain how she can be here dressed like royalty. What do you really want from me, Aksel? To learn the family business or bed my daughter behind my back, or both? Merry fucking Christmas to me! When the two of you get your stories straight, send me the memo." Grant stormed off with his empty glass.

"Grant, wait," Ginger attempted to stop him, but Aksel pulled her back.

"Give him some time, *Madame.*"

Ginger sighed.

"If you don't mind me asking," Aksel continued, "You knew about us?"

"Yes."

"How?"

"Lyla."

"Then I must beg for your forgiveness. You see, when we were in Chicago, I…we…"

He looked away from Ginger's face.

"If you are referring to her pregnancy, I know about that too."

He coughed as he almost gagged on his drink. "You do? How long have you known?"

"I knew something was up the first night I saw you both together at Nick's. When I asked her the next day, she fell apart and told me everything. Aksel, she loved you and was devastated that you deserted her. Frankly, before we continue this conversation I need to know *if* you deserted her." Her beauty was magnified as she came to Lyla's defense, Aksel thought, unable to look away from her piercing stare.

"I did not desert her. I even told her that at the Labor Day picnic. But it didn't seem to change her heart." He ripped at a cocktail napkin.

Ginger's crystals shimmered when she shook her head. "I had a feeling there was more to the story, Aksel. I will assume that Margo kept you two apart?"

Aksel nodded. "I shouldn't have let it happen."

"I can't believe I didn't see that sooner," she said. "Aksel, do you know what Lyla's been doing? She's an—"

"Exotic dancer," he said, cutting her off. "Yes, I know."

"Oh, she's more than an exotic dancer." Ginger's eyes didn't release him.

"What do you mean by that, *Madame*?"

"She's a gentleman's escort."

"A what? Are you certain?" His body slumped as guilt filled his heart.

"Trust me. I was…exposed to that life early on in my career as a model. I've seen the signs of it with her, and tonight was all the proof I needed."

"Oh, Lyla what have I done to you?" Aksel hunched over his drink.

They sat there in silence, sipping thoughtfully.

"Are you still in love with her now that you know what she has become? I would understand that this is more than you bargained for." Ginger tilted her head back with pressed lips as she waited for his response.

"I don't care about what she has become or done," he said somberly. "Our love transcends this life."

Ginger perked up. "What did you say?"

"I love her more than you can imagine. I…" He hesitated, then looked into Ginger's eyes. "I have tried to learn to live without her. But it is I who ruined her! It is all my fault and I have tried to make it up to her. I even know why she will not allow herself to trust me. I discovered I let her down in my past…" his voice trailed off and he looked away.

Ginger shifted toward him. "Past? What do you mean you let her down in your past, Aksel?"

"Past. Just the past." He ran his fingers through his thick hair.

Ginger spoke sternly. "Aksel, are you going to be honest with me? If you have any idea how to save her from the self-destructive path she's on, you have to tell me."

"It seems pointless—probably not even realistic." His heart ached with sadness.

"Aksel, are you referring to past lives?" Ginger stared into his face.

"*Madame* Ginger, do you believe that past lives exist?" He suddenly felt very insecure about sharing the subject.

"You have no idea how much," she said, not breaking eye contact with him.

"In therapy, I was regressed. I…" He couldn't quite explain what he knew, and now that he was talking about it aloud, it sounded ridiculous. "You must think I'm insane."

Ginger grabbed his hand. "No, I don't. Tell me."

"Well, I learned that I had wronged her…in a past life, and then again in this one. That may be why it is so hard for her to trust me."

"That's the answer then," Ginger said. "You must explain that to her, convince her of who you are, who you both used to be. It might help bring her back to the reality in this lifetime and save her from being trapped in her past."

Aksel scoffed. "It sounds so unbelievable. And she doesn't listen to me anyway."

She squeezed his fingers. "I never said it'd be easy. But the best things in life, the things worth fighting for, are never easy."

Aksel remained silent, attempting to wrap his head around their conversation.

"Please don't give up," Ginger finally said. "It may save her life. Jesus! I never thought I'd have to worry about her being an expensive call girl."

"And you are certain about that as well?"

Ginger twirled her empty glass. "Yes. Very certain."

"Why do you believe she would listen to me? Obviously, you saw how she treated me tonight."

"Consider this a rescue mission. I once lost a best friend because she gave up hope. I can't live with the thought of losing Lyla."

Aksel stood up and took a deep, centering breath.

"*Madame* Ginger, I love her. We should work together for her sake. I met the people involved with the gentleman's club she works at, and they make me fearful for her safety."

"Probably how she ended up as an escort. I know how it works. So please reach out to her as soon as possible. You may be her only hope."

"How do we tell *Monsieur* Grant, though?"

"*We* don't." Ginger's eyes glittered like her crystals. "I will handle him."

Chapter 44

After hours of sex, drinking, and doing cocaine with Nathaniel, Lyla was lying naked on his king-sized bed overlooking Times Square from the window on the twenty-fifth floor. Emotionally and physically spent, Lyla looked forward to going home and sleeping with her kitten. *At least he made me cum tonight, and I get paid for it!*

Nathaniel returned to the bedroom after taking a shower and stretched out his tall, tan, athletic body, rustling his fingers through his damp dark-brown hair—he could have been a model posing for hair products. Next to her in bed, he pulled her against his toned body. "My God, Lyla.

That was even better than our last time! The madam must have given you lessons." His words were slurred since he was still high.

"Is that supposed to be a compliment?" She sneered at him, irritated by his comment.

"Well, I guess so. You were a newbie when we first fucked." He gave her a tight-lipped smile. "Right?"

Wound up from drugs and the evening's emotional upheaval with Aksel and her doppelganger as his date, she sat straight up. "Fuck you!"

He propped himself on one elbow while looking at her. "It seems to me like you learned what a man really wants, that's all I'm trying to say."

"You're an asshole." She got up to gather her belongings and get dressed.

"Oh, relax. Jesus. What are you getting so worked up over? I have more coke on its way." He rose from the bed and pawed at her, but he lost his balance since he was too high.

She slapped his hand away and pushed him, hard, backwards onto the bed. "I'm done with you for the night."

He started laughing. "Come on, Lyla. You certainly seemed to be enjoying yourself tonight."

Her hands were on her hips as rage filled her from his laughing at her. "Are you saying it's only acceptable for men to enjoy sex?"

"No, of course not." He feebly attempted to get up but fell back on the bed. "You *always* enjoy your work, don't you?" Sarcasm laced his voice.

"I do, most of the time. But guess what, you fucking piece of shit, I faked all my orgasms with you! You couldn't get me off if you doubled what you paid for me!"

His face turned red. "Get off your high horse, you little fucking whore! Who do you think you are *talking* to?"

"I am the whore who's *walking* out on you." She finished dressing and grabbed her bag.

"No, you're not. I paid top dollar for you!" He got up, pulling on his boxers. "I'm not done with you!"

She hurried to the door. "I believe I've fulfilled my duties for the night. No wonder you have to pay for sex! I doubt you've ever actually pleased a woman. And I'm not a cheap whore, you stupid motherfucker!"

"Don't open that door, you fucking cunt!" He lunged at her.

"Watch me." She slammed the hotel room door behind her.

Riding down from the twenty-fifth floor on the elevator her thoughts were erratic: *Just because I'm from the brothel doesn't mean I deserve to be treated like a slut! He made me feel like a cheap prostitute when I am an expensive commodity! And God knows I don't need his judgment.*

Fucking Nathaniel was right… it was better tonight! Probably because the madam expected perfection from me while I'm on probation. I like being the naughty, highly sought-after escort, 'the diamond in the rough.' So what if I amped my sexiness for that loser to keep my job? Ugh! Do I even want this job? I probably just lost it anyway. Fuck me!

Maybe I can tell her just not with Nathaniel. But I'm on probation! And this is what I wanted, right? Just meaningless, errant sex for financial support.

Lyla began to sob as tears rolled down her cheeks. Things were crumbling around her with the lifestyle she'd chosen. Between being an escort, perhaps a porn star, and drug addict, she'd fallen far in the last six months since she'd been the class valedictorian. *Something's gotta give and it's going to be me.*

She waited outside the hotel for a cab. *I'm glad I left that asshole's suite. I'm going home to enjoy my apartment, my own hot shower to wash Nathaniel away, then a soothing, hot bubble bath, until I fall asleep. Maybe the time has come for me to OD.* She sobbed in the back of the taxi. *But who would take care of my Misty and give her catnip?*

⊷⊱◉◈⊰⊶

When she arrived home, Wally stood outside on the steps in the cold smoking a joint. She didn't let him speak, and held up her palm with attitude. "Alone time, got it?" She entered her apartment and locked the door.

Lyla followed her plan with a hot bath but fell asleep and woke in very cold water. Misty stared at her from the bath mat. "Shouldn't fall asleep in the tub, Misty." Lyla sighed. "Aksel is with some stupid bitch who mirrors me— she seriously could be my twin. He must still be in love with me...why else would he have gone out of his way to talk to me? I may have just thrown my job out the window. My family hates me. Aksel..."

She used all her strength to pull herself out of the tub—she had overdone it with the drugs. She dried off her freezing cold, shivering body and wrapped herself up in a thick robe.

"Think I should do a drive-by, Misty? Evan knows where Aksel lives..." She passed out on the couch.

A knock at four a.m. startled her from her sleep. Still woozy from the drugs and alcohol, she got up and stumbled to the door in her robe. *God I should have gone to college, then I'd be home on break.* She opened the door ready to ream out the doorman. "Wally! I thought I made it clear."

Nathaniel looked her up and down. "I see you're all ready for me. Great minds and all that..." He was in his tux with no tie.

She tightened the belt of her robe. "What are you doing here? How did you find me?" She tried to shake off her buzz, but her words were slurred.

He brushed passed her. "Money talks. My grandfather runs the cabbies. Just relax. I wanted to finish our conversation."

"Well, *I'm* not in the mood to talk. You should go." Lyla didn't want him here.

"I wasn't planning on doing much talking anyway…other than telling you what to do." He reeked of alcohol and could hardly keep his balance—it was clear to her that he wasn't in full control of his faculties; neither was she. "C'mon. I paid for the full night," he begged sweetly.

"The night is over, Nathaniel! The sun is coming up soon, you idiot!" She kept her distance, wondering how the hell he'd gotten by Wally.

"It's over when I say it is!" He snapped back into the asshole she knew him to be.

"Who do you think you are, showing up at my apartment at this time of night?"

"I will pay extra." He pulled out a wad of hundreds and tossed it on the counter. "Let's just start with a drink and talk a little. I didn't mean to offend you earlier. I'm sorry." He regained his gentlemanly composure. "Let's just talk."

Lyla exhaled. *This may be a way to keep my job. Maybe he hasn't told the madam yet, and I can salvage the night.* "Fine." She pointed at the kitchen. "You make the drinks while I use the restroom."

She ran to her dressing room. *Okay, I need to cover myself.* She dug through her drawers. *Something unflattering. I have nothing to cover up? PJs? Flannels? It's cold. Yes! This should make it obvious that I'm not interested in anything more than talking and a drink.* She grabbed a pair of jeans, a ratty old sweatshirt, a bra and socks.

She walked out of her dressing room and thought to herself, let's get this over with…

⊸⫤◈⫥⊷

Early Sunday morning, Ginger woke up to an empty bed. After they'd returned home from the gala the night before, riding the whole way in silence, Grant grabbed a bottle of scotch and had fallen asleep in his jacket on a chaise lounge on the balcony.

She put on a robe and shuffled out to the balcony. He was passed out in the chair, with an empty whiskey bottle on the small patio table. She made a pot of coffee and sat on the couch in the front room and read the *New York Times*. Among the many photographs and blurbs on Page 6, there was a photo of Lyla and Nathaniel from the night before.

Eventually, she heard the balcony door open and watched Grant stumble in. He poured himself a cup of coffee and headed to the bedroom, passing Ginger without looking at her or saying a word.

"Grant, we need to talk." She stood up and dropped the paper to the coffee table. She understood his anger, but he had to hear her side too.

Grant rubbed his forehead. "Talk about what, Ginger? I feel betrayed in the worst way." His eyes were bloodshot and glazed over by the amount of liquor he'd consumed the night before.

"Please."

Grant begrudgingly sat on the couch, still in his overcoat, just out of her reach. "I'm listening."

She sat back down. "There's a lot going on," she said. "And honestly, I'm not sure that right now is the time to explain it to you. But what you do need to do is trust me. And you need to apologize to Aksel." She reached over and grabbed his freezing hand, pouring her love for him into the touch. "It's getting very complicated."

He shook his head. "Why should I apologize to *him*? He lied to me which doesn't make a bit of sense."

"You're right, but I suppose you forgot when you were young and afraid to tell a girl's father that you were in love with his young daughter?"

He sighed.

"This much you should know: Margo is a big part of this mess. She did something unforgiveable to Lyla and Aksel."

"What did she do?" His eyes widened.

"I can't tell you that right now because I promised Lyla I would not repeat it."

"Here we go again. She is *my daughter*, Ginger!" Frustration emanated from his voice.

Torn, Ginger pleaded with Grant to understand. "I can't betray her now—no matter how she acts. I need her to know she can always trust me."

"Fuck, Gin! This isn't fair!" Grant got up from the couch and started to walk away.

"Fair?" Ginger was filled with hurt and she clenched her hands into fists. *"Fair!?"*

Grant must have heard her tone because he stopped and turned back to face her.

"Grant, when is life *fair?* Was it *fair* what you read in the journals—when Tommy sacrificed himself on *FiFi* and left me brokenhearted? Is it *fair* that I even said that to you?" Ginger's voice trembled. "You know Alex would have helped you off the plane! I wouldn't have lost you, or Izzy, or eventually commit suicide. *Fair?* Don't you dare throw that word at me!"

"You're right." Grant took his coat off before sitting back down next to her and wrapped her in his arms. "I still

471

can't forgive myself for leaving you in our last life. But I *do* trust you." Her heart beat rapidly as he held her, her anchor. "I'll call Aksel and apologize for my behavior—blame it on the alcohol or something."

"Thank you, my sweet Tommy."

Grant winced. "Aksel and Lyla. How did I not see that?"

Ginger shrugged. "He really loves her, Grant. I think they may have meant something to one another in a past life." Her voice trembled with emotion as her eyes filled with tears.

"What?" Grant asked, and their gazes locked. "I gave Aksel Dr. Ritzius's card when he asked for a therapist. I didn't realize it would lead to a regression."

That explained some, but not all, Ginger thought. "I really don't know more than that—he was reluctant to go into details. He only hinted at it."

"Then whatever I can do to help, I will." He held Ginger closer.

"Just love her, Grant. And be patient." She started to cry as she recalled Lyla's words the night Ginger had discovered her secret, and the glimpse of hope in Lyla's eyes when Ginger proclaimed her love, no matter what. "When she's ready, she'll come back to us. I just know it."

"I hope you're right."

Me too. Ginger wiped her eyes.

"Let me take care of as much as I can. Trust me, when the time is right, you will be a part of everything. And she will be back in our arms."

They stayed wrapped in each other's embrace knowing their relationship was their greatest strength, especially when they were on the same page.

Chapter 45

Lyla woke up with her naked body only half-covered and her head pounding in a deep fog. Squinting in her semi-dark room she saw Misty staring at her, her purr a rumble. "Hi baby." She sucked in a breath at the instant pain from a swollen lower split lip. Rolling over, a shooting pain in her side made her wince. "What the hell happened last night, Misty?"

Misty meowed, as if in response.

Her throat and neck were sore. Memories of the night before were fractured and indecipherable, like a box of puzzle pieces thrown on the floor. As she sat up, pain poured from her brain down her spine and onto her muscles and bones. Tumbling out of her bed, she painfully wrapped herself up in her robe. Her vision was blurred in her left eye. She remembered having a few drinks with Nathaniel, but after that it was a blank. She just managed to make it into the kitchen to grab a can of cat food when she saw the marks on her wrist. What the hell?

After filling Misty's dish, she went to the bathroom, struggling to keep her balance from her hangover and full-body pain. Standing in front of the sink in the bathroom she saw her reflection in the mirror, and peed right where she stood. Two black puffy eyes, a cut on her left eyebrow that possibly needed stitches, with some dark dried blood under her swollen nose. Beneath her matted hair, she felt a tender spot that had a slightly raised knot.

Looking away from her horrifying reflection, she examined the purplish-blue bruises on her wrists. *What the fuck happened to me? I need help. Who can I call? Not Ginger or Grant or even Aksel.*

She made her way into the living room and collapsed on the couch next to the phone. She pushed the speed dial button for Candy and began describing to her what she looked like. She could barely talk as she began blubbering uncontrollably.

"Jesus Christ, Lyla! Who did this to you?"

"It must have been my John from last night, or maybe even Wally, since he always comes to my apartment. I don't remember! I'm so scared! Help me, please!"

"Don't do anything," Candy said. "Slim and I are on our way."

"But I have to shower," Lyla said through heavy sniffs. "I peed on myself."

"Ohmigod, honey! Just change your clothes and wipe yourself with a wet towel. We'll be right there. Slim's already getting dressed."

"Ooh, okay." Sobbing, she gently touched her cheek. "My face! My body! Why would somebody do this to me? I look—Oh God! I can't even look at my face!"

"Get yourself a drink and we'll be right there."

"Hurry, please!"

⊷═◉═⊱

When Candy hung up the phone she filled Slim in on the details of their conversation as they were getting dressed.

"That motherfucker! I'll call da boys, you finish getting dressed."

"Slim, I think we should call Dr. Singhal. He can meet us at her apartment. We can't take her to the hospital."

"Right, right—too many questions. No police."

Arriving at Lyla's apartment a half hour later, Slim and company met the doctor on the steps of the building.

"Dr. Singhal, thanks for coming so quickly on a Sunday. Did you ring the super's bell, Doc?"

"Yes, and no one came to the door."

"Peetie, Paulie, I think you better go find that asshole Wally!"

Unlocking the entrance to the building with his master key, Slim and Candy rushed up the stairs to Lyla's second floor apartment with the doctor in tow. Slim unlocked Lyla's door and found her crying hysterically in the living room. Her hands covered her tear-soaked face and she was curled into a ball on the couch. Misty immediately scattered from Lyla's lap at the entourage of people walking through the door unannounced.

"Honey, we're here. We brought our doctor." Candy sat down next to Lyla and began to wipe her hair from her face. "Oh, sweetheart, Candy's got you. Shh, shh, shh. I'll wait here while the doc checks you out."

"Jesus Christ," Slim said as he looked around, "this place is a fucking disaster."

Slim grunted at a champagne flute that had been shattered against the wall near the fireplace, and shards of glass in another spot—the remains of another flute. He saw blood spots leading into the kitchen, a ball of Lyla's hair on the ground near the refrigerator. Blood-smeared handprints sporadically lined the wall to her dressing room, bathroom, and bedroom. Every drawer in the vanity was opened and the contents were tossed on the floor.

"You coulda picked up the place if you were expectin' company," Slim said. He hadn't been in the apartment since Sarah had lived there.

"I know! And I—" Lyla stumbled over her words, her voice low and weak. "I, I don't keep it like this. It must have happened last night, Slim. I'm so sorry. I wish I could remember more than what I already told you. But I-I— think Nathaniel must have drugged me. I've never blacked out before. I swear! Ever! I, I swear, Slim! You gotta believe me!" Panic filled her swollen face and he wanted to kill the bastard who'd blacked her eyes.

"Shh, shh. Don't yooz worry. We'll get to the bottom of dis fucking story. Peetie and Paulie are wit' Wally right now. Say, where's your stash?"

"I don't think there's much left. I can't see that well..." She pointed at the floor near the couch. "You know I like getting high, but I swear! I swear to you I can't remember what happened! You believe me, right, Slim? Candy? Right?" Still sobbing, she attempted to hide her face from view and wept against Candy's shoulder.

"Of course, we dos. You know I trust yooz. Yooz did the right ting by calling Candy and me, we're here now. The doc will fix yooz right up. Give her somethin' extra strong, eh, Doc?"

"I'll take care of her pain, Mr. Slim," the doctor replied.

"Thanks, Doc. She's important to us. She's family." The doctor nodded, then gently helped Lyla up and assisted her to her bedroom.

Peetie walked in and pulled Slim to the side.

"Wally looks like he got in a catfight."

"That motherfucker!" The veins in Slim's neck and forehead throbbed with fury.

"He couldn't even answer the door because he was as high as a fucking kite. Oh, and get this shit, Boss, the master key don't work on his apartment! Paulie had to kick his fucking door in."

"Is he conscious?" Slim's eyes bulged and rage filled his body.

"Yeah, Boss, but we kicked his ass good. Paulie's got him tied to the bed." Slim's breathing turned heavy and he smacked a fist into his open palm. "Uh, you want us to take care o' him?"

Slim shook his head. "Pack that dumb motherfucker up!"

"Sure thing, Boss." Pettie nodded like he was a dashboard ornament.

"No, no. Wait a second, Peetie. Now, let's be gentlemen about this. Anybody knows when yooz work for me, they what?"

"They don't mess around with Slim," Peetie replied while cracking his knuckles.

"I'll handle this one myself. Where's my fucking crowbar?"

"Downstairs in the car."

"Go get it! That piece of shit can't follow simple instructions!" Slim ranted. "And my poor lil' starlet didn't deserve any of dis fucking shit! Jesus, Peetie, you didn't even see her! She looks like a raw piece of meat! How am I gonna get her into porno now lookin' like she does? It's gonna take forever, if ever, for her to look like she did before that stupid shit decided to—Peetie! When I'm done wit him, you make him disappear! Yooz got it? He's costing me a fucking fortune over here! That motherfucking stupid ungrateful piece of shit!" Slim followed Peetie down to Wally's apartment.

⊹⊱◈⊰⊹

After Lyla was sedated in her bedroom and Dr. Singhal left, Slim called the Manhattan Madam. Candy sat close to him to listen to the conversation.

"Madam, we needs to talk. Yooz got a few minutes?"

"For you, Slim? Always."

"We got big troubles," he said when she answered, skipping any pleasantries. "Somebody busted up our girl Lyla."

"Oh, dear," the madam said coyly. "How is she?"

"Ever see a piece of raw fucking meat after it's been beaten to a pulp?"

There was silence.

"That's right. We had big fucking plans for this girl—movies! Now we'll be lucky if any guy'll wanna look at her mug eva again!"

"This is…disappointing news." Janice's voice conveyed no emotion, which pissed Slim off.

"Disappointing? This is a fucking travesty! Yooz know how much I'm gonna lose on this deal?"

"You are well aware of the nuances in this line of work, Slim. Beyond reporting to me that I will be a number down, is there any other information I need to know?"

"We think the mayor's idiot grandson may have had something to do wit' it."

"But when he paid this afternoon, he reported he had a very nice time last night."

"Oh, he did, did he? How *delightful*. Did he tell yooz he followed her home, busted into her apartment, and drugged her? Was dat part of his fucking report?"

"Are you certain your facts are correct?"

"I'm looking at the facts as we speak, and the super of dis here building she lives in told me a lot more," he said as he eyed the busted up room with disgust. "And let me tell yooz, I ain't fucking happy here. Yooz keep that entitled son of a bitch away from MY girls! And I don't wanna hear no more shit about her being on no fucking probation. Because as far as I'm concerned, that motherfucker is on probation wit me! Yooz better get word to that little asshole weasel, if I ever see him in or around my club, he's dead, yooz unnerstand? *Dead.* He better not ever shows up at her apartment. And you tell em he ain't invited at the brothel no more neither."

"But Slim-"

He cut her off. "But Slim, nothin'! And if for some dumbass reason he finds himself back here, I'll be happy to gift wrap his cock and send it to his fuckin' grandfather!"

Candy tried not to laugh out loud at his ranting but failed. She buried her face in a pillow on the couch and slapped his leg, laughing hysterically.

He looked at her, raising his arms out, "Wha?" He winked. "Do I make myself clear? Did I articulates everything clearly enoughs for yooz, *madam?*"

"Now, now, Slim."

"Now, now what? How am I supposed to act?"

"Just calm down for a second and—"

He cut her off again. "Calm down? I'm just warming up! Either yooz tells that pretty boy he ain't no longer allowed at your brothel, or I take all my A-list girls outta there! Got it?"

"First off, Slim, you do not own me."

"I don't own yooz?" he roared, and his round face trembled. "Bitch, don't make me come down there and- "

"Secondly," she continued, unfazed by his animosity, "his family is a major contributor to our co-op."

"It's only a co-op 'cause I cut yooz in when I funded his grandfather's elections. And that's why the cops look the other way! Or have yooz forgotten?"

She didn't respond.

"Maybe yooz forgotten—you know what? I'm so fucking pissed off right now I couldn't give a damn about no cops or nobody. You know how much I'm gonna lose on dis deal?" Slim took a deep breath. "Tell ya what," he said, "if that mayor's grandson goes missing one day, I suggest yooz don't go asking questions or remember this conversation. You're right, though... I don't *own* yooz but don't forget how I protect you and provide you customers!"

He slammed the phone down.

Chapter 46

For the first few days after the attack, Candy stayed with Lyla night and day. Dr. Singhal had Lyla on an IV morphine drip with saline liquid to control the pain and keep her hydrated. Candy, who had once been a private nurse, took care of her, changing out the IVs and bandages. During the first week Candy began to feel like a real mom. The duties of washing clothes and making Lyla's meals she enjoyed, but what she looked forward to the most was the time they spent talking, or watching a chick flick together. *God*, she said to herself one afternoon after checking on a sleeping Lyla, *I wish I'd been a mom.* How silly was that?

Slim seemed relieved when Candy told him that their girl didn't remember much of the details about what had happened. The following week, as Lyla improved rapidly, Candy only spent the mornings with her, yet still on a daily basis. She brought Lyla and her kitten food; even cleaning the litter box when needed. She gave daily updates on Lyla to Slim and told him she was concerned about how frightened Lyla had become of unexpected, loud noises— even a police car driving by blasting their sirens had Lyla on edge. She found herself wanting to protect Lyla and told Slim that Lyla's recovery might take longer than expected.

A new super named Uncle Jimmy arrived from Chicago. Candy reassured Lyla that he was not like Wally, just someone who would keep an eye on things—the proper way.

After leaving Lyla's apartment on the afternoon of December 21st, Candy's birthday, Candy reached over to touch Slim's knee as they rode together for a birthday shopping spree.

"She's healing physically," Candy told Slim, "but not so good emotionally."

"Eh, she's young. She'll bounce back. Just like we used to. Don't be negative. It's the holidays, Christmas is around the corner. Hopefully she'll be able to visit with her family. But oh God, that motherfucker fucked her face up!" He punched the seat in his new Cadillac as they were chauffeured to the shopping district, headed straight for 5th Avenue.

"Slim!"

"Wha?" His face tightened with anxiety and anger.

"I'm not being negative here." She worried about his blood pressure and gave his knee another squeeze.

"What yooz tink?" Slim glared at her intensely.

Candy had a mother's instinct to protect Lyla as if she was her daughter—Lyla wasn't ready to get back into the biz. She hesitated. "I'm not sure she ain't changed."

"In what way?"

"I feel like she's different now." She knew this wasn't the answer he wanted to hear.

"She's family, and she knows it," he replied gruffly.

"If you say so. Just be patient with her."

"We'll see. Trust me. I've been in this biz foreva. She's hooked on the money and drugs. And us." Slim's laughter filled the car as it stopped in front of Sak's. "Come on, birthday girl." Opening the door to the limo, Slim grabbed her hand and helped her out. Would she and Slim have this life, if they'd decided to have kids of their own? Probably not. "I want a new ring, Slim. Something sparkly."

The next morning, Candy received a call from Lyla, who said she needed to get out, wanting a change of scenery after weeks of hiding inside her apartment, plus she wanted to do some Christmas shopping.

"That's a good idea, baby," Candy said. "I'm glad you're feeling well enough. I can send a driver over."

"That'd be great. I just want to spend a few hours on 5th Avenue, my shopping Mecca."

"Of course, sweetie. Oh, I like chocolate if you're shopping for me," she teased.

"Good to know. And Slim?"

"He likes everything. Just that you're feeling well enough to step outside will be a gift to him."

"How about a nice scarf? Gloves?"

"Sure, baby. He'll love that."

"Thanks, Candy. And by the way, I won't be getting you a candy cane!" They both laughed. "I'll call you when I get back, okay?"

"Enjoy. Sonny will be on his way."

Hanging up the phone with Lyla, Candy looked at Slim. "Maybe she *is* okay. She wants to do some Christmas shopping. I guess you were right."

"See? I told yooz." Slim slapped his hands together while smiling from ear to ear. "You worry too much."

⊷⟾◉⟾⊶

Lyla applied more makeup than a regular night at the club, but nothing could hide her injuries, and she grimaced at the image in the mirror. She attempted to convince her brain that she didn't look as bad as her reflection. Today was the first day she was going out in public to do Christmas shopping, or so she had told Candy. Really, she just wanted to get out from under Slim's thumb.

She put on Gloria Vanderbilt jeans, a white cashmere sweater, knee-length brown boots, a red scarf wrapped around her neck and over her hair, and a full-length chocolate-brown wool coat. She slipped on a pair of Jackie O sunglasses, which hid her scar over her brow and leftover bruising around her eyes. "Much better," she said, lying to herself.

After an hour of actual shopping to cover her story, she meandered down 5th Avenue and admired the holiday window displays. The smells and decorations of the season sparked memories of her childhood, moments she cherished—moments with Grant. She watched the ice sculptor in action through the window at Barney's, as she recalled being a child—a happier and younger version of herself in the city. Now she didn't even know if she had a future.

She was overwhelmed with regret and loneliness, unable to fight the urge to talk to Aksel any longer. With an armful of shopping bags, she found a payphone and dialed Aksel's apartment, hoping he was there and not in France for the holidays.

When he answered, her heart skipped a beat and she stuttered, "A-Aksel? Hey, it's—"

"Lyla! How are you?"

"Cold. Hungry. Do you have time to eat?"

"*Oui!* Where? When?"

"Nick's, and as soon as you can." Her voice cracked.

"Are you well? You sound—"

"I need to get a cab. I'll see you there."

"*Oui.*"

Lyla hung up, wiped the tears from her eyes, and looked around to see if she was being watched. Not feeling safe going straight to Nick's, she took a cab to Sak's, walked through the department store to the opposite side of the building and exited, immediately hailing another cab.

Aksel was already waiting for her outside of the restaurant when she arrived. His face lit up when he saw her step out of the cab. Carrying bags and looking like an upper-class shopper, she smiled at him and he ran up to her.

"Hi, Aksel," she said somberly.

He wrapped his arms around her in a warm hug, and she dropped her bags on the sidewalk. She began to softly cry as she buried her face in his chest to hide her tears.

"Lyla, what's wrong? God, let me help you, I will get these. We should go inside, *oui?*"

"*Oui.*"

When they walked into the restaurant, Nick saw them immediately and greeted them from behind the kitchen counter. "Ah, bambina! Merry Christmas! It's been too long! And welcome back, uh, Frenchie! Good to see you two. Pick a table and go sit! Let me grab a bottle of vino."

They chose a booth in the corner, far from the windows. Lyla removed her scarf and gloves but kept her sunglasses on.

"How can you see through those things?" Aksel said. "It's so dark in here."

"They're to shield you from how I look."

"Lyla, you are always beautiful to me. I don't understand."

She removed her sunglasses, revealing her cut-up and bruise-faded eyes. She finally looked up at him. "You still think I'm beautiful?" Tears trickled down her cheek.

Aksel opened his mouth to say something but just then Nick walked up with the wine.

"I hope you're thirsty, because—" As soon as Nick saw Lyla's face, he lost his breath and he placed the bottle of wine on the table. He stood still, in obvious shock.

There was a moment of uncomfortable silence and Lyla looked down at her napkin, unable to speak.

Aksel reached out his hand to shake Nick's. "Thank you for the wine. It is good to see you also, Nicky."

Nick ignored his greeting and said, "I think I'll bring yooz two some water." Then he glared at Aksel. "And maybe some ice, eh?" Nick stalked off.

Aksel poured two glasses of wine. "What happened?"

Lyla sobbed into her drink.

"Please, Lyla." He touched her hand. "You can tell me anything. What did you suffer to cause this to happen to your beautiful face? An accident?"

She shook her head and whispered, "No. Far worse."

"Please, please, you reached out to me. I am here with no judgment, Lyla. Tell me what happened to you."

Holding her hands up in the universal 'time out' sign, she gathered herself and began to explain why she looked so battered. He listened, as promised, without judging her but she feared losing his love forever.

⤙⟶⟵⤚

Nick stormed into the kitchen like an Italian raging bull and started to throw and kick anything in his path, whatever he could get his hands on.

"Nicky? What da fuck is wrong wichya?" Tony jumped out of his way as a pot landed on the floor.

"Tony! Call my cousin Sal! I'm gonna have him beat that fucking son of a—nobody messes wit my family!" He pounded the wall.

"Nicky! Calm down! You gonna have a coronary right here in da fucking kitchen! Jesus Christ! Your eyes are poppin' outta your head like a fucking cartoon character! What da fuck is wrong wichya?"

"I just saw her face! Take the fucking water over there and look at her. Tell me she didn't get her ass beat by that French croissant son of a bitch she's wit!?"

"Hey, hey, Nicky! Before we go all Mafioso on his ass, we betta call Grant and Ginga. I got their number here in the book. Fuckin' A! Calm down, Nick! And breathe a goddamn minute, for Christ sake! You tink I wanna run this place by myself?"

"Oh fuck you Tony, eh?"

Tony went to the black book and dialed G Squared as Nick ranted all around the kitchen.

"Yeah, Ms. Ginga. Dis is Tony, from Nicky's."

"Ah, Tony yes," Ginger said. "How are you?"

"Not great. Nick just burst into the kitchen, swearin' up and down. He's out for blood, that one. You betta get over here straight away! Nicky can't even talk—he's foaming at the mouth! Looking for a fuckin gun or somethin—pardon my French and all, but thank God I hid the bullets months ago—"

"What's happening?" Ginger asked.

"Lyla is here wit that French boyfriend of hers." He spoke slowly so she would understand him better. "She's all bruised up, like she was in a fight or somethin'. And Nicky tinks the boyfriend kicked her ass. So's I tell Nicky before he goes knocking somebody's teeth out, maybe we should call yooz guys. I think you otta come down here quickly before I can't hold Nicky back no mores."

"I'm gonna kill him!" Nick shouted.

"I'm already out the door and tell Nick not to do anything."

⊷⊶

Ginger, heart pounding, shrugged into her coat and scarf to get out of the office. Grant glanced up from his phone call and saw her, then placed the call on hold. "Ginger? Where are you—"

"Not now, Grant!" She knew he'd be angry but he'd promised to trust her.

"Are you okay?" Sue asked as Ginger sped by the reception desk.

"Oh! Sue, I'll be back um, when I get back! Hell, I don't know when, but I'll be back!" She forced a smile as she stepped into the elevator.

Fifteen minutes later, Ginger burst through the doors of Nick's restaurant. She surveyed the room and finally spotted Aksel and Lyla at a booth in the corner; they didn't see her. She went in back and found Nick sitting in his office with an icepack on his neck. He saw her and said, "Tryin' to calm down but it ain't working."

"Nicky. Let me do my momma thing, okay?" She touched his beefy shoulder and spoke softly. He let out a low guttural growl in response but stayed put.

Ginger and Aksel made eye contact as she returned to the dining room and she stopped in her tracks. The pair were sitting next to each other on the same side of the corner booth. Aksel had his arms wrapped around Lyla, gently rocking her. Her face was buried in his chest and she hadn't seen Ginger yet.

He nodded for Ginger to join them.

"Lyla," Aksel said, "someone is here to see you."

When Lyla looked up and saw Ginger, she started sobbing again. Releasing a fresh wave of tears, she hid her face against Aksel's chest.

"Ly. It's okay. You're with Aksel. He's got you. And if you want, I'm here for you too, okay?" Her heart wrenched.

"Don't look at me, Gin," she said between sobs. "I'm an unlovable mess!"

"You are not unloved, Ly. Ever. What happened? I told you before, sweetheart, we're kindred spirits. We've always been connected. I will do whatever you need. But only if you want me to."

"You ever have the crap beat out of you?"

"No." Ginger shook her head for emphasis.

"I-I really messed up. I need help, but I am afraid for you. All of you. I love you so much! But I am beyond saving now."

"No one is beyond saving when they ask for help. We'll figure everything out—I promise. Now why don't you start from the beginning? I'm not here to judge you. I only want you to be safe and happy. I love you, Ly!"

Lyla looked up at Ginger and then Aksel, who said, "Tell Ginger everything, Lyla. You need her help. And I will never leave you again. I promise. I will help you also."

Taking a deep sigh, Lyla said, "Where do I begin? Sarah introduced me to…" Ginger heard the whole gory tale from beginning to end.

Chapter 47

Nick had waited for nearly two hours and couldn't contain himself a second longer. He grabbed his favorite baseball bat, and took a few practices few swings in the kitchen, making Tony duck a couple of times.

"Don't go out there with that, Nick!" Tony pulled the bat from his hands.

"Fuck off, you Tony Balony!" Nick pushed him aside. "That's my goddaughter out there and I gotta know what the fuck is goin' on, okay?"

"Sure, sure. Go ahead. But I wouldn't use the bat until you check with Ginga first."

Nick stormed out of the kitchen into the dining room using his bat as a back-scratcher.

"Hey, Ms. Ginga, good to see ya." Nick eyed Aksel and Lyla.

"Good to see you, Nicky. Thanks for having Tony call me." She put her hand up as she gestured to stop with the bat in his hand. "Everything is fine. Or it will be."

"Are you sure? 'Cause I don't mind personally introducing this young man here to Cleon Jones if need be." He gave Aksel a hard stare while smacking the end of the baseball bat into his open hand.

"That's not necessary. Let's go talk."

Ginger excused herself from the table and pulled on Nick's arm. He sighed and lingered long enough to muster a smile for Lyla, then followed Ginger into his office.

"Okay, so what's da deal? Who's gettin' a beatin'? Whoever the motherfucker is that beat on her, he's gonna pay for it!"

"Nicky, God, I adore you! Well, it seems Lyla got herself into some trouble," Ginger said with a serious look on her face.

"With who? She's too fucking young."

Ginger shook her head. "You're never too young. She got into drugs, dancing at a strip club in Williamsburg, and it looks like she's involved with some very scary people."

"A strip club in Williamsburg, eh? Did she mention any names?"

"Nicky, don't judge her. She got in and can't get out. I don't know what to do to help her…other than give her a new identity and send her off to another country. Grant doesn't even know what I've told you, or anything she's been doing. Don't say—"

"Did. She. Mention. Any. Names?" Nick repeated himself in a stern, no-nonsense tone. "Drop the drama and adds some names. I grew up here, remember? I know a lot of dem greaseballs."

"She mentioned somebody named Slim."

Nick's gut twisted. "Are you sure she said Slim?"

"Yes. Why? Do you know him?"

"Yeah, I know him." He sighed. "Okay, let me take care of this. You get my goddaughter outta here. Hide her for a while. She can't go back to wherever she was living. Got it, Ginga? Let me handle this."

"Jesus, Nicky, you're scaring me. Don't make this worse for her."

"Trust me, okay? That greaseball Slim owes me big time. I'll let you know when it's taken care of, okay?" He stared into her eyes until he saw her nod.

"What do I tell Grant?"

"Nothin'. Not yet. Just get her outta wherever Slim's been putting her up. I know how he works and what happens to the girls in the end when he's finished with them. He's not a good man, Ginga."

He promised her everything would be okay as he led her out of his office and she kissed him on the cheek. Once Ginger was out of earshot he said under his breath to Tony, "Get Sal on the phone NOW! We've got to save my goddaughter."

⁘

Ginger returned to the table. "Nicky knows Slim," she told Aksel and Lyla. "He said he can get you out. But he doesn't want you going back to your apartment if Slim is paying for it. Is he, Lyla?"

"Yes, but what about all my stuff? My cat?" Lyla's eyes filled with tears. "I can't leave Misty behind."

"I'll ask Nick if we can go back to get your cat," Ginger said.

"Slim always keeps an eye on the building so he knows when you come and go. How am I supposed to leave with my cat? And where am I supposed to go, Ginger?"

"You can come and stay with us," Ginger said.

Lyla shook her head. "I don't want Grant seeing me like this."

"Stop calling your father 'Grant'! He's your real, biological father, Lyla. We've got proof from Howard that I can show you another time. Okay, okay, let's think."

Ginger rubbed her temples. "I'll book you a room at the Carlyle Hotel where we designed all their uniforms."

"But what about my kitten? Can she stay there?"

"No, they don't allow pets, but I know the General Manager and I'm sure I can get him to make an exception." Money talked.

Lyla perked up. "I know how to get Misty. I'll call Candy and tell her I must take her to the vet. And you can be in a cab waiting for me down the street from my building."

"Good idea," Ginger said. She picked up her full glass of red wine and downed half of it before waving to Nicky, waiting by the kitchen, to join them. He attempted to hide his tears as he hugged Lyla, who started to cry softly.

"Nicky, I'm so sorry," Lyla said.

"I've made many mistakes," Nick said to her. "Everybody does—just learn from 'em and don't repeat them." Ginger's heart warmed—she couldn't ask for a better friend.

Nick turned to Aksel. "Frenchie, what's your name again? Jesus Christ, I wanted to kill you an hour ago! Now I wanna kiss ya!"

"Aksel," Lyla said. "His name is Aksel. And you'll always be my favorite, Nicky!"

"I gotcha, bambina. Don't yooz worry no more. Let Nicky sort this out for yooz, okay?"

"Nicky, we'll need extra time to get her cat," Ginger said.

"A fucking cat?" Nick turned to Lyla. "How's about I get you three new ones?"

"No!" Lyla said emphatically. "Misty loves me. She needs me."

"Okay, okay. Sal won't be here for another half hour. And we'll have to feed him first, so it'll be an hour and a half before I catch him up to speed, that fucking piece —" Nicky put his hand over his mouth. "Excuse my manners, ladies." He smacked Tony on the arm. "Tony! Why you let me say things like that in front of these beautiful ladies?"

They all laughed, half from nervous anticipation of what was to come and half from Nicky's antics.

"So anyways, that gives you about an hour and change. Just be careful, little girl. This ain't no game, okay? These guys play rough and for keeps. Get your cat and nothing else. And get the fuck outta there."

"Thank you, Nicky." Lyla gave him another hug.

"Thank me when we're through with this business." Nick pulled an aged black and white picture of a man in uniform from his pocket and placed it on the table in front of Lyla.

"Who's that?" Lyla asked.

"This is your ticket out. You can thank my brother Micky for this one; it cost him a lot. He woulda loved you, just like I do." He kissed the photo before returning it to his pocket.

Ginger blinked back tears at his generosity.

"What happened here just now, ain't nobody gonna hear about from us, right?" Nick asked. "To the grave wit it?"

Tony chimed in, "To the grave."

Ginger squeezed Nick hard. "Thank you so much for this, Nicky. Grant always said you were an interesting and wonderfully complex man."

"He said dat about me?" Nick laughed and blushed a bit.

"And let me add incredible to the list."

"Now Ginga, get outta here already! All of yooz!"

⊹⟶◉⟵⊹

Once inside the cab, Lyla softly admitted, "I don't know if I should be alone at the hotel. I know I have to wean off all the drugs, but what if I can't do it? What if I screw up and-"

"Or," Aksel interrupted her with his solution to the problem. "You can stay with me. Only if you want to, but I have two bedrooms. I told you I'm not leaving you."

"And what about your family, Aksel? Weren't you going home for the holidays?" Ginger asked.

Aksel shrugged. "So, I won't go to France."

"France?" Lyla asked in a panic. "When?"

"Tonight."

Overwhelmed, she perched on the edge of the rear seat. "I-I can't ask you to stay with—"

"You are not asking me. It's been decided."

He sounded so certain, which is what she needed. Ginger nodded at her with encouragement.

"Aksel, you would do that for me," Lyla said, "after the way I've treated you?"

"I will even let you pick your room. You and your feline are welcome in my home."

Lyla didn't say a word and hugged him tight. And for the first time in a very long time, she felt safe. "Thank you."

"We need to make this happen." He touched the back of her hand. "Cat carrier, correct?"

"Correct," Lyla said, smiling at Aksel. *After all that I've put him through, he knows everything about me, and he still wants to make sure I'm okay... Even my cat? Why do I deserve him?*

"We should treat your feline to the whole *cat* and caboodle as they say...a new litter box, food, toys, *oui?*" Aksel's voice was as triumphant as his expression.

"*Oui!* Help me pick out her new stuff? You'll love her."

"But of course, *ma cherie.*"

Chapter 48

Ahey stopped at a pet store a few blocks away from
Nicky's. Lyla and Aksel scurried into the shop for
everything needed to set up Misty's new temporary abode.

Ginger waited in the cab with Lyla's shopping bags
from earlier that day and kept looking at her watch. *Jesus,
hurry up already! I've been gone for two and a half hours
and Grant has no idea why or where I am.* She didn't see a
pay phone to call him.

Finally, Lyla and Aksel exited the pet store, each
carrying two bags. Ginger jumped out of the cab to meet

them as the cabbie opened the trunk of the checker cab. "How much crap does one cat need?"

"That's what I said! Blame him!" Lyla responded, smiling at Aksel.

"I just want her to be comfortable." Aksel looked at Lyla, then back at Ginger, his mouth tight. "*Madame* Ginger, you seem worried."

"Of course I am! We have so much to do and I haven't talked to Grant! He must think I—"

"Do not worry. After Lyla gathers what she needs, we will drop you off at your apartment or back at the office. From there, Lyla and I will go to my apartment." Ginger was glad they were in an old checker cab, making it easy to accommodate the carrier for Misty.

"Okay. But the clock is ticking on when Lyla won't be able to get inside her place!" Ginger was desperately trying to stay calm as the driver headed toward Brooklyn in rush hour traffic, her heart pounding as fast as if she was in an all-out sprint.

"You know what?" Lyla said. "Let's just go straight to my apartment instead of me arranging for a pickup—it will save us a half hour at least. I'll go in with the carrier, call Candy, tell her Misty is throwing up, and she's got to see the vet. I'll turn on all the lights, so it looks like I'm returning."

"I wish I felt good about this," Ginger fretted—so many things could go wrong. Perspiration dotted her forehead.

"Driver, 15 Roebling Street, please," Lyla said.

Filled with anxiety, Ginger leaned forward, and tapped the cabbie's shoulder. Trying not to sound pushy, she said, "As fast as you can and I will give you a triple tip! Okay, sir?"

"Yes, ma'am!"

⤖⚏⤖

Around the same time that Ginger and Aksel were discussing their timeline with Lyla, Sal parked his Lincoln Continental in the alley behind Slim's club. Nicky got out of the back seat, holding a box of cannolis—a specialty from his restaurant.

"Sal, be careful out here. Whatever yooz do, don't come in."

"Yooz wants my gun?"

"Get fucking serious. I got dis." Nicky walked toward the two bouncers guarding the doors to the club. He'd worn his black leather jacket, black trousers, black wingtip shoes but the final touch was the black fedora on his head.

Paulie eyed Nick as he approached. "What's with the box, buddy? You're awfully well dressed for a fuckin' delivery boy."

"Do I look like a fucking delivery man to yooz?" Nicky said. "How's about yooz do your fucking job and go tell your boss that his old pal Nicky's here." He lifted the box and pointed. "I even brought 'em some dessert." Nick stared up at Paulie. "I'll wait right here so make it snappy since I havs other tings to do before fucking New Year's. Make sure yooz say it's Nicky from the old hood."

"And who's that?" Paulie looked down the alley at the new black Town Car.

"My fucking car and driver, Sal. What's wit all the questions? Do ya need to know the name of my dog too? It's Killa. Get to it, asshole. Slim knows who I am."

Paulie rolled his eyes. "Gimme a minute," he said with an attitude.

"Take your time, big guy."

⤐══◉══⬱

Lyla walked up to her building and buzzed the super's apartment. All the residences that lived in Slim's building now had to call up to be let in after the incident with Wally.

"Yeah?" Peetie said through the speaker.

"Hey, Peetie. Where's Uncle Jimmy?"

"He's at a Christmas party. Who's this?"

"It's Lyla, Peetie. Can you buzz me in?"

"You bet, sweetheart. Sorry I didn't recognize your voice."

Once inside her apartment, Lyla gathered her drug supply as she called for Misty. She tossed everything she could into her oversized purse. "Misty…" While waiting for Misty to come out of hiding, she dumped some cocaine on the counter and snorted it. *God what am I doing? I'm not ready to give up my drugs.*

"Where are you, Misty?" She kept her voice sweet but felt nervous at the thought of her endless drug supply actually ending. Her hands were beginning to shake when she grabbed the catnip bag and placed some catnip in the opened cage. Misty came out from under the couch and stretched as if the kitten had all the time in the world before entering the carrier. Lyla locked it. Fingers trembling, she dialed the club, following the plan.

"Candy, I'm home safe and sound."

"Did you have fun, sweetie?"

"Of course—only, Misty's sick."

⊷⩵◑◖⩵⊶

Nick waited less than five minutes before Paulie reappeared from the club and held the door open to the hallway that led to Slim's office. Once inside, Paulie stuck his thumb in the air. "Arms up. I gotta make sure you ain't packing, okay?"

"Yeah, yeah, no problem. I ain't no disrespectful dumb fuck," Nicky scoffed.

Paulie frisked him, then checked inside the dessert box and laughed when he saw the cannolis.

"They're delicious." Nicky closed the box. "But ain't none for yooz."

Paulie led him down the hallway to a door at the far end, just as a guy sprinted passed them.

"What's the rush, Sonny?" Paulie yelled after him.

"I gotta pick up something for Candy, then take dinner over to Peetie, who's fucking babysitting that bitch who got her ass kicked. You believe this bullshit?"

"That's why we get paid the big bucks, right?"

Listening to their exchange, Nick's stomach churned. *Oh fuck me! Those two idiots are talking about my goddaughter!*

Lyla was sitting on the couch as she hung up the phone and took in her surroundings. Not all her memories here were bad. She started feeling melancholy for the easier days, the days before her life became so complex with Aksel and Darby and Sarah.

She walked to her bedroom and looked at all the things she'd acquired in the short time she'd lived there. *I wish I could take some of this stuff with me. I worked so hard for it all.*

Lyla sat on her bed and hugged her pillow as doubts began to creep into her head. *Do I really want to leave all this behind? I was really free here...*

"No!" *I was never really free. It was a twisted illusion of freedom, and now it's time to move on to happiness...*

Chapter 49

Paulie escorted Nick into a room that still had a fresh paint smell—and soft green walls the color of celery. Slim leaned back in his black leather chair behind a cherry-wood desk, the office newly decorated with a wet bar, refrigerator on the far end, and a black leather loveseat under a large mirror. Added to the paint was the scent of heavy perfume, and a haze of cigar smoke from Slim's cigar. As he approached Slim's desk, Nick saw a medium-sized mirror that had a lot of white powder on it, which he assumed was cocaine. Candy, a woman Nick immediately recognized from grade school, sat next to Slim with her arm draped over his shoulder. She whispered something into Slim's ear as Nick got closer.

Paulie said, "Your guest, Boss. You want me to stay?"

Nick placed the dessert box on the desk and took a few steps back as he looked around the office. He pursed his lips and nodded in approval. "Very nice."

Slim was obviously trying to connect the face of the man in front of him with the name from his past. He slowly stood up and walked from behind his desk. Candy took a puff on her cigarette as she watched the two men stand about two feet away apart, sizing each other up.

Nick's gut twisted as he waited.

To his relief, Slim started laughing. "You look good, you fucking greaseball! C'mere." He grabbed Nick's face and kissed both his cheeks. "Seems like you did well for yourself, just like me, eh?" Slim eyed him from head to toe.

"Yeah, I done, okay." Nick took off his hat.

"Paulie, I got dis." Turning to Candy, Slim said, "Candy Cane, get over heres and say hello to Nicky. Remember him?"

Candy held out her hand. "From the old neighborhood."

"Nice to see you again, Ms. Candy." Nick kissed her knuckles.

"Have a seat, Nicky," Slim said, and Nick sat on the couch. "So, what's the pleasure of a fucking visit after all dees years?"

Nick looked at Candy, then Slim, and nodded toward the door with his lips tightly pressed together. This was a private conversation.

Slim got his signal. "Uh, Candy Cane," he said, "Why don't you give us the room here for a bit?"

"Sure thing, Slim," Candy said. Nick stood up as she grabbed her smokes. "It was good seeing you, Nicky." Turning to Slim, she said, "I won't be too far away if you need me, Slimzee." She left on a tide of floral perfume.

Slim sat back in his chair and took a big puff of his cigar. "Can I offer you anythin'? A Cuban Cohiba?"

"No tanks."

"Okay. Some fresh-cut Columbian cocaine?"

Nick waved him off. "Maybe another time."

"If dat suits ya." Slim put his cigar in the ashtray and Nicky watched as he cut a few lines. They looked at each other in silence. Slim snorted his lines and grabbed his drink.

"How about a drink then? Don't tell me you're too good now to drink with an old friend."

Nick lifted his shoulder in a shrug. "How could I decline such an offer?"

Slim poured a neat Macallan whiskey and handed it to Nick. Nick raised his glass. "To the old times."

"To the old times." Slim drank. "So it's been, wha? Twenty years? You know I hardly recognized you. We've all grown up now, haven't we?" Laughing, Slim took another sip of his whiskey. "So to what do I owe the pleasure of your company after so many fucking years?"

Nick leaned back into the black leather couch as he fumbled around with his hat, purposely ensuring what he was about to say would have a huge impact. "It's personal."

"Whatever you need. You know I owe you big time! Cash? Girls? Whatcha you want? Somebody in the city busting your balls over something at your restaurant? I got a lot of dem dumbass politicians in my pocket." He stared at Nicky, who held his gaze.

Nicky pointed to the box of cannolis he'd placed on his desk. "Before we talk biz, Slim, I brought you a gift from my kitchen. I made dem myself. Remember how my momma made 'em? Same recipe."

Slim opened the box, took a big bite of one on the end, and his face lit up as he chewed. "Fuck me." He swallowed, eyes half-closed. "Just like I remember. Delizioso! You stole your mamma's cannoli recipe? You fucking greaseball you!" He wiped ricotta from his chin.

"No, no. Mamma died awhiles back. May she rest in peace." Nick made the sign of the cross. "Unfortunately, she was never the same after Micky's death, as I'm sure you could imagine. Ain't none of us ever been the same since.

Doc said she died of heartbreak." Nick signed deeply. "You ever end up with kids of your own?"

Slim was caught off guard by Nick's reference to Micky. "Yeah, uh, yeah, I gotta daughter. I can't imagine losing her. I'm sorry to hear about your motha. What a fucking slob you must tink I am. I woulda come and paid my respects if I'd known. May she rest in peace." They did the sign of the cross over their chests and glanced to the ceiling with their hands in a prayer position, then returned to silently looking at each other.

Slim took a long drag off his cigar and a deep sip of whiskey. Nicky reached inside his pocket and pulled out the picture of his older brother, Micky. He walked over to Slim's desk and kissed it before placing it right in front of Slim.

Slim studied the photo, did the sign of the cross again and kissed the picture himself. "Micky, may he rest in peace."

"Amen," Nick replied.

The two men looked at each other and did not speak. Tears filled their eyes, but neither would allow the tears to spill over their cheeks.

"Nicky, bambino, your brother Micky was a good man. If it weren't for him…" Slim shook his head, taking a deep breath, and held his hand over his heart.

"Which brings me to why I'm here. So yooz remember when you got back to the States after Korea? Remember what yooz said to me?"

"Yeah, of course I do. Just 'cause I'm older don't mean I lost my memory or nothin' for Christ sake!"

Nicky continued in a serious tone, "You said that if I ever needed anything, all I had to do was ask, right?"

"Yes. Now, whatcha need?" Slim picked up Micky's photo and shot Nick an intense look.

"You told me back den dat you owes me a life, so here's the deal. Unfortunately for me, my goddaughter stopped by my restaurant for a late lunch today. I took one look at her and I fucking lost it! Seems she got beat within an inch of her life! What da fuck, I say to her, what da hell happened to your beautiful face? I was about to call my cousin Sal and let him loose! Remember Sal?"

"Yeah, yeah. Course! Who could forget Sal? All he did was eat."

"He's out in the alley waiting on me."

"Oh, okay. How's dat greaseball doin anyways?"

"He's da same old Sal. Too many cannolis, but still a badass though. If he ain't whacking somebody, he ain't happy." Nick waved his hands in the air. "Believe me, I know when he ain't happy, he eats half my kitchen! I wants to kill him sometimes." Nick pulled his finger across his neck.

"Jesus Christ!" Slim laughed at Nick's antics. "So you wanna whack Sal? I'm getting confused here, Nicky."

"No, no. Jesus fucking Christ." Nick continued with his very animated hands and speech—it was all part of the game. "So, I sit down with my goddaughter and I ain't seen her in almost six months, you know? Sos I says to her, what da fuck happened to you? I mean, I didn't say it like that to her, I used gentleman words and all, you know, the words we use around ladies."

"Of course. Being a greaseball gentleman," Slim observed cynically.

"Exactly. So now da next thing I know, she's crying. Now I'm crying. And I ain't even know why I'm crying! Thank God ain't nobody else sees us crying 'cause they woulda been crying too. Fuck! My asshole partner is looking at me from the kitchen and wondering what the fuck's going on…" Nick paused for a breath as he brought his hands together like he was praying.

"Anyways, I'm getting carried away here. I'm sorry, Slim. I'm a little emotional over all dis fucking shit goin' on." He put his hand over his heart while shaking his head back and forth.

"I gotcha. Actually, no I don't know what da fuck you're talking about here! You ain't making no sense, Nicky! No wonder you turned down my premium Columbian cocaine. What kinda meds yooz been taking?"

Slim started laughing with a wheezing cough at the end. "Or not? Did yooz miss a dose or somethin? What da fuck, Nicky? Where are we going with all this shit? I ain't needin no fuckin bedtime stories! Just them cannolis is fine. You need a shrink or something? I gotta one of dem, too. Jesus!"

Nick held up both hands. "No, no, no. I ain't needin one of them head shrinks. But anyways, she starts telling me some shit about exotic dancing and working as a lady of the night, you know, I ain't gotta say no more about it. Now I'm crying harder to tink she's doing this. And then she goes on about not being allowed to see her family. And I'm thinking what da fuck? Who am I talking to for Christ sake? It's Christmas and my goddaughter can't see—"

Slim put up his hand to stop him. "Nicky, where are yooz going with dis?"

"Well, Slim, lets me cut to the chase. Some fucking how, between her tears and my tears, I put two and two together and figured out my beloved goddaughter got wrapped up in your business." Nicky stopped joking and leaned toward Slim. "Which by da way, I ain't got no problems with your business. In fact, if it was anybody else, I woulda looked the otha way, but…"

"I don't know your goddaughter," Slim replied with a stern but bewildered look on his face, shaking his head.

"I believe you do, Slim. Here's her picture. Her name is Lyla. Lyla Robinson. I want her out. No questions asked. Especially 'cause her parents don't know nothin."

Slim's face turned red. "You fuckin kiddin me or somethin? What kind of shit you trying to pull wit me?" He stood and leaned on his desk with both hands.

Nick knew not to flinch. "I want her out of your business."

Slim picked up his drink and downed it. Nick almost jumped when he slammed his glass on the desk and poured himself another.

Nick continued, "I ain't here to do nothing but collect on a debt. Blood for blood. Life for life, right? Hell, I wouldn't even be having dis gentlemanly conversation wit you if my dear brother, Micky—God bless his soul," he crossed his chest again, "didn't pull your sorry ass to fuckin' safety. And what kind of reward did he get for calling the fuckin medics to save your ass, Slim? Eh? A motherfucking bullet in the head!"

Slim remained silent, as if in shock. Nick suddenly realized the magnitude of calling in this debt. How much had Slim invested in Lyla?

He had to say something fast. "She ain't gonna be any problem to you, Slim. I want her out. Out, with her life and everybody she loves intact. You can do that, right? I'm sure ain't nobody wanna hear that Slim would go back on his word, you know what I mean?"

Slim stared at him and remained silent as Nick watched his emotions visibly change from rage to irritation, realization, and then finally angry acceptance.

His old friend slowly nodded and raised his chubby pointer finger at Nick across the desk, his voice a deep growl. "Nicky, I'm only gonna tells yooz dis just once."

Nick braced himself.

Slim took a deep breath, trying to contain his anger. "I'm a man of my word. I have always honored my debts. And now, especially for yooz because of your brother, Micky. But after this, yooz and me are square; forever."

Nick swallowed hard as he nodded, feeling like he'd just made a deal with Satan himself.

"So understand dis—if that little whore comes back here looking for work or drugs or anything else," Slim's voice graveled as it raised, his body shaking, and veins stuck out on his neck. "Don't yooz show your ugly mug here again asking for her back! Got it? Because den she's all mine, understood? This is a one-time deal! And I don't wanna hear about dis from nobody. Because if I do, then the deal is off. I'll find that little bitch and what happens to her, happens to her. *Capisce?*"

"*Capisce.*"

"You even know what I did for her? I took care of her after she took dat beatin. And this is how she repays me?"

"Hey, don't blame the kid. She ain't knowin' what's going down here, Slim. She's only eighteen. I'm doing dis for her family. And yeah, if she comes back to you, fuck it! I ain't gonna beg you for nothing. Slim, please understand I have no disrespect for you and your business in any way. You want some money to cover any—"

Slim cut a line of cocaine, snorted it and quickly chased it with some whiskey. "Take her. She cost me a fucking fortune, so I don't ever wanna see that stupid little bitch again!"

Nick got up and boldly slapped Slim's hand, which made him drop the straw. "Watch your mouth. That's my goddaughter you're talking about now."

Slim rose and the two men stared at each other, unspoken resentment sizzling in the air. After a few minutes, Slim nodded at the door.

"Get the fuck out, and keep your bitch goddaughter away from my club."

When Lyla opened the door to her apartment to leave, Peetie was there, his hand out, his face crimson with anger. Lyla froze.

"Gimme your fucking keys," Peetie demanded. "You've been evicted. Now get the fuck outta here."

Lyla shook with fear.

"And you don't get to take any of your things. You're cut off."

Lyla grabbed the cat carrier. "I'm not leaving Misty."

"We don't want your ugly fucking cat. Now one last time—give me the fucking key and get your boney ass outa here."

Her hand shook as she handed him her key and tried with all her might not to cry as he followed her down the stairs, slamming the door behind her. She ran outside and hustled down the street toward the waiting cab.

Chapter 50

Ginger looked at her watch—it was just after six p.m. and the sun had already set with no sign of Lyla. Peering out the iced-up window of the cab, she watched the bundled-up, last-minute Christmas shoppers hurry through their lists, since Christmas was only three days away. Despite the temperature outside in the mid-teens, Ginger was perspiring as fear filled her heart that something had gone wrong. It had been over a half hour since Lyla had entered her apartment and Ginger was getting up the nerve to go to her rescue. "What's taking so long?"

"There she is, *Madame* Ginger!" Aksel opened the cab's door. Brisk, cold air blasted her. *I must be strong,* she told herself as relief filled her entire body.

Aksel quickly crossed the street to help Lyla, who was trying to keep her balance as she ran on the icy sidewalk toward the cab. She jostled the cat carrier back and forth as she picked up her pace. Aksel grabbed the cage, helping Lyla, who slid next to Ginger in the back of the taxi.

Lyla shivered, and Ginger placed a comforting kiss on her cheek, resting her head on Lyla's as she whispered, "I love you and you're safe now." She kissed her head again and held her tightly. Leaning forward, she said, "Driver, Sixty-Eighth and Broadway, please." She returned to Lyla. "What took so long? I was getting worried."

"Sorry, I had trouble with Misty and I grabbed a few things."

Ginger saw the drugs through the open top of the bag. "Jesus, Lyla."

Lyla looked down, away from Ginger or Aksel.

Ginger reminded herself of her promise not to judge. "We'll work all this out. Here," she handed Lyla a tissue. "You need to wipe your nose." White powder crusted Lyla's nostrils.

Lyla wiped off the powdery remnants from her last sniff. "I-I'm sorry. I...I know I have a problem."

"Obviously. And we'll deal with that. But right now, we need to focus on the next phase of this mission. The first thing we must do is drop me off at my apartment. It's almost seven o'clock. Your father is probably pacing the floor by now. I wouldn't be surprised if he's already entertained the idea of enlisting the National Guard to find me."

"God, Ginger, I'm so sorry." Lyla nestled into Ginger, who would have done anything for her.

"Stop apologizing. I told you that we won't judge you." Ginger rubbed Lyla's knee. Now that they had Lyla out of that apartment, she'd need living supplies. "I can lend you some clothes for tomorrow."

"We will buy some," Aksel said. "After we drop you off, we'll stop by a store. *Oui*, Lyla?"

"No, Aksel. I can manage." Lyla smiled wanly. "You still have those ratty NW T-shirts? They were so big on me, they can act as a top and a bottom."

Aksel shook his head. "No, you should sleep in something comfortable."

"Since when did you consider me a princess, Sir Aksel?"

Aksel would have his hands full but his love for Lyla was evident. "Okay, so that's the plan," Ginger said with a relieved laugh. "Now I need to get home. Driver, step on it. Please." It was after seven when Ginger rode the elevator to the thirty-fourth floor. *I know my love for Lyla isn't just because she's my stepdaughter. There is something about her...I am sure we've been together before in a past life. I would jump off a building to save her, even if I had just met her on the street.*

Unlocking the door to the apartment, she walked in to see Grant, in his favorite boxer briefs and his holey UW T-shirt, with a tumbler of vodka on the rocks in hand, waiting for her in the foyer.

"Where have you been, Gin? I was moments away from calling the police," he said, slurring his words as he spoke. "But instead I filled my glass up again." He raised his drink. "Although..." she watched him sway, almost losing his balance. "I should tell you, there isn't any left. In the bottle, I mean."

She moved toward him to steady him—Grant rarely lost control. "I love you, sweetheart."

He staggered over, put his arms around her, and kissed her cheek. "Do you know how worried I was? But, I remembered you need me to trust you more than ever right now and I just knew you would come home safely."

"Grant, baby, listen—"

He cut her off by placing a finger on her lips. "I only need to know this: if you want some of this drink"—he raised his glass—"now is the time to speak up. I can't walk down to the liquor store for more yaka." He was slowly swaying back and forth, holding the tumbler up. He leaned his weight on her and the wall at the same time for stability.

"If you're offering—but let's get comfortable on the couch, my love." She held onto him as she helped him to the soft cushions. "Now, where were we? Yes, I am drinking, and it looks like you've had more than your share. What I really need is another hug from you." She sighed in relief that he was more than half in the bag and she wouldn't need to tell him about the last six hours till morning.

He handed her his drink, and she chugged it in one swallow.

"Must've been one hell of a night," Grant said.

She put her arms around him and kissed him deeply, bringing a grin to his handsome face. "It's getting better. You're Lyla's dad again! Merry Christmas, Grant." She wasn't sure if he heard her when she heard a soft snore escape his nose, as he had laid his head on her lap with his eyes closed... the smile still on his face.

⋅⊷⚍◉⚍⊶⋅

"That'll be a hundred seventy-five," the cabbie told Aksel as they parked in front of his building in SoHo.

Aksel handed over two hundred and fifty dollars in cash. "Keep the change."

The cabbie smiled at his seventy-five-dollar tip. "Merry Christmas, sir! Here's my personal card for the future and ask for me, Sammy. It'll be a pleasure to accommodate you again, sir."

"*Merci beaucoup*, Sammy. Merry Christmas."

How generous, Lyla thought, but she wasn't surprised. Aksel opened the rear door to the cold night air that quickly filled the cab. He grabbed the carrier, along with the pet store purchases. Lyla shivered and shouldered her purse and two large Saks shopping bags.

"This way," Aksel said. Once up to the sixth floor, Aksel unlocked the door and Lyla followed him in. She saw a fireplace, and a navy couch that had a purple blanket with two purple throw pillows, and a white lacquer dining table and chairs close to the open kitchen. The apartment was small but quaint.

"Do you have any idea how many times I almost asked Evan to bring me here? I didn't because I couldn't face you. But here I am." She giggled. "And what a train wreck I am. *Merci*, Aksel."

"I am happy you are here. While you shower off the day, I will set up Misty's things."

"Just leave the carrier open. When she's ready, she'll come out."

"The towels are in the linen closet next to the bathroom. I will leave your clothes on the bed. Wait, which bedroom do you prefer?"

"Aksel, this is your place. I will take the guestroom."

After her long and soothing shower, Lyla examined her drug stash. *This will only last a week or so. I guess I can get more when I need to.* She dumped the full contents of an ecstasy capsule into her mouth and washed it down with a glass of white wine that Aksel had left on her bedside table.

She changed into a pair of soft cotton pajama pants and a T-shirt. Aghast at her image in the mirror over the dresser, she touched a fingertip to a bruise on her cheek. Who had she become through all this? *But now I'm safe!* She spun in a circle. *It feels amazing! And I'm with Aksel! Thank you! Thank you! Thank you!*

As she walked into the living room, she discovered that Aksel had built a fire in the oversized fireplace, and Misty was rubbing her head against his calf.

"There you are," he said. "Dinner should be here any moment. I ordered Italian from Ray's."

"Actually, I'm not hungry at the moment."

"Then shall I refill your glass?"

"Yeah, that would be great."

He looked so adorable, standing before the fire. He was the love of her life and she couldn't lose him again, so she had to be careful with how she treated him.

"Let's finish the bottle," she suggested as she settled on the couch.

He handed her a purple blanket and laughed at Misty, who made a beeline for Lyla's lap. When the Italian food arrived, the aroma hit her, and she realized how hungry she really was. They shared a comfortable silence as they ate, both deep in thought about the events of the day and the near future.

After the meal, Aksel cleaned the dishes, and Lyla curled up with the blanket on the floor near the fireplace. Misty formed a furry ball on her chest.

She was nearly asleep when Aksel whispered into her ear, "I believe the bed is more comfortable, *ma chérie.*"

"No, thank you. I'm fine right here," she replied without opening her eyes.

Aksel gently placed a pillow from the couch under her head.

"Better, *oui?*"

"Better if you sleep next to me," she whispered.

"Misty is on top of you, and I do not want to disturb this peaceful moment. But I will be on the couch watching over you."

"But Aksel, what if—?"

"No one can hurt you now. You are safe."

Safe—she felt it as he watched her slip back into slumber. "Sweet dreams, my knight."

Chapter 51

A beam of light shone from the small opening in the shades and landed on Grant's half-opened eyes. He and Ginger cuddled in the master bed under the white, feather-filled comforter. The clock on the nightstand read a little past seven and he turned over to watch Ginger as she slept on her side, with her back toward him. She was just a few inches away and he stroked her long, auburn hair that rested on the pillow. He finally pulled back the comforter enough to slide over her naked body. He softly kissed her shoulder and woke her up.

"Mmmm, guess you're feeling better? We have so much to talk about," she whispered. He felt his cock growing against her bare ass.

"Oh, yeah. But let's talk about all that later."

She pushed the comforter back and wrapped her hand around his rock-hard cock. "I want to taste you, my sweet Tommy."

"Just let me devour you first, baby." He pushed the covers off the bed. His tongue slid along the lowest part of her flat belly and he spread her legs. Within seconds of him spreading the soft lips of her pussy, he mouthed her clit. She relaxed into the waves of pleasure as they filled her body. Ginger got lost in the sensation that Grant's tongue and fingers ignited in her as her first orgasm took over her body and mind.

She softly cried out, "Yes, baby...There, yes, there, uhhhh-huhhhh..." She thrust her hips into his face. He continued sucking her clit, matching her slow but quickening rhythm while plunging his fingers deeply inside of her, playing with the inner walls of her pussy as she began to climb, peak, and fall into blinding ecstasy.

Her tremors eventually ceased even as her inner walls tightly clutched around his fingers. He gently caressed her clit with his soft lips and warm breath.

"You are...so good...to my body..." she panted.

"I love your body," he said, sliding up to kiss her face.

She murmured, "In a minute or two, when I'm able to see again, I want you to do as I say this time…"

"Tell me what you want, Rach."

"I want to have you inside my body."

"Whatever you wish." His body pulsed with lust.

She pushed him onto his back, then climbed on top of him. Kissing him tenderly, she gently bit his bottom lip with a wicked, sexy look in her eyes. She licked a trail from his chin to his huge dick and stroked his cock with her hand while swallowing as much as she could of him…

After an hour of countless sensuous positions, they lay next to each other breathlessly.

Ginger eventually crawled back on top of Grant and played with his nipples. "You own my mind, body, and soul."

"You own mine as well," he said, feeling it in every fiber of his being.

⊷⊱○⊰⊶

Lyla woke up to Misty licking her nose and purring loudly. It was the soundest sleep she'd had in weeks. The embers from the fireplace warmed her from her position on the floor. Over on the couch, Aksel was wrapped up in the Northwestern blanket, softly snoring. Trying to be as quiet as she could, she fed Misty and then grabbed her purse from her room, taking it to the bathroom. At the bottom, she had hidden two important things: her extra drug stash and a safe deposit box key.

Aksel was still asleep when she came out of the bathroom and she decided to look in the refrigerator, where she found an opened bottle of wine—no champagne. *Beggars can't be choosers.* She emptied the contents of the ecstasy capsule into her mouth. She wanted to keep her usual morning routine of drugs and made a ZeZe Zippie out of the leftover wine. She brought her morning cocktail back into her new room where she sprinkled catnip on the floor for Misty. Once she and her feline were sufficiently satisfied with their mind-altering intake, they climbed into the comfortable bed.

She petted Misty as she looked around the undecorated, dull, off-white room. The bare walls made her feel angry about all the nice things she'd had to abandon.

"Don't worry, baby cat, this is only temporary," she said fiercely. "Mommy will figure out how to get another place—a better place. And you'll love it. I promise."

Misty seemed indifferent as she stretched, mewed, and then scampered off.

"You ungrateful brat cat! Where are you going?"

Lyla was physically and emotionally exhausted but mentally wound up from the drugs. Hoping for an early morning nap, she closed the door to her room and surrounded herself with pillows. The fluffy pillow she placed between her legs touched her clit perfectly.

"Mmmm." She grinded into it, hoping to reach an orgasm to soothe her mind. After twenty minutes of masturbating, Lyla was irritated when she couldn't climax.

"Godammit! I need BOB!" she yelled and tossed the pillow across the room, hitting the door with a thud.

"What was that?" Aksel said through the closed door. "Are you well, Lyla?"

"I'm just fucking fine, Aksel! You need something?"

"No, I was just using the bathroom and heard you. You sounded upset." His footsteps padded away from the door.

Crap. Lyla got out of bed and walked into the living room to apologize.

"Sorry if I woke you up. I'm used to living alone."

"No, I was awake. I didn't mean to bother you. I need to telephone my parents and tell them that I will not be coming home for the holidays." He smiled at her from ear to ear. "I just made coffee if you like. Please help yourself."

"Thank you, but I'm not much of a coffee drinker." Taking a sip of her ZeZe Zippie, she sat down on the couch. "I'll be glad to stay here alone while you're in France if you'd like to go." She hoped he would catch her hint—she could find a place before he returned.

He frowned. "Lyla, that isn't what we discussed with *Madame* Ginger last night."

"Whatever, Aksel, call your parents. I need some alone time."

She went back to her room as she listened to Aksel speak with his mother in French on the phone and felt her moods swinging all around.

He rescued me. I shouldn't be so rude. It's the fucking drugs. But I'm not sure what my heart wants. Why did I call him anyway? Because he owes me, that's why! I lost my job—my whole life—to protect him from Slim. Fuck you, Alex! Alex? I mean Aksel!

She shuffled out of the bedroom and saw him standing in the kitchen, running his hands through his hair, and her sweet side kicked in again.

"Aksel?" Lyla said softly with tears in her eyes.

"What is wrong? Why are you crying?"

"I didn't mean to be ungrateful. You've done so much for me. Please forgive me." She began to sob and he pulled her into his arms.

"You are overtired, and you slept on the floor. I do not hold any anger toward you. Here, let me pour you a café?"

She backed away and went to the fridge. "No, thanks. I'll just make another Zippie and try to get some solid sleep."

Lyla jumped with delight at seeing a bottle of champagne hidden behind the milk. She opened it without a second thought and poured some into a large tumbler.

"Champagne? This early?" Aksel crossed his arms.

"Is that a problem? I thought you fucking French drank all day."

"Some do, I guess."

"Please don't judge me, Aksel." This wasn't going to work. Lyla stormed off to her bedroom.

⊰══◐══⊱

Ginger hung up the phone. Aksel had called her immediately after Lyla blew up at him; he was worried about Lyla's mood swings. She found Grant in the shower and she filled him in on some of the details from the day before.

"So, to answer your question earlier about England for New Year's..." It would have been fun, but maybe next year.

"Any chance?" he asked. Steam warmed the room.

"We can't go," she said. "I just got off the phone with Aksel." Ginger hesitated, trying to find the right words. "Lyla has a drug dependency problem and we need to get help for her."

"Uh…okay?" Grant turned to look in her eyes. "Is this when you need me to trust you about a certain child?"

537

"Yes, darling. You do understand that she needs me and Aksel? She's coming around, love, trust me." Lyla was a powder keg, and Ginger didn't want Grant to get injured when she blew.

"Yes, Gin. I do. Even though I feel completely helpless right now."

"In a way, we all do. I'm sorry she's been through so much, but at least she knows you are her dad and you love her. If I can't handle her, I will tell you. I promise."

"Children are so rewarding," he said sarcastically.

Chapter 52

Lyla struggled as she attempted to braid her long, deep-brown chestnut hair in front of the medicine cabinet mirror in the bathroom. "I wish I had my makeup table," she mumbled to herself. The bruises were coverable by lots of makeup, but the four stitches just above her left eyebrow were still easily noticeable. She rummaged through the drawer to see if Aksel had a small scissors or tweezers so she could remove them.

Annoyed, she left the bathroom and called down the hall, "Aksel, do you have scissors around?" She found him in the open kitchen, making something that smelled like breakfast.

He turned around, a dishtowel over his shoulder. "For what?"

"I want to remove these stitches." She waited impatiently by the dining table.

He examined her face. "I don't have anything that small—besides, this is your face. Don't you want a doctor to make sure they're okay before you remove them?" His deep voice held concern.

"I hate this." Anger overtook her emotions. "I look like shit. I need a drink!" She stepped past him and went to the refrigerator, grabbed the opened bottle of champagne and poured what was left into a water glass.

"I'm sorry you had this happen to-"

"Don't," she cut him off. "Feel sorry for me. I don't want you or anyone to feel sorry for me." She pushed by without another word, returned to her room and shut the door. She got out two X capsules but realized her supply was lower than she originally thought and only took one. She put the X in her mouth and washed it down with some of the wine. *I'm out of control.* She lay on her bed waiting for the X to take effect and decided to examine the clothing she and Aksel had bought for her the night before. After doing a few lines of cocaine she wished she had a cigarette. *I can buy a pack of smokes when I go to the bank.*

Aksel was lying on the floor playing with Misty when Lyla walked out into living room in a red sweater, skinny black jeans, and black knee-high boots. She held a matching scarf, hat, and gloves all in a similar hue of red.

"Lyla, you look *fantastique!*"

"*Merci beaucoup, monsieur.* I guess we did well on our shopping spree last night." She curtsied sweetly.

"Are you going somewhere?"

"*Oui.*"

"But *Madame* Ginger is on her way here."

She stopped by the door and turned to look at Aksel with suspicion.

"Yesterday you said you wanted out of the drug addiction and party lifestyle," he said cautiously. "Ginger and I jumped through fiery hoops for you."

"I have a few errands to run! I'll be back. Is that a problem?" She grabbed the doorknob, but it wouldn't budge. She fiddled with the lock. "What the fuck is wrong with your door?"

"You cannot unlock it without the key."

"Open it up! I have things to do!" Panic rose.

"Lyla, please." Aksel lifted his palm.

"Where the fuck is the key? You son of a bitch! Let me out of here!"

"*Madame* Ginger will be here shortly. I need you to wait to speak with her first." He walked toward her, and she smacked him across the face.

"Fuck you, Aksel!" Lyla stomped off, out of control. "This is all your fault!"

He held his hand against his bright red cheek.

"I'll be in my room when *Madame Ginger* comes calling for me, warden!"

She slammed her bedroom door.

⊹══◐◖══⊹

"I can't thank you enough, Doctor," Ginger said to Dr. Ritzius. The two of them sat in the limo heading to Aksel's apartment. "Lyla is a mess. The drugs are screwing up her mind. She got mixed up with a dark lifestyle, and now she's trapped in a scary cycle of alcohol and drugs."

"Mrs. Robinson, I will help as much as I can today, but I will not treat her regularly. However, my partner, Dr. Lebow, works well with addiction. Especially at isolating the root for initial use and eventual abuse."

"How about past life therapy? I believe there may be a connection between her and Aksel."

"If needed, yes. Dr. Lebow is a highly skilled professional with past life regression therapy like myself. However, that therapy is only used if the patient wants to open that door."

"I understand. Either way, she needs help." Ginger wished the limo would hurry and sat forward on her seat.

"I can't promise you immediate results. I may be able to treat the initial physical and mental withdrawal symptoms through medications. After I consult with her, and if I decide that she needs further medication and traditional therapy, I will recommend that Dr. Lebow take over her treatment. He has privileges at the Betty Ford Rehabilitation Center. There is a special location for young adults in Tribeca. It's very close to SoHo."

⤞══◎◎══⤝

Twenty minutes later Aksel greeted Ginger and Dr. Ritzius.

"What happened to your face, Aksel?" Dr. Ritzius asked with concern.

"Nothing." Aksel looked away, covering his face with his hand as if to hide the red handprint on his cheek. Ginger sighed and searched the apartment for Lyla, but didn't see her.

"Was Lyla physical with you?" Dr. Ritzius waited for Aksel to lower his palm.

"But it is not in her nature to act so violently," Aksel said in defense of Lyla.

"I don't know if that's true anymore," Dr. Ritzius replied. "Drug addiction has many different effects on people's behavior. Where is she?"

Ginger butted in before Aksel could respond. "I think I should see her first. Lead the way, Aksel. I don't want her to feel betrayed."

Dr. Ritzius sat on the couch as Ginger followed Aksel down the short hallway to Lyla's bedroom and knocked on the door.

"What now?" Lyla boomed from within.

"It's Ginger. Can I come in?"

Lyla swung the door open, allowing Ginger in. "As long as you leave your judgment outside, you're welcome." Ginger entered the room. Lyla stood by the dresser with her rolled up hundred-dollar bill in hand. "Want any?" She pointed at her small pile of cocaine on the dresser.

"Ly, I thought you wanted out of that world. If you go back, we can't help you anymore. It has to be your choice." Ginger walked toward her, keeping her voice monotone to avoid showing a reaction to Lyla's flighty attitude.

"Yes!" Lyla screamed. "I want out! But unlike you, I need to do a bump to get through a fucking day. It's only been since last night that I made the decision. Why don't you people get it? I just want a few days to float in my real freedom. And if that means I want to be under the influence of something then you should just leave me alone for a few days. You don't get it, do you?"

"Do you think I've never snorted? Who was my roommate? Did Sarah tell you about her other roommate who overdosed on heroine? The same Sarah that brought you into this world of drugs and self-destruction." Ginger caught Lyla off guard as she stood inches away.

"I don't know! I don't care!" Lyla cut lines on the dresser.

"Go ahead. If you think that's freedom, who am I to say otherwise? I'll have Evan drive you back to Slim, if that's what you want."

Lyla defiantly snorted the cocaine and drank straight from the wine bottle. "Ahhhh, yes. It is freedom."

"For how long? Until the money runs out and then what? Continue to sell your body for more?" Ginger asked. Lyla had to see reason!

"As long as it lasts and then..." Lyla burst into tears and fell on her bed. "Help me, Gin. I want to be better. I want to be loveable again! I'm so awful!"

Ginger wrapped Lyla in her arms. "Shh. No matter the high you feel right now, there is nothing better than unconditional love."

"Nobody should love me unconditionally. You shouldn't. Daddy shouldn't. Jason shouldn't. Why should Aksel? And my mother? I'm not worthy of love. I nearly put all of you in harm's way!"

"That's the white powder talking. It wants to own you. It will, if you let it; but, you're stronger than that. I know you are. I've seen what you can do. Please don't give up."

"I don't even own me! Don't you fucking understand? Everyone, including you and Daddy, has always told me what to do! Fuck you! Fuck all of you!" She pounded her fists on the bed.

"Lyla, I'm not telling you to stop. This is your choice."

"But, didn't we agree that I should wean off? I just need a little more…"

"I brought a friend of mine to talk to you. His name is Dr. Ritzius. He's a psychiatrist."

"You brought a fucking shrink here? Fuck you harder, Gin!"

"Hold on, my sweet girl. Hold on."

"Get out!" Lyla screamed into her pillow, face down on the bed.

"Just talk to him." She rubbed Lyla's trembling shoulders.

"Fucking fine! Whatever! Go get him."

◦◦◦

Lyla didn't recognize the ugliness that spewed and boiled within her. Ginger, who she loved and yet treated terribly, left the room and returned with Dr. Ritzius. They entered and he said, "Hi, Lyla. My name is Dr.-"

Her world was changing and she had no control. "I don't care what your name is. Fuck off!" she yelled. "Can everyone give us some privacy?" Ginger, mouth tight, shut the door behind her.

The doctor waited by the edge of the bed.

She glared at the older man with glasses. "What do you want from me?"

"I am interested in having a conversation with you. I'm here to help you."

"I have nothing to say. Want a hit?" She walked over to her cocaine pile.

"No, thank you."

Lyla snorted two lines of cocaine, then held up an ecstasy capsule. "Let me tell you something, Doc. This shit is the best. When you're down or tired, just a few hits of this and wham! Hello!" She laughed and sat on the bed. "It should be a prescription!"

Dr. Ritzius nodded. "I see."

She pushed a strand of hair behind her ear. "You're judging me."

"Not at all."

"So then tell me, Doc, why are you here?"

"To help a friend in need."

"I'm not your friend."

"I wasn't referring to you, Lyla. And if I make you uncomfortable, I won't be coming back." He spoke very factually—non-threatening.

"Typical male."

"I can refer you to Dr. Lebow, my partner, but only if you wish."

"I-I just need one more hit. But I'll think about it."

"Okay. I'll be waiting in the living room. One more thing, though—one must love oneself before you can accept another's love. Do you love yourself, Lyla? Only you know the answer to that question."

Dr. Ritzius left the room and Misty sneaked in. The kitten jumped on the bed, startling Lyla. Lyla scooped up her cat. "Oh, baby girl. I don't know if I love myself, but I certainly love you. Yes, I do." She kissed Misty's head. "Now, what are we going to do?"

Misty slowly blinked her eyes and hopped down on the floor.

"Got no opinion on the matter?"

Misty waited in a perfect cat posture, looking at her while closing her eyes halfway, softly purring. Lyla knew she was giving her the "I love you" cat gaze.

"Do you have an opinion about this? You like to get high too, you know?"

"*Meow*," Misty replied, keeping her big green eyes locked with hers. Lyla said nothing, captivated by her cat's expression. Misty's little engine roared and she looked toward the slightly open bedroom door.

"What?"

Lyla watched in disbelief as her feline turned her head toward the door again, then slowly walked over to her and rubbed against her leg, after which Misty strutted to the doorway before running out. Lyla followed Misty out of the bedroom and found her sitting on Dr. Ritzius's lap, purring and rubbing her ears into his hands. Misty started kitty-stomping on his lap and butting her furry head against his body.

The future came into focus instantly when she saw what was happening. "Okay, do what you have to do," Lyla said to the doctor. "Fix me."

Chapter 53

Lyla drew another :) on the calendar: January 21, 1990. She had been sober now for over three weeks at the Hazelden Betty Ford Center in Tribeca. Ginger and Grant had visited her almost daily, Aksel hadn't missed a day to see her, even when his classes at NYU started again, and she spoke to her brother Jason three times a week.

Conversations with her mother were unfruitful and tough since all Mom wanted was to blame her father for his failure to keep her out of trouble and of course her for choosing to live in New York. It angered Lyla that her mother accepted no responsibility. When she asked about why her mother had lied about Aksel, Mom insisted that her version of the story was the truth. Lyla had Ginger make a copy of Howard Golden's medical file and mailed it to her mom with a letter telling her to never mention the subject of Grant not being her biological father again. Lyla looked in the mirror and smiled—her blue eyes were once again clear and bright, her skin looked healthy, and she'd gained back some weight. She applied only lip gloss and mascara to her face and put her hair in a ponytail that trickled down to her lower back. She was dressed in a relaxed pair of jeans, a blue long-sleeved T-shirt, and white canvas Keds.

Dr. Lebow walked into Lyla's rose-colored private room for her therapy session at twelve thirty p.m. He was a kind man in his mid-fifties who favored sport coats and dress pants. He had short curly gray hair, thin-rimmed glasses, and a soothing soft voice that was always calm. When he looked into her eyes with his hazel irises, she felt he could see all the way to her soul. They had an honest and easy doctor-patient relationship.

"Hi, Doc. How are you?" She sat down in one of two gray recliners facing each other. Misty immediately jumped into her lap and curled up.

"Very well. You are looking great, Lyla. I am very pleased with how you are progressing. And obviously Misty agrees." He chuckled.

"Couldn't have done it without her." She rubbed Misty's chin.

"You are very lucky that the clinic allowed you to have her with you during this time. Your dad had to pull a few strings, but I think everyone can agree it was a good choice."

"Definitely."

"So, this is the beginning of your fourth week, Lyla. Have you given any thoughts about going home?"

"Home?" She blinked in surprise.

"Not for another week or so, mind you. But soon."

"I don't know if I want to move back to Chicago with my mother, and I'm not ready to live with my dad and Ginger."

"I understand you still have issues with your parents which we haven't fully addressed. But living alone is not heathy after rehab. It could possibly open the door to a relapse, Lyla. Is there anyone you can live with? Family, or a friend, even if it's only a temporary arrangement?"

"I guess I could ask my Uncle Andrew. Maybe Aksel."

"Good. Now, we've been exploring the issue you have regarding people controlling your life during our sessions, but I am not convinced we've found the root cause. We've pinpointed a lot of the issues that stem from your relationship with your mother, but in some way or another you were always able to deal with it. No, she was not a loving mother, but you always got your way eventually; for example, your job at Victoria's Secret."

"She's always made it a contest between us. When I took the job at VS, she would remind me how I could never be a model like the ones in the catalogs. She would sit with me looking through a new catalog that came in the mail and page through it just to point out what was wrong with each model. I was asked to model in a summer catalog but declined at just the thought of hearing her tear me apart."

"Yet you seem to think that others have been, and possibly still are, making decisions about your life or "controlling you", when in truth, these people, for example your father and Ginger, have had your best interest at heart all along."

Lyla scratched Misty's ears, feeling her resistance start.

"Although it may seem like they're attempting to have control over you, *you* are actually in control, because *you've* chosen what to do or not," the doctor said. "You have already decided not to live with your parents after you leave here. Maybe the real issue has been that you want to please everyone? And giving control to others is a way to be accepted. But what you really wanted, you didn't get and so it's their fault for your pain."

"I understand what you are saying. It makes sense to me." Lyla felt her smile fade with the thought of what she had put herself through over the years.

"However, I think your issues with feeling controlled might dwell deeper than just this lifetime. They could stem from a past life experience or relationship. Have you given any thought to having a past life regression done?"

"What is that?"

"It's a new area of psychoanalysis where you are brought to a semiconscious state in an attempt to go back into your past life to understand the meanings of the issues in the present. The belief is that some of the issues in our current life might be brought on by a past life experience that wasn't resolved and has travelled with your soul into this current life. In a lot of cases, once those issues are identified and faced, the healing process begins. If you are interested, we can explore that option since it is one of my fields of expertise. Please realize there are no guarantees that it will open a door, but I've had plenty of patients that have opted for past life regression therapy and they were satisfied, even mystified, at times."

"But what if I don't believe in past lives? I mean, so I had some crazy flashback after the bombing at the club, but I thought it was drug-related." She'd tried hard not to think about that time at all.

"Have you ever been drawn to someone that you just met? Or the opposite—repelled by his or her very existence?"

"Yes, my first lover, Aksel. But isn't that normal?"

"People who pay attention to those unexplained connections oftentimes can delve into their past lives through regression. Frankly, you may not even find a past life. But if you do, it may release you from some of the issues that have been plaguing you."

"Sold!" She clapped her hands together, causing Misty to jump off her lap. "So, let's get started!"

Dr. Lebow held his hands up in a stop position, all the time smiling at her enthusiasm. "Okay, but before we explore that avenue let's settle the issue regarding where you are going to live first. The other thing you need to consider is what you want to do when you leave."

"Well, stay sober for starters."

"That's always good to hear, but I was referring to you becoming focused on school again, or at least getting a job in a healthy environment for the sake of your sobriety. What would you be interested in doing?"

"I had thought about fashion design, maybe modeling, but definitely business. I really liked working for Uncle Andrew. Barbizon was a great school, so maybe I'll look into F.I.T."

"Great start. Just toss around some ideas. Think about what you are passionate about. It is important that you create a healthy daily routine."

Ten days later she was released from the center. Lyla rode in her father's limo with Aksel, who had come to help her pack and take her home—to his apartment.

"Thank you, Aksel," she said, sitting next to him. "I can't tell you how grateful I am for all you've done."

"You mean a lot to me. We will always be friends."

The limo pulled up to Aksel's building, and Evan helped carry her bags up to the apartment. When Evan dropped the bags in the foyer, he embraced Lyla. "I'm so happy to see you like this again, Miss Lyla. I am not sure how my big heart fits in my chest right now."

"Evan! Don't make me cry!" She hugged him back. "You are just as special to me."

"You're in good hands—your own." Evan patted her shoulder.

"See you soon. And thank you again."

Misty darted to her cat castle that Aksel had built for her on their first night in his apartment. She meowed loudly and batted at her stuffed mice. *Home.*

Later, Aksel joined Lyla as she sat quietly on the bed in her room. The walls were covered with uplifting and brightly-colored artwork, and the windows were freshly dressed in blue sashes, which matched the new bedding. There was a makeup station in the corner overflowing with Chanel and Estée Lauder products, including perfumes and face and body lotions.

"You like?"

"It's beautiful, Aksel."

"*Madame* Ginger had fun in here."

"I can only imagine." She snickered. "But, Aksel, I don't deserve all this."

"Yes, you do. You have been through a lot, Lyla. You made some bad choices in the past but look how far you have come."

"We *all* have been through so much—because of me." Her eyes began to water as her expression turned bittersweet. "I just can't believe all she did to make me feel comfortable."

"We all helped."

"We?"

"Your father and me. You want to see a funny sight? Just watch your father hang curtains…" He chuckled.

"He did? Not Ginger?"

"And what a sight that was! He's good with designing clothes, but with a drill? I was frightened!"

Lyla and Aksel burst into laughter. After they fell into a companionable silence, Aksel sat next to her on the bed and handed her a blue box with a white ribbon.

"What's this?"

"Your freedom."

"Tiffany's is freedom, isn't it? At least that's what Holly Golightly would say." She opened the box. Inside was a key on a Tiffany & Co. heart-shaped key ring.

"You can come and go as you please, Lyla. You are not captive here. I believe in you."

"*Merci*, Aksel. I love you—I mean, it! I love *it*!" She leaned toward him and gave him a tight hug. "I do love you, my friend." She pulled back and rested her forehead against his.

Their lips were within inches of each other. Sighing deeply, Aksel gently held her hands, kissed them, and forced himself to stand up.

"Nicky is sending over a Hawaiian pizza. Your favorite, right?"

"Yum! How sweet of him! I need to call and thank him again for all he did." She looked at Aksel. "And, thank *you*, Aksel."

"Oh, I didn't make the pizza." He smiled.

"Not for that, dork." She punched his arm lightly. "For not giving up on me. Thank you for helping me find myself again. If it weren't for you, I…"

"Lyla, I never gave up on you." He knelt before her.

"But you should have. I was awful to you, so awful!"

"Sh, sh, sh. I do not keep score. Life is an endless opportunity of do-overs."

She leaned over and kissed the top of his head.

Chapter 54

A week had passed since Lyla had left the rehab center, and life slipped into a comfortable groove. She finally felt amazing in her own skin—drug free, stripper free, brothel free…the version of herself she had forgotten existed but had found again.

She caught up with Jason and made plans for him to visit her. For their first outing, Aksel and Lyla went to the movies and she ate a whole tub of popcorn—something Aksel loved teasing her about. She had dinner with Ginger and Grant at their apartment one night. All the small events reminded her of the things in life that were truly important.

Monday morning, Lyla lay in the soft blankets with Misty snuggled up next to her. She didn't want to leave the warm cocoon of her bed, but she forced herself to move.

"Unfortunately, it's time for us to get up, Misty."

She hopped out of bed and grabbed her robe and plush slippers. Misty buried herself farther under the covers, leaving only her eyes and whiskers visible and mewing belligerently.

"Oh, come on, you brat cat. If you want to eat, now is your chance. I have a doctor's appointment."

When Lyla walked into the kitchen to make tea, she found a note next to the fresh croissants and preserves on the counter.

Ma chérie,

Good morning. I am off to classes and will see you later this afternoon. Enjoy your breakfast and your day.

Aksel
PS I already fed Misty while you were sleeping. She has become quite a demanding little princess! :)

She took the note and kissed it, meowing at Misty when she peeked into her bedroom. "I'm not the only one who knows you are a spoiled brat cat!"

Lyla ate her breakfast, showered, dressed, and then wrote a note to Aksel.

Monsieur,

You have been a wonderful host. If you dare, I would like to cook for you tonight. :)

Love, Lyla

⤙══◉══⤚

It was her first therapy session with Dr. Lebow since she'd left the rehab center. Her heart pounded, and her palms were clammy as she sat in his waiting room.

Once inside his office, the basic beige and neutral surroundings and minimalistic décor helped her to relax and she breathed a bit easier. She settled into one of the plush recliners, which matched the couch along the wall.

"Lyla, you seem nervous."

"Yes, I am."

"What are you nervous about?" he asked in his usual soothing voice.

"I guess it's just because this is a new chapter in my life." She held the arms of the chair so tightly that her knuckles turned white.

"That's fair. How was your first week matriculating back into society?"

Lyla filled the doctor in on what her week was like and how she was feeling, and they agreed it was a good day to dig deeper and hopefully uncover some of the roots of her issues.

She found a comfortable position in the recliner. Dr. Lebow closed the curtains of his office window, lowered the lights, and played soft new age music to make her relax even more. He began to talk softly as he guided her into a deep, relaxed state of mind. He asked her if she could find a time in the past where she felt she was being controlled by those in charge.

Her breathing hitched almost immediately upon his question. Lyla gasped for air as if she was choking, and he gently guided her to look back to a calmer moment.

"What do you see now, Lyla?"

Lyla responded in a thick British accent, "My Auntie Margaret is the head parlor housemaid. She assigned me as a lady's maid to journey across the ocean with Lady Beatrice.

I did not want to go, but at this moment, I am bloody happy to be here."

"Do you know your name?"

"Helene."

"Why are you so happy, Helene?"

"Him. Love. I fell in love with him instantly."

"Who did you fall in love with?"

"He's a strong, tall fireman who works in the engine room of the boat. It's a big boat. Me new friend onboard, Megan, is a lady's maid as well. Our Ladies' staterooms are next to each other and we just got on right from the start; she feels like a sister to me. She's in love with me beau's boss. I think he's the head engineer. On the first night at sea, she invited me to a late-night crew party down below. She introduced me to my beau."

"What is his name, Helene?"

"Spencer," she said with a smile on her face. "He kissed me the next morning. He is very bold." She shook her head, still smiling.

Dr. Lebow waited a while before he said, "Helene? Let's go forward slowly. How do you know you are in love with him?"

"I am with Lady Beatrice, an older woman who barely reaches five feet tall, but very fancy and intimidating. Me lady sees the smile on me face. I tried to hide it from her while I dress her for bed. She presses me to tell her why I've appeared so gay over the last two days.

"I tell her it is a man who has put me in this state. He is well-spoken and handsome. But I am bashful." Lyla laughs and covers her closed eyes with her hands. "She knows I am giddy and teases me. She can be a very intimate, sweet woman—she doesn't show this side of herself often—who speaks of her past lovers freely with me. She's had so many. Lady Beatrice encourages me to spend time with Spencer again after I finish attending to her."

"Do you feel controlled by her?"

"Yes. It is my station to do as she says. However, I am following my heart...I am smitten."

"Where does your heart take you next?"

Lyla's happy expression quickly shifted to distress and fear. She again gasped for air. "He's not here! Spence! Where are you, Spencer? I'm here! Spencer? It's so cold...I'm freezing..."

"Helene, let's move forward now."

Lyla slowly stopped gasping for air, and her sobs subsided. After a few moments, Dr. Lebow asked, "Helene, did you find Spencer?"

After searching her mind's eye, she responded peacefully with no accent, "I believe his soul is nearby, but not with me at the moment. His soul is with the other spirits."

"You have finished with that lifetime then?"

"Yes, I died in the freezing water."

"How do you feel now?"

"Welcomed. Safe. Warm. Loved. Such incredible love. Happiness. Peace." Her breathing was calm.

"Do you recognize who Spencer is in your current life?"

"He's so familiar. I know him. But I cannot tell you who he is right now." She remained quiet then added, "The spirits tell me when the time is right…" Her voice faded as if she was listening to someone else in her trance-induced state.

"So, you are with the spirits as well?"

"Yes."

"Can you describe where you are? What it looks like?"

"White, it's soft but at the same time so bright."

"What are they telling you?"

Again, she listened, then nodded. "It will all unfold in its natural course. I need to be patient and keep my heart open. I have more healing to do. Once I forgive, they will allow me to recognize him."

"Do you recognize Auntie Margaret or Lady Beatrice from your current life?"

After a moment, Lyla began to quietly laugh. "Yes, yes, of course. Auntie Margaret is Candy."

"Does she love you in your current life?"

"She shows me love the only way she knows, but she also seeks to control me."

"Are you ready to let go of her being in control of you?"

Lyla sighed in relief. "I already have. I am free of her."

"Good. I am going to count to three and bring you back to your present life. When you are ready, open your eyes. One. Two. Three."

Lyla's mind transitioned from Helene to Lyla. When she opened her eyes, although the lighting in the room was dim, she felt like some darkness had left her being.

"Lyla, how do you feel now?"

"Serene and hopeful."

Chapter 55

When Lyla left Dr. Lebow's office it was after one thirty, so she decided to walk a few blocks and breathe in the wintery air of Manhattan. She barely noticed her feet crunching the icy patches on the sidewalk along Madison Avenue; a warmth deep within kept her from physically feeling the cold winds.

New confidence filled her from inside like a bright star in the cover of night to guide her home. Peace and hope for a new tomorrow grew stronger with each step she took. *How can one session of regression heal me so much?* She sat down on a bench in the park and then laughed out loud when she recognized where she'd inadvertently ended up—the path leading to what she had referred to as the Garden of Eden inside Central Park.

How in the world did I end up here? Is this some kind of sign that I'm on the right path?

Lyla took a deep breath to sort her thoughts.

I never thought of Candy as someone who had control over me. It makes sense, though. She took care of me only because I was their golden ticket. I must have had a guardian angel watching over me during that mayhem…I got out of it alive! I can't say the same for Sarah, though. She didn't have people like Aksel, Ginger, and Daddy for support like I did. They were never trying to control me this whole time—they only loved me. How can I ever tell them that I get it now without sounding like I'm just trying to appease them?

She checked the time on her watch. *I gotta get to the grocery store!* What the hell am I going to make Aksel for dinner?

Lyla flagged down a cab and rode to G Squared. Grant leapt from his chair when he saw her walking into his office unannounced. He grinned and opened his arms wide, making her feel like a little girl when he hugged her tightly.

"Baby girl!" He wrapped her in his arms and lifted her off her feet.

"Daddy! I mean, *Dad*, can you pick a new nickname for me already? And *bitch* is not an option." She laughed in his ear, hugging him back.

"Okay, sassy girl. How about that?"

"We need to work on it. Where's Gin?"

"In her office; she's swamped right now."

"Love you, Dad."

"Love you too, ba—sassy brat. Better?"

Lyla blew him a kiss and walked to Ginger's office. Seeing the door opened, she tapped on it.

"Ly! Hey, come on in and close the door. How are you?"

"I'm good. Just saw Dr. Lebow. We did something called a past life regression. Ever hear of it?"

Ginger, sitting behind three stacks of papers drinking a latte, nearly spat it out. "Y-yes. I have."

"Do you believe in it?"

"I do, actually," she said, her brow arched in astonishment. "What did you think?"

"I was kinda skeptical at first, but wow, it's pretty amazing. Have you ever done it?"

"I have."

Lyla couldn't tell if Ginger was reluctant to talk about it or caught up in her work, and decided to change the subject.

"I wanted to cook dinner tonight for Aksel. He's been so amazing. I was thinking of making him my favorite soup, tomato bisque, and—"

"It's after three, kitten!"

"Already?"

"Think maybe you should swing by Uncle Andrew's instead of making it from scratch?"

Lyla laughed. "Good call, Gin. Kind of a one-stop shopping then. Will you call him and let him know what I need and include blueberry cobbler?" Ginger came around her desk and hugged her tightly.

"Will do. Nice to have you back. Oh, by the way. Would you be interested in assisting me with a few patterns over the next couple of weeks? I could use a fresh opinion and an extra set of hands."

"I think so."

"Just let me know."

"Tell him to throw in a salad too. Muah!" She left, her peace-filled heart beating faster as she took the stairs rather than the elevator to the street level. Ginger had just offered her a chance to work with them! No judgments, no questions about how it was going, only love. It was almost as if the last six months were nothing more than a bad dream.

Lyla's cab was caught in traffic two blocks away when she decided to hop out and walk, hoping to beat Aksel home. She carried the bags back to the apartment building and charged up the stairs. When she opened the door, Misty was in her direct path, and she had to hopscotch over the cat to avoid stepping on her while holding the bags of food.

"Misty!" she screamed.

Misty hissed, pounced sideways to avoid being crushed, and ran for safety.

"You almost killed me!" Lyla yelled.

Misty leapt to the top level of her castle and hissed. Her tail twitched back and forth as she crouched in attack mode.

"You were trying to greet me, weren't you?" she said to Misty. "Come here, you little ninja!" When she scooped up the cat, she realized Aksel had been watching her from the hallway entry. He leaned against the wall with his arms crossed and head tilted, a sexy smile in his eyes and on his lips.

"Good evening, *mademoiselle*. You certainly know how to make a grand entrance."

"And how long have you been standing there?" Lyla replied.

"Long enough to know that you have successfully foiled an assassination attempt by the devious Misty the Ninja."

Aksel mimicked her moves like he was avoiding the cat, and Lyla laughed so hard her sides hurt.

Aksel finally asked, "Can I help with anything?"

"No, no. I have a grandiose idea in place for preparing your dinner tonight."

"*Oui*, I read your letter, and I am looking forward to it."

She placed Misty in his arms. "Great. Now please get lost, I have things to do."

"Shall I put some music on?"

"Sure. But then scram while I cook, please. And no peeking!"

When Aksel carried Misty into his room, Lyla watched him disappear. *God he looks extra hot tonight...*

She spent the next hour in the kitchen making enough noise to sound like she was creating a meal, when in reality she was just warming up the food and plating it. Then she set the table precisely the way she was taught while working at The Nue and lit some candles. She couldn't help herself from dancing to the music as she prepared their dinner. The lightness in her heart radiated from inside her body.

She stood back to admire the table and nodded with contentment, then changed into a plaid skirt, knee-high socks, and a white argyle sweater. Her hair was in a braid off to one side and she added an extra dab of lipstick.

When she was ready, she grabbed a bottle of merlot and poured a single glass. "*Monsieur*! Dinner is ready."

Aksel's mouth dropped when he saw her before noticing the table—it made her feel pretty.

"Lyla…you're beautiful …I mean, wow. Should I put a tie on with a dinner jacket?"

"No!" She savored his sweet smile as they sat down. "Thank you," she said, and lifted her glass of sparkling water. "I propose a toast—to new beginnings."

"Does it bother you that I am drinking wine?"

"Not at all. As long as you're okay with me drinking bubbly water from a wine glass."

"Cheers."

Aksel practically lapped up the tomato bisque soup and devoured every crumb of the grilled triple-cheese sandwiches. Each one had different cheeses, one had bacon on it, the other had honey-roasted turkey, but all had perfectly sliced tomatoes. *Thank you, Uncle Andrew.*

"*Dessert, monsieur?*"

"*Oui.*"

Lyla took the warm blueberry cobbler from the oven and cut two pieces, adding a scoop of French vanilla ice cream on top.

Aksel offered to clean since Lyla had cooked, and she agreed. She curled up on the couch with Misty on her lap and watched the logs crackling in the fireplace while listening to music Aksel had put on earlier.

After Aksel was done, he joined her on the couch. "I think you need to be in charge of the cooking from now on. It was delicious, and the blueberry cobbler was superb. Where did you learn to cook so well?"

"Oh, come now. It was nothing." She waved him off. "You are much more of a chef than I am."

"Oh, no, no, *ma chérie*, you—"

Lyla smirked.

"What is so funny?" Aksel asked.

"Well…" She tapped her lips. "There's something you should know. The delicious food you just ate? It all came from The Nue, except for the grilled cheese sandwiches. Honestly, I am only good at ordering."

Aksel guffawed and straddled her. "You little stinker!" He started to tickle her midsection and around her knees as desire began to fill her. "And you admit this after I did the dishes!"

She laughed carelessly as he teased her and the sexual tension between them grew. Once the giggling subsided, their noses were only inches apart, and they were breathing heavily. She could feel his desire growing in his pants. They looked into each other's eyes, and Lyla kissed him with all her pent-up passion for him.

For a long, intimate moment, they easily melded into each other. Aksel wrapped his arms around her, resting his hands on her ass cheeks. She pulled her sweater off and struggled to unhook her bra.

Suddenly, Aksel grabbed her arms. "*Ma chérie*, please stop for a moment. After everything we have been through…we mustn't satisfy ourselves for the sake of physical pleasure."

"Don't you want me?" Instantly she felt rejected and turned away from him.

"*Oui*, a thousand times over. But that is not the point. You see, I too have been on a journey, and I have come to realize that it is my soul that needs to find love as well."

She looked at him when she heard him mention his soul.

"Therefore, before we do anything physically pleasurable, I must ask you, Lyla, do you love me? Or do you just need physical pleasure? Or do you want me *because* you love me?"

Lyla slowly regained her emotions and sat up, putting her sweater back on. "Aksel, your friendship is important to me. Maybe I let this newfound feeling of forgiveness and freedom today get the best of me. I also need to focus on my future. I do love you. But on some level, and I can't understand why, honestly I am afraid to trust you completely."

"Thank you for your honesty." Aksel turned his head and cleared his throat.

"Should I move out? Maybe it is too complicated for both of us right now," she suggested meekly.

He shook his head and grabbed her hand. "Maybe we should just take it slow and see where it goes."

"I'd like that. For the record, I wholeheartedly believe you about my mother and what she did to you…to us. How she lied to me. But my brain is still spinning from my recent lifestyle and I'm still adjusting."

Aksel put his arms around her. "*Mi amour*, you are vulnerable right now. And as gorgeous as you look, I don't want to take advantage of that. You will always own my heart and soul forever and ever. If we are to end up as a couple, as I hope it will be, maybe one day I will own your heart and soul the same way."

"Perhaps," she said coyly. He already did but she had answers to find yet.

He kissed her on the lips and she returned the kiss gently. They spent a few more moments embraced in a comfortable silence and then he announced he needed to study before going to bed. He retired to his room for the night.

She hugged the pillow on the couch and then went into the bathroom with Misty in tow. Lyla showered and lay on her bed, reliving what had happened earlier. "Misty," she spoke softly, "he really is in love with me, isn't he? He's always been so special to me. We are connected beyond just what we went through a few years ago. Or even recently."

Lyla pet Misty's furry head. "You know what, baby girl? I need advice from Mommy Gin on this one. She offered me a job today, and I think we should take it."

Lyla and Misty yawned almost simultaneously and drifted off to sleep. Eventually, colorful dreams about a time where she was playing as a happy young girl in a field of hay on a farm somewhere filled her head. In the morning, she opened her eyes and quickly shut them, trying to reenter the dream that made her heart so happy.

Chapter 56

"Good morning, sweetheart. How'd you sleep?" Ginger asked Grant as he shuffled into the kitchen in his bathrobe.

"Perfectly. How about you, Gin?"

"Great." She lowered the issue of *Women's Wear Daily* she was reading on the couch and stretched.

"Holy shit," Grant said as looked at the kitchen clock. "It's almost nine! Why'd you let me sleep so late?"

"I figured you needed the sleep deposit. Anyway, I had a surprise call this morning and thought we should talk about it before we get to the office."

Grant poured himself coffee and took a few sips as he sat down on the couch. "Is this good news or bad?"

"Definitely good. Remember when I said I could use an extra pair of hands right now? Well I found someone."

"Anyone I know?"

"Oh, you know them."

"*Them?* As in plural?"

"Yup."

Ginger returned to the magazine as he waited for her to continue. "Hey, babe," she said, "you need to read this article about the new trade agreements that are being made with Mexico."

"C'mon, Gin! Don't leave me in suspense here. Who are the new assistants?"

"Well, one of them has four paws and is really furry…"

⊷⊷◉⊜⊰

Lyla walked the few blocks from the subway that afternoon and enjoyed the sunny, mild winter day. She had on a light-weight jacket as she entered The Nue carrying a Barney's shopping bag. Grant was already seated at a table with a window view and she walked toward him with a smile. She kissed her dad on the cheek, and when they both sat down, she put the bag under the table.

"Hi, beautiful. I hear that you and Misty will be on the payroll starting tomorrow," Grant said, looking at her with anticipation. "I didn't realize that you were interested in this end of the fashion industry."

"Yeah. I really am. Dad, living with Mom was difficult for me and I've only started realizing how damaging it was--Mom hated you and wanted to keep us apart, so she told me all the bad stuff about the fashion business. I have always wanted to know how you make your magic happen and dreamt as a child that someday I would be designing my own clothes."

Grant reached across the table and held Lyla's hand. "Sweetheart, I can't tell you how proud I am of you and having you work with me is more than a dream come true."

She studied her dad's face and could read the happiness on it. "God, Daddy, I've been a major pain your ass, haven't I?"

Before he could answer, their server walked up to take their order.

After ordering their iced teas and two Cobb salads, he shrugged. "Major pain in my ass? Yes. But nothing has changed between us. You still own my heart, baby girl. Uh, sorry, Lyla."

She winced. "Daddy, I always want to be your baby girl, okay? Thank you for my second chance."

Grant squeezed her hands, then reached into his coat pocket and put an envelope on the table.

"What's this? Employee paperwork already?" She picked it up and laughed when she saw H&M Designs on the envelope.

"God, I love it when you laugh. I've missed that so much. It's all the paper work from Howard Golden. I think you should have it."

"I already sent a copy to Mom and told her to never refer to Howard as my father."

"Gin told me. Thank you for sending it to your mom."

Lyla took the envelope and stuck it in her purse, and nothing further was spoken about Howard Golden. She had always known in her heart that Grant was her real father. "I'm sorry that you had to endure my childish fits—I wish I could take back all the terrible words I said to you."

"Don't worry about that. We need to press forward and not look back."

The waitress brought them their salads.

Lyla pushed aside a piece of hardboiled egg. "Dad, I still have some ways to go and I'm afraid I will slip." Her heart filled with sadness. What happened if she wasn't strong enough?

"Lyla, I know that." He put his fork down and looked at her. "But you are doing everything you can by attending drug abuse meetings and going to counseling. If you do relapse we will never give up on you and will always be there *no matter what*."

She absorbed the strength, love and determination on her father's face. It reminded her of when she'd tried to learn to ride her new pink Schwinn Sting-ray Lil Chik bike. It had been a warm day in May in Central Park and she was on her bike; he had just taken off the training wheels. She was so scared of falling but there he was running alongside her, "Pedal, baby girl, I won't let go. You can do this!" Tears welled in her eyes.

"Sweetheart, are you okay?" He reached across the table and she took his hand.

"More than you can imagine, Dad." She sighed. "I love you for always being there for me." Taking her napkin, she patted her tears. "Thank you, Daddy."

"For what?"

"Everything…from teaching me how to ride a bike, to still loving me after everything I put you and Ginger through." *Yes, life only has beginnings.*

After enjoying their dessert, Lyla felt it was time to finish off the past and reached under the table for the handle of the Barney's bag. With a glance around the restaurant to make sure nobody was paying attention, she placed it on the table.

"Oh, a gift for me?"

"Not exactly." The bag was filled with shoeboxes of money. "I need you to take this and put it somewhere safe until we can decide what to do with it."

"What is it?"

"It's some cash I saved from my...previous...occupation. I suggest you don't deposit it at the bank; it may raise a few eyebrows. One day, the three of us will figure how to best use it. But I gotta run, Daddy. I have a few things to do at home—I mean, at Aksel's."

His brow arched at the full shopping bag.

Lyla stood up and kissed him on the forehead. "Thanks again, Daddy, for everything. I love you."

"I love you, too."

She slipped her jacket on and started toward the exit, taking a quick glimpse over her shoulder. He looked up at her with astonishment after peeking inside the top box. "Holy. Fucking. Shit." She blew him a kiss and got the heck out of there.

Lyla arrived at Aksel's and put on some music. She washed their clothes, towels, and bed sheets. She vacuumed and made the beds. She dusted and wiped down the windows. When she finished all the cleaning, she headed out to the grocery store, excited about going to work—a definite fresh start.

Walking down the busy street, she realized how much emotional weight she'd lost just by giving Dad her naughty cash stash. Handing over her hard-earned dirty money allowed her to emerge from yet another dark abyss. She was grateful for everyone in her life who loved her, even after the heartache she put them through during the last six months.

She picked up some milk, bread, eggs, and fried chicken for dinner. On the way home, her breath hitched, and she halted when she spotted Slim's Caddy driving down the street in her direction. Bile rose up her throat and she feared she might vomit. The car passed without slowing down, and Lyla shook off her terror, running back to Aksel's.

She burst into the apartment, locked the door, and shut off all the lights. She knew she was safe, yet she didn't *feel* safe. Fear had shaken her to her core. Where she'd used drugs before to calm down, she instead decided to sleep it off.

She lit a candle and wrote a note for Aksel.

Aksel,

I cannot thank you enough for last night. For you, your understanding, your honesty, and your respect. I will always be your best friend.

XOXO,

Ly

PS… There are wings in the fridge in case you need a late-night snack.

She took a prescribed sleeping pill and curled up in bed with Misty. Tomorrow was her first day at G Squared, the first time she'd be able to express herself creatively in a healthy work environment—her thoughts no longer were on naughty nights and dancing. She closed her eyes and drifted into a place from long ago.

Chapter 57

"Good morning, Aksel."

Aksel jumped at the sound of Lyla's voice, pouring the coffee creamer onto the counter instead of his cup. She snickered.

"Well, somebody needs to switch to decaf." Smiling at him, she grabbed a paper towel to wipe up the mess.

"Good morning. What are you doing up so early?" He had a quizzical look on his face. She'd been sleeping in for the past week.

She thought about telling him they would be working together for a few hours a day. *Nah, I love teasing him...* "I decided to do some community service hours today."

"Oh, I didn't remember that you had to do that." He took a sip of his coffee. "Well, you look splendid. Where are you volunteering?"

She looked at her watch to avoid giving him details. "Oh crap, I gotta run. Misty? Come here, baby girl." She turned to Aksel. "I'll catch up with you later."

Aksel watched her while she quickly slipped on her coat, corralled her cat into the carrier and left, closing the door behind her.

"Um, okay? Bye."

⊷⊶⊙⊜⊷⊶

Lyla walked into G Squared just before nine a.m. toting the cat carrier in one hand and a box of pastries in the other.

"Good morning, Sue!"

"Good morning, Ms. Robinson. Welcome aboard. And what's your cat's name again?"

"This is my partner in crime, Misty." She placed the carrier on Sue's counter for her to see.

Misty blinked at Sue. "She's adorable! Mrs. Robinson prepared a work space for you in her office."

"Thanks, Sue." Lyla deposited the pastries on the countertop by the coffee pot in the lobby for all to share.

Lyla knocked on the door to Ginger's office.

"Come in!"

She opened the door and stopped in astonishment. On the far side of the room there was a door with a nameplate that read, "Lyla and Misty." Ginger smiled but didn't speak, just winked at her as she finished up on the phone.

Ginger had turned the private office space that Grant and Ginger used to share into Lyla's own office. Under the window was a new desk. Every colored pencil imaginable was displayed inside a large coffee mug next to a framed picture of Misty. Pads of drawing paper and layers of colored fabric swatches were neatly organized in open shelving on the wall opposite of the window.

"Misty, look at what we have here!" Lyla put the carrier down and opened it. Misty peered out at her new surroundings.

Ginger had decorated Lyla's office perfectly. The walls and shelves were filled with photos of Lyla and her family. In one corner, there was a cat climbing castle and food and water bowls; in the other corner, a litter box hidden inside a faux small cabinet that had a swinging door, and cat toys lay on the floor in the shape of a heart.

Lyla finally sat down in her black leather chair and swiveled around in circles while taking it all in. Then there was a light knock on the door.

"Uh, come in?" She laughed.

"Do you like it?" Ginger beamed.

"Like it? I love it! And I think Misty's pretty happy too."

They hugged, and Grant walked in.

"Welcome, baby girl—Ms. Robinson."

"Thanks, Daddy—Grant. I should call you Grant and Ginger here, right? Or Mr. and Mrs.?"

"First names are fine," Grant replied.

"I thought this was a temporary gig, but looking around…"

"It is temporary. Or permanent, if you decide you really like the biz," Ginger replied with a gleam in her eyes.

"Well, I have a lot to learn."

"We all do," Grant chimed in. "Fashion is forever changing."

"So where do I start?" Lyla looked from one to the other.

"That's up to Ginger. She's the one who needed the extra paws."

Lyla spent the next three hours with Ginger touring the entire eleventh and twelfth floors and meeting the staff. She looked at design notes during lunch at her desk, sharing her turkey sandwich with her little piggy brat cat.

She reminded Ginger that she had an appointment with Dr. Lebow at 1:30 and would return right after. Lyla stood in the lobby of G Squared, waiting for the elevator.

The doors opened, and she almost collided with Aksel as he stepped off, not paying attention to where he was going.

"Pardon me, *madame*—Lyla? I didn't expect to see you here! How did your volunteer work go today?"

"Really good, since they hired Misty, also. I'll tell you all about it when I get back." She hopped in the elevator and smiled at him as the doors closed.

Lyla walked the ten blocks to Dr. Lebow's office organizing her thoughts about things she wanted to talk about before her regression session. She sat in the waiting room, rummaging through her purse for a pen, when Dr. Lebow opened the door and led a tall man with white hair and a stoop out.

"Larry, please call me before your next appointment if you need to."

"Thank you, Doctor."

Then Dr. Lebow turned to Lyla. "Hello, Lyla." He gave her a hug in greeting. "Come on back."

She followed him down the short hallway to his office and he closed the door behind them as she sat down in one of the tan recliners.

"How have you been since I saw you last?"

"Actually, great. So many things have happened that I'm not sure where to begin."

He laughed. "It's only been two days."

"Yeah, but what a couple of days they've been!"

They discussed the job she was starting at G Squared and her experience with Aksel, how she was still unable to trust him. "I want to."

Dr. Lebow counseled, "I believe that the root of all your issues do have beginnings. We just need to unearth those events, some of which are from this lifetime and some are from your past lives."

"I'm ready to understand more about my life. I'm ready to trust Aksel."

"I'm happy for your enthusiasm, but please do not be disappointed if it takes a few more sessions. Trust is a big issue, and we cannot control how events play out during the regression. Let's begin, shall we?"

She snuggled down into the chair, her eyes closed.

After the doctor had relaxed her, he asked, "Do you know where you are?"

"At my home, waiting for Father to return from work." She spoke again with a British accent. "He always has a new surprise for me on this day of the week. Last week was a pretty rock in the shape of a heart. I can't wait to see what he'll bring me today!"

"What is your name?"

"My name is Isabella. But everyone calls me Izzy."

"How old are you, Izzy?"

Lyla hesitated, thought for a moment, then proudly held up both hands with all fingers splayed and said, "Ten!"

She was silent, then shared, "Uncle Kenneth and Auntie Helen are here now. They are sad. My Auntie is crying." Lyla suddenly burst into tears. "No, no, no!"

"Why are you crying, Izzy? What happened?"

"Uncle and Auntie say he's gone...my father. I hear them say that they are sorry for our loss. My brother, Shelby, will not cry in front of anyone. This isn't the surprise I wanted from Father! He's not coming home. Ever again. Father..." She quietly wept.

"Izzy, let's move forward to a happy moment."

Lyla regained her composure again and Dr. Lebow waited for her breathing to become relaxed as she searched within her REM state. A smile slowly formed on her face. "Happy birthday!"

"Is it your birthday?"

"Oh no. My best friend's. We always pretend we are sisters. I love her so much. I gave her the heart-shaped rock that Father gave me as a birthday present. She promised to take care of it forever and ever." Her happiness radiated throughout her being, expressed in her childlike body language.

"Who's your best friend?"

"Rachel." Her smile softened and then turned to a frown.

"Izzy, are you upset?"

"Mum is angry all the time since Father died. It's only been a few months. I have so many chores to finish, and I'm already late because of Rachel's party. Mum will be cross again. I have to leave but I don't want to."

"Did you leave the party then?"

"Not yet." She covered her ears. "I don't want to hear her say how terrible our life is or how Father let us down, so I'm staying a little longer. Why does she say bad things about Father like that? But she isn't mean to Shelby. Just me. She loves Shelby more."

"What makes you think she loves him more than you?"

"She tells me all the time that I am too hefty and not pretty. Shelby just came to the party to fetch me. Now I *have* to leave."

"What happened when you return home?"

"She is very mad at me. It's the same thing again and again. She tells me I have to work hard and keep learning the laundry cycles. That I will end up just like her but probably childless. She says that whether men die or leave us, don't ever forget that they will always let you down. I am so sad."

"Okay, Izzy, let's move forward to a happy moment."

Lyla smiled and took a deep breath. "Mum died and now I get to live with my Auntie. It's nice here. I love Auntie Helen. She is so kind but lives alone."

"Where is Uncle Kenneth?"

"He passed away a long time ago, just after Father."

"How old are you now, Izzy?"

"Fifteen."

"Is your brother younger or older?"

"Older. He's away. He joined the Royal Navy."

"Were you ever close to him?"

"Oh, yes, always. He is very soft on Rachel. He writes both of us all the time. She shows me his letters."

"You are able to spend time with Rachel?"

"Every day now that I live with Auntie. We go to school together."

"Okay. So let's move forward a few years to when you are finished with school. What do you see yourself doing?"

"I work with Rachel and her parents at their public house, their pub."

"A pub, like a drinking establishment, or a bar?"

"Yes. I think there is another war beginning. There are a lot of young soldiers who visit. Shelby wrote that he's mastered flying a plane."

"Let's keep moving forward. Look for a place that makes you happy."

A naughty smile crossed her face. "I enjoy all the fly-boys. That's what Rachel calls them." She laughed. "She isn't like me, and I laugh when she calls me a harlot. I know she is toying with me. We have fun with them…I have more fun than she does…I'm not at all what my mother predicted," she said defiantly. "I'm not hefty—I'm voluptuous."

"Are you happy with who you find yourself to be?"

"Oh, yes!"

"Now it is time to talk to Lyla again. Do not let go of how happy you are, okay?"

"Okay."

"We have covered a lot today. How do you feel right now?"

"Peaceful. Aware."

"Good. You can open your eyes when you are ready, and we will discuss what we've learned."

Chapter 58

Lyla chose to walk back to G Squared so she could absorb what she and Dr. Lebow had discussed after her regression therapy. The cold temperature invigorated her, and as she neared the building, she realized she'd been humming "Baby, It's Cold Outside" by Ray Charles and Betty Carter. *I really can't stay…But baby it's cold outside…The answer is no…But don't you see…How can you do this thing to me…Get over that old doubt…Oh, but it's cold outside…"* She understood the significance of a few words worming through her brain, *"Get over that old doubt…"*

Grant spotted her as she passed by his office door and called out, "Lyla, may I speak with you please?"

"Yes, Da—Grant." She shut his door behind her.

"I'm going to have to get used to that," he said. "Here, I need you to fill out some paperwork. It's a tax form."

"Got it."

"That's only if you want to stay a little longer than a couple of weeks."

"I'm excited about being here and hope it works out."

"Great. On a different note, I put your bag of cash in the safe over there. Have you, uh, thought of how you want to spend it?" He narrowed his eyes.

"My rehab cost a lot of money. Why not take some to recover what you spent to help—?"

"Your mental health has no price tag."

"Hmmm, then maybe we can donate it to the center?"

Her dad smiled at her with pride.

"Anyway," Lyla continued, "let's discuss it with Gin later. I want her opinion." She looked around. "Where's Aksel?"

"Somewhere around here. Hey, how about Nick's for dinner? The four of us if that's okay?"

"Sounds great, Daddy." She walked to her office and closed the door behind her.

Lyla picked up Misty, who was napping on her desk, and went to find Aksel. His desk was in the shipping office which was down the hall from Ginger's office. She saw him standing at the work counter through the door window and for a few moments she just *watched* him. He was always a treat for the eyes, being so gorgeous with his dark hair and square shoulders covered in an off-white fishermen's sweater with jeans. So caught up in his work, she debated if she should bother him. But she wanted to see his face and sexy eyes. She finally tapped on the glass window of the door. He turned and his face lit up as he waved her in.

She opened the door and entered the office. "Hi!"

"Hi!" He walked up to her, stopping within inches of her personal space. Her cheeks flushed.

"Guess you figured out where I went this morning?"

His eyes twinkled with humor. "*Oui.*"

"Are you okay with us working together?"

"You and Misty?" he teased.

"You know what I mean." She placed Misty on the floor and the kitten sat at her feet.

"Actually, I am glad you are here. Ginger really needs the help, and you have always had a great eye for fashion."

"Thanks, Aksel. We're having dinner tonight at Nick's, just the executives." She chuckled at the thought of her words. "That means you, me, Ginger and Grant."

He was standing so close to her that the scent of his skin filled her head.

"I am a bit nervous considering the last time we had dinner there, Nicky was ready to beat me to a pulp."

"Then you'd better be good." Trying to back away from his magnetic hold on her, she changed the subject. "I'll have to stop by the apartment to drop Misty off. I doubt she'd be welcomed at Nick's."

"Are you kidding?" Aksel said. "I would just put a plate of spaghetti and fish balls in front of her."

She smirked, peering into his eyes. "And what—hook her up with a boy cat named Tramp? Is life really a Disney movie, with happily-ever-afters and magical princesses?"

"I think you should look in the mirror for the answers to those questions, *Princess* Lyla." He stepped into her space, curving his palm over her shoulder. "As for the happily-ever-after, that is always within our reach. It's a choice."

Struck speechless, she couldn't move until he winked at her.

"See you later, princess."

⊷≡◐◑≡⊶

Evan picked up the two couples and they cheerfully talked all the way to Nick's. She enjoyed watching Aksel laugh and interact with Grant and Ginger. Misty was inside her carrier, purring loudly and preparing to take a nap as she kitty-stomped the plush pink blanket that Ginger had chosen.

"Evan, would you mind keeping Misty with you?" She didn't feel comfortable bringing the cat into the restaurant.

"Miss Lyla, it would be my pleasure."

"You really don't mind keeping an eye on her, Evan?" Lyla asked again, just to be sure.

"No, Miss Lyla. You know I love animals. I wonder if she would get along with my dog? My daughter named him Rascal."

"We should probably introduce them sometime."

Evan laughed. "Yes, yes. Enjoy dinner."

"Thanks, Evan. I'll bring you your favorite lasagna to take home," Grant said.

Grant, Ginger, and Lyla, followed by Aksel, walked into Nick's.

"My favorite Robinsons! And you, Mr. Francisco Treat. Tony! They're here!" Nick yelled from behind the counter.

"I can see that, Nicky, you tink I'm blind or somethin? Jesus."

Nick reached out for them. "Ginga, Grant."

They all hugged Nick and Ginger whispered, "Thank you again."

Nick peered closely at Lyla. "Ahh, bambina, you look boo-tee-ful!"

"Thanks, Nicky."

Nick squeezed her tighter.

"Nicky—air," Lyla squeaked out.

"Sorry. It's just so good to see yooz all put togetha, ya know? My God." He did the sign of the cross and looked above to the ceiling, clasping his hands together.

"I feel good. Thank you." Lyla laughed softly and tucked her fingers into Aksel's coat, while he reached out to shake Nick's hand.

"Good to see you too, Mr. France. Jesus. Forgive me. What's your name again? I wish I could get it right."

"*Monsieur* Nicky—"

"I see yooz been takin' good care of our girl here?"

Lyla felt a closeness to Aksel and for the first time openly interacted affectionately toward him.

"Nicky, *paesan*, his name is Aksel. And it sure looks like it, doesn't it?" Grant replied before Lyla had a chance.

"Yes, sir." Aksel looked back and forth between Grant and Nick, Lyla leaning on his shoulder.

"Sit! Sit! Ginga, red, white? Both?"

"Both, Nicky. We're celebrating Lyla's first day of working with us at G Squared."

"I'll take a bubbly water, Nicky," Lyla quickly chimed in, basking in his nod of approval.

Chapter 59

After a lovely meal filled with laughter and conversation, they sipped their espressos as Nick embellished yet another story involving his bat with an ornery customer regarding the fish special. He loved the Robinsons like they was blood. The door opened and a group of three men and a woman entered the restaurant.

Nick was first to notice the look on Lyla's face, "Jesus, Lyla, you look like you seen a ghost or somethin'." Nick followed her line of sight and immediately jumped up. "Excuse me, folks," he said, then whistled to get Tony's attention as he approached the four customers who stood at the entryway: Slim, Candy, Peetie, and Paulie.

Slim nodded and looked around then back to Nick. "Nice place you got here, you fuckin greaseball!"

Nick led them to a table on the opposite side of the restaurant from where the Robinsons were seated. As Slim sat down, he eyed Nick up and down. "Look at ya. Yooz look like Chef Boyardee! What happened to your leathers?"

"I save that for special occasions. You shoulda told me yooz was comin' Slim. I coulda prepared something extra nice just for yooz."

Slim shook his head. "So, what, now I gotta call ya ta tell yooz I'm eatin' at your fine dining establishment?" He waved his hands all around. "Get outta here. Now who do I have to blow ta get some fucking grub here?"

Peetie and Paulie guffawed at the joke, while Candy lit a cigarette and rolled her eyes.

Nick bit his lip, holding back his anger, and said, "How about some wine?" Tony walked up and took the bat out of Nick's hand, and started scratching his back with the short end of it.

"Eh, Nicky, who's dis? You spendin alota time ova heres. I ain't never met nobody at dis table. I'm Tony, Nick's partner." He shook hands with everyone at the table after Nick introduced him. "It's a pleasure to make your acquaintances."

"Let me tell yooz, Nicky, the food better be amazing, 'cause the help ain't no good." Slim chuckled and winked at Candy.

Nick took a deep breath, then smiled. "For yooz, only the best," he said through gritted teeth. He turned, walked into the kitchen, and yelled at his kitchen staff, "Hurry da fuck up! I ain't happy right now!"

⟡

Lyla slouched in her chair, hoping to remain out of view of Slim and his crew. Her fingers dug deeper into Aksel's leg by the second. Ginger and Grant seemed oblivious to her state of mind as they had their backs turned to her and Aksel, talking to some of Nick's patrons they knew at the next table.

Aksel whispered, "*Bébé*, what is wrong?"

Lyla nodded to Slim's table and Aksel looked over.

"Do not fret; I do not believe they saw you. Nicky has placed them across the restaurant, and I'm sure he'll keep them distracted. Plus, I am here now, so you are safe. No matter what." He handed her his glass of wine without thinking about her sobriety and Lyla winced. "Oh, sorry." He exchanged the wine for her water.

Their noses were inches apart, and a single tear spilled over her cheek. He kissed it away before it reached her chin, then wrapped an arm around her and pulled her into his chest after she swallowed some water from her glass. She melted into his embrace.

⊷═◉═⊶

Near the large ovens toward the back of the open kitchen, Nick hastily prepared a special plate of bread with antipasto and stuffed artichokes for Slim's table.

After delivering the starters, he whispered to Tony, "Jesus fucking Christ, Tony! Why in the fuck did he pick tonight to show up? Is that motherfucker having Lyla followed?"

Tony tossed some garlic into a frying pan and shrugged. "Maybe he's just here ta eat, ya know?"

Nick shook his head. "You don't know this fucker like I do. We need to get my extended family outta here safely."

As Nick and Tony were leaving the kitchen with their arms full of dishes and more wine bottles for Slim's table, Nick saw one of the men from Slim's party returning from the restroom. Just as Slim was biting into a garlic roll, the beefed-up man leaned over to Slim's ear and whispered something. Slim dropped the bread onto the plate, splashing olive oil and pepper over the dish, and threw his napkin onto the table. He got up, looked toward the Robinsons' table, and stalked over.

Tony and Nick looked at each other in shock.

"Fuck me," Nick said and hurried to intercept, but to no avail as Slim charged right past him.

"What a lovely family you have here, Miss," Slim said to Lyla, his hands leaning on the edge of the table top.

"Th-thank you," Lyla stuttered.

Grant looked at the short, menacing man who spoke sweet words laced with animosity. He'd caused his daughter to turn as white as the bleached tablecloth. Did she know him?

"Well, aren't you gonna introduce me?" the man said.

Aksel stood up and stepped around Lyla to stand face-to-face with the man. Seconds later, two thugs were at the man's side, like a bad gangster movie. Nick and Tony moved between the two parties. Grant tried to stand, but Ginger pulled him down.

"Hey, hey, now," Nick said, arms placating as if attempting to prevent a scuffle. "There ain't no problems, right? We're all just here having my great Italian food. How's about a bottle of wine? Just follow me back to your table, Slim."

Slim?

The man got himself under control and straightened his jacket. "Oh, right, I thought you were a movie star, Miss. Excuse the interruption of your family dinner."

"Thank you for being a gentleman, sir," Aksel said cryptically before he sat down, and wrapped his arm around Lyla's shoulder.

"Can I be a *gentleman*?" Slim looked at his thugs. "Peetie, Paulie?" He faked a laugh.

"Of course, you are," the one he'd called Peetie blurted out.

The other, Paulie, patted his pocket and Grant would bet the thug was packing.

Nicky stood face to face with Slim. "Slim," he said softly, "I knows yooz follow da gentleman's rules."

Slim nodded slowly. "Right, right. Well then, alls I got to say is you should be in da movies." He pointed at Lyla, then grabbed Nick's arm. "Nicky, bambino, I'm starving. If you'll excuse me and my boys, we're gonna finish our fine Italian cuisine."

Lyla remained pale and quiet, her eyes down.

Slim tapped the table before her and she jumped. "Enjoy your night, Miss."

After they left, Grant turned to Ginger and whispered in her ear, "Jesus Christ, is that an 'as need to know basis'?"

"Yes," she quietly replied and nodded toward Lyla, who was being comforted and protected by Aksel. "She'll be fine."

"Those guys were scary. That's all I'm going to say for now." He wanted the story—someday. He had a feeling he owed Nicky the world.

"Good idea."

Chapter 60

It was obvious that no one wanted to speak as they rode in silence. Evan would drop off her dad and Ginger first, since they were on the way. The events at Nick's had taken the wind out of Lyla's sails and she tucked herself into Aksel's chest. What if Slim had hurt him? She pushed away and retrieved Misty from the cage.

Her dad's brow lifted in wonder. "Ly, you've got her trained like a dog, huh?" They all laughed lightly.

"I sometimes think she is a dog trapped in a cat's body," Aksel said as he scratched Misty's ears.

"How was the steak pizzaiola, Aksel?" Her dad patted Aksel's knee.

"Always good. Nick is an amazing chef. Don't you agree, Lyla?"

Lyla twirled Misty's tail around her finger, taking solace from her soft fur. "Yes. But my favorite is the Hawaiian pizza."

Her dad chuckled. "I will forever struggle to call that Italian food since it has pineapple on it. But it's on a lot of Italian menus, so I guess it is."

"Daddy, a Hawaiian Italian could have created it..."

The limo arrived at Grant and Ginger's apartment building. When Ginger was getting out after Grant, Lyla grabbed her arm. "Since you're the boss-lady and all, I was wondering if we could leave work early tomorrow and hook up for some Ly and Mommy Gin time?"

"Sure, sweetheart." Ginger searched her face as if to make sure Lyla was all right, so Lyla nodded.

"Say we leave around three?"

"Great," Ginger said. We can have a late lunch..."

"Okay. Perfect! Goodnight, Gin."

When her dad shut the door, the limo drove off and there was a moment of silence before Lyla said furiously to Aksel, "That was incredibly stupid, Aksel. Why would you ever risk your safety like that for me?"

"Lyla, once in a while when the odds are against you, *showing no fear is all you have*, therefore you *just do it.*" His reply held strength.

"But Aksel—"

"For you, I would do anything."

Tears welled in her eyes as her body trembled. Misty purred and snuggled closer. "Don't risk your life for me like that ever again. I'm not worthy of it."

"Lyla, I wish you could understand how much you are worth to me." There was no doubting the loving expression in his eyes.

"You can't go to war with him. This is not a playground with a big, bad bully. He's a person who makes things he wants to, just, um, disappear." Suddenly she began crying and hyperventilating all at the same time.

He pulled her into his arms. "I love you so much," he whispered.

"Love can't conqueror all." She gained control of her emotions as he just held her silently. "Slim's reach is far and wide. I don't want to lose you."

"But he can't hurt you anymore, Lyla." The car stopped as it arrived at the apartment.

"Maybe. Will you sleep next to me tonight?"

"Sure." He kissed her cheek as they gathered all their stuff.

She lifted her palm to their driver. "Thank you, Evan."

"Your welcome, Miss Lyla."

Aksel led her up the stairs, and at their doorway, she investigated his face for any signs of her taking advantage of him. "I just don't want to sleep alone. I'm not trying to be a tease or anything, I just—"

"Sh. I understand. You are asking me to sleep *next* to you, not *with* you, my princess."

⊷═◉═⊶

In the morning when Lyla woke, Aksel was no longer next to her. She slipped her hand to where he had been sleeping, but the sheet was cold. She snuggled under the covers. Where was Misty? She finally looked at the clock and saw that it was already eight thirty in the morning.

She quickly climbed out of bed, put on her robe and slippers, and made her way to the kitchen.

"Misty, baby, where are you?"

Lyla went to Aksel's room where she found Misty curled up on his sweater from yesterday, in the center of his bed. "So now you're under his spell too?" She stood in the doorway with her hands on her hips. "I know how you feel, baby. How does he do that to us?"

Sipping her tea as she got ready for work, Lyla reran the events of the previous night in her mind, and how Aksel had stood up to Slim—terrifying! Had anyone ever done that for her before? *Well, brave or foolish, it is a first for me, and it makes me really feel good but scares the hell out of me.*

She stared out the window for a few minutes at the cloudless blue sky. *Would I have done the same for him? I'd like to think so, despite the way I have treated him over the last seven months...*

After feeding Misty, she decided to go pick up a bagel for her breakfast. There was the best shop a block away, and worth the cold. "I'll be right back Misty," she called out.

Lyla took a deep breath as she went out into the chilly morning breeze—emotionally content. She stood at the corner of Spring Street and Broadway waiting to cross when a black Caddy screeched to a halt in front of her—almost instinctively she knew it was Slim's. The tinted window of the back passenger's seat rolled down, her heart began to race, and she pivoted to walk in the opposite direction, hoping to avoid a confrontation with Slim.

"Hey, Lyla!" a female voice yelled.

Lyla turned to see Candy wave, her winter coat snugged up around her neck, her red lipstick in a smile.

"Uh, hi, Candy," Lyla said, fearful after the previous night's events.

"Come here a sec, Lyla. I just wanna talk." Candy gestured Lyla over. "Slim's not here, honey, just your Candy."

Lyla hesitated a moment, then peered inside—Candy was indeed alone in the back seat.

"Baby, I'm so sorry that Slim made such a scene last night. He can be such an idiot. He's just hurt that you left him…us. But if you ever need anything, you can call me. You know that, right?"

Lyla didn't speak.

"Anyway," Candy said as she handed Lyla a small brown paper bag. "Here's a little gift from your Candy to make up for last night. Just to say how sorry I am about what happened."

Lyla looked inside the bag and saw three vials of cocaine and countless ecstasy capsules. "Candy, I-I don't know if I should—"

"Oh, just take it. I only want you to be happy."

Lyla's addictive brain quickly rationalized it as an opportunity to slip from reality which she really craved. "O-okay, thanks."

"If you need anything, just call me. No strings attached, and I mean that. I love you, sweetheart."

The window went up, and the Caddy sped away.

⊷⟊⟊⊶

An hour later she called and spoke with Ginger at work. "Gin, I'm not feeling well today."

"Leftover nerves from last night?"

"Probably. I'll call you later and let you know if I feel any better."

"You can still come over if you're up to it. I cleared my calendar this afternoon."

"I'm going to call and see if I can get in with Dr. Lebow first," she lied. "I'll let you know."

A few hours later, Lyla was dancing around in front of the fireplace. *I'm in total control of this. This is easy!* She had a glass of club soda laced with ecstasy in one hand which swished back and forth as she swayed to the music. When the door unexpectedly opened, she jumped, her heart pumping hard.

"Lyla? I thought you would be at work," Aksel said as he walked in. He tossed his keys on the table. "Are you okay? You look a little off…"

"Aksel, hi. I'm, um, just trying to relax. How about you?"

"I was in the mood for some of last night's leftovers. I did not expect to see you."

"I took a mental health day, if you know what I mean." She winked.

"Ah, the perks of being the bosses' daughter."

She held his hand. "Come with me. I want to talk to you about something." She led him to the couch, and they both sat, facing each other.

"So, what is happening in that amazing mind of yours, *mi amour*?" he asked.

"A lot of things. But most importantly, you. Or us."

"What do you mean?"

She grabbed both of his hands and looked into his eyes. "Aksel, in the last twenty-four hours, I have come to realize how much you love me. What you did at the restaurant, and how you slept with me last night, so I would feel secure without taking advantage of me…" She paused to drink from her glass. "I want you to know I'm deeply in love with you."

Aksel sat there in shock. Something seemed off with her, but he *needed* her to be just as in love with him as he was with her.

Lyla stood up before he could say anything and pulled her robe off her shoulders, revealing her body to him.

He was hesitant, but all his protective inhibitions dissipated immediately, leaving his heart unguarded. Even his fear that she was always a miniscule moment away from breaking his heart again left him.

"Make love to me, Aksel. I can't wait any longer."

She sat on his lap and kissed him, her bare breasts pressed against his chest.

"Are you sure –" he said between kisses, "we should—"

She stood up and removed her panties.

"I need you." She took his hand and placed his fingertips between her legs. His fingers slid easily inside her wet lips. She was slowly grinding into his hand, begging him with her body. He couldn't hold back any longer, his doubts burnt away by his passion. Within seconds, they were in each other's arms, kissing and fondling the other's body.

"Love once brought us together," she whispered, panting heavily, "so this time, love can *keep* us together."

Aksel lifted Lyla up in his arms and carried her to his bed. He unbuttoned his shirt as she unbuckled his belt and lowered his pants. His swollen cock was hidden only by his boxer briefs, and she yanked them to his knees and wrapped her hand around his thick shaft. Then her tongue danced softly around the tip of his cock, licking his precum.

He looked at her spectacular naked body lying in front of him as she began to suck his rock-hard cock. He pulled her hair into two knots—two fists full of hair so he could rhythmically slide her head up and down his hard length. Finally, he picked her up, and set her on her back so he could stretch next to her.

He slid his fingers inside the slippery lips between her thighs. He loved how wet she was for him, and he sucked on her nipples before he spread her legs. Lyla looked at him with desire in her eyes when he bent down and sucked her clit. She pulled his head into her. He slid two fingers inside her while his tongue gently circled her clit, bringing her to a mind-shattering climax.

He crawled up to her face with his cock resting against the lips of her pussy, looking into her beautiful blue eyes. At last, feeling free of all his fear-driven inhibitions, he gently slid his cock inside her. Slowly he pushed into her as deeply as he could, feeling the back of her pussy. He attempted to keep control of his primal desire for her, just trying to soak in the fact that they were one again, both physically and emotionally.

Aksel began to thrust in and out of her, slowly at first and then feverishly. She pushed her hips toward him as they both began their ascent to an intensely overwhelming climax. His ass and thighs tightened with each thrust. Her legs were locked around his back. Both her clit and the inner walls of her pussy were wrapped around his cock as if sucking it when she began to cum. Aksel let out a guttural moan as he exploded inside her. He tried to focus on her eyes as he filled her.

They lay there for a while, exhausted from the physical and mental pleasure they'd just shared. He wouldn't move off her; he couldn't. He just quietly listened to her heartbeat. As it slowed, and their breathing returned to normal, he whispered, "I love you, *bébé*." She just purred in response, holding him tight.

An hour later, after making love again, he whispered, "I must return to class. Will I see you later at work?"

"I don't think I'm going in today. It's so cozy. Can you just forget class and stay in bed with me? Forever?"

"Back away, you temptress!" he teased her. "I would love to. But I do need to use the restroom first."

When Aksel returned to the bedroom, Lyla wasn't in bed. He found her in the kitchen and silently walked up behind her to embrace her naked body again. Before he could, though, she turned, and he saw her empty two capsules into her glass of club soda.

"Lyla? What are you doing? Drugs!?"

Lyla looked up, startled. "Aksel! You scared the shit out of me!"

"Answer the question, Lyla."

"This? This is nothing. It just gives me a nice high. It's not the same as before."

He was frozen, his eyes welling up.

"*Bébé?*" she whispered. He just stared at her...through her. "Are you okay? Are *we* okay?"

He covered his eyes with his hands. "I don't know. I…just don't know." He shook his head and returned to the bedroom where they'd just made love.

She followed him and begged, "Please, please forgive me. Please forget all the horrible things I've said to you in the past. *Please* know that what I said to you today is the truth."

"The things you said today were all spoken while you were high, right? If so, then they are all lies. I must leave."

He tried to get dressed, but she wouldn't let him go without protesting. "No, don't! Don't do this, Aksel! Please! Don't leave me! It was just a momentary lapse. Please don't—"

He pushed her away, and she landed on the bed. He dressed in silence as she lay there sobbing. "Oh, Aksel, please try to understand…"

"I will talk to you in a few days." His heart shattered.

"No! I hate those words! It brings me right back to when I was the only one in love. We've come so far since then, haven't we?"

"The problem is, Lyla, you were never the only one in love. I…I just need to think this through. I want to be with you but being with me does not seem to fulfill *you*. My love for you is pure, but you turn to mind-altering substances to *feel* your love for me."

He turned and left. Lyla got up to chase after him, but she crumbled to the floor and sobbed. She was broken and alone.

Chapter 61

"**M**ommy Gin?" Lyla said on the phone. She was sniffling, and Ginger knew immediately by the sound of her voice that something was wrong.

"Ly? What's wrong?" Ginger replied.

"I need to see you. Can we still meet at your apartment ASAP?"

"I'll be right there."

At the office, Ginger told Grant that she was meeting Lyla and gathered her things to leave. She decided to tell Grant how desperate Lyla sounded and that she was heading to their apartment to meet her.

While Ginger waited for the elevator, a million thoughts raced through her mind. When it opened, Aksel almost ran her over as he stepped out with such haste.

"Pardon me, *Madame* Ginger," Aksel said as he turned to face her. "Is *Monsieur* Grant available?"

"He's in his office. Are you okay?"

"No. Not in the least." Aksel walked away, and Ginger stepped onto the elevator, knowing in her heart that his actions had everything to do with Lyla.

⤝⫘⫘⤞

Aksel walked down the hall and knocked on Grant's open office door. "*Monsieur* Grant, may we speak?"

"Come in, Aksel. What's up, my friend?"

Aksel sat down in front of Grant's desk. "*Monsieur*, please accept my apologies, but I have decided to resign my intern position with you. Effective immediately."

Grant looked at him in disbelief. "I'm in shock, Aksel. What happened in the last twenty-four hours? Please tell me it's nothing we have done to upset you. Or is this about last night's table visit from those thugs?"

Aksel held back the truth; all he could do was shake his head, no. "I have personal reasons. Please except my apologies."

Grant got up from his chair, walked around his desk, and sat next to him. "What's going on, Aksel?"

Aksel cleared his throat. "*Monsieur* Grant, I cannot tell you how much you mean to me, but I cannot talk about it." He stood up and handed Grant his keys. "I will call you in a few days to tell you where to send my final check. I am sorry."

They shook hands, and Aksel stumbled out of his office.

⁘⟴⟶⟵◆⟶⁘

Ginger rode the elevator up to the apartment, unable to get the look on Aksel's face out of her head. She thought about calling Grant as she unlocked the door, but when she opened it, she spotted Lyla's coat and purse in a heap on the floor by the door.

"Ly, where are you?" There was no answer. Ginger walked into the front room and found Lyla curled up on the couch like a little child, sobbing, with tissues on the floor and all around her.

"Oh, Ly!" Ginger ran over and held her sweaty, overheated body.

"I screwed up badly," Lyla said between broken sobs while trembling in her arms.

Ginger gently rocked her back and forth. "I'm here now. It's okay. Just let it out, my sweet girl. I love you." She held her shaking body with Lyla's head buried against her chest and attempted to calm her down. She began to pet her hair with one hand while she rubbed Lyla's back with the other. Ginger wished now that she had gone back to the office to ask Aksel what the hell had happened.

"I messed up bad, Gin. I need to use the bathroom—I think I'm going puke!"

"Okay, honey." Ginger helped her to the bathroom and thought about calling Grant again, but she could hear Lyla gagging through the bathroom door. "Would you like some water?"

"Yes, please. Cold water sounds good. Thanks."

While Ginger poured Lyla a glass of water, she opted for something stronger to soothe her own nerves and made a vodka tonic. *I wish I knew what Aksel wanted to see Grant about. It obviously has everything to do with Lyla.*

She waited in the living room for Lyla to return.

⊹⊱────◈────⊰⊹

Lyla looked at her face in the mirror in the bathroom. Just as she suspected: red, blotchy cheeks, and puffy eyes that reflected her broken heart. "I'm so stupid! Look at you! You stupid, stupid girl! I hate YOU!"

And how do I tell her what I did? How many times are they going to be willing to help me when I slide right back into it within a few weeks of being out of the center? FUCK ME! And oh, Jesus, I have to tell her about having sex with him. Shit, maybe I am just a fucked-up piece of shit and not the lucky girl that Slim said I was…that's probably what he was thinking anyway.

"Okay, I can do this. I have to do this for my future happiness."

Splashing cool water on her face and blowing her nose helped until she walked back out and saw Ginger and then a fresh wave of tears started to flow again.

"I-I'm so sorry, Mommy Gin," Lyla said. "I thought I had myself back together."

"Ly, tell me what happened."

"I will, but I don't want to upset you."

"How many times do I have to tell you that I don't judge you?"

Lyla filled her in on running into Candy and how she gave in to the temptation of drugs again, that she thought she was over her addiction and was going to partake in it for recreational use only.

Ginger silently listened to her as she told her what happened. She got up and poured Lyla another glass of water. "Here, drink this, my love."

Lyla sipped from the glass and put it on the coffee table. She sensed nothing but love from Ginger.

When Lyla finished talking, they faced each other on the couch with their legs crossed, and Ginger held Lyla's hands. "My turn to talk?"

Lyla nodded.

"You know honey, I'm so confused. I know that Aksel loves you, he's told me. And now you've told him you love him too, and then you made love, and then he left after he saw you doing drugs? He didn't even talk about it with you?"

"You think it is okay that I took drugs again? What's wrong with you?"

"Oh, wait. What? I—"

"Well? You can say it. I'm a horrible piece of shit. I know it already."

"Stop that, Lyla." Ginger held her hand tightly. "Do I want you using drugs? No. But self-pity never helped anyone."

"The man I love thinks *I needed* drugs to tell him I love him."

"Is that true, Lyla?"

"I love him, Gin. I do. But I guess I still need to work on me."

"I agree."

Lyla handed Ginger a brown bag. "This is everything that Candy gave me that I didn't use."

Ginger looked at the bag of pills and cocaine. "This is a start," Ginger said. She closed the bag and tossed it aside.

Lyla cried again and collapsed into Ginger's arms. They were silent for a while.

"Thank you," Ginger said.

"For what?"

"For being honest with me, for trusting me enough to share everything."

"Gin, I'm sorry to have put you through all this shit. You've always been so special to me."

"And you've always been someone beyond special to me. Okay, so you swear this is all the drugs, right?"

"Yes."

"And when you see someone like Candy again—?"

"I will remember exactly how I feel right now and turn the other way."

"Because you need to stay focused on what you want out of your life. And you have to realize how slippery this slope is for you right now."

"I know. I have to take responsibility for my dreams to come true."

"Good. As for Aksel, he said he needs space to figure things out. All you can do is honor that. What you did, hurt him deeply. If he truly loves you, though, he will return."

"You think there's a chance? I mean, you don't think I screwed it up beyond repair?"

Ginger smiled. "That depends on how good the sex was."

"Gin! Jesus!" Lyla finally lightened up and laughed while blushing. "I don't think we have a problem there."

Chapter 62

"Grant, you're taking this really hard," Ginger said as she handed him his cup of coffee.

"I know. I'm going to make an appointment with Dr. Ritzius. I don't understand why Aksel's resignation has cut me so deeply. I feel like I lost a limb or something."

"You two have always been very close, especially since he started working with us. He just needs time. Lyla blindsided him."

"But, Gin, you should have seen his face, the heartbreak in his eyes. He could barely talk."

"I know. Lyla's going to lose it when she finds out he quit. She doesn't know yet. What are we going to do?"

"Kids…" He shook his head.

"Your eyes have lost their light, baby."

"I can *feel* their pain. It shouldn't hurt so badly. It's beyond business, is it possible that he's from my past?"

"Ask Dr. Ritzius when you see him. I love you, my sweet Tommy."

"I love you too, Rach."

⟶═◉═⟵

Lyla sat on the recliner the next day in Dr. Lebow's office. "Lyla, do you feel like you want to go back into the rehab center for treatment?"

The question he'd just posed was one she had feared the whole time—of going back to rehab. But she had decided before the appointment that if the doctor suggested it, she would do it—anything to heal herself and have a real chance with Aksel and her dream to be a clothing designer like Ginger and Grant.

"I don't know. You're the doctor. What do you think?"

"Honestly, you had one slipup, which it not unusual. Moreover, you admitted to it right away. You also did not go hunting for the high—it found you."

"I really don't even know why I did it. I guess I wanted to prove to myself that I am no longer an addict and could use drugs recreationally. But the result made me unhappier than I could have ever expected. It's just not worth it. I might have lost Aksel forever."

"You will always be an addict, Lyla. Can you promise yourself if you find that you feel differently that you will page me? Can we make that agreement? I'm your first call, not a dealer?"

"I can do that." She spoke softly yet sternly.

"Then I do not feel at this time that you need to go back to the rehab center just yet. You seem to have learned a valuable lesson. Drugs are always going to be a kink in your armor. Don't kid yourself, though—you will never be able to use drugs recreationally."

Lyla nodded. "I understand. Thank you. Just being able to tell you calms me."

"Good, then I suggest we continue with the regression therapy."

"I'm ready."

Dr. Lebow shut the curtains, played the music, and instructed her to relax her body and control her breathing.

When she was ready, he guided her to search for where they'd left off, the life she led as Izzy.

"We are working at the pub, Rachel and me. We are very forlorn because Shelby died."

"Shelby was your brother, correct?"

"Yes."

"How did he die?"

"He was a fighter pilot. His plane was shot down. I hate this bloody war. Rachel's heart is broken also. She was his sweetheart." Lyla started to cry.

"Okay, Izzy, when you are ready, let's move forward to another significant event in this lifetime."

She stopped crying momentarily, but then started up again.

"Izzy, why are you crying now?"

"Rachel's parents were killed in a bombing raid in London. They had gone to visit her mum's sister. Rachel is beyond heartbroken. I don't know what to do for her. I try to be strong, but this war has taken so much…from all of us. They left the pub to her. And their cottage. We spend a lot of time together. I stay there with her most nights, although I have my own flat."

"I would like for you to search for a happy time in this lifetime."

She smiled, then laughed.

"What do you see?"

"It's the first night we met. He's so bloody handsome… and shy. Oh, I like this. He's very sweet on me. But he can't hit a bull's-eye to save his arse!" She laughed harder.

"Who are you with?"

Her British accent had kicked in at the beginning of the conversation between Dr. Lebow and Lyla. "A yank. He's friends with Rachel's fly-boy. They are cute together. But I know I'll shag my guy before she does hers."

"Do you know his name?"

"Alex. Alex Calder. He's from Minnesota. Got that silly accent, almost makes the rest of the Americans sound proper. But what a kisser! Mmmm."

"Look ahead and see if you end up in a relationship of any kind with him."

"Yes, I'm in love with him. He's in love with me. I was the first girl he ever made love to. I've never been so in love. He asks me to marry him, but I tell him that we will discuss it when he gets back from his next mission. I know I will tell him yes, as soon as he finishes all his missions."

"When he gets back, do you marry him?"

She began to sob again. "He doesn't come back. And I die. Actually, I kill myself. They are gone for so long, and I know I can't help Rachel through another loss, especially if I lose the only one I ever really loved."

"Do you see how your life ended?"

"During a bombing raid in London, I slip away from Rachel and run to the bridge. The bombs are dropping. One hits close to me."

"When you leave that life, are you with anyone, any spirits?"

"Yes, the Masters. They tell me I should have waited for him because he wasn't dead like I thought. They tell me I can go back again, but that I would have to learn to trust him when we next meet."

"Do you recognize Alex from your present life?"

"Oh, yes! It's…oh my God! It's Aksel!"

Suddenly Lyla opened her eyes. "I need to talk to him. I now know why!" She shot up and ran to the door. "I thought he left *me*, but actually, I left *him*!"

"Lyla, we're not finished," the doctor called after her.

"I'll call and make my next appointment. Thank you, Doctor!"

She grabbed her bag and coat and stumbled over herself to get to the elevator. She ran out of the building and hailed the first cab she saw.

⋆⇥◉⇤⋆

How am I going to tell him we were together in a past life? Lyla rode the elevator as it slowly ascended to the eleventh floor which housed G Squared. She pushed the button several more times in hopes of speeding up the process. *Ginger believes in it…maybe Daddy does too. They can help me convince him. Oh, God, hurry up already!*

Finally, the elevator doors opened, and she sprinted directly to Aksel's office. The light was off, and it was empty. She huffed out a large sigh.

Lyla went to see Ginger, in her office. "Hey, Gin, any idea what time Aksel will be in today? I had a major breakthrough in my therapy, and I need to talk to him right away."

Gin just shook her head with an expression of deep sadness on her face.

"What?" Lyla asked. "What's wrong? Is he okay?"

She didn't answer.

Lyla shut the door. "Spill it, Mommy Gin. What's the deal?"

"Aksel resigned yesterday."

"What? Why?" She rubbed her temples. "It's all my fault, Gin. I know I screwed up, but enough for him to quit? What did Daddy say?"

"He's pretty broken up about it."

"But…I should be the one who quits! *He* should stay! I'll find something else to do. He's better at this than I am."

"Ly, it won't make a difference."

"Why not?"

"You'll have to ask your father when he gets back. Let's talk about your therapy. Was it more past life regression?"

Lyla nodded. "I finally figured out why I had trust issues with him. Aksel and I were in England during World War II, and we were lovers. We were supposed to get married when he finished his missions. He only had four or five left."

"During World War II?" Ginger choked out her question.

"Yes. The war battered me and my best friend so badly that I gave up hope. I thought he was dead, so I killed myself during an air raid. The Masters told me that he wasn't in spirit yet, that he had been coming back for me. I fucked it up during that life. And now look, I've done it again!"

Ginger held her for a few minutes and cried with her. Then she wiped the tears from her eyes and walked to her safe in the corner of her office. She pulled out an old cigar box that she'd brought back with her from the cottage in England.

She sat in front of Lyla and placed the box on her lap.

"Lyla, there's more to your past life story than you realize. I knew we were connected. Connected beyond just being family. I can't explain how or why our paths have crossed again but look inside and I think you will understand."

Ginger handed her the old tattered box, and Lyla sifted through the contents. There was an old journal. When

Lyla opened it, a name was scribbled on the first page—
Rachel. *Is that my Rachel—?* She looked through the rest of
the mementos. She found old photos, pictures of people she
could almost remember. She saw a picture of two attractive
young women in a pub. She touched the picture.

"This…this is me," she said, tears in her eyes. "Izzy.
And Rachel."

Ginger nodded. Lyla pulled out a picture of two
couples: Izzy, Alex, Tommy, and Rachel.

"Alex," she whispered.

Finally, she found the heart-shaped rock Izzy had
given Rachel for her birthday. Lyla held the rock against her
chest.

"Impossible. Does Daddy know?"

Ginger nodded, then pointed at the picture of the
couple. "That's your father right there. His name was
Tommy then. He and Alex were best friends."

"Where did you get this?"

"From the cottage we bought in England." She held
Lyla's hands. "There's so much we need to talk
about…Izzy."

⊹⊱═◯═⊰⊹

Aksel dialed G Squared and asked Sue if Grant was
available.

"He is in a meeting with a potential client. But Mrs. Robinson is here. Would you like to speak with her?"

"*Oui.*"

"Hold, please."

Aksel waited a moment in silence, then there was a click. "Aksel, hi, it's Ginger. How are you?"

"Not well. I told *Monsieur* Grant that I would let him know where to send my final check. I decided I do not want it. Please inform him." His voice was thick and heavy with sadness.

"What are your plans? I know you are hurting…"

"I plan to move back to France for a while. Lyla can have everything. I thought time could help, but now I am not sure. Although I love her, *Madame* Ginger, I am not good enough for her."

"Aksel, please don't –"

"This will not affect the Portier and Robinson business. That will stay intact."

"Aksel, before you leave, someone very important needs to talk to you. Can you hold for a moment?"

"Alex, it's Izzy…" Lyla said.

Chapter 63

Lyla kissed Aksel good morning, while Misty purred loudly between them on their bed. "Do you mind taking Misty to work for me, *bebe*? I have to complete my enrollment this morning and pick my classes."

"Of course, *mi amour*. When I enrolled at NYU last year they were very helpful."

"Let's hope I get the same registrar."

They went about their morning routine and finally Lyla was ready to leave and kissed him good-bye. "See you this afternoon."

The door closed, and he said, "Perfect timing." He called Grant.

"G Squared, how may I direct your call?" Sue's sweet voice asked.

"Good morning, *Madame* Sue. May I speak with *Monsieur* Grant?

"Good morning, Aksel. Hold please."

His heart thumped against his chest while he waited for Grant to pick up the phone.

"Hey, Aksel, are you coming in late today?"

"*Monsieur,* no. I just wanted to know if you and *Madame* Ginger will be in the office for a while—I must speak with you both."

"All day long. Is everything okay, Aksel?"

"*Oui, oui!* I shall be in shortly."

⊷⋙◯⋘⊷

Grant walked straight to Ginger's office and tried to keep his breathing under control. Ginger looked at him, her eyes round with concern. "My God! Are you okay?" Grant's stomach was flipping, recalling the last time Aksel had sounded so serious. It was when he'd almost left their lives forever.

"I'm having a flashback to when Aksel quit all those months ago when Lyla relapsed."

"Why? She's been clean for almost six months. What could possibly make you feel like that?"

"I just spoke with Aksel and he sounded so, just so serious... He wants to see us *both*."

"Hmmm," she purred as she walked closer to him, rubbing his chest and leaning in for a soft kiss.

"Mmmm, Gin?"

"Don't jump into the negativity pool just yet...we'll wait and see what it's about, okay, my sweet Tommy?" She tugged at his tie, loosening it just a bit.

He followed her instructions while she nibbled his ear—telling him to inform Sue to hold their calls. Ginger locked the office door. She kissed his neck and he further loosened his tie and the first few buttons of his shirt while she led with her lips to the sensitive flesh around his nipples. She undressed in front of him, after pushing him back on the office couch, where the last thing she took off were her panties, leaving her heels on. For the next half-hour they were physically lost in each other.

⊹⊷≡◉⊜≓⊹

They were nearly finished dressing when Sue informed them via intercom that Aksel had arrived and was waiting for them in the conference room.

Putting his tie back on, Grant said, "He wants to talk to us both. I'll have Sue send him in here."

"No! It smells like sex in here! Let's go to the conference room." Ginger unlocked the door, "Coming?" Grant checked himself in the mirror and slapped her ass as he walked past her into the hallway.

"Aksel!" Grant said as they entered the conference room.

Aksel stood up with a nervous smile on his face. "*Monsieur* Grant, *Madame* Ginger, thank you for meeting me." Ginger hugged him while Grant sat down in one of the leather conference room chairs, next to Aksel.

"What's on your mind, Aksel?"

Aksel returned to his seat. Ginger sat next to Grant. They both waited for his response.

"I know how important Lyla's happiness is to you, and I don't want to do anything to change things between us…"

Grant cut him off, "I hope this isn't going where I think it is…" He stared at him, fearing that the next words out of Aksel's mouth would be that his daughter had relapsed again. His heart thundered.

Aksel cleared his throat. "I'm, sorry I didn't…" He paused then blurted, "Can I have your daughter's hand in marriage?"

"Her hand?" Silence echoed until Grant said emphatically, "No!"

Aksel vibrated with tension in his seat.

Ginger hit Grant's shoulder hard. "Grant, he wants to marry Lyla!" She looked at him in disbelief.

He rubbed his shoulder and grinned. "No, he only wants her hand." Grant turned to Aksel, "You can have her hand in marriage *but only* if you take the rest of her too," he smirked.

Aksel laughed with relief. "But of course! *Oui!*"

He stood up, smiling from ear to ear.

"I must ask you a favor since I have not proposed to Lyla yet, please don't speak of this—I wish to surprise her."

"You haven't asked her yet?" Grant shifted on his chair. Lyla and Aksel, married. He couldn't imagine his daughter saying no.

"No, I wanted to be sure to have your blessing."

"And our blessing, you have." Grant stood up and hugged Aksel.

"When are you planning to propose?" Ginger asked him excitedly.

"Today! I am leaving this card on her desk to meet me in a special place in the park where we once met before. It's been four years ago today. I need to make sure everything is in place, *Madame* Ginger, *Monsieur* Grant. May I leave you now with your blessing?"

"Yes, yes! Go and take care of everything." Grant pushed him toward the door.

Aksel went to Lyla's desk and placed the card on it and then left for the park.

⊹⟶◉⟵⊹

Lyla walked into her office that afternoon, speaking briefly with her father to update him on her new schedule for NYU, which included a business course that required a change of hours at G Squared.

On her desk she found a folded note that read "Izzy" across the front, so she opened it.

Mi amour, with every look, every smile, every touch, I fall in love with you all over again. Please meet me at the entrance to Eden at four-thirty… just past Shakespeare's Garden. All my love, Alex.

Excitement rushed through her body like a tidal wave and she felt dizzy. It immediately reminded her of the place she would forever refer to as *The Garden of Eden*.

She went straight to Ginger's office as soon as she caught her breath. She found Ginger on the floor, waist-deep in orders for spring. Gin looked up when Lyla walked in. "Hi, what's going on?"

"Here, read this. Then you'll know what I want…" Lyla handed Ginger the folded notecard.

Ginger smiled while asking, "What's Eden?"

"Oh, God, it's kind of an intimate thing, I don't know if I'm totally comfortable telling you the gory details…" Her cheeks heated with a blush.

"Come on, Ly, just tell me what Eden means."

"It's a secret place in the park where we've made love. It was wild and one of my favorite memories with Alex-I mean, Aksel." She covered her eyes from embarrassment.

Ginger got up off the floor and hugged her. "If you want to leave to get ready, just go! I'll tell Daddy."

"You'll tell him nothing!" Lyla coughed out, snapping at Ginger.

"NO! I wouldn't *tell* him! I'll just tell him you're running some errands for me."

"Much better. Thanks, Gin."

⊷══◉══⊶

Lyla reminisced about the first time she'd played the scavenger hunt with Aksel while walking toward the stone path of Shakespeare's Garden. She went home, showered and put on a sundress that she knew Aksel especially liked. She twisted some pieces of her long hair into multiple layered braids, leaving the rest of her thick locks flowing.

Like before, Aksel had left another note for her to find taped to the park bench… she discovered him waiting around the corner behind the tree. He held a bottle of water and a small compact mirror.

She laughed at the mirror after kissing him. "What's this for?"

"You said to me four years ago today that you wished we had a mirror. This should work, *our?*"

"Not exactly what I was picturing, love of my lives."

"By the way, I love that dress on you."

"You say that every time I wear it. Thanks, love."

She jumped on his back again and he bobbed and weaved through the underbrush to their final destination. To her surprise he had recreated the day from so long ago that she'd fantasized about, thinking it would only ever remain a memory. The blanket was spread over hay as he had done previously. This time there was an ice bucket with a bottle of bubbly Pellegrino and two champagne glasses. An old full-length mirror rested horizontally against the tree that still hid them.

"I love it!"

She stood and looked for the heart-shaped carving on the tree trunk he had done years before. Time had aged the tree and it was barely visible, so Aksel went to work on it right away with a pocket knife to freshen their mark in Central Park.

"Do you remember that this was the first surprise I gave you?" he asked as he carved. She kissed his neck from behind with her arms wrapped around his waist, feeling his stomach muscles through his T-shirt.

"Mmmm, yessss."

"I have another surprise for you."

"Do I have to hunt for it like last time?"

"No… it's in my pocket. You can feel it through my jeans."

"Oh, this?" She cupped his cock that was growing by the second in his jeans.

"No—yes! I mean no. But mmmm, that feels great, *bebe*."

"I know how you like it." Lyla purred and rubbed his hard-on through his jeans until he shifted and moved a bit to the right and her hand landed on a square shape in his pocket. "What's this?" She reached into his pocket to retrieve it.

He turned around, held her hand that wasn't holding the little blue box, and knelt before her. "Lyla, Izzy, you and I are connected in a way that goes beyond romance, beyond friendship, beyond what we've ever had before. It has defied all the changes and discoveries of ourselves and our past lives. And now at this time in our lives, I know purely and simply, we're soulmates."

He took the little blue box from her hand and opened the Tiffany & Co. ring box.

"We have discovered that we cannot live happily without each other. The sound of your voice brings me joy in a way I cannot explain…the way we laugh at exactly the same things…or how just a look from your beautiful face melts my heart. Everything about us has made me understand that we have a once-in-a-lifetime connection. Will you grant me the honor of spending the rest of this lifetime with me as your husband and you as my wife?"

Before she even looked at the ring box holding the sparkling brilliance of the two-carat square-shaped Tiffany diamond ring she would wear forever, she knelt into his arms and cried, "Yes, yes, yes!"

"I love you, *ma cherie*, I told you I would never give up on you, or us."

"I'm glad you're as stubborn as you are. I love you too, Alex…Aksel…whoever you are."

He slipped the ring on her finger and they kissed in the afternoon light. "*Merci, mi amour.* I will honor and love you forever."

"As I will you."

They kissed again, and she squealed as she looked at the ring on her finger. "It's extraordinary, Aksel! Look at how perfect it fits on my finger! You picked out a beautiful ring. I love all the little diamonds encasing the big sparkly square! It looks old, but modern. Which makes me think ahead already—I can't wait to plan our wedding…"

"I'm sure you and *Madame* Ginger will have fun in the months to come. It will probably be more of an event than a wedding."

"Oh, how well you know me." Her eyes morphed from pure bliss to intense sexual desire. "But at this moment all I want is you. Naked. Now. Let's try out the mirror you so thoughtfully placed here for us, *mi amour.*"

"My pleasure." He unbuttoned his shirt.

She lifted her sundress. "*Our* pleasure, Alex. I love you."

"God, I love you too, Izzy."

En tracte…

Like We Always Do

A Note from Ray and Deb

Visit MysticScribblers.com for updates and interesting past life information. Have you had past lives? Find out. Take the past life questionnaire.

If you enjoyed this book, help others find it so they can enjoy it too.

- **Recommend it:** Please help other readers find this book by recommending it to friends, readers' groups, and discussion boards.
- **Review it:** Let other potential readers know what you liked about this book.

> Thank you.
> Life Only Has Beginnings,
> Ray and Deb

Printed in Great Britain
by Amazon

82330673R10376